CLOUD HOWE

to George Malcolm Thomson

James Leslie Mitchell, 'Lewis Grassic Gibbon', (1901–35), was born and brought up in the rich farming land of Scotland's North East coast. After a brief and unsuccessful journalistic career, he joined the Royal Army Service corps in 1919 serving in Persia, India and Egypt. Thereafter he spent a further six years as a clerk in the RAF. He married Rebecca Middleton in 1925, and became a full time writer in 1929. The young couple settled in Welwyn Garden City where they lived until the writer's death in 1935.

Mitchell published a number of short stories and articles and his first book, *Hanno, or the Future of Exploration* appeared in 1928. Seven novels followed under his own name, *Stained Radiance* (1930); *The Thirteenth Disciple* (1931); *Three Go Back* (1932); *Image and Superscription* (1933); *The Lost Trumpet* (1932); *Spartacus* (1933); and *Gay Hunter* (1934). In the same year Mitchell collaborated with Hugh MacDiarmid to make *Scottish Scene*, which contained three of Mitchell's best short stories, since collected in *A Scots Hairst* (1969).

He adopted his mother's name for his finest work, the trilogy *A Scots Quair*, which comprised *Sunset Song*, *Cloud Howe* and *Grey Granite* written between 1932 and 1934. Dogged by ill health at the end, Mitchell died of a perforated ulcer at the age of only thirty-four. An unfinished novel, *The Speak of the Mearns*, was publised in 1982.

Lewis Grassic Gibbon

CLOUD HOWE

Edited with an introduction by Tom Crawford

CANONGATE
CLASSICS
19

First published in 1933 in Great Britain by Jarrolds.
This edition first published as a Canongate Classic in
1988 by Canongate Publishing Limited, 17 Jeffrey
Street, Edinburgh EHI 1DR. Introduction © 1989
Tom Crawford.

The publishers gratefully acknowledge general sub-
sidy from the Scottish Arts Council towards the
Canongate Classics series and a specific grant towards
the publication of this volume.

Set in 10pt Plantin by Hewer Text Composition
Services, 152 Leith Walk, Edinburgh. Printed and
bound in Great Britain by Cox and Wyman, Reading.

Canongate Classics
Series Editor: Roderick Watson
Editorial Board: Tom Crawford, J. B. Pick

British Library Cataloguing in Publication Data
Gibbon, Lewis, Grassic, *1901–1935*
Cloud howe
I. Title
823′.914[F]

ISBN 0-86241-227-7

Contents

Introduction vii

Note on the Text xvii

Map of Segget xviii

PROEM I

I Cirrus 7

II Cumulus 35

III Stratus 109

IV Nimbus 158

Notes 213

Glossary 221

Introduction

American reviewers were as impressed by *Cloud Howe* on its
first appearance as they had been by *Sunset Song*. The *New
York Times*, *Herald Tribune*, and *North American Review*
praised it to the skies, but the best account I know of a
first reading comes from Herschell Bricknell, in a letter of
14 February 1934 to Gibbon's American publishers:

> I read until I went to sleep Saturday night and waked
> half a dozen times thinking of what Gibbon was saying.
> Early Sunday morning—very early—I finished it,
> and all day yesterday I was under the spell of it. It is
> a perfectly extraordinary book—I don't know what
> people will do with the dialect, but I hope everybody
> able to be turned upside down by a piece of writing will
> read it.[1]

Gibbon's peers among contemporary Scottish novelists
—Compton Mackenzie, Naomi Mitchison, Neil Gunn, and
George Blake—hailed it as a masterpiece, although one
writer of the older generation, the poet Lewis Spence, who
had been delighted by *Sunset Song*, saw its successor as merely
'a deliberate misconception, a capricious guffaw' (*Scottish
Field*, October 1934). As might have been predicted, many
Scottish newspapers were as scathingly contemptuous as
they had been over *Sunset Song*. 'Those who like a simple
clean story will not find it here', wrote the Aberdeen *Press
and Journal*'s critic on 3 August 1933. 'If life in a Mearns
town is compounded of indecencies, sneers, ill-will, spying,
gossiping, downright cruelty, then this Mearns town is con-
sistent.'

These hostile judgments are worth recalling because they
were a response to an essential feature of the book. Seen from
one angle, *Cloud Howe* is a brilliant picture of a small country
town set in a consummately rendered fictional region. There

is nothing on the map of Kincardineshire that corresponds to Segget in the place where Segget is supposed to be, though certain features, such as the jute mill and the owner's management of it may be based on Inverbervie. The ruined Kaimes are compounded from various sources, not least Fenella's castle near Fettercairn; Frellin, Culdyce Moor, and Quarles seem to be inventions, though marvellously plausible ones. But Gibbon, in the interests of solidity, also features many genuine place names from the real region of which the fictional one is an emanation. Segget, like so much in the book, is fictional in order to be *typical*—more typical than a photographic documentary of any real community could be; and it is typical of a community gone wrong. It has gone wrong because it is infected with 'those little prides and those little fortunes' which Robert told of in his sermon by the war memorial at the end of *Sunset Song*, the 'new oppressions and foolish greeds of the world that we seem to inherit'. That is why the narrative voices of the community—the Segget voices—are often cruder and more strident than the Kinraddie voices, and why Chris's voice never fuses with the Segget ones but is always separate, just like her essential inner self, 'Chris alone'.

Yet it is not only what has happened since the war that has made Segget the obscene pit that it is; it is the whole history of class society, all the millenia of man's inhumanity to man, as we see from Chris's thoughts during a confrontation with Mowat, the degenerate mill-owner:

> . . . suddenly she'd seen so much she didn't say, all the pageant of history since time began up here in the windy Mearns Howe: the ancient rites of blood and atonement where the Standing Stones stood up as dead kings; the clownings and cruelties of leaders and chiefs; and the folk—her folk—who kept such alive—dying frozen at night in their eirdes, earth-houses, chaving from the blink of day for a meal, serfs and landworkers whom the Mowats rode down, whom the armies harried and the kings spat on, the folk who rose in the Covenant times and were tortured and broken by the gentry's men, the rule and the way of life that had left them the pitiful gossiping clowns

that they were, an obscene humour engraffed on their
fears, the kindly souls of them twisted awry and veiled
from men with a dirty jest . . .

What Lewis Spence and the *Press and Journal* reviewer did
not appreciate was that there are still kindly souls in this
community, a point made cogently by Chris in a dialogue
with Robert which extends the discussion from region to
nation, from the Mearns to the whole of Scotland:

[Robert said], 'My God, were there ever folk like
the Scots! Not only THEM—you and I are as bad.
Murderous gossip passed on as sheer gospel, though
liars and listeners both know it is a lie. Lairds, ladies,
or plain Jock Muck at the Mains—they'd gossip the
heart from Christ if He came, and impute a dodge for
popularizing timber when He was crucified again on
His cross!'

Chris said 'That's true, and yet it is not. They would
feed Christ hungry and attend to His hurts with no
thought of reward their attendance might bring. Kind,
they're so kind. . . . And the lies they would tell about
how He came by those hurts of His . . .'

Throughout the novel, the voices of Segget are not uniformly
mean and petty. True, there is the vile voice that reports the
long agony of Meiklebogs' injured horse; but there is also
an essentially decent voice that is proud of Cis Brown and
refuses to believe she has taken up with Dod Cronin. This
same voice is later full of honest radical indignation at the
sufferings of the unemployed:

And there were worse cases than these, far worse, God
damn't! you had never much liked the spinners, but
the things that were happening near turned you sick,
it was kicking in the faces of the poor for no more than
delight in hearing the scrunch of their bones.

One of the triumphs of *Cloud Howe* is its magnificent
'orality'. There are indeed many voices other than the community voices—not merely the voice of Chris's interior
thoughts with its subtle use of 'self-referring you', or Else
Queen's intensely Scots inner voice and Ewan's cool English
one, which we occasionally hear as vehicles of the narrative;
not merely Robert's ministerial conversation (we hear him

only in dialogue, he is never given interior monologue);
but the more public voices of oral folk tale, sermons, and
open-air speeches. There is at times a quite extraordinary
orchestration of folk-narrative technique within the Segget
voice, where one must assume an anonymous *individual* in
the traditional role of tale-teller with an audience around
him. It is such a person (though malicious and mean of
spirit, one feels), who tells how Else Queen's bairn was
born among the sheaves in the corn-loft; and into *his* tale
is set another, a folk anecdote about Burns and the Virgin
Mary, assigned to a named individual and perfectly suited to
his character: 'That was a real foul story to tell, it showed
you the tink that Ake Ogilvie was, interrupting the real fine
newsy tale of the happenings down at the Meiklebogs.' Of
course Gibbon's irony intends us to approve of Ogilvie's racy
irreverence and condemn the tone of the newsy tale-teller.

A more sublime orchestration is heard in Robert's contrast-
ing sermons—the militant sermon about Samson and the
Philistines which got him the Segget kirk, though the congregation hadn't a clue what it meant; the crusading sermon
with which he opens his campaign to clean up Segget and
which puts the tradespeople against him; the namby-pamby
quietist sermons he preaches after the defeat of the General
Strike (we only hear about these, they are not quoted
directly), and the fine rousing sermon at the very end of
the book which looks away from Christianity altogether to the
Communism of *Grey Granite*. Within this pattern of public
oratory we also have the evangelical sermons of the hypo-
critical McDougall Brown (these are merely referred to,
not quoted at length); and the dialectic between Robert's
sermon at the Memorial on Armistice Day and the socialist
address of Jock Cronin, the spinners' leader, after their
procession has broken in on the official service. If Gibbon
had included an Episcopal minister and his wife, as was
once his intention,[2] he might well have given us even more
sermons than he did. And if he had followed the idea he once
had of ending not with Robert's death in the pulpit but with a
grand trial scene in which he would have been expelled from
the Kirk for his politics,[3] public oratory would surely have
bulked even larger in the total design.

Such oratory necessarily belongs, given the nature of society and public life in the Mearns and Scotland of the 1920s, to the world of men. But the book's greatest achievement does not belong to the world of men at all, except peripherally; it lies in the continued development of Chris's character, so brilliantly begun in *Sunset Song*. Robert's career has the shape and emotional impact of a tragedy of character in which the hero redeems himself at the close and destroys himself in so doing. But we experience the tragedy mainly through its effect on Chris—the breakdown of her originally happy marriage, her agonised spectator's response to his desertion of Christ the Tiger for Creeping Jesus after the defeat of the Strike, and the final act of heroic mercy that brings about his death. We are false to the book if we read it as *primarily* historical allegory; if it were, it would not turn non-Scots readers upside down the way it does. Like all the greatest characters in narrative and drama, Chris is both a unique individual and profoundly typical. George Malcolm Thomson, to whom the book is dedicated, wrote that 'this Chris of yours is surely the greatest woman character in Scottish fiction . . . She is intensely Scottish and yet universal (Letter of 23 July 1933)[4]. In this respect Chris is like Natasha in *War and Peace*, for she exhibits the most positive, the most enduring aspects of the national character in a complex form. This, surely, is what Robert means when he says 'Oh Chris Caledonia, I've married a nation!', and Stephen Mowat when he says that the first time he met her 'he felt he was stared at by Scotland herself.' In her brief confrontations with Mowat she is representative, not of Scotland as an abstraction, but of the Scottish *people*, as Jeanie Deans is in her interview with the Queen in Scott's *Heart of Midlothian*, and it is this aspect of her—her independence, lack of affectation, hatred of oppression, and love of freedom, which leads Robert to say that she will outlast him by a thousand years.

Gibbon's remarkable presentation of female experience has been freshly examined recently, notably by Isobel Murray and Deirdre Burton.[5] Burton in particular has observed that Gibbon's techniques for rendering Chris's separate selves—the first, second, third and fourth

Chris—and the precise ways in which she is aware
of these splits and is able to look down at herself 'as
though she looked at some other than herself'—are
like those employed by many women writers: they are
almost an identifying characteristic of women's writing in
this century.[6] Female perceptiveness, or rather a remarkable
fusion of male and female perceptiveness, also informs the
cloud imagery that runs through the novel. The whole
book as we now have it is structured around clouds.
It moves from the high bright wispy clouds of Cirrus
with their shapes like locks of hair, through the rounded
heaps of Cumulus with darker horizontal bases, to the
low, wide Stratus, and finally to the looming rain-clouds
of Nimbus with their connotations of tragedy and despair.
A thoroughgoing allegorical reading might however ponder
the other meaning of nimbus—'a cloud or luminous mist
investing a god or goddess.'

One of the most beautiful moments in the book is a
purely female exchange, an incident in sisterhood, when
Chris has commented on the plight of the pregnant Cis
Brown:

> Oh, we're such fools—women, don't you think that
> we are now, Cis? To worry so much about men and
> their ploys, the things that they do and the things that
> they think!

Immediately after this, there occurs one of the strongest
statements of the metaphysical significance of the title and
its associated imagery. The clouds are linked in Chris's
mind with the deepest layers of woman's biological being,
'when it came on women what thing they carried, darkling, coming to life within them, new life to replenish the
earth again, to come to being in the windy Howe where
the cloud-ships sailed to the unseen south'. The Howe,
the vast vale of the Mearns, is hollow, feminine. But the
clouds transform themselves to pillars, symbols of male-
ness on a Freudian reading—'those clouds that marched,
terrible, tenebrous, their pillars still south.' Then follows
the great Mosaic emblem which reverberates throughout
the book and is associated with the best in Robert and
the Kirk: 'A pillar of cloud by day and a pillar of fire by

night.' On one level Chris thinks that the ideals, creeds, and theories which men have followed throughout history are insubstantial—'mere' clouds, and Robert's not the least of these—compared to the underlying creativity of the universe, to which she is instinctively attuned. But on another the pillars of fire are not confined to one sex, they body forth the energy of the *general* unconscious, the libido, while the pillars of cloud are the superego and its rationalizations. Gibbon continues:

> The wind was coming in great gusts now, driving the riven boughs of the broom, in times it rose to a scraich round about and the moor seemed to cower in its trumpet cry. Cloud Howe of the winds and the rains and the sun! All the earth that, Chris thought at that moment, it made little difference one way or the other where you slept or ate or had made your bed, in all the howes of the little earth, a vexing puzzle to the howes were men, passing and passing as the clouds themselves passed: but the REAL was below, unstirred and untouched, surely if that were not also a dream.

What is meant by 'the REAL' and what are we to understand by 'below'? The answer, at this stage of Chris's pilgrimage, is perhaps provided by comparison with an earlier passage where she speaks of 'something that was bred in your bones in this land—oh, Something: maybe that Something was GOD', and where it is clear that 'land' does not signify an abstract geographical entity, but rather the soil and the rocks and the trees and the heath as made out of the one solid reality, a base that is obstinately *there*. She continues, in that same earlier passage, with the thought that it is at the moment of death that Scots folk 'face up to the REAL at last, neither heaven nor hell but the earth that was red'. (The soil of the Mearns is bright red in colour, which makes the fields when freshly ploughed glow with a peculiar richness and warmth). For Chris, the Earth itself abides *below* all the ephemeral forms that arise in the course of evolution and of history. Neil Gunn was struck by 'mystical' passages such as this, when he wrote to Gibbon on 17 July 1933:

> I don't think I have ever been put under the illusion

before of the Earth's having a voice. Writers have tried to give it a voice, of course, often enough. But here the black thing speaks serpent and curlew, prehistoric gloaming (wan or fey, you get it when you want it), and in it for the most part an irony that never fails in an economy that is an echo-speech of the humors of your part of that world, but is often enough deep as horror.[7]

Gunn's phrase about the Earth's having a voice applies most of all to Chris, and she can be said—not to *equal* the Earth or the Land as a term in an allegorical equation—but to be aware of it as no other character is, to be thirled to it with every part of her:

> She had found in the moors and the sun and the sea her surety unshaken, lost maybe herself, but she followed no cloud, be it named or unnamed.

After Robert dies in the pulpit, with all the pages of his Bible soaked in the stream of blood from his lips, Chris speaks to the congregation in Christ's words that come unbidden; 'It is Finished!' At that moment of tragedy she takes upon herself the priestly role reserved for men in her society. In the second last paragraph, as she leaves Segget for good, she once more mimes Robert, shaping her hands into the gesture with which he would bless the folk of Segget on Sabbath. The very last paragraph begins with an echo of her words in the kirk: 'Then that had finished.' She turns back to look at the hills, bare of clouds for once—the clouds of past doctrines and ideologies, 'the pillars of mist that aye crowned their heights, all but a faint wisp vanishing south, and the bare, still rocks upturned to the sky.'

What she sees in that epiphany is the reality of the high places and their granite peaks, not necessarily truer but certainly different from the REAL that is 'below'. It was perhaps those perceptions of Chris that Neil Gunn called 'wan or fey', and that led Hugh MacDiarmid, the day after it first went on sale, to end his review with the challenging and provocative conclusion: 'Cloud Howe is the only really religious book Scotland has produced for a century and a half.'[8]

Thomas Crawford

NOTES TO INTRODUCTION

MSS in the National Library of Scotland are quoted by kind permission of the NLS and of Gibbon's daughter. Mrs Rhea Martin.

1. Quoted in Ian S. Munro, *Leslie Mitchell: Lewis Grassic Gibbon* (Edinburgh, 1966), p.120.

2. Early list of 'Dramatis Personae' for *The Morning Star*, the first title that occurred to Gibbon for *Cloud Howe*, in NLS MS Acc. 26040.

3. Ian Campbell, *Lewis Grassic Gibbon* (Edinburgh, 1985), p. 95.

4. In NLS MS Acc. 26064.

5. See 'Action and Narrative Stance in *A Scots Quair*', in *Literature of the North*, ed. David Hewitt and Michael Spiller (Aberdeen 1983), pp. 109–20; and Isobel Murray and Bob Tait, 'Lewis Grassic Gibbon's *A Scots Quair*', in *Ten Modern Scottish Novels* (Aberdeen 1984), pp.10–31. Also Deirdre Burton, 'A Feminist Reading of Lewis Grassic Gibbon's *A Scots Quair*', in *The British Working-Class Novel in the Twentieth Century*, ed. J. Hawthorne (1984), pp.35–46

6. 'A Feminist Reading', p.38.

7. In NLS MS Acc. 2064. Gunn may have written 'humans' rather than 'humors'.

8. In *The Free Man*, 29 July 1933.

Note on the Text

The present text follows that of the first edition as scrupulously as possible, except in such matters of typographical styling as the use of roman, not italic, capitals for words emphasised in direct speech. Misprints that were not picked up in later editions have been corrected. We have gone back to the original paragraphs of 1933, and the map of Segget has been prepared from the one in the first edition.

MOUNTAINS

The KAIMES

MEIKLE BOGS

SCHOOL HOUSE

The KIRK

T.MUIR

The MANSE

S.SMITH

A.OGILVIE Joiner

The SCHOOL

THE SOUROCK'S HOUSE

P.PEAT, TAILOR

D.PEAT, GROCER

H.HOGG, SHOEMAKER

GRANTS GARDENS

R MOULTRIE SADDLER

EAST WYND

THE SQUARE

THE WAR MEMORIAL ANGEL

RAILWAY STATION

THE SEGGET ARMS

BRIDGE

BOROUGH of SEGGET

THE BOROUGH of Segget stands under the Mounth, on the southern side, in the Mearns Howe, Fordoun lies near and Drumlithie nearer, you can see the Laurencekirk lights of a night glimmer and glow as the mists come down. If you climb the foothills to the ruined Kaimes, that was builded when Segget was no more than a place where the folk of old time had raised up a camp with earthen walls and with freestone dykes, and had died and had left their camp to wither under the spread of the grass and the whins—if you climbed up the Kaimes of a winter morn and looked to the east and you held your breath, you would maybe hear the sough of the sea, sighing and listening up through the dawn, or see a shower of sparks as a train came skirling through the woods from Stonehaven, stopping seldom enough at Segget, the drivers would clear their throats and would spit, and the guards would grin: as though 'twere a joke.

But God alone knows what you'd want on the Kaimes, others had been there and had dug for treasure, nothing they'd found but some rusted swords, tint most like in the wars once waged in the days when the wife of the Sheriff of Mearns, Finella she was, laid trap for the King, King Kenneth the Third, as he came on a hunting jaunt through the land. For Kenneth had done her own son to death, and she swore that she'd even that score up yet; and he hunted slow through the forested Howe, it was winter, they tell, and in that far time the roads were winding puddles of glaur, the horses splashed to their long-tailed rumps. And the men of Finella heard of his coming, as that dreich clerk Wyntoun has told in his tale:

As through the Mernys on a day
    The kyng was rydand hys hey way;
Off hys awyne curt al suddanly

I

Agayne hym ras a cumpany
In to the towne of Fethyrkerne
    To fecht wyth hym thai ware sa yherne
And he agayne thame faucht sa fast,
    Bot he thare slayne was at the last.

So Kenneth was dead and there followed wars, Finella's
carles builded the Kaimes, a long line of battlements under
the hills, midway a tower that was older still, a broch
from the days of the Pictish men; there they lay and
long months withstood the folk that came to avenge the
death of Kenneth; and the darkness comes down on their
waiting and fighting and all the ill things that they suffered
and did.

The Kaimes was left bare and with ruined walls, as
Iohannes de Fordun tells in his time, a Fordoun childe
him and had he had sense he'd have hidden the fact, not
spread it abroad. Some kind of a cleric he was in those days,
just after the Bruce drove out the English, maybe Fordoun
then had less of a smell ere Iohannes tacked on the toun to
his name. Well, the Kaimes lay there in Iohannes' time, he
tells that the Scots folk halted there going north one night to
the battle of Bara; and one man with the Scots, a Lombard
he was, looked out that morn as the army roused and the
bugles blew out under the hills, and he saw the mists that
went sailing by and below his feet the sun came quick down
either slope of a brae to a place where a streamlet ran by a
ruined camp. And it moved his heart, and he thought it an
omen, in his own far land there were camps like that; and
he swore that if he should survive the battle he'd come back
to this place and claim grant of its land.

Hew Monte Alto was the Lombard's name and he fought
right well at the Bara fight, and when it was over and the
Bruce made King, he asked of the Bruce the lands that lay
under the Kaimes in the windy Howe. These lands had
been held by the Mathers folk, but they had made peace
with Edward the First and given him shelter and welcome
the night he halted in Mearns as he toured the north. So
the Bruce he took their lands from the Mathers and gave
them to Hew, that was well content, though vexed that he
came of no gentle blood. So he sent a carle to the Mathers

lord to ask if he had a daughter of age for wedding and bedding; and he sent an old carle that he well could spare, in case the Mathers should flay him alive.

For the Mathers were proud as though God had made their flesh of another manure from men; but by then they had come to a right sore pass in the mouldering old castle by Fettercairn, where hung the helmet of good King Grig, who first had 'stablished the Mathers there, and made of the first of them Merniae Decurio, Captain-chief of the Mearns lands. So the old lord left Hew's carle unskinned, and sent back the message he had more than one daughter, and the Lombard could come and choose which he liked. And Hew rode there and he made his choice, and was wedded and bedded to a Mathers quean.

But short was the time that he had for his pleasure, the English again had come north to war. The Scots men gathered under the Bruce at a narrow place where a black burn ran, the pass of the Bannock burn it was. And Hew was a well-skilled man in the wars, he rode his horse lathered into the camp, and King Robert called him to make the pits and set the spiked calthrops covered with earth, traps for the charge of the English horse. So he did, and the next day came, and the English, they charged right brave and were whelmed in the pits. But Hew was slain by an English arrow as he rode unhelmed to peer at his pits.

Before he rode south he had builded a castle within the walls of the old-time Kaimes, and brought far off from his Lombard land a pickle of weavers, folk of his blood. They builded their houses down under the Kaimes in the green-walled circle of the ancient camp, they tore down the walls of that heathen place, and set their streets by the Segget burn, and drove their looms, and were well-content, though foreign and foolish and but ill-received by the dour, dark Pictish folk of the Mearns. Yet that passed in time, as the breeds grew mixed, and the toun called Segget was made a borough for sake of the Hew that fell at the Burn.

So the Monte Altos came to be Mowat, and interbred with the Mathers folk, and the next of whom any story is told is he who befriended the Mathers who joined with other three lairds against the Lord Melville. For he pressed them right

sore, the Sheriff of Mearns, and the four complained and
complained to the King; and the King was right vexed,
and he pulled at his beard—*Sorrow gin the Sheriff were
sodden—sodden and supped in his brew!* He said the words
in a moment of rage, unthinking, and then they passed from
his mind; but the lairds remembered, and took horse for
the Howe.

There, as they'd planned, the four of them did, the
Sheriff went hunting with the four fierce lairds, Arbuthnott,
Pitarrow, Lauriston, Mathers; and they took him and
bound him and carried him up Garvock, between two stones
a great cauldron was hung; and they stripped him bare and
threw him within, in the water that was just beginning to
boil; and they watched while he slowly ceaed to scraich,
he howled like a wolf in the warming water, then like a
bairn smored in plague, and his body bloated red as the
clay, till the flesh loosed off from his seething bones; and
the four lairds took their horn spoons from their belts and
supped the broth that the Sheriff made, and fulfilled the
words that the King had said.

They were hunted sore by the law and the kirk, the
Mathers fled to the Kaimes to hide, his kinsman Mowat
closed up the gates and defied the men of the King that
came. So they laid a siege to the castle of Kaimes; but
the burghers of Segget sent meat to the castle by a secret
way that led round the hills; and a pardon came for the
Mathers at last, the army withdrew and the Mathers came
out, and he swore if ever again in his life he supped of broth
or lodged between walls, so might any man do to himself as
he had done to the Sheriff Melville.

And for long the tale of Segget grows dim till there came
the years of the Killing Time, and the Burnesses, James
and Peter they were—were taken to Edinburgh and put
to the question that they might forswear the Covenant and
God. And Peter was old, in the torment he weakened, but
by him his son James lay on the rack, and even when the
thummikins bit right sore and Peter opened his mouth to
forswear, his son was before him singing a psalm so loud
that he drowned the voice of Peter; and the old man died,
but James was more slow, they threw him into a cell at last,

his body broken in many places, the rats ate him there while he still was alive; and maybe there were better folk far in Segget, but few enough with smeddum like his.

His son was no more than a loon when he died, he'd a little farm on the Mowat's land. But he moved to Glenbervie and there took a place, and his folk had the ups and down of all flesh till the father of Robert Burnes grew up, and grew sick of the place, and went off to Ayr; and there the poet Robert was born, him that lay with nearly as many women as Solomon did, though not all at one time.

But some of the Burneses still bade in Segget. In the first few years of King William's reign it was one of them, Simon, that led the feud the folk of Segget had with the Mowats. For they still owned most of Segget, the Mowats, a thrawn old wife the lady was then, her sons all dead in the wars with the French; and her wits were half gone, it was seldom she washed, she was mean as dirt and she smelt to match. And Simon Burnes and the Segget minister, they prigged on the folk of Segget against her, the weaver folk wouldn't pay their rent, they made no bow when they met the old dame ride out in her carriage with her long Mowat nose. And at last one night folk far from Segget saw sudden a light spring up in the hills: it wavered and shook there all through the dark, and from far and near as the dawn drew nigh, there were parties of folk set out on the roads to see what this fairely was in the hills. And the thing they saw was the smoking Kaimes, a great bit fire had risen in the night and burned the old castle down to its roots, of the stones there stood hardly one on the other, the Segget folk swore they'd all slept so sound the thing was over afore they awoke. And that might be so, but for many a year, before the Old Queen was took to her end and the weaving entirely ceased to pay and folk went drifting away from the Mearns, there were meikle great clocks in this house and that, great coverlets on beds that lay neist the floor; and the bell that rung the weavers awake had once been a great handbell from the hall of the Mowats up on the Kaimes high hill.

A Mowat cousin was the heritor of Kaimes, he looked at the ruin and saw it was done, and left it there to the wind and the rain; and builded a house lower down the slope, Segget below, yew-trees about, and had bloodhounds brought to roam the purviews, he took no chances of innocent sparks floating up in the night from Segget. But the weavers were turning to other things now, smithying and joinering and keeping wee shops for the folk of the farms that lay round about. And the Mowats looked at the Segget burn, washing west to the Bervie flow, and were ill-content that it should go waste. But it didn't for long, the jute trade boomed, the railway came, the two jute mills came, standing out from the station a bit, south of the toun, with the burn for power. The Segget folk wouldn't look at the things, the Mowats had to go to Bervie for spinners, and a tink-like lot of the creatures came and crowded the place, and danced and fought, raised hell's delight, and Segget looked on as a man would look on a swarm of lice; and folk of the olden breed moved out, and builded them houses up and down the East Wynd, and called it New Toun and spoke of the dirt that swarmed in Old Toun, round about the West Wynd.

The spinners' coming brought trade to the toun, but the rest of Segget still tried to make out that the spinners were only there by their leave, the ill-spoken tinks, with their mufflers and shawls; the women were as bad as the men, if not worse, with their jeering and fleering in Segget Square; and if they should meet with a farmer's bit wife as she drove into Segget to go to the shops, and looked neat and trig and maybe a bit proud, they'd scraich *Away home, you country cow!*

But the Mowats were making money like dirt. They built a new kirk when the old one fell, sonsy and broad, though it hadn't a steeple; and they lived and they died and they went to their place; and you'd hear the pound of the mills at work down through the years that brought the Great War; and that went by and still Segget endured, outlasting all in spite of the rhyme that some coarse-like tink of a spinner had made:

Oh, Segget it's a dirty hole,
A kirk without a steeple,
A midden-heap at ilka door
And damned uncivil people

ONE

Cirrus

SEGGET WAS wakening as Chris Colquohoun came down the shingle path from the Manse. Here the yews stood thick, in a starlings' murmur, a drowsy cheep on the edge of the dawn; but down the dark, as you reached the road, you saw already lights twink here and there, in the houses of Segget, the spinners' wynds, a smell in the air of hippens and porridge. But she'd little heed for these, had Chris, she went quick as she looked at the eastern sky, the May air warm in her face as she turned, north, and went up the Meiklebogs road. So rutted it was and sossed with the carts that there was a saying in Segget toun: *There's a road to heaven and a road to hell, but damn the road to the Meiklebogs.*

But that didn't matter, she wasn't going there, in a while she turned by a path that wound, dark, a burn was hidden in the grass, over a stile to the hills beyond. And now, as she climbed swift up the slope, queer and sudden a memory took her—of the hills above the farm in Kinraddie, how sometimes she'd climb to the old Druid stones and stand and remember the world below, and the things that were done and the days put by, the fun and fear of the days put by. Was that why the Kaimes had so filled her sky the twenty-four hours she had been in Segget?

Now she was up on the lowermost ledge, it lay dark about, the old castle of Kaimes, no more than a litter of ruined walls, the earth piled high up over the stones that once were halls and men-shielded rooms. There were yews growing low in a corner outbye, they waved and moved as they heard Chris come. But she wasn't feared, she was country-bred, she wandered a little, disappointed, then laughed, at herself, to herself, and the place grew still.

Maybe it thought, as did Robert Colquohoun, that her laugh was a thing worth listening for.

She felt her face redden, faint, at that, and she thought how over her face the slow blood would now be creeping, she'd once or twice watched it, bronzed and high in the cheek-bones her face, and a kindly smoulder of grey-gold eyes, she minded how once she *had* wished they were blue! She put up her hand to her hair, it was wet, with the dew she supposed from the dark Manse trees, it was coiled over either ear in the way she had worn it now for over two years.

She turned round then and looked down at Segget, pricked in the paraffin lights of dawn. They were going out one by one as the east grew wanly blind in the van of the sun, behind, in the hills, a curlew shrilled—dreaming up here while the world woke, Robert turning in his bed down there in the Manse, and maybe outreaching a hand to touch her as he'd done that first morning two years ago, it had felt as though he wakened her up from the dead . . .

SO STRANGE IT had seemed a long minute she'd lain, half-feared, with his hand that touched her so. Then he'd moved, quiet-breathing, deep in his sleep, and the hand went away, she reached out in the dark and sought it again and held to it, shy. It was winter that morning, they both had slept late from their marriage night; and, as the winter light seeped grey into the best bedroom of Kinraddie Manse, Chris Colquohoun, who had once been married to Ewan, and before that time was Chris Guthrie, just, had lain and thought and straightened things out, like a bairn rubbing its eyes from sleep. . . . This was new, she had finished with that life that had been, all the love she had given to her Ewan, dead, lost and forgotten far off in France: her father out in the old kirkyard: that wild, strange happening that had come to her the last Harvest but one there was of the War, when she and another—but she'd not think of that, part of the old, sad dream that was done. Had that other remembered the happening at all, his last hour of all in a Flanders trench?

And she thought that maybe he had not at all, you did this and that and you went down in hell to bring the fruit of your body to birth, it was nothing to the child that came from your womb, you gave to men the love of your heart, and they'd wring it dry to the last red drop, kind, dreadful and dear, and deep in their souls, whatever the pretence they played with you, they knew it a play and Life waiting outbye.

So she lay and thought, and then wriggled a little—to think these things on her marriage-morn, the hand she held now never held so before! And she peered in his face in the light that came, his hair lay fair on the pillow's fringe, fair almost to whiteness, his skin ivory-white, she saw his brows set dark in a dream, and the mouth came set in a straight line below, she liked his mouth and his chin as well, and his ears that were small and lay flat back, so, and the hand that had tightened again in his sleep—oh! more than that, you liked all of him well, with his kisses in the night that had only just gone, his kisses, the twinkle-scowl in his eyes: *And now it's to bed, but I don't think to sleep.* She had laughed as well, feeling only half-shy. *An awful speak, Robert, for Kinraddie's minister!* and he said *Don't ministers do things like that?* and she'd looked at him swift, and looked quick away. *Maybe, we'll see;* and so they had seen.

She stretched then, softly, remembering that, warm under the quilt her own body felt queer, strange and alive as though newly blessed, and she smiled at that thought, in a way it had been, one flesh she was made with a kirk minister! Funny to think she had married a minister, that this was the Manse, that she was its mistress—oh! life was a flurry like a hen-roost at night, the doors were banging, you flew here and there, were your portion the ree or the corner of a midden you could not foretell from one night to the next.

She got from bed then and into her clothes, agile and quick, and not looking back, if ministers ate as well as they loved, Robert would be hungry enough when he woke. Down in the kitchen she came on Else Queen, ganting as wide as a stable-door, she stopped from that, the Manse's new maid, a handsome quean, and she said *Hello!* Chris felt the blood in the tips of her ears, she saw plain the thing in the great lump's mind. *You call me Mrs Colquohoun, you know, Else. And you get up smart in the morning as well, else we'll need another maid in the Manse.*

Else went dirt-white and closed up her mouth. *Yes— Mem, I'm sorry,* and Chris felt a fool, but she didn't show it, and this kind of thing had just to be settled one way or the other. *My name's not Mem, it's just Mrs Colquohoun. Get the water boiling and we'll make the breakfast. What kind of a range is this that we've got?*

THAT WAS THAT, and she had no trouble at all with meikle Else Queen in Kinraddie Manse, though the speak went out and about the parish that Chris Tavendale, the new minister's new wife, had grown that proud that she made her maid cry *Mem!* every time they met on the stairs, a fair dog's life had that poor Else Queen, it just showed you the kind of thing that happened when a creature got up a bit step in the world. And who was she to put on her airs—the daughter of a little bit farmer, just, and the wife of another, killed in the War. Ay, them that were fond of their men didn't marry as close as that on the death of the first, the Manse and the minister's silver the things that the new Mrs Colquohoun had had in her mind.

Chris heard those stories in the weeks that went, if you bade in Kinraddie and any ill tale were told about you—and you fair had to be an angel in breeks if that weren't done and even then, faith! they'd have said there were unco things under your breeks—the very trees rose and sniggered it to you, the kye lowed the news from every bit gate. But she paid no heed, she was blithe and glad, happed in her Robert and the nearness of him, young Ewan as well, a third by the fire as they sat of a night and the storms came malagarousing the trees down the length and breadth of the shrilling Howe. Behind and far up you would hear the hills quake, Robert would raise up his head and laugh, the twinkle-scowl in his deep-set eyes—*The feet of the Lord on the hills, Christine!*

Ewan would look up, staring and still, *Who's the Lord?* and Robert would drop his great book and stare in the fire,

That's a tough one, Ewan. But He's Something and sure, our Father and Mother, our End and Beginning.

Ewan's eyes would open wider at that, *My mother's here and my father's dead.* Robert would laugh and upset his chair, *A natural sceptic—come out of that chair, there's over many of your kind already squatting their hams in the thrones of the mighty!*

So the two of them would crawl round the floor and would growl, play tigers and beasts of like gurring breeds, Ewan with his coolness and graveness forgot, Robert worse than a bairn, Chris sitting and watching, a book in her hand or darning or knitting, but not often those. Robert got angered when she sat and darned. *What, waste your life when you'll soon be dead? You're not going to slave for me, my girl!* And she'd say *But you won't like holes in your socks?* and he'd laugh *When they're holed we'll buy a new pair. Come out for a tramp, the storm's gone down.*

And out they would tramp, young Ewan in bed, the night black under their feet as cold pitch, about them the whistle and moan of the trees till they cleared the Manse and went up by the Mains, with the smell of the dung from its hot cattle-court, and the smell of the burning wood in its lums. You'd see and hear little about you by then, just the two of you swinging up the hill in the dark, till the blow of the wind would catch in your throats as you gained by the cambered edge of the brae.

Around them, dry, the whistle of the whins, strange shapes that rose and were lost in the dark, Robert would stop and would fuss at her collar, pretending he did it to keep out the cold. But she'd grown to know him, the thing that he'd want, she'd put up her arms round close by his throat, and hug him, half-shy, she was still half-shy. He'd told her that once and Chris had been vexed, lying in his arms, for a sudden moment she had touched him with lips fierce and sudden with a flame that came up out of her heart, up out of the years when she still was unwed: and he'd gasped, and she'd laughed *Do you call that shy?* Then she'd been half-ashamed and yet glad as well, and fell fast asleep till the morning came, and they both woke up and looked at each other, and he said that

she blushed and she hid her face and said that one or the
other was a fool.

But best she minded of those night-time walks the first
that took them up to the hills, a rousting night in December's
close. They came at last on Blawearie's brae, and panting,
looked down on the windy Mearns, the lights of Bervie a
lowe in the east, the Laurencekirk gleams like a scattering
of faggots, Segget's that shone as the blurring of stars, these
were the lights of the jute mills there. So they stood a long
while and looked down the brae, Kinraddie below them
happed in its sleep; and Robert fell into a dreaming muse,
as he often did, with his mind far off. Chris said nothing,
content though she froze, after one peek at his stillness
beside her. Queer with *him* here on Blawearie brae, that
once was hers, if they walked down over that shoulder
there they'd come to the loch and the Standing Stones to
which she had fled for safety, compassion, so often and oft
when she was a quean. . . .

She could smell the winter smell of the land and the
sheep they pastured now on Blawearie, in the parks that
once came rich with corn that Ewan had sown and they
both had reaped, where the horses had pastured, their kye
and their stock. And she minded the nights in the years of
the War, nights such as this when she'd lain in her bed and
thought of the times that would come yet again—Ewan
come back and things as before, how they'd work for
young Ewan and grow old together, and buy Blawearie
and be happy forever. And now she stood by a stranger's
side, she slept in his bed, he loved her, she him, nearer
to his mind than ever she had been to that of the body
that lay mouldering in France, quiet and unmoving that
had moved to her kisses, that had stirred and been glad
in her arms, in her sight, that had known the stinging of
rain in his face as he ploughed the steep rigs of Blawearie
brae, and come striding from his work with that smile on
his face, and his clumsy hands and his tongue that was shy
of the things that his eyes could whisper so blithe. Dead,
still and quiet, not even a body, powder and dust he with
whom she had planned her life and her days in the times
to be.

In a ten years time what things might have been? She might stand on this hill, she might rot in a grave, it would matter nothing, the world would go on, young Ewan dead as his father was dead, or hither and borne, far from Kinraddie: oh, once she had seen in these parks, she remembered, the truth, and the only truth that there was, that only the sky and the seasons endured, slow in their change, the cry of the rain, the whistle of the whins on a winter night under the sailing edge of the moon—

And suddenly, daft-like, she found herself weep, quiet, she thought that she made no noise, but Robert knew, and his arm came round her.

It was Ewan? Oh, Chris, he won't grudge you me!

Ewan? It was Time himself she had seen, haunting their tracks with unstaying feet.

BUT THE SPRING was coming. You looked from the Manse at the hills as they moved and changed with each day, the glaur and the winter dark near gone, the green came quick and far on the peaks the blink of the white snow-bonnets grew less, swallows were wheeling about the Manse trees, down in the fields of the Mains you could hear the click and spit of a tractor at work, far up by Upperhill parks rise the baa of the sheep they pastured now on Bridge End. It seemed to Chris when those first days came that she'd weary to death with a house and naught else, not to have fields that awaited her help, help in the seeding, the spreading of dung, the turning out of the kye at dawn, hens chirawking mad for their meat, the bustle and hurry of Blawearie's close. But now as she looked on the land so strange, with its tractors and sheep, she half-longed to be gone. It had finished with her, that life that had been, and this was hers now: books, and her Robert, young Ewan to teach, and set a smooth cloth on the Manse's table, hide in the little back room at the top and darn his socks when Robert didn't see.

He was out and about on the work of the parish, marrying this soul and burying that, christening the hopeful souls new-come to pass in their time to marriage and burial. He'd come back dead tired from a day of his work, Chris would hear him fling his stick in the hall and cry out *Else, will you run me a bath?* And because of those strange, dark moods she had met, Chris seldom met him now on the stairs, she'd wait till he changed and was Robert again, he'd come searching her out and tell her the news, and snatch the book from young Ewan's hand as Ewan squatted in the window-seat, reading. *A prig, a bookworm!* Robert would cry as he flung the book the other side of the room; and Ewan would smile in his slow, dark way, and then give a yell and they'd scuffle a while, while Chris went down and brought up the tea. From that room you could see all Kinraddie by day and the lights of Kinraddie shine as night came, Robert would heave a great sigh as he sat and looked from Chris to Kinraddie below. *Wearied?* she'd ask, and he'd say, *Lord, yes,* and frown and then laugh: *Looks everywhere that would sour the milk! But my job's to minister and minister I will though Kinraddie's kirk grows toom as its head.* And would think a while, *It's near that already.*

FAITH! SO IT was, nothing unco in that, there was hardly a kirk in the Mearns that wasn't, the War had finished your fondness for kirks, you knew as much as any minister. Why the hell should you waste your time in a kirk when you were young, you were young only once, there was the cinema down in Dundon, or a dance or so, or this racket or that; and your quean to meet and hear her complain she's not been ta'en to the Fordoun ball. You'd chirk to your horses and give a bit smile as you saw the minister swoop by on his bike, with his coat-tails flying and his wee, flat hat; and at night in the bothy some billy or other would mock the way that he spoke and moved. To hell with ministers and toffs of his kind, they were aye the friends of the farmers, you knew.

All the farmers now of Kinraddie were big, but they had as little liking as the bothy for the Reverend Colquohoun and the things he said. Would a man go up to the kirk of a Sabbath to sit down and hear himself insulted? You went to kirk to hear a bit sermon about Paul and the things he wrote the Corinthians, all of them folk that were safely dead; but Kinraddie's minister would try to make out that

you yourself, that was born in Fordoun of honest folk, were
a kind of Corinthian, oppressing the needy, he meant those
lazy muckers the ploughmen. No, no, you were hardly so
daft as take that, you would take the mistress a jaunt instead,
next Sunday like or maybe the next, up the Howe to her
cousin in Brechin that hadn't yet seen the new car you
had bought; or maybe you'd just lie happed in your
bed, and have breakfast, and read about all the divorces
the English had from their wives—damn't, man! they
fair had a time, those English tinks! You wouldn't bother
your head on the kirk, to hell with ministers of the kind of
Colquohoun, they were aye the friends of the ploughmen,
you knew.

AND CHRIS WOULD stand in the choir and sing, and
sometimes look at the page in her hand and think of the
days when she at Blawearie had never thought of the kirk
at all, over-busied living the life that was *now* to bother at
all on the life to come. Others of the choir that had missed
a service would say to her with a shy-like smile, *I'm so sorry,
Mrs Colquohoun, I was late;* and Chris would say that they
needn't fash, if she said it in Scots the woman would think,
Isn't that a common-like bitch at the Manse? If she said it in
English the speak would spread round the minister's wife
was putting on airs.

Robert's stipend was just three hundred pounds, when
he'd first told Chris she had thought it a lot, and felt deep
in her a prick of resentment that he got so much, when
the folk on the land that did all the work that really was
work—they got not a third, with a family thrice bigger.
But soon she was finding the money went nowhere, a maid
to keep and themselves forbye, this and that charity that
folk expected the minister should not only help but head.
And they didn't in vain, he'd have given the sark from his
back, would Robert, if Chris hadn't stopped him, and syne
given his vest. When he heard of a cottar that was needy or
ill he'd wheel out his old bike and swoop down the roads,
he rode with old brakes and they sometimes gave way, and
then he would brake with a foot on the wheel, his thoughts
far off as he flew through the stour, if he hadn't a broken

neck it was luck. That was his way and Chris liked him for it, though she herself would as soon have thought of biking that way as of falling off the old tower by the kirk, and lippening to chance she would land on her feet.

Well, so, and most likely sparked up with glaur, he'd come to the house where the ill man lay, and knock and cry *Well, are you in?* and go in. And sit him down by the bed of the man, and tell him a story to make him laugh, never mention God unless he was asked, and that was seldom enough, as you knew, a man just blushed if you mentioned God. So Robert would talk of the crops and fees, and *Where is your daughter fee'd to now?* and *The wife looks fine,* and *I'll need to be off.* And syne as he went he'd slip a pound note into the hand of the sick bit man; and he'd take it and redden up, dour, and say *Thank you;* and after Robert went they'd say, *What's a pound? Him that gets paid as much as he does.*

Chris knew that they said that kind of thing, Else told her the news as they worked in the kitchen; and she knew as well how the news went out from the Manse of every bit thing that was there—Ewan, her son, how he dressed, what he said; and the things they said and the things they sang and how much they ate and what they might drink; when they went to bed and when they got up; and how the minister would kiss his wife, without any shame, in the sight of the maid—Oh, Chris knew most and she guessed the rest, all Kinraddie knew better than she did herself how much she and Robert might cuddle in bed, and watched with a sneer for sign of a son. . . . And somehow, just once, you would hate them for that.

You knew these things, it was daft to get angry, you couldn't take a maid and expect her a saint, especially a lass from a cottar house, and Else was no worse than many another. So in time you grew used to knowing what you did—if you put your hair different or spoke sharp to Ewan or went up of an evening to change your frock—would soon be known to the whole of Kinraddie, with additional bits tacked on for a taste. And if you felt sick, once in a blue moon, faith! but the news went winged in the Howe, a bairn was coming, all knew the date, they would eye you keen as you stood in the choir, and see you'd fair filled out this last week; and they'd mouth the news on the edge of their teeth, and worry it to death as a dog with a bone.

But Chris cooked and cleaned with Else Queen to help, and grew to like her in spite of her claik, she'd tried no airs since that very first time, instead she was over-anxious to *Mem!* Chris couldn't be bothered in a while to stop her, knowing well as she did that in many a way she was a sore disappointment to Else.

IN OTHER BIT places where a quean would fee, with the long-teethed gentry up and down the Howe or the poverty put-ons of windy Stonehive, the mistress would aye be glad of a news, hear this and that that was happening outbye, you'd got it direct from so-and-so's maid. But Mrs Colquohoun would just listen and nod, maybe, polite enough in a way, but with hardly a yea or a nay for answer. And at first a lassie had thought the creature was acting up gentry, the minister's wife: but syne you saw that she just didn't care, not a button she cared about this place and that, and the things that were happening, the marryings and dyings, the kissings and cuddlings, the kickings and cursings, the lads that had gone and the farmers that broke; and what this cottar had said to his wife and what the wife had thrown at the cottar. And it fair was a shock, the thing wasn't natural, you made up your mind to give in your notice and go to a place where you wouldn't be lonesome.

So you'd have done if it hadn't been Ewan, the laddie that came from *her* first bit marriage, so quiet and so funny, but a fine little lad, he'd sometimes come down and sit in the kitchen and watch as you peeled the potatoes for dinner, and tell you things he had read in his books, and ask, *What's a virgin princess like—like you, Else?* And when you laughed and said *Oh, but bonnier a lot,* he would screw up his brows, *I don't mean that, is she like you under your clothes, I mean?*

You blushed at that, *I suppose she is,* and he looked at you calm as could be. *Well, that's very nice, I am sure*—so polite you wanted to give him a cuddle, and did, and he stood stock still and let you, not moving, syne turned and went out and suddenly went mad in the way that he would, whistling and thundering like a horse up the stairs, with a din and a racket to deafen a body, but fine for all that, you liked a place with a bairn at play; though not aye making a damned row, either.

So you stayed at the Manse as the summer wore on, and you liked it better, and sometimes you'd stop—when outbye or gone up home for a day—in the telling of this or that at the Manse, and be sorry you ever had started the tale. And your father would growl *Ay, and what then?* and you'd say, *Oh, nothing*, and look like a fool, and whoever was listening would be sore disappointed. But you'd minded sudden the face of the mistress, or young Ewan, polite, who thought you looked nice: and it didn't seem fair to tell stories of *them*.

And then, in the August, you were ill as could be, and they didn't send you off home to Segget, as most others would, to the care of your folk. Faith! you half thought as the mistress came in and dosed you with medicine and punched up your pillows and brought you your breakfast and dinner and tea, that she was well pleased to do all the work, you heard her singing washing the stairs, the minister himself went to help in the kitchen, you heard of that through the half-open door, then laugh as the mistress threw water at him and the scamper of feet as he chased her for that. When next dinner came the minister himself came in with the tray and his shirt-sleeves up, you blushed, and tried to cover your nightie, he cried, *All safe, Else, you needn't be shy. I'm old and I'm married, though you're pretty enough.*

And somehow you just didn't tell that outbye, folk would have said that he slept with you next. So you lay in your bed and had a fine rest but that they tormented you to read books and brought great piles to put by your bed, and themselves were so keen that you fair were fashed, they would read you out bits, the mistress or minister, sometimes them both, and you never had had patience with books in your life. You could never get in them or past the long words, some thing there was that stood fast between, though you knit up your brows and tried ever

so hard. And you'd drop the damn book when a minute
was past and listen instead to the birds in the trees, as the
evening drew in and they chirped in their sleep, and the low
of the kye in the parks of the Mains, and see through the
swinging of the casement window the light of the burning
whins on the hills, smell—you smelled with your body
entire—the tingle and move of the harvesting land. And
then you'd be wearied and lie half asleep, wondering what
Charlie was doing to-night, had he taken some other quean
out to the pictures, or was sitting about at some bothy fire? .
And would he come to see you as he'd written he'd come?

He came that Sunday, and the mistress herself it was
brought him up, he stood with his cap in his hands and
he blushed, and you did the same, but the mistress didn't.
Now sit down and talk and I'll bring you both tea. And off then
she went, and you thought then, as often, she was bonny in
a way, in a dour, queer way, with her hair dark-red and so
coiled, and the eyes so clear, and the mouth like a man's,
but shaped to a better shape than a man's, you stared at the
door even after she'd gone, till Charlie whispered, *Do you
think she'll come back?* And you said, *No, you gowk,* and
peeked at him quiet, and he looked round about as slow as
a sow and then cuddled you quick, and that was fair fine,
and you wanted a minute to cry in his arms, because you
were ill and weak and half-witted. You told yourself that
and pushed him away, and he smoothed his hair and said,
You're right bonny, and you said, *Don't haver,* and he said,
Well, I don't.

The mistress and Ewan brought up the tea, then left you
enough together alone for the two of you to have wedded
and bedded, as you thought in a peek of a thought that
came. And you looked at Charlie, he was sitting there
douce, telling of his place and the hard work there was,
he'd as soon have thought ill as of dancing a jig. Like a
fool you felt only half-pleased to know that, of course you
didn't want anything to happen, but at least he should try
to make out that *he* did, it was only nature a man should
want that, especially if you looked as bonny as he said. So
you were fell short with him in the end, and he took his
leave and the mistress came up. And you suddenly felt a

fool altogether, you were weeping and weeping, with her arm about you, safe you felt there and sleepy and tired. She said, *It's all right, Else, sleep, you'll be fine. You're tired now you've talked so long with your lad.*

But you knew from her look she knew more than that, she knew the thing you yourself had thought; and you said to yourself when she left you that night, *If I ever hear any speak ill of the Colquohouns, I'll—I'll—*and afore you'd decided whether you'd blacken their eyes, or their character, or both, you fell fast alseep.

SOMETIMES A BLACK, queer mood came on Robert, he would lock himself up long hours in his room, hate God and Chris and himself and all men, know his Faith a fantastic dream; and see the fleshless grin of the skull and the eyeless sockets at the back of life. He would pass by Chris on the stairs if they met, with remote, cold eyes and a twisted face, or ask in a voice that cut like a knife, *Can't you leave me alone, must you always follow?*

The first time it happened her heart had near stopped, she went on with her work in a daze of amaze. But Robert came from his mood and came seeking her, sorry and sad for the queer, black beast that rode his mind in those haunted hours. He said that the thing was a physical remembrance, only that just, and Chris not to worry; and she found out that near the end of the War he'd been gassed by an awful gas that they made, and months had gone by ere he breathed well again, and the fumes of that drifting Fear were gone. And sometimes the shadows of that time came back, though his lungs were well enough now, he was sure, though 'twas in the months of his agony he'd known, conviction, terrible and keen as his pain, that there was a God Who lived and endured, the Tortured God in the soul of men, Who yet might upbuild the City of God through the hearts and hands of men of good faith.

But also Chris found it coming on Robert that here he could never do good or do ill, in a countryside that was dying or dead. One night he looked at Chris and said, *Lord! But for you, Christine, I was daft to come here. I'll try for a kirk in some other place, there's work enough to be done in the towns.* And thought for a while, his fair head in his hands. *Would you like a town?*

Chris said, *Oh, fine,* and smiled reassurance, but she bit at her lips and he saw, and he knew. *Well, then, not a town. I'll try to find something betwixt and between.*

So he did ere a month was out, news came from Segget its minister was dead, Robert brought the news home: *I'm to try for his kirk.* And Chris said, *Segget?* and Robert said *Yes,* and Chris quoted the bit of poetry there was, somebody they said in Segget had made it:

Oh, Segget it's a dirty hole,
  A kirk without a steeple
A midden-heap at ilka door
  And damned uncivil people!

Robert laughed, *We'll make them both civil and clean,* Chris said, *But you haven't yet gotten the kirk,* and he said *Just wait, for I very soon will.*

Three Sundays later they set out for Segget, Robert to preach there and Chris to listen, it was April, quiet and brown in the fields, drowsy under a blanket of mist that cleared as the sun rose, leaving the hills corona'ed in feathery wispings of clouds, Chris asked their name, and Robert said, *Cirrus. They bring fine weather and they're standing still. There's little wind on the heights to-day.*

And Chris on her bicycle suddenly felt young, younger far than she'd felt for years, Robert beside her on his awful bike, it made a noise like a threshing machine, collies came barking from this close and that; but Robert ground on and paid them no heed, scowling, deep in his sermon, no doubt. But once he swung round. *Am I going too fast?* and Chris said, *Fast? It's liker a funeral,* and he came from the deeps of his thoughts and laughed, *Oh, Chris, never change and grow English-polite! Not even in Segget, when we settle in its Manse!*

Syne he said of a sudden, a minute or so later, they were past Mondynes and Segget in sight: *Do you mind how Christ was tempted of the devil? And so was I till you spoke just now. I'd made up my mind I'd butter them up, in the sermon I preached—just for the chance of getting out of*

*Kinraddie, settled in Segget, and on with some work. Well, I
won't. . . . By God, I'll give them a sermon!*

THE OLD MINISTER had died of drink, fair sozzled he was,
folk said, at the end; and his last words were, so the story
went, *And what might the feare's prices be to-day?* No doubt
that was just a bit lie that they told, but faith! he'd been
greedy enough for his screw, with his long grey face and his
bleary eyes and his way that he had of speaking to a man,
met out in the street or down by the Arms, as though he
were booming from the pulpit itself: *Why didn't I see you
in the kirk last Sabbath?* And a billy would redden and
give a bit laugh, and look this way and that, were he one
of New Toun. But more than likely, were he one of the
spinners, he'd answer: *Maybe because I wasn't there!* in
the awful twang that the creatures spoke; and go off and
leave old Greig sore vexed, he'd never got over the fact that
the spinners cared hardly a hoot for kirk session or kirk.

Ah well, he was a dead and a two-three came to try for
his pulpit, more likely his stipend, two old men came,
each buttered up Segget, you'd have thought by the way
the creatures blethered the Archangel Michael could have
come to Segget, and bought a shop, and felt at home as
he sat at the back and sanded the sugar. Folk took that
stite with a dosing of salts, then the third man came and
some stories came with him, 'twas the Reverend Robert
Colquhoun of Kinraddie, he'd been down there only a
bare two years, and half his congregation had gone, they'd
go anywhere but listen to him, he was aye interfering and
preaching at folk that had done him no harm, couldn't he
leave them a-be? Forbye that he'd married a quean of the
parish, and if there's a worse thing a minister can do than
marry a woman that knows the kirk folk, it's only to suck
sweeties under the pulpit in the time he's supposed to be
in silent prayer.

Well, Mr Colquhoun, he didn't suck sweets, but he
did near everything else, folk said, and most of Segget,
though it thronged to hear him, had no notion to vote for
the creature at all.

But when he was seen stride up to the pulpit, and he

leaned from the pulpit rails and he preached, the elders
were first of all ta'en with his way, and the old folk next
with the thing that he preached, not the mealy stuff that
you'd now hear often, but meaty and strong and preached
with some fire—and man! he fairly could tell a bit tale!

For he took his text from a chapter in Judges, his sermon
on Gath and the things that that Jew childe Samson did,
how at last the giant was bound to a pillar, but he woke
from the stupor and looked round about, and cried that
the Philistines free him his bonds; and they laughed and
they feasted, paying him no heed, sunk in their swine-like
glaurs of vice. Their gods were idols of brass and of gold,
they lived on the sweat and the blood of men, crying one to
the other, *Behold, we are great, we endure, and not earth itself
is more sure. Pleasure is ours and the taste of lust, wine in our
mouths and power in our hands;* and the lash was heard on
the bowed slave's back, they had mercy on neither their kith
nor their kin. And Samson woke and looked round again,
he was shorn of his hair, bound naked there, in the lights of
the torches, tormented and chained. And then sudden the
Philistines felt the walls rock and they looked them about
and saw the flames wave, low and sharp in a little wind;
and again about them the great hall groaned, and Samson
tore down the pillars of the roof, and the roof fell in and
slew him and them. . . . And Samson was rising again in
our sight, threatening destruction unless we should change,
and free both him and the prisoners chained in the littered
halls of our secret hearts.

And maybe it was because it was Spring, new-come, the
sun a long, drowsy blink in the kirk, and folk heard the
voice of the Reverend Colquohoun like the wind they'd hear
up under the hills, fine and safe as they listened below, and
who could he mean by Samson but them, ground down by
the rents they'd to pay the Mowats? Maybe it was that
and maybe it was because folk aye had prided themselves
in Segget in taking no heed of what others said, that they
licked up the sermon like calves at a cog; and a fair bit
crowd watched Robert Colquohoun, him and his wife, she
seemed decent and quiet, mount on their bikes and ride
home to Kinraddie.

ROBERT SAID TO Chris, *That's the end of my chance. But I'm glad I preached what I felt and thought.* But Chris had a clearer vision than his, *They liked the sermon and I think they liked you. They hadn't a notion what the sermon meant—themselves the Philistines and someone else Samson.*

Robert stared. *But I made it plain as plain.* Chris laughed, *To yourself; anyhow, we'll see.* And they rode to Kinraddie, and the days went by, Robert didn't believe he would head the leet. But he found out, for fun, all he could about Segget, from papers and Else and lists and old books, there was less than a thousand souls in Segget, and most of them lost, if you trusted Else. Half of the Segget folk worked at the mills—the spinners, as the rest of Segget called them; the others kept shops or were joiners or smiths, folk who worked on the railway, the land, the roads, and the gardens of Segget House. Robert found an old map of the place and renewed it, playing as a boy with a toy town.

Chris leaned on his chair and looked over his shoulder, his fingers nimble in limning New Toun (where the folk had gone when the spinners came), Old Toun and its winding jumble of lanes that bunched and clustered around the West Wynd. South was the Arms, in the Segget Square, the East Wynd dotted with a joiner's, a school, a tailor's shop, a grocery, a sutor's—*and the Lord knows what*, Robert said as his pen swopped down the Wynd to the Segget Square. Then it wheeled about and went up The Close to the post-office-grocery-shop combined, dotted the Segget smiddy beyond, and syne lost itself in the Segget slums. . . . Chris saw on the northern outskirts of Segget two dots for the Manse and the steepleless kirk, and over to the west another one still, Segget House, where the Mowats lived, the old mill-owner new-dead, said Else, and his son, young Stephen, at an English college.

And Robert would whistle as he looked at his map— *What mightn't a minister do in Segget, with the help of young Mowat or the folk of the schools? And sutors are atheists, bound to have brains, and extremely religious, all atheists are. One could do great things with a village League . . .*

Then he would laugh, *Just playing with bricks! Ewan, where are those toys you've outgrown?*

The news that he'd topped the leet at the poll was brought to Robert by an elder of Segget, it was Else who opened the door for the creature, she knew him well, but she didn't let on. It was wee Peter Peat, the tailor of Segget, his shop stood mid-way the wind of East Wynd, with his house behind it, he thought it a castle. And he spoke right fierce, and he'd tell a man, before you were well in the lithe of his door, that he made a fine neighbour to those that were good, the best of friends to his friends, he was, but God pity the man that fell out with him, he'd never forgive an injury, never. And he was the biggest Tory in Segget, the head of the Segget Conservative branch, and an awful patriot, keen for blood; but he'd loup in his shoes as he heard his wife, Meg Peat that was slow and sonsy to look at, come into the shop, she'd cry *Peter, I'm away. Mind the fire and have tea set ready;* and he'd quaver, *Ay Meg,* like an ill-kicked cur. But soon's she was gone he'd look fierce as ever, ready to kill you and eat you forbye, and running his tape up and down your bit stomach as though he were gutting you and enjoying it.

Well, here he was standing, fierce as a futret. *Is the Reverend Mr Colquohoun indoors?* And Else said, *I'll see; what name shall I tell him?* And he said *Gang and tell him Peter Peat's here.*

Else went and found the minister in his study, and the minister said *Peat?* and looked at the mistress; and the mistress smiled in the quiet way she had, and shook her head, and the minister shook his. *Still, kindling or peat, I suppose I'd best see him!*

Else went down the stairs to where Peter stood. *Come in, and wipe your feet on the mat.* He looked as though he'd have liked to wipe them on *her,* but he came in, fierce in his five feet two, the minister was waiting and rose when he came. *I've come from Segget,* Else heard the thing say, and the minister answer as she closed the door, *Oh, yes? Well, won't you sit down, Mr Peat?*

And then, a half hour or so after that, Chris heard the closing of the Manse front door and syne the scamper of feet on the stairs, she thought it was Ewan come in from his play. But instead it was Robert, he burst into the room, his face was flushed and he caught her arms, and plucked her up from the chair she sat in, and danced her half round the great-windowed room. She gasped, *What is't?* and he said *What, that? Peter Peat, the tailor of Segget, of course.* Then he dropped in the chair from which he had plucked her, and sat there panting, still holding her hands. *Christine, you're now looking at Segget's minister. And he's promised that never as long as he lives he'll pray for All-but the Prince of Wales!*

HE TOLD THE story he'd gotten from Peter, and Chris heard it later amended by Else, a warning that folk in a pulpit speak plain. He was fell religious, wee Peter Peat, an elder of the kirk and twice every Sunday he'd nip up and down the pews with the bag; and look at you sharp to see what you put in. And once he cried out to Dalziel of Meiklebogs, that was stinking with silver but fair was right canny, *No, no, I'll not have a button from you!* And Meiklebogs reddened like a pig with rash, and dropped a half-crown in the bag by mistake, he was so took aback and affronted-like. That was back a good while, in the days of old Nichols, the last minister but one, he was, as proud and stuck-up as a hubbley-jock, English, and he never learned to speak right; and his prayers at first had fair maddened Peat. For when he came to the bit about Royalty, and he'd pray for the birn with might and with main, he'd finish up *And all but the Prince of Wales.* Now Peat he was Tory and fond of the Prince, he went home to his wife in a fair bit stew, *What the hell ails him at the Prince of Wales that he blesses all but him, I would like to know?* And at last he tackled old Nichols on the matter, and the creature gave a bit sniftering laugh, and said to Scotch ears he supposed that *All-but* was how it sounded when he said *Albert.* And he spoke this slow, in a sneering bit way, as though he thought Scotch ears were damn poor ears, mostly bad in the need of a clean—when manners were being given out he hadn't even the manners to stay and receive his, Peter Peat said.

CHRIS WOKE ON the morning of the move to Segget with a start of fear she had over-slept. It was May, and the light came round about five, red and gold and a flow of silver down the parks that she knew so well, she got from bed at the very first blink, Robert yawned and sat up and remembered the day, and dived for his clothes, no bath this morning she told him as each struggled into clothes. He said, *Ah well, I'm not very foul*, and she thought that funny, and giggled and tangled her hair with her dress; and he said, *Let me help*, and his help was a hinder, it was only an excuse to take her and kiss her, this day of all!

She pushed him away at last and he went, whistling, two steps at a time down the stair, Chris heard Else moving already in the kitchen and when she got down found breakfast near ready, and Else all excitement, and young Ewan up, his knickers pulled on the wrong way in his hurry. She'd to alter that and try answer his questions, and run to help Robert with the very last kist, full up to the brim with books and such-like; and he swore at the thing and Chris sat on the top, and Ewan came running and jumped there as well, and it closed with a bang, and they all of them cheered.

They sat down to breakfast, famished already. Suddenly Else came running in—*Mem, it's started to rain!* with her face as though it were raining ink, and thick ink forbye. So Chris had to quiet her, and see Ewan ate, and Robert forbye, excited as Else. Then they heard down the road the burr of a lorry, and Else came again: *It's Melvin from Segget.*

So it was, they'd hired him to do the Manse flitting, and had heard his character redd up by Else. He kept the only hotel in Segget, the Segget Arms that stood in the Square, the other inn down at the foot of West Wynd had been closed when the local option came. Will Melvin had been right well pleased over that, he said if this was their Prohibition, then he for one was all for the thing. He'd a face like a cat, broad at the eyes, and he'd spit like a cat whenever he spoke; he aye wore a dickey and a high, stiff collar and a leather waistcoat, and leggings and breeks, and he drove the two cars on hire in Segget, and carted folks' coals and attended the bar when Jim the potman, that folk called the Sourock, was down with the awful pains in his wame. Will Melvin had married fell late in life, an Aberdeen woman,

right thin and right north, she kept a quick eye on the bar
and the till. And if she heard a billy give a bit curse, as
a spinner or a cottar might do from outbye, knowing no
better, they weren't Segget folk, she'd cry out sharp in the
thin Aberdeen: *None of your Blasting and Blaspheming in
here*. So folk called her the Blaster and Blasphemer for short,
and if thoughts could have burned she'd have needed to go
and take out a life insurance for fire.

Well, here was Will Melvin, he sat in the kitchen, but
got to his feet when Chris came in. *Good morning, Mem,* and
Chris said Good morning, and he asked, *Will I start then to
load her up?* meaning the lorry, Chris saw, not herself. And
he said he had Muir, the gravedigger, to help, and Chris
called in Robert, and he came and scowled because he was
thinking of some other thing. But he said, *Hello, then, are
we all ready? Would you like a dram before we begin?* Will
Melvin said, genteel, *Just a drop,* and would have sat and
waited for the dram by himself but that Chris asked, *Isn't
there another with you?*

So John Muir was brought in from his seat in the lorry,
he was big and cheery and buirdly, John Muir, a roadman
of Segget, and the two had their dram, and John Muir as
he drank began to tell them of the awful time he'd once had
with a grave. He'd aye had a horror of premature burial,
a fell few there were that were buried like that, when you
dug up the coffins of folk of old time and the boards fell
agley you would sometimes see, through the shrouds, the
bones all bulging and twisted, the creatures had struggled
down there in the earth, not dead at all, gasping for breath.
. . . Well, he'd been thinking of that one night as he went
to dig a new grave by the kirk, it was windy weather on
the winter's edge. He'd only finished digging the hole, and
turned about, and straightened his back, when the earth
gave way and his feet as well. Next minute his head went
over his heels and flat in a puddle of red earth he went,
right down at the bottom of the grave he had dug, his head
half-jammed in under his shoulder. He nearly fainted with
the awful shock, syne cried for help as loud as he could.
But he heard long nothing, it was winter time, the light
was waning up on the hills, he looked up and knew before

long he'd be dead. And he cried again and as luck would
have it the old minister heard his bit yowl, and came canny
and slow down through the graves, and looked in the hole
where John Muir was lying. And he said: *Who is't?* and
John Muir was sore vexed. *Oh, ay, we've been introduced*, he
cried back, *so stand on no ceremony—damn't, get a ladder!*

Maybe that was why he still gleyed that way and went
with a kind of twist to his shoulder, Chris thought; but
Robert just laughed and looked at his watch. *Well, this is a
flitting, not yet a funeral.* John Muir set down his glass and
gleyed cheery, *Ay, well, it'll end in that, come time*, you'd
have thought he had something wrong with his stomach.
But he gleyed at Chris cheery as a cock on a ree, and fell to
with a will, him and Will Melvin, and carried out tables and
presses and chairs, and kists and beds and boxes of dishes,
and piled them up till the lorry groaned. Will Melvin near
did the same at the sound and went spitting around like a
startled cat. Then they drove off, Robert went with them
to help, Else went as well in the back of the lorry, clasping
the best tea-set to herself, and giving young Ewan a wave
as she went.

The rain had cleared and Chris watched the lorry lurch
down by the Mains in the flare of the sun, they'd got a fine
day after all for the flitting. She liked John Muir, if not
Melvin much; but then it was daft to judge folk at first
sight. Young Ewan came running and asked for a piece,
they sat together in the half-tirred rooms, and ate some
biscuits and looked at each other, with the bizz of a fly
on the stripped window-panes. Ewan asked why they were
moving to Segget, Chris tried to tell him, and he listened,
polite, and then went out and drowsed in the grass till he
heard the lorry returning from Segget.

They loaded up the last of the stuff, John Muir climbed
gleying up in its midst, and Chris locked the door and left
the key for the folk of the Mains to come up and get, hid
in a little hole in the wall. Then she went to the lorry where
Melvin was waiting, young Ewan beside him, and climbed
in as well; and the lorry wound out through the bending
of yews where long, long ago the knight Wallace had hidden
as the English were looking for him in the wars.

They saw not a soul as they passed the Mains, then they swung out into the road that led south; and so as they went Chris turned and looked back, at Kinraddie, that last time there in the sun, the moor that smoothed to the upland parks Chae Strachan had ploughed in the days gone by, the Knapp with no woods to shelter it now, Upperhill set high in a shimmer of heat, Cuddiestoun, Netherhill—last of them all, high and still in the hill-clear weather, Blawearie up on its ancient brae, silent and left and ended for you; and suddenly, daft, you couldn't see a thing.

BUT THAT WENT by, Chris glad to be gone; and the lorry switched from the main road's ribbon up by the old thatched toun of Culdyce, and she saw the Howe spread out like a map, there was Drumlithie down in its hollow, a second Segget, but steepled enough. Mondynes that stood by the Bervie Water, Fettercairn, where the soldiers of the widow Finella had lain in wait to mischieve King Kenneth. All the parks were set with their hoeing squads, four, five at a time they swung by the drills, here and there the hindmost man would stop, and straighten up slow, a hand at his back, to look at the lorry—whose could it be? And all the long line would straighten up, slow, and catch a glimpse of Chris, in her blue, and young Ewan in his, with his straight, black hair.

And there, as they swung by the Meiklebogs farm, the hills to the right, at last lay Segget, a cluster and crawl of houses white-washed, the jute-mills smoking by Segget Water, the kirk with no steeple that rose through the trees, the houses of the spinners down low on the left, though Chris didn't know that these were their houses. Then the lorry puffed up to the old kirk Manse, on the fringe of Segget, and Chris saw the lawn piled in a fair hysteria of furniture. She jumped down and stood a minute at gaze, in the shadows, the shadows the new yews flung, the grass seemed blue in the blaze of the heat.

Then as Melvin backed back the lorry and Ewan went running out over the lawn to the door, Robert came out and saw Chris and waved, and was pleased as though they'd been parted a year. He dropped the end of the press he'd picked up, near dropped it down on the toes of Muir (who gleyed as cheery as though 'twas a coffin) and cried to Chris, *Come and see the new study*. And nothing could content him but up she must go, leaving Melvin below to glower after the gowks.

Then two men came taiking up the Manse drive, Dalziel of the Meiklebogs and one of his men, Robert went down to see who they were. Dalziel said *Ay, you'll be the minister?* and smiled, he was bad in the need of a shave, of middle height though he looked a lot less, so broad in the shoulders, hands like hams; and he smiled slow and shy with his red, creased face, and he said that he'd seen the lorries go by, and he knew right well the sore job it was to do a flitting without much help. And all the time he was smiling there, shy, he looked to Chris like a Highland bull, with his hair and his horns and maybe other things: there was something in his shyness that made her shiver. Beside him, Robert seemed like a boy from school, thin and tall with his slim, thin face; and back of Robert was Else as she looked, not slim at all but big and well-made, her head flung back in that way she had and a look on her face as much as to say, *Good Lord, what's this that has come to us now?*

Then they all fell to carrying in the Manse gear, and Chris fled here and there in the house, a great toom place that shambled all ways, there were stairs that started and suddenly finished and steps that crumbled away into gloom, down to old cellars that never were used. And sometimes you'd think you would come to a room, and you didn't, you came slap-bang on another, the windows fast-closed and stiff with the heat. Chris told where and how to place all the things, and Meiklebogs and Else carried up the beds, and set them together, Chris heard Else give orders and Meiklebogs answer, canny and shy, *You'll be the new minister's bit maidie?* Else said, *There's damn the* MAIDIE *about me;* and Chris didn't hear more, but she guessed a bit.

John Muir came to her and asked where to put a press and a bed and some other things she'd brought from Blawearie the first flit she made. And she didn't know, in that crowding of rooms, till he said *Would you maybe like the gear altogether?*

and she said, *Just that, in a small-like room.* So he carried
the bed up and back through the Manse, to a high-built
room, it was three stairs up. The place was so lost that the
cleaners had missed it, there were cobwebs looped from the
walls like twine. But through the window, when you swung
it out wide, you saw sudden hills rise up in your face, with
below you the roll of long, grass-grown mounds. John Muir
let down the bed with a bang, the great heavy bed that had
once been her father's. Chris asked him what were the ruins
up there, and he said, *You've heard of the Kaimes of Segget?*

Chris leaned from the window and looked to the west.
*And what's that to the left, that hiddle of houses?—Where
the spinners bide,* he told her, she stared, she had thought
them abandoned byres or pig-styes. But Muir just gleyed
and said they were fine—*good enough for the dirt that's
in them. If you gave good houses to rubbish like them, they'd
have them pig-rees in a damn short while. They're not Segget
folk, the spinners, at all.*

Chris said *Oh?* and looked at him, quiet, then they went
down to bring up the rest; and there was Meiklebogs met
on the stair, smiling shy at that sumph of a maid. And John
Muir thought, *You'd think he'd have quieted by now. A man
that can't keep off the women by the time he's reaching to sixty
or so should be libbed and tethered in a cattle-court.*

Near twelve they'd the most of the furniture in, all but
a long table brought from the north, from the Manse of
Robert Colquohoun's old father, solid and oak and a hell
of a weight. And then Else called that the dinner was ready,
Chris said they all must stay and have dinner. Robert said
Let's eat it out on this table.

So Else served them the dinner in the shade of the
yews, and sat down herself when she'd finished with that,
Meiklebogs waiting to see where she sat, and sitting down
next with a shy-like smile. Robert came out, getting into his
coat, and stood at the end of the table a minute and bent
his head, fair in the sunny weather, and said the grace, the
grace of a bairn; and they bent and listened, all but young
Ewan:

> God bless our food,
> And make us good.

And pardon all our sins,
       For Jesus Christ's sake.
Then they all ate up, Muir, Melvin, and Meiklebogs, and
the fee'd man that blushed and was shy, not just looked
it, Chris liked him best, with that sudden compassion that
always came on her as she looked at one of his kind—that
conviction that he and his like were the REAL, they were the
salt and savour of earth. She heard him, shy-like, say *Ay,
I've a spoon*, as Else was asking, and knew by the way that he
mouthed the *spoon* that he came from the North, as she did
herself. And faith! so he did, like her 'twas from Echt, and
he knew fine the place where once she had bidden, Cairndhu
in the Barmekin's lithe. And he fair buckled up and he lost
his shyness, *Ay, then, you're a Guthrie?* and she said that she
was, and he said that they minded him long up in Echt, John
Guthrie, her father, the trig way he farmed: and Chris felt
herself colour up with sheer pleasure, her father could farm
other folk off the earth!

Then she fell in a dream as she heard them talk, the
rooks were cawing up in the yews, and you thought how
they'd fringed your pattern of life—birds, and the waving
leafage of trees: peewits over the lands of Echt when you
were a bairn with your brother Will, and the spruce stood
dark in the little woods that climbed up the slopes to the
Barmekin bend; snipe sounding low on Blawearie loch as
you turned in unease by the side of Ewan, and listened and
heard the whisp of the beech out by the hedge in the quiet
of the night; and here now rooks and the yews that stood
to peer in the twisty rooms of the Manse. How often would
you know them, hear them and see them, with what things
in your heart, in what hours of the dark and what hours of
the day, in all the hours lying beyond this hour when the
sun stood high and the yew-trees drowsed?

But she shook herself and came out of her dream, back to
the table and the sun on the lawn, daft to go prowling those
copses of night where the sad things done were stored with
the moon. Here was the sun, and here was her son, Ewan,
and Robert, the comrade of God, and those folk of Segget
she had yet to know, and all the tomorrows that waited
her here.

BUT THAT NIGHT she had slept in fits and in starts, waking early in that strange, quiet room, by the side of Robert, sleeping so sound. Then it was the notion had suddenly arisen, to come up to the Kaimes, as here she was now, watching the east grow pale in the dawn.

Pale and so pale: but now it was flushed, barred sudden with red and corona'ed with red, as though they were there, the folk who had died, and the sun came washed from the sea of their blood, the million Christs who had died in France, as once she had heard Robert preach in a sermon. Then she shook her head and that whimsy passed, and she thought of Robert—his dream just a dream? Was there a new time coming to the earth, when nowhere a bairn would cry in the night, or a woman go bowed as her mother had done, or a man turn into a tormented beast, as her father, or into a bullet-torn corpse, as had Ewan? A time when those folk down there in Segget might be what Robert said all men might be, companions with God on a terrible adventure? Segget: John Muir, Will Melvin, Else Queen; the folk of the grisly rees of West Wynd—

Suddenly, far down and beyond the toun there came a screech as the morning grew, a screech like an hungered beast in pain. The hooters were blowing in the Segget Mills.

TWO

Cumulus

CROSSING THE steep of the brae in the dark, by the winding path from the Manse to the Kaimes, Chris bent her head to the seep of the rain, the wet November drizzle of Segget. Then she minded a wall of the Kaimes still stood, and ran quick up the path to stand in its lee. That gained, she stood and panted a while, six months since she'd been up here in the Kaimes—only six months, she could hardly believe it!

It felt like years—long and long years—since she'd worked as a farmer's wife in Kinraddie. Years since she'd felt the beat of the rain in her face as she moiled at work in the parks. How much had she gained, how much had she lost?—apart from her breath, she had almost lost that!

She felt the wall and then leant against it, wrapped in her ulster, looking at Segget, in its drowse of oil-lamps under the rain. Safe anyhow to go home this time. . . . And she smiled as she minded last time she had climbed to the Kaimes, and Segget had seen her go home—by the tale they told all Segget had seen her and stared astounded, a scandalled amaze——

BUT INDEED, IT was only Ag Moultrie that morning, as ill-luck would have it, who saw her go home. She had gone out early to the school to redd up, she went heavy with sleep and her great mouth a-agant, as you well might believe, though she didn't tell that. Folk knew her fine, all the Moultries forbye, Rob Moultrie had once been the saddler of Segget, his shop lay down by the edge of the Square. And as coarse an old brute as you'd meet, was Rob Moultrie, though a seventy years old and nearing his grave. 'Twas only a saddler's shop in name now, the trade

35

had clean gone this many a year. There was still a britchen or so in the shop, and a fine bit bridle Rob Moultrie had made in the days long syne when he still would work. But his trade had gone and his sweirty had come, he was never a popular man in the toun; he couldn't abide the sight of the gentry, or the smell of the creatures either, he said, and that was why he was Radical still. And if he went on a dander somewhere, along the road and he'd hear a car, toot-tooting behind him, would he get off the road? Not him, he'd walk on bang in the middle, dare any damn motorist try run him down. So sometimes he'd come back to Segget from a walk, step-stepping cannily along the bit road, with a two-three motorists hard at his heels, toot-tooting like mad, and the shovers red-faced. Mrs Moultrie would be looking from the window and see, and cry as he came, *Losh, Rob, you'll be killed!* And he'd stop and glower at her with his pocked old face, and his eyes like the twinkling red eyes of a weasel, and sneer, the old creature, shameful to hear. *Ay, that would be fine—no doubt you'd get up to your old bit capers. Get out of my way!* And he'd lift his stick, maybe more than do that, syne hirple over to his armchair, and sit there and stare in the heart of the fire or turn to the reading of his old bit Bible.

For he'd never forgiven Jess Moultrie the fact that more than a forty years before, when he'd met her and married her, she'd been with a bairn. She told how it was before she would marry, and he'd glowered at her dour: *More fool that I am. But I'm willing to take you and your shame as well.* And he took her, and the bairn was born, young Ag, no others came and maybe that was why he still kept up the sneer at his wife. But she would say nothing, she was patient and bowed, little, with a face like a brown, still pool; and she'd say not a word, getting on with her work, making ready the supper for Ag when she came. She cleaned out the school and the hall and such places, did Ag, and in winter made the school broth, as nasty a schlorich as ever you'd taste. She looked like a horse ta'en out of a plough, and her voice was a neigh like a horse's as well, and she'd try to stand up for her mother with old Rob. *Don't speak that way to my mother!* she would cry, and he'd look at her dour, *Ay, ay, no doubt she's precious in your sight. You had only one mother, though three or four fathers;* and Ag more than likely would start to greet then, she wasn't a match for the thrawn old brute, though a good enough one for most other folk. And faith! she'd a tongue for news that was awful. Ake Ogilvie called her the Segget Dispatch, she knew everything that happened in Segget, and a lot that didn't, but she liked best to tell of births and funerals and such-like things; and how the daughter of this or that corpse no sooner looked on the dead than broke down—*and fair roared and grat when she saw him there.* So folk called her the Roarer and Greeter for short.

Well, then, it was her, to get on with the tale, as she blinked her way in that morning in May, saw a woman come down the hill from the Kaimes, and stopped dumbfoundered: Who could she be?

Ag was real shocked, for the Kaimes was the place where spinners and tinks of that kind would go, of a Sabbath evening, and lie on the grass and giggle and smoke and do worse than that—Ay, things that would leave them smoking in hell, as the old minister said that they would. So no decent folk went up there at night, this creature of a woman was surely a tink. And Ag gave a sniff, but was curious forbye, and crept canny along in the lithe of the dyke that hemmed in the lassies' playground from the lads'. So she waited there till the woman went by, hurrying, bare-headed, with a stride and a swing and a country-like gait. And then Ag Moultrie near fainted with joy, though she didn't tell you that when she told you the story, she saw that the woman was Mrs Colquohoun, the wife of the new minister of Segget.

Well, afore the day was well started all Segget had heard that the wife of the new minister had been seen by Ag Moultrie up on the Kaimes, she'd been out all night with a spinner up there, Ag had seen them cuddling and sossing in the grass. Folk said, *By God, she's wasted no time; and who would the spinner have been, would you say?* Old Leslie heard the story in the smiddy and he said the thing was Infernal, just. Now, he minded when he was a loon up in Garvock—And the sweat dripped off him, pointing a coulter, and he habbered from nine until loosening-time, near, some story about some minister he'd known; but wherever that was and why it had been, and what the hell happened, if anything ever had, you couldn't make head nor tail if you listened; and you only did that if you couldn't get away. Old Leslie was maybe a fair good smith: he was sure the biggest old claik in Segget. He'd blether from the moment you entered his smiddy, he'd ask how the wife and the bairns all were, and your brother Jock that was down in Dundon, and your sister Jean that was in a sore way; and your father that was down with the colic or the like, and your grandfather, dead this last fifty years. And syne he'd start on your cousins, how they were, and your uncles and aunts and their stirks and their stots, their maids and all that were in their gates: till your hair would be grey and your head fair dizzy at the thought you'd so many relations at all. And his face would sweat like a dripping tap as he hammered at the iron and habbered at you and then he'd start some story of the things he'd done or seen or smelt when a loon up in Garvock, and the day would draw in, the night would come on, and the stars come out, he'd have shod all your horses and set all the coulters and you near were dead for lack of some meat; but *that* damned story wouldn't have finished, it would be going on still with no sign of an end, he'd start it the next time he saw you or heard you, though you were at the far side of a ten-acre field—unless you took to your heels and ran.

Well, about the only soul that couldn't do that was his son, Sim Leslie, the policeman of Segget. He had joined the police and had been sent back to Segget, and still bade with his father, he was used to the blether: and folk said if he listened with a lot of care, for a twenty years or so at a stretch, he at least might find out what really *had* happened that time when his father was a loon up on Garvock. Folk called him Feet, Sim Leslie the bobby, he'd feet so big he could hardly coup, there was once he was shoeing a horse in the smiddy, an ill-natured brute from the Meiklebogs; and the creature lashed out at him fair and square and caught him such a clour on the chest as would fair have flattened any ordinary man. But young

Sim Leslie just rocked a wee bit, his feet had fair a sure grip on Scotland.

Well, Feet heard the story of Mrs Colquohoun, from his father, as the two of them sat at dinner. And he kittled up rare, there was something in this, and maybe a chance of promotion at last. So he went and got hold of Ag Moultrie, the sumph, and pulled out his notebook with his meikle red fingers, and asked was she sure 'twas the minister's wife? And Ag said *Ay*, and Feet made a bit note; and then he seemed stuck, and he said; *You're sure?* And Ag said *Ay, I'm as sure as death.* Feet made another note, and scratched at his head, and swayed a bit in his meikle black boots. *It fair was her?* and Ag said *Ay;* and by then it seemed just about dawning on Feet it really was her and nobody else.

But Ag was real vexed, as she told to folk, she hadn't wanted to miscall a soul, *God knows I'm not a body to claik;* and she said when she'd finished with Feet and his questions she went home and sat down and just Roared and Grat, so sorry she was for the new minister. And she'd tell you some more how the woman had looked, her face red-flushed, with a springy walk; and if you were married you well could guess why all of that was—damn't, man, 'twas fairly a tasty bit news!

That night Feet went up and prowled round the Manse, with his bull's-eye held in his hand and his feet like the clopping of a Clydesdale heard on the ground. He didn't know very well what he was there for, or what he would say if Mrs Colquohoun saw him; but he was awful keen on promotion. And he said he was fine at detective-work, like, and if honest merit were given its reward, they'd make him a real detective ere long. And Ake Ogilvie said in his tink-like way *A defective, you mean? God, ay, and certificated!*

Well, Feet had prowled round to the back of the Manse, and had stopped to give his head a bit scratch, when sudden the window above him opened and afore he could move there came a bit splash and a pailful of water was slung down his back. He spluttered and hoasted and his lamp went out, when he came to himself he was shaking and shivering, but the Manse was silent and still as the grave. He thought for a while of arresting the lot—ay, he would in the morning,

by God; and turned and went home, running home stretches
to change his bit sark, in case he might catch a cold from his
wetting.

And, would you believe it, next day as he sat in his office
writing up his reports, his mother said, *Here's a woman to
see you.* And Feet looked up and he knew the quean, Else
Queen, the maid at the Manse it was; 'twas said she'd
been brought up as a lassie in Segget, though her father
had moved to Fordoun since then, now she was fair a great
brute of a woman, with red eyes and hair, and cheeks of like
tint. And she said, *Are you Feet?* and Feet reddened a bit.
*I'm Simon Leslie the policeman of Segget.——Well, I'm the
person that half-drowned you last night; and I've come to tell
you when you want the same, just prowl round the Manse at
such a like hour.*

And she didn't stop only at Feet then, either. She made
for Ag Moultrie and told her the same, she would have her
sacked from her job at the school; and Ag broke down
and just Roared and Grat, she said she'd never said an ill
word of any, but what was the minister's wife doing on the
Kaimes? *Looking at the hills and the sunrise, you fool. Did
you never hear yet of folk that did that?* And Ag said she
hadn't; and who ever had? Folk shook their heads when
they heard that tale, if the woman at the Manse wasn't fair
just a bitch, damn't! you could only suppose she was daft.

DITE PEAT HEARD the story and fair mocked at Feet.
What, you that were once in the barracks? he said, *and lived
in Dundon, and can't manage a woman?* And he told a story,
'twas down in the Arms, about how once when he was living
in London, he'd come there, he said, on a leave from the
Front, he hired a bit lodging near Waterloo.——And
old Leslie that was standing by said *Eh? Would that be
the place the battle was at?* and Dite Peat said, *Oh, away to
hell,* a coarse way to speak to an old bit man.——Well,
Dite had put up in his London room, he saw the landlady
was a gey bit quean, fair young and fair sonsy, her man at
the Front. And he tried this way and that to get round her,
keen for a woman but not a damn fool like some that came
back on leave from the Front, they'd spend all their silver

on whores, but not Dite, he wanted a gratis cuddle and
squeeze. Well, he waited and waited about for a bit, and
half-thought of getting the woman at night, she was only
English and they're tinks by nature, it wasn't as though
she was decent and Scotch. But she locked up her door
and went early to bed till there came one night that he
heard her scraich, and he louped from his bed and he went
to the door, and there she was standing down in the hall,
in her nightgown, the tink, and white as a sheet. She'd a
telegram held in her hands as she stood, and was gowking
and gobbling at the thing like a cow, choked on the shaws
of a Mearns swede. And Dite called down *What's wrong with
you, then?* and she laughed and laughed as she looked up at
him, she was young, with a face like a bairn, a fool, white,
with no guts, like the English queans. And she said *Oh, it's
just that my husband's dead,* and laughed and laughed, and
Dite licked his lips, it fair was a chance, he saw it and took
it. Well, she wasn't so bad, but far over-thin; and God!
she was fair a scunner with her laughing, every now and
then she would laugh like an idiot, he supposed that the
English did that in their pleasure. So he took her a clour
or so in the lug, to learn her manners, and that quietened
her down. Oh ay, she was tasty enough in her way.

Some folk in the Arms asked what happened next, did
he bide there long? Dite said *Damn the fears. I nipped
out next morning, afore she awoke. She might have tried on
to get me to marry her.* And he went on to tell what tinks
were the English, they'd rob right and left if you gave
them the chance. He gave them damn few, but once out
in France——

That fair was a sickener, you put down your glass, or
finished the dram and rose up and went out; and Will
Melvin looked mad as he well could look, Dite sitting and
telling a story like that, sickening customers away from
their drinks. But you couldn't do much with a billy like
Dite, a dangerous devil when he got in a rage. He looked
a tink though he kept a shop, he and his brother, wee Peter
the tailor, hadn't spoken for years, though they lived next
door. His father had lived with Dite till he died, Dite saw
to that dying, some said helped it on. The old man had

been one of the road-mender childes, he worked with old
Smithie and that fool John Muir, he'd come back with his
wages at the end of the week and maybe he'd have spent
a shilling on tobacco. And soon's he saw that Dite Peat
would fly up and take him a belt in the face, most like,
and send him to bed without any meat; and as he lay
dying the old man cried to see his other son, wee Peter,
the tailor. But Dite snapped *Be quiet, damn you and your
wants. You'll see him in hell soon enough with yourself.* That
was hardly the way to speak to your father, him dying and
all; and some folk stopped then going to his shop, spinners
and the like, they said Dite should be shot; and collected
below his windows one night and spoke of taking him out
for a belting. But Feet, the policeman, came up and cried
Now, you'll need to be moving if you're standing about here;
and the spinners forgot the thing they'd come on, and took
to tormenting the bobby instead, they carried him down the
Drumlithie road and took off his breeks and filled him with
whisky; and left the poor childe lying drunk in the ditch;
and went back and fairly raised hell in the Arms, the Blaster
and Blasphemer near scraiched herself hoarse, the spinners
had new got a rise in their pay.

Ah well, that was how Dite Peat had escaped, spinners
and their like wouldn't trade with him now, though most
other folk weren't foolish as that. You went on as before
and waited the time when he and Ake Ogilvie would yet
get to grips, Ake hated Dite Peat as a dog hates a rat.

CHRIS FOUND IT took nearly a fortnight to settle, the
whole of the Manse wanted scrubbing and cleaning, she
and Else Queen were at it all hours, Robert laughed and
locked himself in his room. But he came out to help rig
the curtains on rods, both he and Else were handy and
tall, they spent the most of one long afternoon tacked up
to the walls like flies in glue; and Chris handed up rods
and curtains and pictures, and this and that, and hammers
and nails; and Else and Robert would cling to the walls, by
their eyebrows sometimes, or so it would seem, and push and
tug and hammer and pant. Else was willing and strong and
enjoyed it, she'd poise on the edge of a mantel and cry *Will*

that do, Mem? and near twist her neck from her shoulders to catch a look at some picture or other. Chris would cry *Mind!* and Else: *Och, I'm fine!* and nearly capsize from her ledge, and young Ewan, watching below, give a yell of delight.

But at last all things were trig and set neat. That evening, with Ewan bathed and to bed, Chris found Else yawning wide as a door, and sent her off to her bed as well. Chris felt she was almost too tired to rest as she sat in a chair in Robert's room; and Robert knew and came and made love; and that was nice, and she felt a lot better. In the quiet and hush of the evening below you could see the touns drift blue with their smoke, as though it was they that moved, not the smoke. Robert sat in his shirt-sleeves, smoking his pipe, planning his campaign to conquer Segget, as Chris supposed, but she closed her eyes. In a minute she'd get up and go to her bed.

But Robert jumped up sudden and picked up his coat. *I know! Let's go and see Segget at night.*

Chris thought *If it wasn't that I am in love—Goodness, how far I could tell him to go!* But she said not a word of that, but went down, and he groped in the dark and found her coat, and she his, and next they were out on the shingle, it crunch-crunched under the tread of their feet, the moon had come and was sailing a sky, lilac, so bright that the Manse stood clear as they turned and looked back, the yews etched in ink, beyond them the kirk that hadn't a steeple, set round with its row upon row of quiet graves, the withered grass kindled afresh to green, in long, shadowy tufts that whispered like ghosts. An owlet hooted up on the hill and through the quiet of the night round about there came a thing like a murmur unended, unbegun, continuous, the hum of the touns—and that was queer, most folk were in bed! Chris thought a thought and put it from her mind—an awful woman to have wedded a minister!

The she slipped her arm in Robert's, beside him, Segget stood splashed in the light of the moon like a hiddle of houses a bairn would build. Their feet were quiet on the unpaved street, they smelt the reek of the burning wood, and Robert said sudden, his voice not a whisper, *It's like walking a town of the dead, forgotten, a ruined place in the light of the moon. Can you think that folk'll do that sometime, far off some night in the times to be, maybe a lad and his lass, as we are, and wonder about Segget and the things they did and said and believed in those little houses? And the moon the same and the hills to watch.*

Chris thought it most likely they would find these enough, the hills and the moon, and not bother about Segget, that lad and that lass in the times to be. So they passed quiet down through the wind of East Wynd, over to the right the hiddling of lanes where the spinners bade, nearer the road and black in the moon the school and the schoolhouse set round with dykes. They passed a joiner's shop to the left, Chris peered at the name and saw ALEC OGILVIE, then came to a place with shops all around, a grocer's shop with D. PEAT on the sill, fat lettering over a shoe-maker's—HOGG; and a narrow little front that barked PETER PEAT. Beyond, to the right, a lane wound down to the post-office kept by MacDougall Brown, so Chris had been told, she hadn't been there.

East Wynd to the left was now bare of houses, beyond its dyke was the garden of Grant. And once they heard through the night a crying, some bairn frightened or waked in the dark, and a voice that called it back to its sleep, all in a drowsy hush through the night. *There's honeysuckle somewhere*, said Chris, and stopped to smell, as they came to the Square, *over here by the saddler's shop*.

But Robert was giving no heed to smells, he had stopped and he said *My God, what a slummock!* And Chris saw the thing that had now ta'en his eyes, the War Memorial of Segget toun, an angel set on a block of stone, decent and sonsy in its stone night-gown, goggling genteel away from the Arms, as though it wouldn't, for any sum you named, ever condescend to believe there were folk that took a nip to keep out the chill. . . . Chris thought it was fine, a pretty young lass. But then as she looked at it there came doubts, it stood there in memory of men who had died, folk of this Segget but much the same still, she supposed, as the folk she had known in Kinraddie, folk who had slept and waked and had sworn, and had lain with women and had lain with pain, and walked in the whistle of the storms from the Mounth, and been glad, been mad, and done dark, mad things, been bitter for failure, and tender and kind, with the kindness deep in the dour Scots blood. Folk of her own, those folk who had died, out in the dark, strange places of earth, and they set up THIS to commemorate THEM—this, this quean like a constipated calf!

Robert said *May God forgive them this horror! And look at the star on its pantomine wand. But still it's a star; not a bundle of grapes. Folk'll think it a joke when we've altered things, this trumpery flummery they put up in stone!*

His dream again he could alter things here! *But what kind of change, Robert, what can you do? Things go on the same as ever they were, folk neither are better nor worse for the War. They gossip and claik and are good and bad, and both together, mixed up and down. This League of the willing folk of Segget—who'll join it or know what you want or you mean?*

He leaned by the angel, looked down at her, smiled cool and sure of his vision to-night. *Chris, if ever we've a child, you and I, and when it grows up it finds that that's true—what you've said—then I hope it'll come here with Ewan, and a host of others of their own generation, and smash this Memorial into smithereens for the way that we failed them and left God out. Change? It's just that men must change, or perish here in Segget, as all over the earth. Necessity's the drive, the policeman that's coming to end the squabbling stupidities of old——*

Then he laughed. *What, sleepy as that? Let's go back.*

HE FAIR HAD plenty on his hands that summer, Feet, the policeman, as the days wore to Autumn. First, 'twas the trouble in the roadman's place, old Smithie and the hay he nicked from coles and carted home at night to his kye. His house stood side by side with John Muir's, both under the lee of the kirk and the Manse, their back doors opened out on the land that stretched east under the scowl of the hills to the lands that were farmed by Meiklebogs. Muir kept no stock and he bought his milk, but old Smith on the chap of dawn would be out, up out of his bed and round to the byre, where his cows and his two young calves were housed, none knew where he bought the fodder to feed them; and that wasn't surprising, he stole the damned lot.

He'd look this way and that, he'd a face like a tyke, thin, and ill-made, with a bushy moustache; and then, as swack as you like he would loup, canny and careful in over a fence, and make up a birn of somebody's hay; and be back and breaking his stones as before when the next bit motor appeared on the road. Syne at night he would load the lot on his bike and pedal canny without any light, and nip up through Segget as the Arms bar opened and folk had gone in for a bit of a nip, rone out to see; and syne he was home, and the cows, as hungry as hawks, would low, old Smithie would give a bit low as well, and stuff them with hay and pat at their shoulders, daft-like, he near was crack about kye, he liked the breath of the creatures, he said.

Folk said that the cows couldn't be so particular, else they'd fair get a scunner at *his* bit breath. For he liked a dram and he took what he liked, he'd no more than peek round the door of an evening (though the house was his and all the gear in it) than his daughter would cry *Here's the old devil home!* and her bairns, the bairns of Bruce the porter, would laugh and call him ill names as they liked. And he'd smile and stand there and mumble a while, though he wasn't a fool in the ordinary way; and syne he'd go down to the Arms in a rage and swear that before another night came he'd have Bruce and his birn flung out of his doors, he was damned if he'd stand their insultings longer. Well, damned he was, for he kept them on, folk would once kittle up with excitement when they heard old Smithie get wild and say that, they'd 'gree with him solemn and say 'twas a shame for a man of Segget to stand what he did; and they'd follow him home when the Arms closed down and stand by the door to hear the din. But all that they'd hear would be Ellen his daughter, fat as a cow at the calving time, cry *Feuch, you old brute, and where have you been?* And Smithie would just mumble and gang to his bed.

He'd another daughter as well as his Ellen, he'd slaved to give her an education; and faith! so he'd done, and made her a teacher. She lived in Dundon and never came south. And the only thing Smithie said that he'd gotten, for all his pains and his chaving for her, was one cigarette: and that wouldn't light.

Well, that Saturday afternoon in July, old Smithie was wearied with chapping at stones, and instead of stealing some hay outbye and rowing it home strapped over his bike, he got on the bike and pedalled near home, till he came to the new-coled hay of Meiklebogs. And old Smithie got off and lighted his pipe and made on he'd got off for nothing but that. There wasn't a soul to be seen round about, the park was hidden, and old Smithie was quick, he nipped in over and pinched some hay, and was back with the stuff strapped on to his bike—so quick that you'd fair have thought it a wonder that his corduroy trousers didn't take fire. But no sooner was he gone than Dalziel jumped up, he'd been hiding all the while in the lee of a cole; and he ran to the close and got his own bike, and followed old Smithie and shadowed him home. Then he went down the toun and collected Feet, and they came on old Smithie as he entered the byre, the bundle of stolen hay in his hands.

And Feet cried out *Mr Smith, I want you;* and old Smithie looked round and near dropped the birn. *Ay, do you so?* he quavered, and syne the old whiskered creature fairly went daft, he threw the birn in Meiklebogs' face. *Take your damned stuff, I wouldn't poison my kye with such dirt!*

Feet said, *Well, I doubt this'll be a case,* but old Smithie was dafter than ever by then. He said, *Make it two, and to hell with you both!* and went striding into his house as he hadn't, striding that way, gone in for years. His daughter, that sumph that was Mistress Bruce, fair jumped as she heard the bang of the door, she cried: *You nasty old wretch, what's the din?* Old Smithie was fairly boiling by then, he said, *Do you know who you're speaking to, Ellen?* and she said, *Ay, fine, you disgrace to Segget;* and at that old Smithie had her over his knee, afore she could blink, she was stunned with surprise. She gave a bit scraich and she tried to wriggle, but she'd grown over fat and old Smithie was strong. And damn't! if he didn't take down her bit things and scone her so sore she grat like a bairn, her own bairns made at old Smithie and kicked him, but he never let on, just leathered his quean till his hand was sore, not so sore as her dowp. *That's a lesson for you, you bap-faced bitch,* he said, and left her greeting on the floor, and went down to the Arms, and near the first man that he met there was Bruce, old Smithie by then like a fighting cock.

Bruce was a dark and a sour-like childe, but he looked near twice as sour in a minute when old Smithie took him a crack in the jaw. *What's that for?* Bruce cried, and Smithie said *Lip*, and came at him again, the daft-like old tyke. Well, you couldn't expect but that Bruce would be raised, he was knocking Smithie all over the bar when Mistress Melvin came tearing in. She cried in her thin Aberdeen, *What's this? Stop your Blasting and Blaspheming in here.* Bruce said, *I haven't sworn a damn word,* she said *That's enough, take your tink fights out, sossing up the place with blood and the like. If you've any quarrel to settle with your relations, go out and settle it where folk can't see.*

And Bruce said *Right;* and took old Smithie out, and gey near settled him entire, you would say. It just showed you what happened to a billy that stole, there's a difference between nicking a thing here and there, and being found out and made look a fair fool.

AND NEXT SABBATH MacDougall Brown, the postmaster, came down to the Square and preached on stealing, right godly-like, and you'd never have thought that him and his wife stayed up of a night sanding the sugar and watering the paraffin—or so folk said, but they tell such lies. He was maybe a fifty years old, MacDougall, a singer as well as a preacher, i'faith! though some said his voice was the kind of a thing better suited to slicing a cheese. During the War he had fair been a patriot, he hadn't fought, but losh! how he'd sung! In the first bit concert held in the War he sang Tipperary to the Segget folk, with his face all shining like a ham on the fry, and he sang it right well till he got to the bit where the song has to say that his heart's right there. And faith, MacDougall got things a bit mixed, he clapped down his hand the wrong side of his wame; and Ake Ogilvie that sat in the front of the hall gave a coarse snicker and syne everybody laughed; and MacDougall had never forgiven Ake that. But he got on well with his post-office place, Johnnie his son was a bit of a fool and MacDougall sent him to take round the letters, it cost him little with a son that was daft and MacDougall kept the cash for himself. Forbye young Jock he'd two daughters as well, the eldest, Cis, was bonny and trig, with a grave, douce face, she went to the College but she wasn't proud, a fine bit queen, and all Segget liked her.

Well, MacDougall had a special religion of his own, he wasn't Old Kirk and he wasn't of the Frees, he wasn't even an Episcopalian, but Salvation Army, or as near as damn it. He went on a Sabbath morn to the Square and preached there under the lee of the angel, that the road to heaven was the way he said. He'd made two-three converts in his years in Segget, they'd stand up and say what the Lord had done, how before they'd met Him they were lost, ruined souls: but now God had made them into new men. And faith! you would think, if that was the case, the Lord's handiwork was failing, like everything else.

Well, that Sunday after the row at Smithie's, he was there at his stance where the angel stood, MacDougall himself with his flat, bald head, and beside him his mistress, a meikle great sumph, she came from the south and she mouthed her words broad as an elephant's behind, said Ake Ogilvie. She thought little of Cis, that was clever and bonny, but a lot of her youngest, the quean called Mabel—by all but her mother, she called her May-bull. Well, they both were there, and the daftie Jock, gleying, and slavering up at the angel, and a two-three more, the gardener Grant and Newlands the stationy, them and their wives; with the angel above with her night-gown drawn back, right handy-like, in case it might rap against the bald pow of MacDougall Brown. Mistress Brown opened up the harmonica they'd brought, it groaned and spluttered and gave a bit hoast, syne they started the singing of their unco hymns, Newlands burring away in his boots and MacDougall slicing the words like cheese.

Syne MacDougall started to preach about stealing, with a verse from Leviticus for the text, though the case of old

Smithie had supplied the cause; and they started singing
another bit hymn, all about being washed in the Blood of
the Lamb, the Lamb being Jesus Christ, said MacDougall,
he was awful fond of hymns full of blood, though he'd turned
as white as a sheet the time Dite Peat had come over to kill
his pig, and asked MacDougall to hold the beast down.

Well, they were getting on fine and bloody, and having
fairly a splash in the gore, when MacDougall noticed there
was something wrong, the words all to hell, he couldn't
make it out. Syne his mistress noticed and screwed round
her head, and she said *What is't?* and saw MacDougall,
red as rhubarb, he'd stopped his singing. The rest of them
had to do the same, for a drove of the spinners had come
in about, with that tink Jock Cronin at their head, as usual,
they were singing up fast and fair drowning MacDougall, a
coarse-like mocking at MacDougall's hymn:

WHITER than—the whitewash on the wall!
WHITER than—the whitewash on the wall!
Oh—WASH me in the water
Where you washed your dirty daughter,
And I shall be whiter than the whitewash on the
wall!

MacDougall waited until they had stopped, then he cried
to Cronin *Have you no respect—you, John Cronin—for
the Lord's Day at all?* And the tink said, *Damn the bit;
nor have you.* And MacDougall nearly burst to hear that,
he'd lived by the Bible all his life. And John Cronin said
You believe all that's in it? and MacDougall Brown said,
Ay, I have faith. But Cronin had fairly got him trapped
now, he said *Well, it says in the Bible that if you've got faith
you can move a mountain. That'll be proof. Move back the
Mounth there in front of our eyes!*

The spinners with him, a lot of tink brutes, all brayed
up then, *Ay, come on, MacDougall! Move a mountain—
you're used to move sand!* MacDougall habbered redder
than ever, then he cried *We'll now sing Rock of Ages.* Jock
Cronin cried *Where's the rock of your faith?* and as soon as
MacDougall and his converts began the spinners sang up
their song as before, about being whiter than the whitewash
on the wall, and about MacDougall's dirty daughter; and

such a noise was never heard before in the Sabbath Square of Segget.

Old Leslie came by and he heard the noise, and he knew MacDougall and was right sorry for him. But when he came over and tried to interfere, Jock Cronin cried *Christ, here's Ananias!* And old Leslie walked away, fair in a rage, and went up to the Manse to complain about them.

He arrived there just after the morning service, the minister new back, and dinner-time done. And old Leslie said 'twas Infernal, just, the way that they treated a man nowadays. In his young days if a loon like that Cronin had miscalled a man he'd have been ta'en out and libbed. Ay, he minded when he was a loon up in Garvock—

But the new minister rose up and said *Well, I'll hear that again, I've no time to waste,* with a look as black as though he could kill you. And afore old Leslie knew well what had happened he was out on the doorstep and heard the door bang.

CHRIS HEARD the door bang and she saw old Leslie, he was turning slow to go down the walk, crunching the shingle under his feet; and suddenly you saw the old man that he was, his back crooked into that queer-like shape, cruel and a shame to get rid of him so, suddenly you wanted to weep, but you didn't, biting your lips as you watched him go. Only a tiring old fool, as you knew, and he'd come on Robert in that mad, black mood. And yet—

Things like that caught you again and again, with a tightening heart, when you had no thought—Robert in weariness half an hour back, his head in his hands, as he said *What's the use?* Robert's head as he prayed to that God of his that you couldn't believe in, though you hid that away, what need to hurt Robert with something that never he or you could alter though you lived forever? So, in the strangest of moments it would come, in a flame and a flash, a glimpse into depths that wrung your heart, you'd see the body of Else as she bent, a curve of pleasure that would curve yet in pain. You'd see—frightening the things if you cared to think in the dark of the night in the quiet of Segget, the hush of the yews out there on the lawn—the

hopeless folly of all striving, all hope. Sudden, in a Segget
shop, maybe, you'd glimpse a face like your father's, near,
alive and keen with its bearded lips, and you'd think of your
father, long ago dead, bones rotted from flesh in Kinraddie
kirkyard—what had life availed him and all his long years
when he hoped for this and he strove for that? He died a
coarse farmer in a little coarse house, hid in the earth and
forgot by men, as forgot as your pains and your tears by
God, that God that you knew could never exist. . . .

Only with Ewan you'd never these glimpses into the
shifting sands of life, bairn though he was there was something within him hard and shining and unbreaking as rock,
something like a sliver of granite within him. Strange that
his body had once come from yours in the days when you
were a quean unthinking, so close to the earth and its smell
and its feel that nearly he came from the earth itself!

From that we all came, you had heard Robert say, but
wilder and stranger you knew it by far, from the earth's
beginning *you yourself* had been here, a blowing of motes
in the world's prime, earth, roots and the wings of an
insect long syne in the days when the dragons still ranged
the world—every atom here in your body now, that was
here, that was you, that beat in your heart, that shaped your
body to whiteness and strength, the speed of your legs and
the love of your breasts when you turned to the kiss of your
Robert at night—these had been there, there was nothing
but a change, in a form, the stroke and the beat of a song.

And you thought how long, long ago with Will, your
brother, that time he came home from France, before he
went back and was killed in France you'd said that the
Scots were never religious, had never BELIEVED as other
folks did; and that was fell true, and not only for you,
MacDougall that brayed by the angel in the Square, the folk
that came to the kirk on a Sunday, Robert himself—even
Robert himself! There was something lacking or something added, something that was bred in your bones in
this land—oh, Something: maybe that Something was
GOD—that made folk take with a smile and a gley the
tales of the gods and the heavens and the hells, the afterlives
and the lives before, heaven on earth and the chances of

change, the hope and belief in salvation for men—as a
fairy-tale in a play that they'd play, but they knew the whole
time they were only players, no Scots bodies died but they
knew that fine, deep and real in their hearts they knew that
here they faced up to the REAL, at last, neither heaven nor
hell but the earth that was red, the cling of the clay where
you'd alter and turn, back to the earth and the times to be,
to a spraying of motes on a raging wind when the Howe
was happed in its winter storms, to a spray of dust as some
childe went by with his plough and his horse in a morning
in Spring, to the peck and tweet of the birds in the trees,
to trees themselves in a burgeoning Spring. You knew, and
you knew that they knew—even Robert, holding to God
in his blackest hour, this God he believed was the father of
men, pitiful, He was Pity and a Friend, helpless even in a
way as men, but Kind and Hero, and He'd conquer yet
with all the legions of hell to battle.

So Robert believed: but now, as you heard his feet
coming down the stairs in haste, out of his mood and
happy again, you knew that he knew he followed a dream,
with the black mood REAL, and his hopes but mists.

CHRIS REMEMBERED THAT dream of her own—she'd
been daft! she thought as she fled about next week's work.
There was jam to make and she thought it fun, and so
did Else, they'd boil pot on pot and fill all the jars, and
forget about dinner. And Robert would come sweating in
from the garden and cry *Losh, Christine, where have you
been? I thought you promised to come out and help. What's
wrong—nothing wrong with you, is there, my dear?* Chris
would say *Only hunger*, and he'd say *Not love?* and the two
would be fools for a moment till they heard the stamp of Else
bringing in the tray. Syne they'd each slip into a chair and
look solemn; but once Else caught them and said to the
minister *Faith, I don't wonder!* and looked at Chris; and
Chris thought that the nicest thing ever *looked* about her.

Ewan ran wild, Chris seldom saw him all the length of the
summer days, he was out in Segget, exploring the streets,
Chris at first had been feared for him—that he'd fall in
front of a horse, or a car, or one of the buses that went by

to Dundon. She tried to tell him to be careful, then stopped, he'd to take his chances with the rest of the world.

On the Saturday she and Robert looked up from their work in the garden, and stood and watched Ewan, hands in his pockets, no cap on his head, go sauntering out through the gates of the Manse, his black hair almost blue in the sun, and turn by the Meiklebogs, going to the Kaimes, Chris wondered what he could want up there?

Robert said *He's seeking the High Places already*, and laughed, and went on with his digging, Chris the same, sweet and forgotten the smell of the earth, you thrust with your spade, the full throw of your body, so, and the drill built up as you dug. Then the rooks came cawing and wheeling in by, and they both looked up from Segget to the Mounth, rain drumming upon it far in the heuchs, cattle, tail-switching, dots on the heath. Chris asked what the clouds were, up there by Trusta, they piled up dome on dome in the sky, like the roofs of a city in the land of cloud. Robert said *Cumulus: just summer rain;* and a minute later—*Look, here it comes!*

Chris saw it come wheeling like a flying of rooks, dipping and pelting down from the heights, she looked left and saw it through a smother of smoke, the smoke stilled for a minute as it waited the rain, all Segget turning to look at the rain. Then Robert was running and Chris ran as well, under the shelter of the pattering yews. There they stood and panted and watched the water, whirling in and over the drills, the potato-shaws a-bend in the pelt, the patter like hail and then like a shoom, like the sea on a morning heard from Kinraddie, *the empty garden blind with rain.* And then it was gone and the sun bright out, and Chris heard, far, clear, as though it never had stopped, a snipe that was sounding up in the hills.

By noon they saw a drooked figure approaching. Chris heard Else cry *Are you soaked!* and Ewan answer *I was; but I dried,* he'd some thing in his hand. Turning it over he came up to Robert. *Look, I found this up on the Kaimes.*

Chris stopped as well to look at the thing, the three of them stood in the bright, wet weather, Robert turning the implement over in his hands, it was rusted and broken, the

blade of a spear. *Did they use it for ploughing?* Ewan wanted
to know, and Robert said *No, they used it for killing, it's a
spear, Ewan man, from the daft old days.*

Then Else came crying them in for their dinner, and in
they all went, as hungry as hawks. Ewan wanted to know
a lot more about spears, 'twas a wonder he managed to ask
all he did, him eating as well, but he managed both fine;
he'd a question-mark for a brain, Robert said!

But the most of his questions he kept until night, when
Chris bathed him and took him up to his room. Why did
the stairs wind? Why weren't they straight? Would it
be long till he was a man? Where was Christ now, and
had Robert met Him? *That's an owl, why don't owls fly in
the day? Why don't you go to sleep when I do? Does Else
like Dalziel of the Meiklebogs much? I like the smiddy of old
Mr Leslie, he says that when he was a loon up on Garvock he
was never let gang anywhere near a smiddy, his mammy would
have smacked his dowp; didn't she like it? I saw Mr Hogg,
he said 'What's your name?' Why is there hair growing out of
his nose? Mrs Hogg is fat, is she going to have a calf? Does
she take off her clothes to have it, mother? Mother, have you
got a navel like mine? I'll show you mine, look, there it is,
isn't it funny? I'm not sleepy, let's sing a while. Why——*

He was sleeping at last, in the evening quiet, the Saturday
quiet, the sun not yet gone. Chris went down to the garden
and took out a chair, and leaned back in it with her arms
behind her, drowsy, watching the gloaming come. Robert
was up in his room with his sermon, he wrote the thing
out when he'd thought of a theme—he would think of a
theme of a sudden and swear because he hadn't a note-book
at hand.

This afternoon it had come on him suddenly. *I know!
That spear-blade that Ewan brought—where the devil has
he hidden the thing?*

At half-past ten next morning, the Sunday, Chris heard
John Muir and looked out and saw him, his shoulder
a-skeugh in his Sunday suit, come stepping up the path
from the kirk. *There's a fair concourse of the folk the day;
and how are you keeping then, mistress, yourself?*

Chris said she was fine, and he gleyed at her cheery,

Faith, so you look, you take well with Segget. Well, well, if the minister hasn't any orders I'll taik away back and tug at the bell.

Chris heard that bell in a minute or so beat and clang through the quiet of the air. It was time that she herself had got ready, she sought out her hymn-book and hanky and Bible, and inspected Ewan, and straightened his collar. Then the two of them hurried through the blow of the garden, and out of the little door let in the dyke, and into the little room back of the kirk. There the sound of the bell was a deafening clamour. Chris brushed Ewan down and went into the kirk, and put Ewan into a pew and herself went ben to the pews where the kirk choir sat, Mrs Geddes, the schoolmaster's wife, there already, smiling and oozing with eau-de-Cologne, whispered right low and right holy-like, *Morning. A grand day, isn't it, and such a pity so few have come up to hear the Lord's word.*

Chris said, *Oh, yes,* and sat down beside her, and looked round as the folk came stepping in, slow, Hairy Hogg, the Provost, and his mistress, Jean, they plumped in their seats and Hairy looked round and closed his eyes like a grass-filled cow. Then the wife and queans of John Muir came in, Chris had heard a lot about them from Else. Else said she could swear there were times when Muir wished he'd stayed where he was when he fell in that grave. His wife was one of the Milton lot that farmed down under Glenbervie brae, she deaved John Muir from morning till night to get out of his job, a common bit roadman, and get on in the world and show up her sister, Marget Ann, that had married a farmer. But John Muir would say *Damn't, we all come to the same—a hole and a stink and worms at the end* and his mistress would snap, *Ay, maybe we do, but there's ways of getting there decent and undecent. And as for stinking, speak of yourself.* And, real vexed, she'd clout Tooje one in the ear. Tooje was her eldest, fairly a gawk, and then clout little Ted when she started to greet because she saw her sister Tooje greeting; and John Muir would get up and say not a word but go dig a grave as a bit of a change.

Then Chris saw Bruce, the porter, come in, with the mark

on his jaw where his goodfather hit him, then Leslie, the smith, paiching and sweating, he dropped his stick with an awful clatter. Then she saw Geddes, the Segget headmaster, sitting grim in a pew midway, his rimless specs set close on his nose, looking wearied to death, as he was. Robert had thought to make him an ally, but he'd said to Robert, *Don't be a fool, leave the swine to stew in their juice*—by swine he meant his fellow-folk of Segget. He would stand hymn-singing with his hand in his pocket, and rattle his keys and yawn at the roof.

Then Moultrie came in, a slow tap-tap, with his stick and his glare, and stopped half-way, his wife, Jess Moultrie, waiting behind, her hand on his arm, gentle and quiet. But when he moved on he shook her away. Chris had heard the story of him and of her and how he had never forgiven her her daughter, Ag, whom they called the Roarer and Greeter.

The others came in, all in a birn, Chris didn't know some and of some was uncertain, she thought that one was Ake Ogilvie the joiner; and a trickle of folk from the farms outbye, a spinner or so, but they were fell few, and Dalziel of the Meiklebogs, red-faced and shy, funny how one couldn't abide him at all.

Syne John Muir finished with the ringing of the bell and came with his feet splayed out as he walked, and his shoulder agley, down the length of the kirk; and went into the little room at the back. Robert would be there and Muir help him to robe. Syne the door opened and John Muir came out, and swayed and gleyed cheerful up to the pulpit and opened the door and stood back and waited. And Robert went up, with his hair fresh-brushed, and his eyes remote, and sat down and prayed, silent, and all the kirk silent as well, for a minute, while Chris looked down at her hands.

Then Robert stood up in the pulpit and said, in his clear, strong voice that hadn't a mumble, that called God GOD and never just GAWD, *We will begin the worship of God by the singing of hymn one hundred and forty, 'Our shield and defender, the Ancient of Days, pavilioned in splendour and girded with praise.' Hymn one hundred and forty.*

Folk rustled the leaves and here and there a man glowered helpless while his wife found the page; and the organ

started with a moan and a grind and the kirk was a rustle
with Sunday braws, folk standing and singing, all straight
and decent, except young Ewan, a-lean in his pew, and
Geddes the Dominie, hand in his pouch.

Chris liked this hymn near as much as did Robert, most
folk stuck fast when they came to pavilioned, Robert's bass
came in, Chris's tenor to help, Mrs Geddes' contralto a wail
at their heels. Then down they all sat; Robert said *Let us
pray.*

Chris wondered what Robert was to preach to-day, his text
was no clue when he gave it out. Folk shuffled in their seats,
and hoasted genteel, and put up their hankies to slip sweeties
in their mouths; sometimes Chris wished she could do the
same, but she couldn't very well, the minister's wife. And all
Segget lifted its eyes to Robert, he flung back the shoulders
of his robe and began, slow and careful, reading from his
notes; and then pushed them aside and began a sermon
on that bit of a spear young Ewan Tavendale had found on
the Kaimes. He'd brought the thing up in the pulpit with
him, folk stopped in their sucking of sweeties and gaped.

And Robert told of the uses the thing had once had, in
the hands of the carles of the ruined Kaimes; and the siege
and the fighting and the man who had held it, desperate at
last in the burning lowe as King Kenneth's men came into
the castle: and the blood that ran on this ruined blade for
things that the men of that time believed would endure and
be true till the world died; they thought they were fighting
for things that would last, they'd be classed as heroes and
victors forever. And now they were gone, they were not even
names, their lives and their deaths we knew to be foolish, a
clamour and babble on little things.

So might the men of the future look back, on this Segget
here, not of antique times, and see the life of our mean-like
streets ape-like chatter as the dark came down. For change,
imperative, awaited the world, as never before men could
make it anew, men of good will and a steadfast faith. All
history had been no more than the gabble of a horde of
apes that was trapped in a pit. *Let us see that we clean our
pit-corner in Segget, there is hatred here, and fear, and malaise,
the squabbling of drunken louts in the streets, poor schools, worse*

houses—we can alter all these, we can alter then NOW, *not waiting the world.*

Robert had launched his campaign on Segget.

THAT SERMON FAIR raised a speak in the toun, as soon's they got out Peter Peat said Faith! they'd fair made a mistake in getting this childe. You wanted a sermon with some body in it, with the hell that awaited the folk that were sinners, and lay on the Kaimes with their unwed queans, and were slow in paying their bills to a man. And what did he mean that Segget was foul? A clean little toun as ever there was, no, no, folk wanted no changes here.

Old Leslie said 'Twas Infernal, just, he minded when he was a loon up on Garvock—

Rob Moultrie said *Well, what d'you expect? He's gentry and dirt with his flat-patted hair; and speaking to God as though he were speaking to a man next door—and a poor man at that. Ay, a Tory mucker, I well may warrant, that would interfere in our houses and streets.*

Will Melvin said *Did you hear him preach against folk taking a dram now and then? And if he himself wasn't drunk then I'm daft, with his spears and his stars and his apes and his stite.*

That fairly got Hairy Hogg on the go. He cried *Ay, what was all yon about apes? And him glaring at me like a thrawn cat. If he comes from the monkeys himself let him say it, not sneer at folk of a better blood.*

Folk took a bit snicker at that as they went—damn't, the minister had got one in there! And afore night had come the story had spread, the minister had said—you'd as good as heard him—that Hairy Hogg was a monkey, just.

Well, it made you laugh, though an ill-gettèd thing to say that of old Hairy Hogg, the Provost. Faith, he fair had a face like a monkey, the sutor of Segget and its Provost forbye. He'd been Provost for years, not a soul knew why, or how he'd ever got on for the job; or what was the council, or what it might do, apart from listening to Hairy on Burns. For he claimed descent from the Burneses, Hairy, and you'd have thought by the way he spoke that Rabbie had rocked him to sleep in his youth. His wife had once been at Glenbervie House, a parlourmaid there, and awful genteel; but a thirty years or so in old Hogg's bed had fair rubbed gentility off of the creature, she was common and rough as a whin bush now, and would hoast out loud in the kirk at prayers till the bairns all giggled and old Hogg would say, loud enough for the pulpit to hear, *Wheest, wheest, redd your thrapple afore you come here.*

She would make him regret that when they got home, she'd little time for any palavers, her daughter Jean that was nurse in London, or Alec her son that clerked down in Edinburgh. Old Hogg he would blow like a windy bellows about Jean and the things she'd done as a nurse. For when the bit King took ill with a cough she was one of the twenty-four nurses or so that went prancing round the bit royalty's bed, she carried a hanky, maybe, or such-like. But to hear old Hairy speak on the business you'd have thought she'd cured the King's illness herself, and been handed a two-three thousand for doing it. Yet damn the penny but her wages she got, said Mrs Hogg; what could you expect? The gentry were aye as mean as is dirt and wasn't the King a German forbye?

Young Hogg was at home now, on holiday like, he meant to attend the Segget Show. You had seen the creature, wearing plus fours, east-windy, west-endy as well as could be, forbye that he said he had joined the Fascists. Folk asked what they were, and he said *they* were fine, Conservatives, like, but a lot more than that; they meant to make Britain the same as was Italy. And old Hogg was real vexed, he cried *But goodsakes! You're not going to leave your fine job, now, are you, and take to the selling of ice-cream sliders?* And Alec said *Father, please don't be silly;* and old Hogg fair flamed: *Give's less of your lip. What could a man think but that you were set, you and your breeks and your Fashers and all, with being a damned ice-creamer yourself?*

Alec said nothing, just looked at his quean, and she and him sniffed, she was real superior, a clerk like Alec himself down in Edinburgh. He'd brought her up on holiday to Segget, he called her his feeungsay, not just his lass: she wouldn't be able to stay for the Show, and if any soul thought that a cause for regret, he'd managed to keep a good grip on himself. The first time they sat down to tea in Hogg's house Alec finished his cup and looked round the table. *Where's the slop-basin, mother?* he asked, to show his quean he was real genteel. But his mother was wearied with him and his airs. *Slop it in your guts!* she snapped as she rose, *and less of your Edinburgh touches here!*

SEGGET SHOW WAS held in a park that was loaned to the toun by Dalziel of the Meiklebogs. He blushed and looked shy, *Oh ay, you can have it,* when Hairy Hogg went out there and asked him. 'Twas a great ley park with a fringe of trees, the hills up above, the Kaimes to the left; and early on the evening afore Segget Show there were folk down there making out this and that, the lines of the tents and the marquees and such; the circle where the bairns would run their bit races and folk that thought they could throw the hammer could stand and show what their muscles were made of. Folk came to Segget Show far and about, from Fordoun and Laurencekirk, Skite and Arbuthnott, early on the Saturday Segget awoke to the rattle of farm carts up through East Wynd, down past the Manse, and so to the park, carts loaded with kail and cabbage and cakes, and hens and ducks in their clean straw rees, and birns of bannocks and scones for show, and the Lord knows what that folk wouldn't bring to try for a prize at the Segget Show.

It was wet in the morning, folk looked out and swore, but by noon the rain had cleared off and soon, as the lines of folk held out from Segget, there came a blistering waft of the heat, men loosed their waistcoats, some took off their collars, and paid their shillings and went in at the gates, all except a crowd of the spinners. They suddenly appeared near the big marquee, and Sim Leslie, him that the folk called Feet, went over and looked at the bunch fell stern, he hadn't seen them pay at the gate. But he wasn't keen on starting a row, just looked at them stern: and the spinners all laughed.

There fair was a crush as the judges began, Hairy Hogg was one, the minister another, Dalziel of the Meiklebogs the third. They started in on the hens to begin with, a lot from MacDougall Brown's of the post-office. MacDougall stood by, looking proud as dirt, he'd won first prize for his Leghorns for years. So he fell near fainted when he got a green ticket, the second prize only and not the red first; and he said to whoever stood by to listen that it was that minister had done this to him, he was scared at the way that MacDougall drew folk away from the Auld Kirk's preaching and lies. But faith! his Leghorns looked none so well, he'd been mixing lime in their feed and the birds had a look as though they'd like to lie down and burst. But they daren't, with MacDougall's eye upon them, they stood and chirawked, as though kind of discouraged when they saw that they'd ta'en only second prize.

By then the judges were through with the hens, the ducks as well, a childe from a farm out near by Mondynes had ta'en every prize there was to be took. Syne the judges turned into the big marquee, to judge the baked stuff and the flowers and the like. The minister was speaking as they went inside; Hairy Hogg turned round to hear what he said; and prompt his elbow knocked over the dish that was set with the cakes of Mistress Melvin. The landlady of the Arms looked at the Provost as though she'd like to bash in his head, with a bottle, and syne carve him up slow with its splinters; but she daren't say anything, seeing it was him, and he'd given the Melvins the catering to do.

So the Blaster and Blasphemer just smiled, genteel, and got down and picked up her cakes from the grass, the minister got down and helped her; and smiled; (what was the creature laughing about?). But Hairy Hogg said, for the marquee to hear, *I want stuff set out plain and decent, not pushed right under my nose when I judge*. He spoke as though he were the Lord God Almighty, and the bannocks sinners on the Judgement Day.

They couldn't make up their minds on the pancakes, there were two fine lots, one rounded and cut, neat-shaped and fine as ever you saw, the other lot not of much shape at all, but bonnily fired, and the judges stopped, and each ate a bit, of the well-cut at first, they weren't so bad, but looked better than they tasted. Syne the judges bit at the ill-cut cakes, they fairly melted in a body's mouth, the minister had eaten up

one in a minute, and Meiklebogs nodded, and Hairy Hogg
nodded, and the Reverend Mr Colquohoun gave a nod. So
old Jess Moultrie had the first prize, faith! that was fairly
a whack in the face for that Mistress Geddes with her fine-
shaped cakes, and her blethering of lectures at the W.R.I.
She was daft on the W.R.I., Mrs Geddes, she said that folk
in a village like Segget wanted taking out of themselves. So
she and some others started the thing, they'd collect at all
hours, the women of the place, and speak about baking and
minding the bairns, and how to make pipes from the legs of
old sofas: and hear lantern-lectures on Climbing the Alps.
Well, damn't! she'd have to do a bit climbing herself ere
she learned to bake cakes like the Moultrie wife.

By three nearly everything there had been judged, most
of the folk had scattered by then, to see the games in the
ring that Ake Ogilvie had set up for nothing, the previous
night. And well so he might, damn seldom he worked, you
couldn't get near to his joiner's shop for the clutter of carts,
half-made and half-broken, lying about, and the half of a
churn, a hen-coop or so and God knows what—all left
outside in the rain and sun while Ogilvie sat on a bench
inside and wrote his ill bits of poetry and stite—he
thought himself maybe a second Robert Burns. He was
broad and big, a fell buirdly childe, and it seemed fell queer
that a man like that couldn't settle down to the making of
money, and him the last joiner left in the place. But he'd
tell you instead some rhyme or another, coarse dirt that was
vulgar, not couthy and fine. He was jealous as hell of the real
folk that wrote, Annie S. Swan and that David Lyall: you
could read and enjoy every bit that they wrote, it was fine,
clean stuff, not sickening you, like, with dirt about women
having bairns and screaming or old men dying in the hills
at night or the fear of a sheep as the butcher came. That
was the stuff that Ake Ogilvie wrote, and who wanted to
know about stuff like that? You did a bit reading to get
away from life.

Well, Ake Ogilvie, him and his poetry and dirt, there he
was, on the edge of the ring. And inside the ring, round
about the hammer, were a pickle of those that would try
a bit throw. And Feet cried *Back, keep out of the way*,

and went shooing bairns at the ring's far side; and folk clustered around fair thick to look on, old Leslie and Melvin the judges here.

The first to throw was a man from Catcraig, Charlie Something-or-other his name, and he swung himself slow and steady on his feet and syne took a great breath and leaped in the air, and swung, and syne as his feet came down his arms let go and the hammer flew out and flashed in the air and spun and then fell—ay, a gey throw, folk cheered him a bit. But one of his galluses had split with the throw and he blushed to the eyes and put on his coat.

Syne another childe threw, a farmer he was, the hammer went skittering out from his hand, he laughed in an off-hand way as to say he was just taking part to encourage the others. Syne folk saw that the third was that tink Jock Cronin, one of the spinner breed, he picked up the hammer and waited and swung, and louped, and the thing went a good foot beyond any of the earlier throws that were made. 'Twould be a sore business if the Cronin should win. His friends all shouted, *That's the stuff, Jock!* they were fair delighted with their champion's throw, with their rattling watch-chains and their dirty jokings, the average spinner knew as much of politeness as a polecat knows of the absence of smell. The worst of the lot, folk said, were the Cronins, they bade in West Wynd, a fair tribe of the wretches, old Cronin had once been a foreman spinner till he got his bit hand mashed up in machinery. He'd fair gone bitter with that, they told, and took to the reading of the daftest-like books, about Labour, Socialism, and such-like stite. *Where would you be if it wasn't for Capital?* you'd ask old Cronin, and he'd say *On the street—where the capitalists themselves would be, you poor fool. It's the capitalists that we are out to abolish, and the capital that we intend to make ours.* And he'd organized a union for spinners and if ever you heard of a row at the mills you might bet your boots a Cronin was in it, trying to make out that the spinners had rights, and ought to be treated like gentry, b'God!

The worst of the breed was that young Jock Cronin, him that had just now thrown the hammer. The only one that wasn't a spinner, he worked as a porter down at the

station, folk said that the stationmaster, Newlands, would
have sacked him right soon if only he'd dared; him and
his socialism and the coarse way he had of making jokes
on the Virgin Birth; and sneering at Jonah in the belly
of the whale; and saying that the best way to deal with
a Tory was to kick him in the dowp and you'd brain him
there. But Jock Cronin worked as well as he blethered, the
sly, coarse devil, and he couldn't be sacked; and there he
stood with a look on his face as much as to say *That's a
socialist's throw!*

It was Newlands, the stationmaster, himself that came
next, you hoped he'd beat the throw of the porter. But faith,
he didn't, he was getting fell slow, maybe it was that or he
wasted his breath singing at the meetings of MacDougall
Brown, the hammer just wobbled and fell with a plop, if
they didn't do better at the second round and third it was
Cronin the porter would grab the first prize.

But syne folk started to cheer, and all looked, 'twas the
Reverend Mr Colquohoun himself, being pushed inside
the ring by his wife. Ay, that was well-intended of him,
now, you gave a bit clap and syne waited and watched.
And the minister took off his coat and his hat and smiled
at the childe that held out the hammer, and took it and
swung, and there rose a gasp, he'd flung it nearly as far
as the Cronin's.

The second bout he landed well over Jock Cronin's, plain
it was between the spinner and him, the spinners stopped
laughing, crying, *Come on, then, Jock! You're not going to
let a mucking preacher beat you?* The Reverend Colquohoun
looked at them and laughed, and syne spoke to Cronin, and
he laughed as well, not decent and low as a man would do
that spoke to a minister, but loud out and vulgar, he wished
folk to think that he was as good as any minister that ever
was clecked. Then the childe with the galluses threw once
again, but he'd never got over the blush or the galluses, he
landed fell short and went off the field, and Else Queen,
the maid at the Manse, was his lass, and she laughed out
loud; and that was ill-done.

Syne Ake Ogilvie threw—ay, not a bad throw, but
shorter than Cronin's, Ake did it with a sneer. Syne Cronin

again, and the hammer was flung with the whole of his
weight and his strength and it fell, crack! a bare foot
short of his very first throw. And as the minister stood
up, arms bared, you knew well enough that he couldn't
beat that; and then everybody knew that he wasn't going
to try, he maybe thought it not decent for a minister to win,
he swung the hammer to give it a good throw, but safe and
not so far as Jock Cronin's.

But the spinners had broken into the ring, a birn of them
down at the farther end; and as the Reverend picked up
the hammer and got ready to swing, one of them cried, you
couldn't tell which, *Jesus is getting a bit weak in the guts.*

The minister gave a kind of a start, you thought for a
minute that he wouldn't throw. But instead he suddenly
whirled him about, and spun and swung and had flung
the hammer, so quickly you hardly saw what he did. And
the hammer swished and twirled through the air, like a
catapault stone or a pheasant in flight, and landed a good
three feet or more beyond the furthest throw of the Cronin:
and struck on a great meikle stone that lay there, and stotted
and swung, the handle swung first, into the middle of the
spleiter of spinners.

They jumped and ran and the hammer lay still, and
there rose such a yell from the folk that watched, your
lugs near burst in the cheering and din. The minister's
face had reddened with blood, the veins were like cords
all over his face; and then he went white as ever again,
and put on his coat and went out of the ring, folk cried,
That was a fine throw, minister, but he didn't say a word,
just went off with his wife.

Chris said, *What's wrong?* Then she saw his hanky as he
took it away from his lips; it was red. He said *Oh, nothing.
Gassed lungs, I suppose. Serves me right for trying to show off.*

Chris said *You didn't; I thought you were fine.* Robert said
*I'm afraid not, only a fool. There, I'm all right, don't worry,
Christine. Come on, we've to watch Ewan running his race.*

The bairns' races were the next things set. Ewan Chris
watched lined up with the others, Geddes the schoolmaster
in charge of the lot, disgusted as ever he looked with the job.
They'd marked out a track through the middle of the ring,

John Muir stood down at the further end, the bairns had
to run to him and then back. Chris watched Ewan, he was
eating a sweetie, calm as you please, his black mop blue in
the sun, his eyes on the Dominie, he didn't care a fig. But as
soon as Geddes cried *Run!* he was off, he went like a deer,
his short legs flying, the other bairns tailed off behind, and
Ewan was first to reach Muir and go round him, swinging
round gripping at John Muir's trousers; and as he went by
the place where Chris stood, he looked at her and grinned
calmly as ever, and shifted the sweetie to the other side of
his mouth, and looked back, and slowed down, no need to
race. He was up at the Dominie first, at a trot, folk round
about asked who he was, as black as all that, he was surely
foreign?

Then somebody knew and saw Chris stand near, and
cried out *Wheest!* but Chris didn't care; she watched
Ewan take the prize and say *Thanks,* calm still, and put
the shilling in his pocket, and come walking back to look
for her, and stand grave in front of her as she smoothed
down his collar. Robert gave him a shake and he smiled
at that (the smile that so sometimes caught your heart,
the smile you had known on the lips of his father). Then
Robert said *Well, since we've won all the prizes, let's go and
look for tea in the tent.*

And the three of them set out across the short grass,
through the groupings and gatherings of folk here and
there, the show was fairly a place for a claik, one gossip
would now meet in with another she hadn't seen since the
last Segget Show, and would cry *Well, now, it's Mistress
MacTavish!* And Mistress MacTavish would cry back *her*
name, and they'd shake hands and waggle their heads and
be at it, hammer and tongs, a twelve months' gossip, the
Howe's reputation put in through a mangle and its face
danced on when it came through the rollers.

There was a great crush in the tent they entered, but
Melvin came running and found them a table, the gabble
of the folk rose all round about, they nodded to the minister
and minded their manners, and reddened when they thought
that he looked at them, and took a sly keek at the clothes
Chris wore—faith! awful short skirts for a minister's

wife. Mrs Hogg was sitting at a table with her son, him that she'd told to slop slop in his guts, his quean had gone back, and folk saw the damned creature trying to catch the minister's eye. But the Reverend Mr Colquohoun didn't see, you were torn two ways with scorn of the Manse for being so proud, and with sheer delight at seeing the Hoggs get a smack in the face.

Then it was time for the band to begin, folk trooped out to see in the best of spirits, well filled with biscuits and baps and tea; but weren't such fools as go over close to the board where John Muir and Smithie were standing, crying, *Come on, folk, now, will you dance?* Behind them the Segget band played up, Ake Ogilvie there at the head of it, fair thinking himself of importance, like, with Jim that served in the bar of the Arms and folk called the Sourock because of his face, tootling on his flute like a duck half-choked and Newlands the stationy cuddling his fiddle a damn sight closer than ever his mistress, or else she'd have had a bairn ere this—not that you blamed him, she'd a face like a greip, and an ill greip at that, though you don't cuddle faces. And Feet was there, he was playing the bassoon, he sat well back to have room for his boots and looked as red as a cock with convulsions. God ay! it was worth going up to the board if only to take a laugh at the band.

But not a childe or a quean would venture up on the thing till at last Jock Cronin, that tink of a porter that came of the spinners, was seen going up and pulling up a quean. She laughed, and turned her face round at last, and folk fair had a shock, it was Miss Jeannie Grant, she was one of the teachers, what was she doing with a porter, eh?—and a tink at that, that called himself a socialist, and said that folk should aye vote for labour, God knew you got plenty without voting for't. Socialists with queans—well, you knew what they did, they didn't believe in homes or in bairns, they'd have had all the bairns locked up in poor-houses; and the coarse brutes said that marriage was daft—that fair made a body right wild to read that, what was coarse about marriage you would like to know? . . . And you'd stop from your reading and say to the wife, *For God's sake, woman, keep the bairns*

quiet. *Do you think I want to live in a menagerie?* And
she'd answer you back, *By your face I aye thought that was
where you came from,* and start off again about *her* having
no peace, she couldn't be sweir like a man, take a rest;
and whenever were your wages going to be raised? And
you'd get in a rage and stride out of the house, and finish
the paper down at the Arms, reading about the dirt that
so miscalled marriage—why shouldn't they have to get
married as well?

Well, there were Jock Cronin and Miss Jeannie Grant,
they stood and laughed and looked down at the folk. Syne
some spinners went up, as brazen as you like, giggling, and
then a ploughman or so, syne Alec Hogg that was son of the
Provost, he had up Cis Brown that went to the College, thin
and sweet, a fell bonny lass, she looked gey shy and a treat
to cuddle. So there were enough at last for a dance, and Ake
waved his arms, and they struck up a polka. There was fair
a crowd when the second dance came, you felt your back
buttons to see were they holding, and took a keek round
for a lass for the dance: and the queans all giggled and
looked at you haughty, till you asked one, bold, and then
she'd say *Ay.*

Charlie, the childe from Catcraig, went to Else, the maid
from the Manse, and said *Will you dance?* and she said
Can you? and he blushed and said *Fine.* Else was keen
for a dance and she left Meiklebogs, he looked after her
shy, like a shy-like stot, as she swung on the board, a fair
pretty woman. God, you hardly saw her like nowadays,
queans grown all as thin as the handles of forks, and as
hard forbye, no grip to the creatures; and how the devil
they expected to get married and be ta'en with bairns you
just couldn't guess, what man in his senses would want to
bed with a rickle of bones and some powder, like?

Well, Else was up with the Catcraig childe, it was *Drops
of Brandy* and the folk lined up, Else saw the minister, he
smiled like a lad with the mistress herself further down the
line. Ake waved his arms and you all were off, slow in the
pace and the glide, then the whirl, till the brandy drops
were spattering the sky, the board kittled up and the band
as well, and you all went like mad; and Else's time when

she did the line she found the minister the daftest of the lot, he swung her an extra turn right round, and he cried out *Hooch!* and folk all laughed—ay, fairly a billy the new minister, though already he'd started interfering with folk, and he'd preached so unco, a Sunday back, that old Hairy Hogg was descended from monkeys. . . . Had he said that, then? Ay, so he had, old Hogg himself had told you the speak, it was hardly the thing to have said of the Provost, fair monkey-like though the creature was. . . . And just at the head of the dance as Else flew round in the arms of her Catcraig childe, he gave a kind of a gasp and his hand flew up to his waistcoat and Else cried *What?* And the childe let go and grabbed at his breeks, his other bit gallus had fair given way, he slipped from the board with his face all red, and went home fell early that evening alone, not daring to stay and take Else Queen home.

The teas were all finished and Melvin had opened up one of the tents for the selling of drams, folk took a bit dander up to the counter, had a dram, and spoke of the Show and looked out—at the board, the gloaming was green on the hills, purple on the acre-wide blow of heather. There was a little wind coming down, blowing in the hot, red faces of the dancers, you finished up your dram and felt fair kittled up; and went out and made for the board like a hare, damn't! you might be old, but you still could dance, you hoped the mistress had already gone home.

There was old Smithie, well whiskied by now. He cried each dance till he got to the Schottische, he stuck fast on that and shished so long you thought the old fool never would stop, his whiskers sticking from his face in a fuzz, like one of the birns of hay he would steal. And just as he paused to take a bit breath his eyes lit down on his goodson, Bruce, and he stopped and said *What the devil's wrong with you, you coarse tink, that lives in my house, on my meal, and snickers like a cuddy when a man tries to speak?* Bruce glunched up, dour, *Be quiet, you old fool,* and that fair roused the dander of Smithie to hear. *Who's a fool? By God, if I come down to you*—and he made a bit step, just threatening-like, but he was over-near the edge of the board to be threatening, even, next minute he was off, on top of Ed Bruce, folk were fair scandalized and crowded about, snickering with delight to see the daft fools, old Smithie and Bruce, leathering round in the grass. But down came the minister and pushed folk aside, angry as could be, and folk stared at *him. Get up there, confound you, the two of you!* he cried, and in a jiffy had old Smithie up in one hand and Bruce in the other, and shook them both. *Haven't you more sense than behave like a couple of bairns! Shake hands and shut up!*

And so they did, but before the night was well done the speak was all over the Howe of the Mearns that the new minister of Segget had come down and bashed Ed Bruce in the face and syne Smithie, and cursed at them both for ten minutes without stopping. And a great lot of folk went to kirk next Sunday that never went afore, and never went again, for no other purpose than to stare at the minister, and see if he'd be shamed of the coarse way he'd cursed.

Well, that was the Segget Show and Games, by eight and nine the older folk were crying ta-ta and taiking away home, the farmers in their gigs spanked down by Meiklebogs, the Segget folk dandered home slow in the light, it lay like the foam of the sea on the land, soft, in a kind of blue, trembling half-mist, a half-moon, quiet, came over the hills and looked down on the board where the young still danced. Else sought out the mistress—should she take Ewan home? But the mistress shook her head, *I'll do that. Dance while you're young, but don't be too late;* she smiled at Else the fine way she had, she looked bonny with that dour, sweet, sulky face, the great plaits of her hair wound round her head, rusty and dark and changing to gold, Else thought *If I were a man myself I'd maybe be worse than the minister is—I'd want to cuddle her every damned minute!*

Young Ewan was beside her, he stood eating chocolate, he had eaten enough to make a dog sick, as Else knew well, but he looked cool as ever, the funny bit creature, and said *Ta-ta, Else. Will Mr Meiklebogs squeeze you under my window?* Else felt herself flushing up like a fire, *Maybe, if I let him,* and Ewan said *Oh, do,* and would maybe have said more, for bairns are awful, but that the minister had hold of his arm—*Come on, or I'll squeeze* YOU. *Ta-ta, Else.*

SO THE THREE went home through the night-quiet park, Robert and Chris the last of the elders to leave. It came sudden on Chris, with her feet in the grass, her hand in Ewan's, that that's what they were—old, she who was not yet thirty years old! Old, and still how you'd like to dance, out under the brightening coming of the moon, drop away from you all the things that clung close, Robert and Ewan and the Manse—even Chris—be young and be young and be held in men's arms, and seem bonny to them and look at them sly, not know next hour who would take you home, and not know who would kiss you or what they would do. . . . Young as you never yet had been young, you'd been caught and ground in the wheels of the days, in this dour little Howe and its moil and toil, the things you had missed, the things you had missed! The things that the folk had aye in the books—being daft, with the winds of young years in your hair, night for a dream and the world for a song. Young; and you NEVER could be young now.

Like a sea you had never seen plain in your life, you heard the thunder and foam of the breakers, once or twice, far off, dark-green and salt, you had seen them play, spouting and high on the drift of the wind, crying in the sun with their crested laughters, hurrying south on the questing tides. Youth, to be young—

High up and over the Kaimes two birds were sailing into the western night, lonely, together, into the night Chris watched them fade to dots in the sky.

THE WHISPER WENT round the minister had gone, the ploughmen and spinners gave a bit laugh and took a bit squeeze at the queans they held; and some of the folk that were hot with their collars pulled the damned things off and threw them in the hedge. In Will Melvin's bar was a roaring trade, old Hairy Hogg's son and Dite Peat were there, the both of them telling the tale, you may guess, Alec Hogg of the things he had seen in Edinburgh, Dite Peat of the things he had done in London. God! 'twas a pity they'd ever come back. Meiklebogs came taiking into the bar, near nine that was, folk cried: *Will you drink?*

and he answered back canny, *Oh, ay; maybe one;* and had two or three, and looked shyer than ever. Dite Peat roared *With that down under your waistcoat, you'll be able to soss up the Manse quean fine.* Meiklebogs looked a wee bit shyer than before, and gave a bit laugh, and said, *Fegs, ay.*

Else had danced every dance since the dancing began. When Charlie from Catcraig, the fool, disappeared, Alec Hogg had taken her up for a while, and half Else liked him and half she didn't, he felt like a man though he spoke like a toff. He asked in his clipped-like way, *You're Miss Queen?* as though he thought it should be *mistake.* Else answered careless, *Oh, ay, so I've heard. You're the son of old Hairy Hogg, the Provost?* He grinned like a cat, *So my mother says,* and Else was fair shocked, a man shouldn't make jokes about his own mother. So after a while she got rid of the creature, and the next dance she had was with Ogilvie the joiner, he'd left the band for Feet to conduct, he swung her round and round in a waltz, his own eyes half-closed near all that time. If he thought your face such a scunner to look at, why did he ask you up for a dance?

Then Feet cried *The last,* and there was John Muir, he'd grabbed Else afore any other could get near, and he danced right well, Else warmed up beside him, he cried out, *Hooch!* and she did the same, if he dug graves as well as he danced, John Muir, he should have had a job in a public cemetery. As Else whirled she saw the blue reek of Segget, and the dusk creep in, it was warm and blue, and the smell of the hay rose up in her face; there was the moon, who was taking her home?

She was over big and scared off the shargars; but one or two childes she knew keen enough for a slow-like stroll up to Segget Manse. But they looked at Dalziel, that was waiting by, and turned away and left Else alone. And the old fool said, with his shy-like smile, *Ay then, will I see you home, Else lass?*

Else said *You may, since you've feared all the rest;* but he smiled as canny as ever and said *Ay,* he didn't seem to mind that she was in a rage. The dances were ended and the folk were going, streaming from the park as the night came down, the band with their instruments packed in their

cases, and their queans beside them, them that had queans,
them that had wives had the creatures at home, waiting up
with a cup of tea to slocken the throats of the men that had
played so well for Segget that afternoon. Here and there in
the park a bit fight broke out, but folk paid little heed, they
just gave a smile, that was the way that the Show aye ended,
you'd think it queer in a way if you didn't see a childe or
so with his nose bashed in, dripping blood like a pig new
knived.

Jock Cronin and his spinners had started a quarrel with
the three fee'd men at the Meiklebogs. Jock Cronin said
ploughmen should be black ashamed, they that once had
a union like any other folk, but had been too soft in the
guts to stick by it, they'd been feared by the farmers into
leaving their union, the damned half-witted joskins they
were. George Sand was the foreman at the Meiklebogs,
a great meikle childe with a long moustache and a head
on him like a Clydesdale horse. He said *And what the hell
better are the spinners? They've done a damn lot with their
union and all? I sit down to good meat when the dirt are
straving,* and another Meiklebogs man cried the same, *Ay,
or a porter down at the station? What the hell has your union
done for you? I've more money in my pouch right the now, let
me tell you, than ever you had in your life, my birkie. I could
show you right now a five and a ten and a twenty pound note.*

Jock Cronin said sneering-like, *Could you so? Could you
show me five shillings?* and the childe turned red, he hadn't
even that on him at the time, it had been no more than an
empty speak, and he felt real mad to be shown up so. So
he took John Cronin a crack on the jaw, by God it sounded
like the crack of doom. Jock Cronin went staggering back
among the spinners, and then the spinners and ploughmen
were at it, in a minute as bonny a fight on as ever you
saw in your life at Segget Show. You'd be moving off the
Show-ground quiet with your quean, till you saw it start
and then you'd run forward, and ask what was up, and not
stop to listen, for it fair looked tempting; so you'd take a
kick at the nearest backside, hard as you liked, and next
minute some brute would be bashing in your face, and you
bashing his, and others coming running and joining; and

somebody trotting to Melvin's tent and bringing out Feet
to stop the fight.

He was well loaded up with drink by then, Feet, and
he'd only a bit of his uniform on. But he ran to the fighters
and he cried *Hold on! What's all this jookery-packery now?
Stop your fighting and get away home.*

But the coarse brutes turned on poor Feet instead, it was
late that night when he crawled from the ditch and blinked
his eyes and felt his head, the moon high up in a cloudless
sky, the field deserted and a curlew crying.

ALL THE FOLK had gone long ere that, even the youngest
and daftest of them gone, home from the Segget Show in their
pairs, there were folk at that minute on the Laurencekirk
road, a lad and his lass on their whirring bikes, the peesies
wheeping about in the moon, the childe with his arm around
the quean's shoulder, the whir of the wheels below their feet,
the quean with her cheek against the hand that rested shy on
her shoulder, so, home before them but still far off; and
the dark came down and they went into it, into their years
and to-morrows, they'd had that.

Some went further in business, if less far in mileage. Near
Skite a farmer went out to his barn, early next morning, and
what did he see? Two childes and two lasses asleep in his
hay. And he was sore shocked and went back for his wife,
and she came and looked and was shocked as well, and if
they'd had a camera they'd have taken photographs, they
were so delighted and shocked to see two queans that they
knew in such a like way, they'd be able to tell the story about
them all the years that they lived on earth; and make it a
tit-bit in hell forbye.

Cis Brown had asked her father MacDougall if she could
stay on late at the dance; and he'd said that she might,
his favourite was Cis; and so she had done and at the
dance end she had looked round about and had blushed
as she wondered would any one ask her to walk home to
Segget? She was over young, she supposed, for all that, a
college quean with her lessons and career, and not to waste
her time on a loon. And she wished that she wasn't, and then
looked up and saw a spinner, a boy, beside her, about the

same age as herself, she thought. He was tall like a calf, and shy and thin, he looked at her and he didn't look—*Are you going up home?*

She said she was and she thought as she said it, *What an awful twang those spinners speak!* She was half-ashamed to walk home with one. But so they got clear of the stamash of the fighting, saying never a word as they went through the grass. Then the boy gave a cough, *Are you in a hurry?* and Cis said *No, not a very great hurry,* and he said *Let's go down by the Meiklebogs corn and home through the moor to the Segget road.*

So she went with him, quiet, by the side of the park, the path so narrow that he went on ahead, the moon was behind them up in the Mounth, below them stirred the smell of the stalks, bitter and strange to a quean from Segget, she bent and plucked up one in the dark, and nibbled at it and looked at the boy. Behind them the noise of the Show grew faint: only for sound the swish of the corn.

Then the path grew broader and they walked abreast, he said sudden, but quiet, *You're Cis Brown from MacDougall's shop, aren't you?* Cis said *Yes,* not asking his name, he could tell her if he liked, but she wasn't to ask. But he didn't tell, just loped by her side, long-legged, like a deer or a calf, she thought, leggy and quick and quiet. They heard as they passed in that cool, quiet hour the scratch of the patridges up in the moor, once a dim shape started away from a fence with a thunderous clop of hooves in the dark, a Meiklebogs horse that their footsteps had feared.

Syne they came to the edge of the moor, it was dark, here the moon shone through the branched horns of the broom, the whins tickled you legs and Cis for a while couldn't find her way till the boy said *Wait. I know this place, I often come here.* And his hand found hers and she felt in his palm the callouses worn by the spindles there, he'd some smell of the jute about him as well, as had all the spinner folk of the mills.

Water gleamed under the moon in a pool. Cis stopped to breathe and the boy did the same, she saw him half turn round in the moonlight and felt suddenly frightened of all kinds of things—only a minute, frightened and curious, quick-strung all at once, what would he do?

But he did not a thing but again take her hand, still saying nothing, and they went through the moor, the low smoulder of Segget was suddenly below them, and below their feet sudden the ring of the road. She took her hand out of his then. So they went past the Memorial up through The Close to the door of the house of MacDougall Brown; and Cis stopped and they boy did the same, and she knew him, remembered him, his name was Dod Cronin. And he looked at her, and looked away again; and again, as on the moor, queer and sweet, something troubled her, she had never felt it before for a soul—compassion and an urgent shyness commingled; sixteen herself and he about the same, daft and silly to feel anything like this! He slipped his hand slow up her bare arm, shy himself, he said something, she didn't know what. She saw him flush as she didn't answer, he was feared, the leggy deer of a loon!

And she knew at once the thing he had asked. She put up her hand to the hand on her arm, and next minute she found she was being kissed with lips as shy, unaccustomed as hers. And a minute after she was inside the door of MacDougall's shop, and had the door closed, and stood quivering and quivering alone in the dark, wanting to laugh and wanting to cry, and wanting this minute to last forever.

ELSE QUEEN OF the Manse had held home with Dalziel. As they gained the road he turned round and said, with a canny glance back to where folk were fighting: *Would you like to come ben the way for some tea?* Else was still in a rage, she didn't know why, or with whom, or how it began, so she snapped: *No, I wouldn't, then. Do you know what the hour is?* Meiklebogs looked shylike—she knew that he did, she could guess the soft-like look on his face, she felt half inclined to take it a clout—and said: *Oh ay, but I thought that maybe you would like to slocken up after the dancing about.*

She might as well do as the old fool said, even though there'd be no one else at Meiklebogs. Oh ay, she had heard the gossip of Segget, about Dalziel and his various housekeepers, though he did his own cooking now, as folk knew: It was said that two hadn't bidden a night, two

others had come to the Meiklebogs alone and left in their
due time, each with a bairn, a little bit present from the shy
Meiklebogs. Well, that didn't vex Else, the stories were lies,
old Meiklebogs—he was over shy ever to find out what a
woman was like, unless it was out of a picture book, maybe:
and even then it was like he would blush the few remaining
hairs from his head. And even were there something in the
Segget gossip she'd like to see the cretaure alive that would
take advantage of *her*—just let him!

So she nodded, *All right, I'll come up for a cup.* Meiklebogs
said *Grand*, and the two went on, the moon was behind
them, in front was the smell from the coles out still in the
hayfield, tall, they'd had a fine crop that year of the hay.
As they came near the house there rose a great barking,
and Meiklebogs' meikle collie came out, Meiklebogs cried
Heel! and the beast drew in, wurring and sniffing as they
passed through the close. In the kitchen 'twas dark and
close as a cave, the window fast-snecked, the fire a low
glow. Meiklebogs lit a candle, *Sit down, will you, Else?
I'll blow up the fire and put on the kettle.*

So he did, and Else took off her hat, and sat down and
looked at the dusty old kitchen, with its floor of cement and
its eight-day clock, ticking with a hirpling tick by the wall;
and the photo of Lord Kitchener that everyone had heard
of, over the fireplace, a dour-looking childe. 'Twas back
in the War-years that Meiklebogs had got it, he'd cycled a
Sunday over to Banchory, to a cousin of his there, an old
woman-body: and she'd had the photo new-bought at a
shop. Well, Meiklebogs had fair admired the fine thing,
he thought it right bonny and said that so often that the
woman-body cousin said at last he could have it. But it
was over-big to be carried in his pouch, and the evening
had come down with a spleiter of rain. But that didn't bog
Meiklebogs, faith, no! He took off his jacket and tied the
damn thing over his shoulder with a length of tow; and
syne he put on his jacket above it. And the cousin looked
on, and nodded her head: *Ay, the old devil's been in a
pickle queer places. But I'm thinking that's the queerest he's
ever been in.*

The dresser was as thick with dust as a desert, Else bent

in the light of the candle above it, and wrote her name there, and Dalziel smiled shy. *Will you get down two cups from the hooks up there?*

Else did, and brought saucers as well, he gleyed at them: *Faith, I don't use them. I'm not gentry, like.* Else said: *Oh, aren't you? Well, I am.*

He poured the tea out and sat down to drink it. And faith! he found a good use for his saucer, he poured the tea in it and drank that way, every now and then casting a sly look at Else as though he were a mouse and she was the cheese. But she didn't care, leaning back in her chair, she was tired and she wondered why she'd come here, with this silly old mucker and his silly looks; and why Charlie had made such a fool of himself. Meiklebogs took another bit look at her then, she watched him, and then he looked at the window, and then he put out a hand, canny, on to her knee.

It was more than the hand, a minute after that, he louped on her as a crawly beast loups, something all hair and scales from the wall; or a black old monkey; she bashed him hard, right in the eye, just once, then he had her. She had thought she was strong, but she wasn't, in a minute they had struggled half-way to the great box bed. She saw once his face in the light of the candle, and that made her near sick and she loosed her grip, he looked just as ever, canny and shy, though his hands upon her were like iron clamps. She cried *You're tearing my frock,* he half-loosed her, he looked shy as ever, but he breathed like a beast.

Ah well, we'll take the bit thing off, Else.

ROBERT HAD GONE to moil at his sermon; Chris heard the bang of the door upstairs. Ewan was in bed and already asleep, hours yet she supposed ere Robert came down. The kitchen gleamed in the light of the moon, bright clean and polished, with the stove a glow, she looked at that and looked at herself, and felt what she hoped wasn't plain to be seen, sticky and warm with the Segget Show. She'd have a bath ere she went to bed.

The stove's red eye winked as she opened the flue, and raked in the embers and set in fresh sticks; and on these piled coals and closed up the flue. In a little she heard the crack of the sticks, and went up the stairs to her room and Robert's, and took off her dress and took off her shoes, not lighting a light; the moon was enough. The mahogany furniture rose red around, coloured in the moonlight, the bed a white sea, she sat on the edge and looked out at Segget, a ghostly place, quiet, except now and again with a bray of laughter borne on the wind as the door of the Arms opened and closed. Far down in the west, pale in the moon, there kindled a star that she did not know.

She stood up and went over and looked in the glass, and suddenly shivered, cold after the dancing; and drew the curtains and lighted the lamp, and took off her clothes in front of that other who watched and moved in the mirror's mere. She saw herself tall, taller than of old, lithe and slim still with the brown V-shape down to the place between her breasts, she could follow the lines of the V with her finger. And she saw her face, high cheekboned and bronze, quiet and still with the mask of the years, her mouth too wide but she liked her teeth, she saw them now as she smiled at the thought her mouth was too wide! She loosed the pins in her hair and it fell, down to her knees, tickling her shoulders, faith! it was worse than a mane, a blanket, she'd cut it one day, if Robert would let her. She caught it aside and suddenly remembered a thing she'd forgot, forgotten for years, and looked for the dimple she once had had, and found it, there still, and saw her face flush faint as she minded, now that she thought of the thing at all, she'd been told that first night two years ago that the dimple was there—

Funny and queer that you were with a man! You did this and that and you lay in his bed, there wasn't a thing of you he might not know, or you of him, from the first to the last. And you could speak of these things with him, and be glad, glad to be alive and be his, and sleep with your head in his shoulder's nook, tickling his chin, you supposed, with your hair—you could do all that and blush at the memory of a daft thing said on your wedding night!

Then she remembered she'd wanted a bath. She seemed to have stood there dreaming for hours, and found her dressing-gown and her slippers, and went down the stairs and turned on the taps. The water came gurgling out with a steam, she saw her face in the shaving glass, and stared at it—something happening to-night?

She splashed for a little thinking of that, the water about her stung quick at first; she saw herself fore-shortened and fragile, but fair enough still, so she supposed—yes, she would think that if she were a man! She lifted an arm and the water ran down it, little pellets, they nested under her cheek; and 'twas then she thought of the thing she would do. Yes, she would do it this very night! . . . And because that wouldn't bear thinking about, here, she splashed herself and got out, Robert's mirror blinded in a cloud of steam. She opened the bathroom door and listened, there was no one to hear or see for this once, she caught up her gear and ran quick up the stairs, in the moving pattern of splashed moonlight high from the window set in the gable, and gave a gasp as she felt a hand on her shoulder, the arm came tight, she was kissed. Robert coming down had seen the light splash as she opened the bathroom door.

She struggled away, *I've no clothes on!*

He said that he'd half suspected that, teasing her a minute, then let her go. Then he said he'd go down and get ready their supper, and went lightly down the stairs as a lad, it was Chris who now stood still and looked down, high in her breast her heart beating fast. She would, and this very night she would, in spite of what he had told her and taught her!

She dressed and went down through the quiet of the Manse, Robert popped his fair pow round the edge of the door, *Supper in the kitchen, or shall we be grand?* She said she would like the kitchen as well and pushed him into a chair as she spoke, and took off Else's apron he'd draped on his trousers, and set to the making of supper herself. He sighed and stretched out and lighted his pipe, and drew at it, looking out of the window. *There's something in the night—or is it in you?* He stood up and walked to the window and peered, and came back and looked at Chris for a while; and put out a finger upon her forearm. *Funny to think that was once monkey-hair!*

She said that it wasn't, whatever his ancestors had been,

hers were decent, like Hairy Hogg's, hers (they'd both
heard the story). Robert chuckled over that as he sat
down again, the only result of his sermon so far to drop
a blot on the Provost's escutcheon. Hopeless, the Provost,
and most of the others, Geddes, poor chap, had mislaid his
guts; but he'd form that Segget League even yet, wait till
this young Stephen Mowat came home!

Chris asked when that was but Robert didn't know, he
thought very soon, then grew puzzled again. *Funny, there
really* IS *something about,* and Chris said *Maybe,* and keeked
at him sly, as he sat there and puzzled, and restrained herself
from suddenly and daftly cuddling him tight. When she
opened the kitchen window wide there came a faint scent
on the tide of the wind, from the garden, the jonquils and
marigolds glowed faint and pale in the light of the moon.

Then Chris set the table and they both sat down, it was
fine to work in her kitchen untrammelled, good though
Else was as a general rule, if it wasn't for the fact that
the Manse was so big they could have done well without a
maid here. She said that to Robert, he said *Yes, I know, I
feel that way myself—for to-night! As though I could turn
our Segget myself into Augustine's City of God. . . . Something
in the night that's making us like this,* and stopped and stared,
Why, Chris, you look different!

She said he was silly—or 'twas maybe the bath! Then
she felt herself colour with his eyes upon her. He shook
his head, *An unusual bath!——A mental one? They're
uncommon in Segget.*

He said *That's the first time I've ever heard you bitter,* and
she said she didn't feel bitter, she was fine; and they washed
up and dried in the moonlight quiet, together and content
and yet more than that, once he brushed her shoulder as he
went to and fro, carrying the dishes over to the dresser; and
he stopped and scowled, sore-puzzled upon her, *It must be
that monkey-hair that's electric!*

And then they had finished and a mood came on Chris.
Let's go out in the garden. And they both went out in the
honey-dark shadows that the hedgerow threw, warm, a
little mist crept up from Segget, under the nets in the
strawberry patches the berries were bending their heads

full ripe, Chris knelt by a bed and found one that was big, and ate half herself, Robert the other, seeing it waiting there on her lips. And, as he laughed and kissed her for that, something caught them both to a silence, foolish and quiet by the strawberry beds. The rooks chirped drowsily up in the yews as they passed beneath to the sheltered wall where love-in-a-mist and forget-me-nots bloomed blue and soft even now in the night, under the wall that led to the kirkyard, just low enough for Chris to look over.

And so for a little she stopped and looked, that third Chris holding her body a while, how strange it was she stood here by Robert, so close that the warmth of his body warmed hers—when in such a short time she would die down there on a bit of land as deserted and left. They were gone, they were quiet, and the tears that were shed and the folk that came and the words that were said, were scattered and gone and they left in peace, finished and ended and all put by, the smell for them of forget-me-nots and the taste of a strawberry eaten at night and the kiss of lips that were hard and kind, and the thoughts of men that had held them in love and wondered upon them and believed in God. All that had gone by, now under the gold of the moon the grass rose from those bodies that mouldered in Segget, the curlews were calling up in the Kaimes, the hay lay in scented swathes in the parks, night wheeled to morning in a thousand rooms where the blood that they'd passed to other bodies circled in sleep, unknowing its debt. Nothing else they had left, they had come from the dark as the dustmotes come, sailing and golden in a shaft of the sun, they went by like the sailing motes to the dark; and the thing had ended, and you knew it was so, that so it would be with you in the end. And yet—and yet—you couldn't believe it!

Robert teased, *Choosing a place for your coffin?* and Chris said *Just that, but don't plant me deep;* and he said with a queer, sudden fear in his voice, he startled Chris and she turned to look, *Lord God, how I'd hate to be 'planted' myself! If I die before you, Christine, see to that: that I'm sent for burning to a crematorium. I'd hate to be remembered once I am dead.* Chris thought in a flash how Segget would take it, should he die and she get him a funeral like that,

They'd say, most likely, that I'd poisoned you, Robert, and were trying to get rid of the evidence, you know. He laughed, *So they would!* and then laughed again, a second laugh that was dreary, Chris thought. *My God, were there ever folk like the Scots! Not only* THEM—*you and I are as bad. Murderous gossip passed on as sheer gospel, though liars and listeners both know it is a lie. Lairds, ladies, or plain Jock Muck at the Mains—they'd gossip the heart from Christ if He came, and impute a dodge for popularizing timber when He was crucified again on His cross!*

Chris said *That's true, and yet it is not. They would feed Christ hungry and attend to His hurts with no thought of reward their attendance might bring. Kind, they're so kind. . . . And the lies they would tell about how He came by those hurts of His!*——

And yet you don't believe in a God. I've never asked you, but do you, Chris?

She bent her head as she answered, *No*, not looking at him; but his laugh was kind. *You will sometime, however you find Him.*

Then he looked at his watch, it was nearly midnight; and suddenly Chris forgot the sad things. She ran away from him and he came after, playing hide and seek, daft bairns both, in the play and wisp of the moonlight's flow, till Chris lost breath and he caught her up: and she suddenly yawned and he said, *Bedtime*. And Chris minded now the thing she had planned, and lingered a minute behind his step, shy as a bride to go with him.

The room was in shadow, for the moon had veered, Robert moved about quiet and lighted the lamp, his close-cropped hair lay smooth on his head till his clothes ruffled it up as he pulled them off. He looked over at Chris, *I'm not sleepy at all*. And said in that voice that he sometimes used *You look very sweet, Christine, to-night. Did you know?*

She reached up then and put out the light, and changed in the dark though he laughed and asked why. She answered nothing, slipped in beside him between the cool sheets; and lying so, still, she heard her heart hammer.

He lay quiet as well, then the curtain flapped and bellied in the breeze, and you saw like a shadow the smile on his face, it was turned to you and you turned to him; and he said in a minute, *Why, Christine!* solemn, and his hands came firmly under your chin to hold you so and to kiss you, stern. And you knew that you stood on the brink of that sea that was neither charted nor plumbed by men, that sea-shore only women had known, dark, with its sailing red lights of storms, where only the feet of women had trod, hearing the thunder of the sea in their ears as they gathered the fruit on that waste, wild shore. . . .

So: and his lips were in yours, and they altered, and you were gladder than you'd been for years, your arm went round his bared shoulder quick . . . and suddenly you were lying as rigid as death. Robert said, *Tired out, after all, Christine?*

For months after that she remembered that moment, her voice hadn't come from her lips for a minute; then she said, *Just a bit*, and heard him draw breath, and she said again, soft, *Not* TOO *tired, Robert*, and had set her teeth fast after that, for an age, the thunder of that sea cut off by a wall, as she herself was, by a wall of fire; but she said not a word of either of these, stroked his hair where it clung to his brow; and he put his head on her breast and slept, after a while: and the house grew still.

She'd sleep soon herself, she'd put that dream by, the dream of a bairn fathered by Robert—not now, maybe never, but she could not to-night, not with memory of that scar that was torn across the shoulder of this living body beside her, the scar that a fragment of shrapnel had torn—but a little lower it would have torn this body, grunting, into a mesh of blood, with broken bones and with spouting blood, an animal mouthing in mindless torment. And she'd set herself to conceive a child—for the next War that came, to be torn like that, made blood and pulp as they'd made of Ewan—*Oh, Ewan, Ewan, that was once my lad, that lay where this stranger's lying the night, I haven't forgotten, I haven't forgotten, you've a Chris that lies with you there in France, and she shan't bring to birth from her womb any bairn to die as you, for a madman's gab*. . . .

Quiet, oh, quiet, greet soft lest he wake, who's so kind and dear, who's so far from you now. But you'll never have a bairn of his for torment, to be mocked by memorials, the gabblings of clowns, when they that remained at home go out to praise the dead on Armistice Day.

FAITH, WHEN IT came there was more to remember in Segget that year than Armistice only. There was better kittle in the story of what happened to Jim the Sourock on Armistice Eve. He was aye sore troubled with his stomach, Jim, he'd twist his face as he'd hand you a dram, and a man would nearly lose nerve as he looked—had you given the creature a bad shilling, or what? But syne he would rub his hand slow on his wame, *It's the pains in my breast that I've gotten again;* and he said that they fairly were awful sometimes, like a meikle worm moving and wriggling in there. Folk said he fair did his best to drown it, and God! that was true, the foul brute would go home, near every night as drunk as a toff, and fall in the bed by the side of his wife, she'd say *You coarse brute, you've come drunken again;* but he'd only groan, with his hand at his stomach, the worm on the wriggle like a damned sea-serpent.

Well, the Sourock and his mistress kept a pig, and the night of November the tenth Dite Peat closed up his shop and came over to kill it. He fair was a hand at a killing, was Dite, and the pig looked over its ree as he came, and knew fine what the knife and axe were for. So it started to scraich, and Dite grinned at the brute, *Wait a minute, my mannie, I'll let that scraich out.* And the Sourock's wife, that was standing by, felt queer as she saw that look on his face, she thought him a tink, but he fair could kill, not useless entirely like that gawpus Jim.

So she asked Dite in for a dram ere he started, and down he sat with his dram and his cake, and he drank down the one like a calf with its milk and ate up the cake like a famished dog. Syne he said it was over late to-night to cut up the beast out there in the ree, he'd come over the morn and see to that, Armistice Day would be a fine time to do a bit cutting about among flesh—*Fegs, mistress, I've seen humans carved up like pigs, like bits of beef in a butcher's shop, and it fair looked fine, as I often thought, you couldn't wonder at those cannibal childes——*

The Sourock's wife asked if he'd like to see her sick, Dite said, *Be sick as you like, I won't mind; you've an uneasy stomach for a potman's wife*. And she broke down and grat then and said what a fool she had been to marry a creature like Jim, her that was a decent bit parlour-maid once, with her wages her own and her fine new clothes, Jim had sworn in those days he was fair tee-tee, now he drank like a drain and stank like one, too, he wouldn't care a fig though he came of a night and found her lying dead in her bed. Dite thought, *B'God, if he'd sense he'd dance!* but he didn't say that, he didn't care a damn for the Sourock's wife or the Sourock's troubles, why should you care about any man's troubles, there were damn the few that had cared for yours—not that you'd asked them, you could manage them fine.

So he rose up and said, *Well, then, I'll go out and have a bit play with that beast in the ree.*

She asked if he'd manage the thing by himself, she was off for the night to her sister in Fordoun, soon's she'd laid his supper for the Sourock: not that she supposed the sot would eat it, he'd come home and just stiter to his bed, as usual. Dite said he would manage fine on his own, and went out, and the Sourock's wife a bit later heard the grunt of the pig turn into a scream, nasty to hear, and then it came shrill, and she put on her hat and took her bit bag and went out and down by the ree as she went, not wanting to look and see Dite at his work of killing her pig for the winter dinners. But something drew her eyes in over the ree, there was Dite Peat, he was covered with sharn, he'd tripped in a rush he had made at the pig, now he'd cornered it up at the back of the ree. Its mouth was open and its bristles on end, and it whistled through its open jaws like the sound of the steam from an engine in Segget station. So she didn't look longer, went hurrying on, it had been a fine beast, the pig, she remembered, would stand on its trough with a pleased-like grumph as she scratched the bristles on its back and lugs, fair a couthy beast, though scared at the rats, it had once near tripped her as she stood in its ree, she thought the creature was making at her: but instead it had caught a glimpse of a rat and was trying to get behind her for safety. So she turned the corner by Moultrie's shop and heard up in Segget the pig

scream again, and she found herself hoast, like a fool of a
bairn, with water in the nose—where was her hanky?
And she suddenly thought of Dite Peat as a rat, a great rat
with its underhung jaw and cruel eyes, creeping on the pig
that was frightened at rats and had run once frightened to
hide behind her—och, she was daft or soft or just both,
and damn it! she couldn't get at her hanky.

But Dite had cornered Jim's pig at last, as it swithered its
head he saw it set fine, and swung the bit axe, the blade of it
up, the pig screamed again and fell at his feet with a trickle
of blood from its snout and its trotters scraping and tearing
at the sharn of the ree. So Dite turned the brute over, slow,
with his axe, and took out his knife and cut its throat, slow,
and held the throat open to let it bleed well. Syne he slung
it on his shoulder and took it to the kitchen, and hung it on
a hook and left it to drip.

It was fell dark then, as he slung the brute up, its flesh
was still warm, and it minded him well of the bits of folk
that a shell would fling Feuch! in your face with a smell of
sharn, out in the War—He had liked it fine; there was
something in blood and a howling of fear that kittled up a
man as nothing else could. So he left the pig to drip in the
dark, and it moved quick once, when the sinews relaxed,
and Dite gave a laugh and gave it a slap.

'Twas near to ten when he took a bit dander back again to
the Sourock's house, a blatter of rain was dinging on Segget,
sweeping and seeping up over the Howe, lying at night on
the winter's edge with its harvests in, its potato-crops with
dripping shaws in the rigs of red clay. Dite pulled down his
cap and lifted the sneck and went into the house of Jim the
Sourock. He cracked a match and looked at the pig, it was
getting on fine, had near finished to drip, he would leave it
now till the morn's night. And then—he was aye a coarse
brute, was Dite Peat, though you couldn't but laugh when
you heard the tale—a grand idea came into his head, and
he sat down and thought it all out and syne laughed, and
took down the pig he had killed from its hook and slung
it over his shoulder and went, ben to the bed the Sourocks
slept in, a great box-bed that was half-covered in.

Dite threw back the blankets and put the pig down, the

near side of the bed where the Sourock's wife slept—all
the wives of Segget slept at the front, a woman aye sleeps at
the front of the bed where she can get quicker out than a man,
that's sense, for the lighting of the morning fire or getting up
in the dark to be sick, as a woman will, when she's carrying
a bairn, and not disturbing her man from his rest.

So Dite dumped down the pig in the bed, and covered it
up, careful and canny. And he took a bit dander up through
Segget, to freshen himself, as he said, for the night; and
syne he went home, for he was fell tired.

'Twas an hour or so later ere the Sourock came home, he'd
had to clear up the bar in the Arms, and lock the doors and
hand over the silver, and stoke up a fire for a traveller childe
that was spending the night in the Arms' best room. What
with one thing and another that night, the drinks he had ta'en
and the heat of the Arms, Jim came through Segget with a
head fair spinning. As he crossed the Square he keeked at
the angel, and damn't! there were two of the things up
there, he stared at the fairely stern for a while; not decent
for angels to cuddle like that. But then he decided he was
fell drunk, and shook his head, two angels still there, and
went slithering up through the lurching East Wynd.

Well, he got home at last through the drift of the rain,
there was hardly a light to be seen in Segget, it cuddled
up close in its beds and slept, with its goodmen turned to
the wall and its wives wearied with a day of bairns and of
claik, the bairns lying three-four in a bed, though five or six
among the tink spinners, they bred like lice and they slept
like them, too, Ake Ogilvie said—an ill bit speak, a man
couldn't help the bairns that came, sometimes a woman was
just of the kind that would take if you gave her no more than
a squeeze, the next was cannier: you just couldn't tell.

Well, Jim the Sourock had been lucky so far, a fell good
thing, one Sourock enough; but he wasn't thinking of that
or aught else, for a while he couldn't lay hands on his sneck.
But he got it at last and let himself in, and sat down on the
chair that stood by the door, and gave a great paich and
rubbed at his middle.

Syne he loosened his boots, not bothering with a lamp, he
knew better than that, he might fire the damned house; so

he got his boots off and left them lie there, and made for the bedroom, holding to the wall, he would know the way in his sleep by now. Then the first thing happened that jaggered his night, his knees went bang 'gainst the side of a tub; he tumbled half-way into the tub, the bottom was full of some sticky soss, the Sourock swore and lurched up to his feet and wiped his hands on the seat of his breeks, he supposed that the wife had been washing fell late—the careless bitch to leave the tub there!

Well, he edged round about it and got to the door, and stitered inside and grumbled out loud, *Do you know you've near broken my neck, eh, woman?*

His wife said nothing, that wasn't surprising, considering that she was a five miles off. But the Sourock had forgotten all about that, he went shoggling and stitering about the room, pulling off his breeks and his socks, nothing else, he aye slept in his drawers and kept fine and warm. Syne he made for the bed and went in by the foot, his left hand on the hump he took for his wife. So he pushed back the blankets and got in below, and felt about with his feet awhile to lay them on his wife and get himself warm. But damn the warmth could he find the night, so he reached out to give the creature a joggle—*Jean, are you wake?*

Well, the hump said nothing and the Sourock by then had his head a bit cleared through the fall in the tub. And he felt in a rage—*Here, answer me, can't you? What's wrong with the like of you, eh, the night?* And he put his hand under the blankets to feel her, so he did, and nearly shot out of the bed. *Jean—God, Jean, but you're awful cold!*

She said nothing at all and he sudden felt ill. He put out his hand, she was cold as a stone—worse than that, the hair frozen hard on her skin, the Sourock was dribbling and yammering by then, *Jean, Jean, waken up; you're near frozen stiff!* And at last he could bear the thing no longer, and got from his bed and found a match and lighted it up and pulled back the blanket. And he saw a great gaping throat in the light, and the spunk went out, his yell maybe blew it.

That was the story he'd tell to folk. For the rest, you gathered he pulled himself together, and went out to get some body go for the doctor: he was maybe a bit fuddled, but he knew what he wanted and was keeping quite calm, or so he would swear. That maybe was so, and maybe it wasn't, 'twas strange anyway if he felt like that, that when Peter Peat heard a bellow and yammer and somebody beat on the door of his house like the angel of God on the Judgement Day—and Peter got from his bed and looked out, there was no angel but Jim the Sourock, in his sark, with no boots or breeks on either, his face and neck all covered with blood. And he yammered in the light of Peter Peat's candle—*Let's in, Peter Peat. Oh, Christ, let me in!*

But Peter wasn't near such a fool as do that. *Go home to your bed,* he said, *and keep quiet. Is this a time to disturb decent folk? Go home and sleep by your goodwife's side——* And he couldn't say more, the creature of a Sourock was fairly daft, he decided, for he yelped like a dog hard-kicked, and vanished from the range of Peter Peat's eyes; and Peter closed down the window and went back, canty, to sleep by his meikle wife's side, like a calf cuddling up to a haystack, folk said.

The Sourock was fair demented by then, he tried the house of old Hairy Hogg, and the Provost came down and keeked through the slit that was set in the door for letters, fair gentry. And the Sourock cried *Let me in, oh, I'm feared.* And old Hogg said *In? To your sty; you drunkard! You're a fair disgrace to Scotland and Segget. Go home like a decent man to your wife.* The Sourock vanished so quickly at that that the Provost was fair convinced he'd obeyed—ay, there still were folk had the power to rule, them that came of the Burnes blood.

Well, where do you think that Jim ended up? Down in the house of MacDougall Brown. MacDougall let him in and heard his bit story, Cis got from her bed and came down to hear. MacDougall cried on her to go back, but she wouldn't, she said *All right, I won't look*—not decent for a lassie to look on a man when he hadn't on breeks, or not at least till she'd married one herself, syne she'd think, said Ake Ogilvie, his breeks were fair the best bit of the bargain, and the Scythian childe that invented the things the greatest benefactor of the human race.

Well, Cis boiled some water to wash the Sourock, and MacDougall, it fair must have been a sore wrench, made

tea for the creature and he drank it up, and his stomach
for once didn't turn at the taste. And he felt a bit better
and washed his foul neck, telling how his wife lay with
her throat cut out. MacDougall said, *Ay, she has met the
Lord, as you yourself one day must do. Repent and come to the
arms of Jesus*—that's what he'd planned from the first,
you gathered. Well, the Sourock said that he would, by
God, he'd be fair tee-tee from that minute, he would; and
MacDougall was pleased as punch and near kissed him, he
was awful fond of bringing souls to God, was MacDougall,
and threatening the souls with the pains of hell if they traded
at any other shop but his.

So he loaned a pair of his breeks to the Sourock, and out
the pair of them went together, and went canny up to the
Sourock's house and ben to the room where the red corpse
lay, MacDougall carrying the lantern he'd lit. And he lifted
the lantern and glowered at the thing that was lying there in
the Sourock's bed, and cried *Hoots, man this is no the mistress*
and pulled back the blankets and showed Jim the pig. And
the Sourock glowered at it, *Well, then, I'm damned. Man,
but it fair looked her image to me*.

THEY WERE INTO Armistice Day by then, though neither
MacDougall nor the Sourock cared, they shifted the pig and
went to their beds, the rain held on through the night, and
morning came soaking laired across the clay parks, the parks
that begirdle Segget in red, in a wheep of gulls driven in from
the coast, if you drove into Segget that day you'd have seen
enough glaur around to make you believe the tale that they
never took a good wash in Segget till the harvest was over
and the bills all paid. That was no more than a speak, you
knew, but it made a fine hit at the Segget folk, them so
damned proud of their Burgh and Kaimes, and their new
bit kirk that hadn't a steeple, not so proud of their mills and
the spinners that made up the most of their population. And
faith! by the time Armistice was out, it was less proud than
ever of its spinners, Segget.

The day had cleared by eleven o'clock, and folk came
taiking in round the angel that stood so bonny in Segget
Square. Ay, fairly a gey bit gathering, impressive—except

for the smell, Ake Ogilvie said. But he aye was sneering something like that, the coarse brute, why couldn't he let folk a-be? And you saw him there in the midst of the lave, with his medals pinned on his waistcoat flap, and his hands in his pockets, looking at the angel as though he wouldn't sleep with the lass though she tried to come down and crawl into his bed. Sim Leslie, the bobby, that folk called Feet, tried to form a half-circle here, the Provost to the right, all hair and horns, with his popping bit eyes and his ancestor Burns, he was telling how Burns was a patriot childe, aye ready to shed his blood for the land. Ake Ogilvie said *Ay. He slew a fell lot of the French—with his mouth. He was better at raping a servant quean than facing the enemy with a musket*. And Hairy Hogg said that was a foul slander, Ogilvie mad with jealousy, just, because the dirt that he wrote himself was worse than dirt, compared with the Bard; and Ake said he'd rather be just plain dirt than slush on a dung-heap, disguised as a flower; and young Alec Hogg, that was home from Edinburgh, cried *Cannot you leave my father alone?*

Ake looked him up and down with a long, cold stare. *I never touch dung except with a fork, but give's none of your lip, or I'll break my rule*. Alec Hogg cried *Try it!* and maybe in a minute there would have been a fine bit fight on the go, right there by the angel in Segget Square, folk round about looking shocked as could be and edging nearer for a better look, when they saw the minister coming from East Wynd, and the choir coming with him; and folk cried, *Wheest!*

'Twas him, the minister, that had started the thing and had you all out in the Square to-day, old Greig, that filled the pulpit afore him, hadn't bothered to hold any service at all, he'd over-much sense to catch cold in the Square. But the Reverend Mr Colquohoun was fell keen, he'd badgered folk to close up their shops and gotten the mills to close down as well, he fair was a go-ahead billy, like, though some folk said he was more than that, he'd barely started interfering yet. 'Twas said he'd already the kirk session against him, with his preaching for this and that daft-like reform; and he'd badgered Hairy Hogg near from his wits—or what little wits were left the old Provost—about the town council and where it might meet, and what it could do, and who were

the members, and why didn't they light Segget at night, did
they know the drains in West Wynd were bad, when were
the mills inspected, and how? . . . Folk said the next thing
you'd find him keen on would be shifting the Kaimes for a
seat in his yard, ay, if the creature went on at this rate he'd
soon have all Segget on his hands to fight.

A raw wind blew down the Howe through the Square and
fluttered the minister's robes as he prayed, his thin white face
down-bent as he prayed, his prayer just said in an ordinary
voice. It made a man kind of uneasy to hear the way that he
spoke to God like that—not as any other ministers would
do, as though they'd only half-swallowed their dinners and
had the remainder still in their throats. No, no, the Reverend
Colquohoun spoke plain, some liked it that way, you were
damned if you did: and he asked the mercy of God on a
world unawakened yet from a night that was past. And he
said that God had made neither night nor day in human
history, He'd left it in the hands of Man to make both,
God was but Helper, was but Man Himself, like men he
also struggled against evil, God's wounds had bled, God
also had died in the holocaust in the fields of France. But
He rose anew, Man rose anew, he was as undying as God
was undying—if he had the will and the way to live, on
this planet given to him by God. *A pillar of cloud by day and
a pillar of fire by night*—they had hung in the sky since
the coming of men, set there by God for the standards of
men, clouds and the shining standards of rain, the hosts
of heaven for our standard by night. . . . A trumpet had
cried and unsealed our ears: would it need the lightning
to unseal our eyes?

And after a bit you stopped listening to that, you didn't
know much about preaching and the like, but was that
the way a minister should speak? You were damned if
you thought so: fair heathen it sounded. And you took
a canny bit keek round about, at the throng of the Segget
folk that were there—hardly a spinner, where were the
dirt? There was Mrs Colquohoun, anyway, bonny in a way,
with a sulky-like face, a common bit quean the minister had
wifed, folk that had known her well in Kinraddie said she
had once been as blithe as bonny; but now she was altered

out of all manner, if they met her and spoke to her and cried, *Chris!* she would smile and speak and be friends enough, but different somehow—ay, she'd grown damned proud. Well, there she was, and her son as well, the son of her first bit man you had heard, with a cool, dark face, but not a bad bairn. Nearby was the Provost and next him his son, the Fasher, rigged out in his baggy breeks. MacDougall Brown was well to the fore, not that he'd fought in the War, but he'd sung; and Peter Peat, the tailor, a terrible patriot; and Dite, the foul tink; and Dominie Geddes, and the three women teachers; and the porters and stationy, Smithie and Ake. Will Melvin you could see near the Station folk, John Muir and Bruce and a birn of the like. Syne the minister held up his hand for quiet, and you knew that it was eleven o'clock.

And faith! The quiet would have been fell solemn, but for a great car that came swishing up, from the south, and turned, and went up East Wynd. Folk had stood still like stooks of rags, but they moved then and stared at the thing go by—all but the minister, he stood like a stone. Then he said, low and clear, *We will now sing the hymn, 'O God, our help in ages past'.*

You cleared your throat and looked right and left, felt shy to be such a fool as stand there and sing without a bit organ to help; and the first few words were a kind of growl, till you heard the minister himself sing up. And just as folk were getting in the swing, the dirt of spinners came down to the Square.

They came marching down through the Close from West Wynd, a twenty or thirty of the ill-gettèd creatures, with their mufflers on, not in decent collars, their washy faces crinkled with grins, marching along there four by four. In front of the lot was that tink John Cronin, and over his shoulder he carried a red flag, and the spinners behind him were laughing and joking, two-three of them women, the shameful slummocks. Well, your mouth fell open, as it damn well might, you had never yet seen such a sight in Segget; and you stopped your singing, and so did some more, and some after that, till the only folk left were the Reverend Colquohoun, and his wife, and Cis Brown, and that gawpus Else Queen. And then Ake Ogilvie that hadn't yet sung took a look round about and started to sing, as loud as could be, as though he'd new-wakened; he did it to be different from others, as usual.

But afore folk could pipe up again to the thing the spinners were close and Jock Cronin cried *Halt!* And they swung round about him and stood in a circle, and next minute they'd started singing themselves, loud as could be and fair drowning the hymn, a song about shrouding their dead in red, and about their bit limbs being stiff and cold: and God alone knows what kind of stite.

Well, that fairly finished the Memorial Service. The minister had turned as white as a sheet, he finished his singing and so did his wife, here and there a man in the crowd cried out, *Have you no manners?*—speaking to the spinners. And Feet, the policeman, went over to them, *Now then, you're causing a disturbance*, he said, he was awful proud of that word, was Feet, that he'd got in a book on how bobbies should speak. But they took no notice, just stood round and sang, till he pushed through the ring round that tink John Cronin; then they stopped and Cronin said *Well, Feet, what's up?*

Feet was fair roused, a patriot-like childe, he hadn't been out to the War himself, they wouldn't let him go with feet like that in case he might block up the trenches, folk said. But he'd fair been a one for the War all the same, and he wasn't to see its memory insulted by a pack of tink brutes that didn't wear collars—them and their song about flinching and sneering from a scarlet standard and God knows what. Who ever heard of a scarlet standard?—Just a tink way of calling their betters bloody. . . . So he said to Jock Cronin, *Aren't you black ashamed to break in on the War Memorial service?* And Jock Cronin said *No, we're not, you see, Feet, we all had a taste of the War ourselves. Take a keek at our chests now, Feet my lad, and then have a look at your own and see if there's anything on it the like of on ours!*

And then you saw plain what he meant, he himself, and all of the spinners that had marched to the Square, had War-medals pinned on their jackets or waistcoats, they were all of them men who had been to the War: except the three women, and they wore medals sent on to them after their folk were dead. Well, that fair staggered Feet, and you felt sorry for him, especially as you had no medal yourself, you hadn't been able to get to the War, you'd been over-busy with the shop those years, or keeping the trade going brisk in the Arms, or serving at Segget as the new stationmaster. And well you might warrant if the King had known the kind of dirt that those spinners were he wouldn't have lashed out as he'd done with his medals.

But Jock Cronin pushed his way past Feet, and jumped on the pedestal under the angel, and cried out *Comrades—not only mill folk, but others as well that I see down there:* WE *went to the War, we knew what it was, we went to lice and dirt and damnation: and what have we got at the end of it all? Starvation wages, no homes for heroes, the capitalists fast on our necks as before. They're sacking men at the mills just now and leaving them on the bureau to starve—that's our reward, and maybe it's yours, that's the thing we must mind to-day. Not to come here and remember the dead, they've a place that's theirs and we'll share it some time, they're maybe the better compared with some that live here in Segget worse-fed than beasts. It's the living that's our concern, you chaps. Come over and join us, the Labour Party. You first, Mr Colquohoun, you were out there, you've sense.*

And as the impudent brute ended up he waved his hand to the Reverend Colquohoun, and for a minute after that there was such a quiet you could near have cut it and eaten it in chunks, it was that damned solid, while all the folk stared. Syne the minister just turned his back and said, cool, *I think we'll go home, Chris,* to his wife; and she nodded and said nothing, they were both cool and calm. It made a man boil to see them so meek, damn't! if you had been a minister, would you let yourself be insulted like that? No, you wouldn't; and neither would any minister in the days before the coming of the War, the War had fair been a ruination, letting tinks like the Cronins find out that their betters ate and smelt just the same as themselves.

Well, next there was near a fight broke out. Ake Ogilvie cried to Jock Cronin, *Oh ay, and where the hell did* YOU *serve in the War?* And Jock Cronin said *Up in the front, my lad, not scrounging behind with the Royal Engineers.*——*No, you hadn't enough brain for them, you poor fool,* Ake Ogilvie said, and would maybe have said more, if the minister hadn't turned round and cried, *Ogilvie!* And Ake went off, and the spinners all laughed. Some folk stayed near to hear what they'd say, most decent bodies went over to the Arms and spoke of the things they'd have done to the spinners if they'd stayed behind in Segget Square.

CHRIS RAN NEARLY all the way from the Square, Mr Geddes and his teachers were coming for lunch (as they called it, but they ate it just as a dinner); and the meat was cooking in the Manse's oven. Else you could see flying on in front, as anxious as you, you'd left Robert behind, he'd laughed and slowed down and lighted his pipe. But you ran up under the drip of the yews, through the Manse front door and through to the kitchen, and there was Else with her face like a fire, leaning panting up by the kitchen back door, and a burning smell from the open oven. Else cried *Well, I was just in time!* and pointed to the chicken out in its ashet, it had just begun to burn at the top. And you said *That was fine, you're a blessing, Else. Sit and rest a minute.* Else took a look at herself in the glass, *I've a face like that flag the spinners were carrying. Did you ever see such nasty brutes?*

Chris said they hadn't much manners, she thought. But she'd never before seen men with that flag, or heard them singing the song about it—hirpling and sad, but it caught you somehow, there was something in it that you knew was half-true, true with a truth that drew your mind back to Chae Strachan far in your younger days, who had said the mission of the common folk was to die and give life with their deaths forever. . . . Like Robert's God, in a way, you supposed.

And maybe that was Robert's own thought, Chris came on him in the sitting-room, standing and staring queerly at Segget, harsh-blue, rain-driven, in its clouded noon. Chris put up a hand on his shoulder, *Not vexed? The service was fine, and I liked what you said.* Robert squeezed her hand, *My vanity's vexed. That's all, I suppose, and those spinner chaps—a perfect devil if they're right, Christine.* Chris said *How right?* and he said *Their beliefs—a war of the classes*

*to bring fruit to the War. Remember the Samson I preached that
day I tried for the kirk of Segget, Christine? I suppose we saw
him in the Square to-day, with a muffler on and a thin, starved
look. If his betters won't mend the world,* HE *may!*

Then his gaze drew in, *Lord, here they come. His
betters—well, well. They're just at the door.*

Chris herself went and opened the door, Mrs Geddes came
gushing in over the mat, Miss M'Askill behind, sharp as
a needle, the second teacher at Segget school. She eyed
Chris up and down as a ferret might, *How d'you do, Mrs
Colquohoun? Disgraceful exhibition down in the Square!*
Chris had heard of Miss M'Askill from Else, straight as a
pole and nearly as bare, and she wore her hair in two great
plaits, low down on her brow, and it gave her a look like a
stirk with its head in a birn of hay; and whenever she saw
a new man in the toun she'd stare at him till the man would
blush, up and down in the line of her stare; and she'd give a
bit sniff (or so said Else), as much as to say *What, marriage
with you?*

But damn the soul had offered that yet, not even for a
night at the furthest gait, Ake Ogilvie had said he would
rather sleep with a Highland steer in the lee of a whin.
Chris tried hard not to remember that, she would laugh
if she did: and so she did not, but shook hands instead
with Miss Ferguson next, her that they called The Blusher
in Segget. And she started to blush as though someone had
couped a jar of red ink on her head at that minute, the blush
came thicker and thicker each second, till Chris felt so sorry
she blushed as well. Then Miss Jeannie Grant, dapper and
trig, with a fresh, fair face, *Hello, Mrs Colquohoun! What
did you think of the fun in the Square?* Last, Mr Geddes, he
looked at you bitter, as though he thought you poor stuff like
the most of mankind, and shook your hand limp, and trailed
after the others, his hands in his pockets, till he tripped on a
toy of Ewan's in the hall, a wooden horse, and it fell with a
clatter and Ewan came running out to see why.

Mr Geddes had nearly fallen with the thing. Now he
picked it up a great splinter of wood torn out of its side.
Ewan said *What a fool, man, why didn't you look?* and
Chris cried *Ewan!* Mr Geddes grinned. *He's right enough,*

I suppose I'm a fool. I'm sorry, young man. Ewan said *So am I.*

Chris wanted to giggle, but again did not, instead looked solemn as a funeral, near—or two funerals if you counted one of John Muir's; and separated the Dominie and Ewan ere worse came; and shooed Mr Geddes in after his wife.

Robert was there, he'd greeted them all, and was standing by with the sherry decanter. Mr Geddes had lost the smile plucked out for Ewan, like a last swede plucked from a frozen field, he said bitter as ever, *A drop, Colquohoun,* and sat down and looked round the room as though he thought damn little of any thing in it.

And then Ewan started to sing outside, in the moment when folk were sipping their sherry; and Miss M'Askill near dropped her glass. Chris got to her feet and felt herself blush, silly to do that, and she called out *Ewan!* and he cried back *Yes?* and opened the door. And Chris felt a fool, the whole room looking at her. *Why were you singing that song just now?*

Ewan said, polite, *I like it, mother. I think it's a bloody fine song, don't you?*

Else saved the situation, as usual. They heard her feet in the hall, Ewan vanished, and the door was snibbed with a sudden click. Miss M'Askill said it was dreadful, dreadful, those spinners corrupting even the children. Didn't Mrs Colquohoun think the authorities ought to take steps to putting it down?

Miss Jeannie Grant was sitting by Robert, showing a fine length of leg, nice leg, she said *What's 'it'? Put a stop to singing the Red Flag, do you mean?* And Miss M'Askill said, *Yes, that for one thing, there are plenty of others—the ongoings in general of those paid agitators.* And Miss Jeannie Grant said, *Well, I'm an agitator, but I get no pay. Where do the others get theirs? I'd like to apply!* And Miss M'Askill looked at her so awful, 'twas a wonder she didn't shrivel up there and then. But instead she just winked blithe at Chris, and drank up her sherry and had some more.

Syne they were all speaking of the scene in the Square, Geddes said bitter that the spinners had behaved as you would expect such cattle to do, neither better nor worse than other Scotch folk. All Scots were the same, the beastliest race ever let loose on the earth. Oh no, he wasn't bitter, he'd got over that, he'd got over living amongst them, even: their gossip that was fouler than the seepings of a drain, there was hardly a soul in a village like Segget but was a murderer ten times over in word—they hadn't enough courage to be it in deed. Spinners were no worse than the rest, or not much. As for this business of a Segget League, well, he voted Tory himself every time, and no League could remain non-political long. His advice: Colquohoun leave the lot alone, if there's anything a hog hates it's cleaning its sty.

Robert asked Miss Ferguson what she might think, Miss Ferguson blushed till Chris feared for her vest, her underthings would sure be on fire in a minute, she stammered that she didn't know, for sure, some of the spinners' children were cruel, they'd get a girl in the playground and tease her, or worse than that—and Miss Ferguson blushed some more, a torrent, till Chris in pity looked away, and thought herself of her own schooldays and those things that were WORSE in the reek of the playground, hot and still on a summer day and a crowd of loons round about you, laughing, with bright, hot eyes and their short, fair hair, and cruel, eager fingers . . . but she hadn't much minded, she'd been able even then to look after herself, it needed a sudden twist of her mind to think, appalled, that Ewan might do that, might stand by some girl and pry beastly in things—

She switched to listening to the talk again, Mrs Geddes was having all the say now, the three teachers had no other course, very plain, but listen to the Dominie's wife with attention. And Mrs Geddes said what was really wrong, with the whole of Segget, not only the spinners, was Refusal to Co-operate in Fellowship. But the w.r.i. was to combat that, and she really didn't think that this League was needed. The w.r.i. was to organize socials, and teach the mothers all kinds of fresh things—basket work, now, that was very interesting. . . . And she shone and wobbled like a jelly from a mould, and Geddes' look of contempt grew deeper. Miss Jeannie Grant put her sherry-glass down. *I don't see anything your League can do. But the Labour Party can here in Segget, if only we make the branch strong enough;* and she looked as sweet as an apple as she said it, and young and earnest, and Chris half liked her, as though she stood on a hill and looked down on her own youth only beginning the climb, half-liking its confidence, pitying its blindness. But she thought for that matter, again and again (and more than ever since their coming to Segget) that she was older than most she met, older even than Robert himself—older than all but her own son Ewan!

Then they heard Else stamping out in the hall, and she rang the bell and they went through to dinner, Mrs Geddes calling it lunch, of course, she was so genteel Chris thought it a wonder she should ever open her mouth for food. But she fair put away a good plateful and more, for the chicken was golden and cooked to a turn, Robert sat and carved when he'd said the grace, the grace that Chris thought so childlike and kind:

> God bless our food,
>   And make us good,
> And pardon all our sins,
>   For Jesus Christ's sake.

Syne Miss M'Askill was asking Chris, sharp, *Are you fond of social work, Mrs Colquohoun?* and Chris said *Not much, if you mean by that going round and visiting the kirk congregation.* Miss M'Askill raised up her brows like a chicken considering a something lying on the ground, not sure if it was just a plain empty husk, or an interesting bit of nastiness, like. Mrs Geddes said she was very disappointed, she'd hoped they'd have Mrs Colquohoun to help—with the work of the W.R.I., she meant; and why didn't Mrs Colquohoun like visiting?

And suddenly Chris understood her and hated her—she minded the type, oh, well, well enough! So she smiled sweet at her and said *Oh, you see, I wasn't always a minister's wife. I was brought up on a croft and married on one, and I mind what a nuisance we thought some folk, visiting and prying and blithering about socials, doing everything to help us, or so they would think—except to get out and get on with the work!*

Robert's face went queer, a half-laugh, a half-scowl, but Miss Jeannie Grant was delighted, she said *And get off your backs, you could surely have added! You're a socialist the same as I am, you know*. Chris shook her head, she knew nothing about it, sorry already she had spoken like that, Mrs Geddes had gone quite white for a minute, Chris knew she had made an enemy in Segget. The Dominie stared at his plate with a sneer; Miss M'Askill looked at Robert, brows up; Miss Ferguson looked at her plate and blushed; only Ewan ate on, as calm as ever, except when he said, *Can I go now, please?*

Chris caught Miss M'Askill's eye when he'd gone, it said, plain as plain, *A very spoilt child*. And you supposed that it really was true, the truth as she'd see it, who never had a child, who didn't know the things that bound you to Ewan, as though his birth-cord still bound you together, he tugged at your body, your heart, at your womb, in some moments of pity it was sheer, sick pain that tore at you as you comforted him. But THAT you could never explain to a woman who'd never had a bairn, had never, you supposed, yet lain with a man, known all the shame and all the red splendour and all the dull ache and resentment of marriage that led to the agony and wonder of looking on the face, sweet and blind as the eyes of love, of a child new-born from your body's harbour. . . . And Chris roused herself, *Mr Geddes—pudding?*

Robert was trying to keep the talk going, but some thing had spoiled the talk at the table—herself, Chris supposed, with telling the truth. And she thought *They're just servant-queans, after all, with a little more education and a little less sense*—these, the folk Robert had thought could save Segget! It was hardly likely he thought so now: what would he do with his League and his plans? Still wait for young Stephen Mowat to come home?

Suddenly in the midst and mid of them all—the words she now used, the thoughts she thought, the clothes she wore and the things she ate—Chris would see her father's face from long syne, the jutting beard and the curling lip—*Come out of that, quean, with your dirt of gentry!* And because she knew in a way it was true, the gentry that or but little more, sometimes she'd stop in the middle of a talk, in the middle of a walk, in the middle of a meal, and stare for so long that Robert would say, *We've lost her again! Ewan, bring back your mother!*

That feeling came over her later that day, when it brought Stephen Mowat to tea at the Manse. Though none of them guessed the fact at the time, it had been his car that passed the service at eleven o'clock in Segget Square: but ere well the car had reached Segget House the news had spread all around the toun, young Stephen Mowat had come home at last, from wandering about in foreign parts after leaving his English university. And his shover told as they passed the Square young Mowat had looked and seen the angel, and had groaned aloud, *Oh Christ, even here—another bitch in a flannel shift!* The shover said they'd seen birns of the statues as they motored up from England that week, lasses in bronze and marble and granite, dancing about on pedestal tops, he'd thought them bonny, Mr Stephen hadn't, he said that Britain had gone harlot-mad, and stuck up those effigies all over the place, in memory no doubt of the Red Lamps of France.

And the shover said he should know about queans, young Mowat, considering the number he'd had since he'd left the college a six months back. No doubt he'd soon have them at Segget House, he intended to bide there and fee a big staff, and bring back the good old days to the toun. He was going to look after the mills for himself, the estate as well, and the Lord knows what.

Chris heard all this when the school-folk had gone, from Else, when she went to the kitchen to help. But Else needed no help, she'd a visitor there, Dalziel of Meiklebogs it was. He smiled shy and rose when he saw Chris come in, and she told him to sit, and Else poured out the news. Chris didn't feel excited, but she thought Robert might. *Well, that'll be fine, no doubt, for Segget. Oh, have we made any cakes for tea?*

Else said they hadn't, but they damned soon would. *Out of the way, there, Meiklebogs, now!* and pushed him into a chair, he sat canny, his cap in his hands, and watched while she baked. Chris went back to Robert and told him the news.

He said *Mowat home? It's an answer to prayer. And just as I heard the black dog come barking! Let's celebrate!* And he caught Chris, daft, and twirled about the room in a dance. So they didn't hear the knocking at the door, Else did, and went and brought Stephen Mowat in. They came to the door of the sitting-room and watched, till Chris saw them and stopped, and Robert did the same. And Else said, *Mr Mowat, Mem,* and vanished.

He'd a face that minded her of a frog's, he was younger than herself by a good few years, with horn-rimmed spectacles astride a broad nose, and eyes that twinkled, and a way of speaking that in a few days was to stagger Segget. His brow went back to a cluster of curls, he was charming, you supposed, as a prince should be, and very likely damn seldom is; and he said he was pleased to be back in Segget, looking at Chris as though she were the reason, Chris had never met in with his like before, and stood and looked at him, cool, in surprise, taller than he was, he was to say later he felt he was stared at by Scotland herself. And once, when drunk, he was to say to the Provost that she couldn't get over her blood and breed, she was proud as all the damned clodhoppers were, still thought in her heart they were the earth's salt, and thought the descendant of a long line of lairds on the level with the descendants of a long line of lice. And he said by God, had it been a four hundred years back, he'd have tamed that look quick enough in his bed, maybe she lost something of her sulkiness there. And Provost Hogg boasted and said *Not a doubt;* and started to tell of his ancestor, Burns. And Mowat said, *Who? Oh, Robbie Burns? A hell of a pity he couldn't write poetry,* and the Provost was vexed, but then, 'twas the laird, just joking-like; and he was the *laird.*

Chris heard of that later, she'd have needed second-sight to know of the gossip that would be in the future: she said she was glad to see him, she wasn't, neither glad nor sad, a funny little thing, was this what Robert depended upon? Funny that the like of him for so long had lived on the rent of folk like hers. Syne she went to the kitchen to see how the cakes came, they were brown and steaming, set on the table, and Meiklebogs, shy, like a big, sly steer, was sitting and eating one by the sink. And because she just couldn't thole him at all, he made her want to go change her vest, Chris smiled at him and was extra polite, and hoped that he'd stay to tea with Else; and helped Else pile the things on a tray; and they carried it through and found Robert and the laird already deep in the talk that was planned by Robert himself when he first saw Segget.

Mr Mowat's English bray sounded so funny that Else gave a giggle and near dropped the tray. *Is the creature foreign?* and Chris said *No;* and Else said no more, but went solemnly in, and took only a keek or so at the creature, a little bit thing in baggy plus-fours. And he said *Oh, thenks!* and *I say!* and *How Jahly!* Else nearly giggled again, but she didn't, till she got to the kitchen and there was Meiklebogs, and she gave him a poke, *I say, how Jahly! You old devil, I've a good mind to make up to the laird. What would you do then, eh, would you say?*

Meiklebogs smiled canny and said he would manage, and Else stared at him and wondered again why she'd ever allowed the old brute to come near her since she'd wept in his bed that night of the Show; she supposed she was still in a kind of a daze at finding the old brute as coarse as they'd said.

Chris sat in the sitting-room and listened to Mowat, and handed him tea, he said he'd come back to look after the mills and Segget in general, the curse of the age was its absentee landlords, not social conditions or unrest or suchlike. He was Jahly well sure he could buck up the village—didn't Mrs Colquohoun approve of that, now? he'd want her approval ever so much. And he flashed her a long, bright, toothy smile, he'd fine teeth and knew it; and Chris said, *I don't know. I'll wait and see what the bucking consists of. My father was a crofter and he used to say you should trust a laird just as far as you can throw him.*

Stephen Mowat said he thought Mrs Colquohoun's father Jahly, and glinted charming, and Chris gave him up, and cleared off the tea things and came back and listened. By then, so it seemed, Robert had told of his plans, and was sitting now harkening to Mowat's reply. And the reply was: The thing that was needed everywhere was Discipline, hwaw? and order, and what not. The hand of the master—all the Jahly old things. He had been down in Italy the last few months and had seen things there, Rahly amazing, the country awakening, regaining its soul, its old leaders back—with a new one or so. Discipline, order, hierarchy—all that. And why only Italy; why not Scotland? He'd met other men, down from 'varsity of late, who were doing as he did, going back to their estates. Scotland a nation—that was the goal, with its old-time civilization and culture. Hwaw? Didn't Mr Colquohoun agree?

But Chris had been listening, and now she must speak, she'd been trying to think as well as to listen, it was hard enough, but words suddenly came: they both turned round with a start as she spoke. *And what's going to happen when you and your kind rule us again, as of old, Mr Mowat? Was there ever the kind of Scotland you preach?—Happy, at ease, the folk on the land well-fed, the folk in the pulpits well-feared, the gentry doing great deeds? It's just a gab and a tale, no more, I haven't read history since I was at school, but I mind well enough what that Scotland was. I've been to Dunnottar Castle and seen there the ways that the gentry once liked to keep order. If it came to the push between you and the spinners I think I would give the spinners my vote.*

Mowat said *Rahly?* staring at Chris, Robert stared as well at her down-bent face—suddenly she'd seen so much she didn't say, all the pageant of history since history began up here in the windy Mearns Howe: the ancient rites of blood and atonement where the Standing Stones stood up as dead kings; the clownings and cruelties of leaders and chiefs; and the folk—her folk—who kept such alive—dying frozen at night in their eirdes, earth-houses, chaving from the blink of day for a meal, serfs and land-workers whom the Mowats rode down, whom the armies harried and the kings spat on, the folk who rose in the Covenant times and were tortured and broken by the gentry's men, the rule and the way of life that had left them the pitiful gossiping clowns that they were, an obscene humour engraffed on their fears, the kindly souls of them twisted awry and veiled from men with a dirty jest; and this snippet of a fop with an English voice would bring back worse, and ask her to help!

And then that went by, she was suddenly cool. It was only a speak, a daft blether of words, whatever else happened to Segget, to Scotland—and there were strange things

waiting to happen—there would never come back that
old darkness again to torment the simple folk of her blood.
Robert was speaking, he knocked out his pipe.

I'm afraid my wife and I think the same—as all folk
worth their salt in Scotland must think. There are changes
coming—they are imminent on us—and I once thought
the folk of some teaching would help. Well, it seems they
won't—the middle class folk and the upper class folk, and
all the poor devils that hang by their tails: they think we can
last as we are—or go back—and they know all the while
they are thinking a lie. But God doesn't wait, or His instruments;
and if these in Segget are the folk of the mills, then, whatever their
creed, I'm on their side.

CHRIS STARTED AND moved, she nearly had frozen, leaning up here while the night went on, she ought to be down
in her bed, she supposed. The rain had cleared and the stars
had come out, frost was coming—there, bright down in
Segget, was a mantling of grey where, the hoar was set,
sprinkled like salt on the cant of the roofs. Beyond them
there rose a red, quiet lowe, from the furnaces stacked for
the night in the mills.

She stamped her feet and drew up her collar, watching
that coming of the frost below. This impulse to seek the
dark by herself! She had left Robert up in his study at
work, Ewan in bed, young Mowat gone, and herself gone
out for a walk through the rain that was closing in the end
of Remembrance Day, wet and dank, as she'd seen it come.
And it might be an age ere she came here again, too busied
with living to stand looking at life, with Ewan at school and
the campaign of Robert to conquer Segget for God and his
dream.

A pillar of cloud by day and a pillar of fire by night.

She raised her eyes and looked where the frost lay bright in
the west, where the evening star wheeled down to midnight
to lead her feet home.

THREE

Stratus

IT WAS funny to think, this forenoon in June, how long it had been since she climbed the Kaimes, here rose the walls, in their mantle of heather, a blackbird was whistling up in the yews, as she turned around slow she saw the light flow up and down the hill as though it were liquid, Segget below lying buried in a sea, as once all the Howe had lain, Ewan said. Still weak, Chris halted and sat on the wall, her hands below her, and looked at Segget, and drew out her hands and looked at those, so thin that almost she could see through them, so thin her face when she put up her hand that the cheekbones that once curved smooth under flesh now felt like twin jagged crags of rock—a long time ere she'd look comely again!

She leant her head in her hand a moment and waited for the hill below to cease reeling—maybe she'd come out too early from bed, this walk, Else had said she mustn't go far. But the Kaimes had called her after those weeks of the smell of medicines, close fires, and the pain that ran up and down her and played hide and seek with every sinew and bone that she had. So up she had come, the sun was up here, she was out of it for an hour or so, out of the winking flash of the days, to sit and look from the high places here, as Christ once had done with the devil for guide.

Idly she minded that and smiled—it came of being a minister's wife. What had the devil said to Christ then? Maybe *Just rest. Rest and have peace. Don't let them tear you to bits with their hates, their cares and their loves, your angers for them. Leave them and rest!*

Yes, He'd said that, there wasn't a doubt, just as He stood by her saying it now, telling her to rest for the first time in years since that night when she last had climbed up the Kaimes, telling her to rest and leave them a-be, her cares for

Robert, for that other who came and yet never came—for
that third, that stranger whom slow through the years she
had grown to half-know as a traveller half-knows the face
of another on a lone road at night, in the summer light of
a falling star. . . . How Segget would snigger if they heard
her say that that stranger desired was her own son Ewan!

BEING YOUNG Ewan Tavendale wasn't all fun, you'd to
get up as early as half-past six in the little room that looked
down on Segget. But it *was* a good room, the best in the
Manse, you could look of a night right into the trees when
the rooks came nesting, they had a great time, fighting and
mating and playing the devil. Once you nearly fell out when
two rooks were at it—mating, you'd wanted to know how
it was done. But that was a long time ago, when a kid, you
knew all about it now, humans or rooks, mother or Robert,
and there wasn't much in it, though the spinner kids of
West Wynd thought so. Charlie Cronin drew pictures in
the lavatories at school, the silly ass couldn't draw at all.
So you drew some yourself to show how things were, he
turned red-faced when you drew IT so well. *Ewan that's
dirty!* What was dirty about it?

You would lie and mind these things of a morning and
stare at the ceiling and hark to the rooks—moving and
chattering and swearing in the cold—how they *did* swear
as the daylight grew! Sometimes you'd wanted to swear
yourself, and you'd tried once or twice when you were a kid,
but it sounded half-witted, so you gave it up. You couldn't
see sense in rubbish like swearing, any more than in speaking
in Scotch, not English, as mother did sometimes, and so did
Robert, and so did Else (but she couldn't help it). Scotch
was rubbish, all ee's and wee's, you didn't even speak it in
the school playground. And the other kids had mocked you
at first, but they didn't long, with a bashing or so.

Chris (and once Else) rigged you out of a morning,
now you did it yourself, nearly twelve years old. The clock
went birr as you looked at its face and you got out of bed
and out of your pyjamas, Charlie Cronin slept in his shirt,
he said only gentry wore things like pyjamas. You were glad
you were gentry, then, shirts got sticky. Then you'd hear

the clock going off down below, where the new girl slept,
she was shy and said *Eh?* A perfect fool, she near fainted
one morning, in summer it was, when she first came here.
You'd thought you'd go down and get a bath first before
either Robert or Chris should be at it. So you'd nipped
down the stairs without anything on, and as you came
back she came from her room, and gave a screech like a
frightened hen, as though she'd never seen folk without
clothes. Charlie Cronin said that his father, old George,
would take off his clothes slow bit by bit, the top bits
first, and cover himself up, and then the lower, and he'd
cover *that*—you'd supposed that Maidie herself was like
that, a fool, maybe frightened to look at herself.

So after that you had promised Chris that you'd wear
some clothes when outside your room, she'd said that she
herself didn't care—and you said *Yes, mother, I know
that you don't. I once saw you with nothing on coming up the
stairs—a night long ago when I was a kid. I think it was
the night of a Segget Show.*

She'd blushed, as though nearly as bad as the others,
but she wasn't: you were glad that your mother was Chris.
She didn't know that you called her that, to yourself, not
aloud, aloud you said *Mother*. But Robert, just *Robert*,
he wasn't your father. Robert was fun when he wasn't
at work, with the kirk or the spinners or his Labour
plans—summers he took you and Chris on your bikes
out on far jaunts up and down the Howe, to Edzell, to
Brechin, to Garvock Hill where they boiled the Sheriff but
not Leslie the smith—you asked Robert what he meant
by that say, and he and Chris laughed like a couple of fools.
But out on picnics he changed and was young, and would
teach you to throw and do the high jump, he could jump
like anything, Robert, and box. Everybody knew that in
Segget now, they hadn't at first, especially the spinners,
and had mocked at Robert till he taught them manners.
Charlie Cronin had been jealous of him and of you, that
was at first when you first went to school, the first day
he came swaggering up and said *Oh, you're the dirt from
the Manse, are you?* And you said *I'm not dirt, I'm Ewan
Tavendale*, and he mocked at you till you hit him a bash,

right on the nose, and he bled and bled, though it was only a baby bash, you were both of you just babies yourselves. But you won that fight all the same, Mr Geddes had watched it all from a window; and he went to the Manse and told Chris about it; and she asked that night *Did he hurt you, Ewan?* and you said *Ay,* all the kids had said *Ay;* and Chris said *Oh, Ewan, that was real like your father!* Father had been killed by the Germans in France.

Time for breakfast: and there was Robert, busy with letters, and Chris, looking sweet. But she always did that, even when she was angry, she could do nearly anything, answer you anything, she couldn't run maybe as fast as you could and she was a perfect fool about flints, but she always told the truth about things, most grown-up people told lies half the time. You didn't yourself, it wasn't worth the bother, explaining, and trying to straighten things later.

And Chris would say *It's nearly schooltime,* and you'd look at the clock, and see that it was, and Robert would say, *He's dreaming about flints!* But you hadn't been dreaming, you'd been thinking of Chris, she'd looked different of late in a puzzling way. Now, if it had been any other woman in Segget, you'd have known—but not Chris! It made a cold water come in your mouth, as though you were going to be sick, that thought. And Chris said *What's wrong? That's a funny-loon stare.* And you said *Oh, nothing. I'll need to be going.*

You kissed Chris every morning, one kiss a day; kisses were sloppy except for that one—like the taste of honey up on a hill, clear, with the wind in the summer south. Robert cried *Ta-ta!* and you did the same, and were out in the hall, where Maidie would be, tweetering about and worrying again, wondering if breakfast were over yet. You hardly ever took notice of her, not since she'd screeched that time on the stairs. She'd call *Master Ewan, is the breakfast done?* and you'd say *I don't know* and leave her to twitter—who wanted to be *mastered* like a kid in a book?

Out from the Manse and down through the shingle, giving it a kick and a plough as you went, under the ferny tops of the yews, the rooks all wakened and screeching, or off—all

but the young ones, pecking, gaping. If it was summer
you passed under quick, they dropped dirt down when
you least expected, they dropped it once on the Provost
of Segget when he came to see Robert and he walked back
home with it white on his hat and everyone laughed, and
he nearly had a fit when he found out about it.

He was frightened to be laughed at, most people were, you
didn't care a button one way or another, they might laugh
themselves blue in the face at you, you were yourself—and
what did it matter?

And there was the land and there were the touns, Segget
half-blue in its early smoke, you started early and with time
to spare to go round the toun and back up to the school.
So you'd stop and pull up your stockings to your knees, in
shorts, and the shirt and tie that Chris tied, you couldn't
get the knack of the thing, she would say *Oh, Ewan, you've
forgotten to tie it at all!* and you'd say *I forgot*, and she'd
ruffle your hair, *Thinking about flints again, I suppose?* She
and Robert were always joking about flints, and calling them
wrong names, and thinking that funny.

Down by Meiklebogs the curlews were calling, you heard
them above the shoom of the Mills, Robert said something
about that once—*Twin daughters of the Voice of God*. You
hadn't bothered to find out what he meant, though you
bothered about most things right to the end, sense to find
out why this went like this, and that was *so*, and the wheels
went round, and some stars twinkled and a lot did not, why
people were ashamed to be seen without clothes and didn't
like girls to go out late at night, and hated capitalists, if they
were spinners, and hated spinners, if they were New Toun.

The curlew called and you stopped and listened, Else
would hear it at the Meiklebogs, you'd liked Else a lot,
though not all the time. Once she'd come to your room
late in the night, harvest, and was sloppy and kissed you
about, you hated slop and threw a book at her, it hit her,
she stared, you were sorry a bit.

There was a seagull up on that post, try a stone at
it—nearly its tail!—and there was Ake Ogilvie's shop
beyond. Most mornings you loitered about at Ake's, he'd
lean from the door with his compass in hand and cry *Well,*

then, have you learned your Burns? 'twas a joke between you, the poetry of Burns, silly Scotch muck about cottars and women, and love and dove and rot of that sort. Ake would recite you some of his own, his green eyes twinkling and his eyebrows twinkling, with a coating of sawdust sprayed on the hairs, and his long moustache going up and down, so, and you'd stare at him and listen a while, it was good enough, better than Burns's rot. Poetry was rot, why not say it plain, when a man kissed a woman or a woman had a baby?

Down past the house of Jimmy the Sourock, the road had a dip and a hollow for years, the rain would gather, deep, in a pool, you used to march through it, your feet close together, and watch the water soak in at the eyelets, and feel it trickling betwixt your`toes: that was when you were only a kid. Then Mrs Sourock would look out and see, and cry she would tell the Mem at the Manse, that was Chris she meant, and you didn't care. It was no business of *hers* to get mad because you liked to wade in the water, especially as she herself was so proud that her husband, the Sourock, drank nothing but water, since he got that fright with the pig in his bed. And every Sunday he went down to the Square, to the service-meeting of MacDougall Brown, and sang about blood, and you thought that funny, he'd been so frightened at the blood of the pig. You'd once played truant from the kirk to go down and watch MacDougall Brown as he prayed, he opened his mouth and looked as though blind, with his eyes like glass and his teeth all black, perhaps he was frightened to go to the dentist.

A dentist came twice a week now to Segget, he hired a room at the back of Dite Peat's: and the first time he came Charlie Cronin was there, hiding and listening under the window to hear the howls when the teeth came out. And the first to come was old Mrs Hogg: she had a wart on her nose like Cromwell and hair growing out of the wart as well, and she groaned like anything, Charlie told. Then she said to the dentist *How much will that be?* and he said *Half a crown,* and Mrs Hogg said *What? Half a crown for that, just pulling out a tooth? Why, old Leslie the smith down there at the smiddy used to pull me all over*

*the place with his tongs, and never would ask a meck for it,
either.*

But you liked Mrs Hogg, she would cry as you passed,
Hello, Ewan lad, is there anything fresh? And you'd show
her the latest flints that you'd got, and she wouldn't just
laugh or blither about Druids, as everyone else in Segget
would do, but would ask what the hunters had done with
the things, and she'd say that that was amazing, just, what
a thing it was to be learned and young. She'd sense, Mrs
Hogg, more sense than her son, who sometimes came home
on a holiday; he spoke bad English and wore bad breeks,
and patted your head and said *Little man*, or tried to pat
you, you just stepped aside.

Sometimes you'd look into Peter Peat's shop, where he
sat on a table making a suit, he'd frown and motion to you
to get off, he came every Sunday and listened to Robert and
hated his sermons and Robert as well. You'd heard him one
Sunday say to the Provost the minister was nothing but a
Bolshevik, just, as bad as that tink John Cronin, the porter.
Bolsheviks lived in Russia, you knew, they'd closed all the
kirks and they all worked together and they hadn't a king:
and it sounded sense.

By now you'd got to the end of East Wynd, to the Square
where the War Memorial stood, the angel that looked like
Miss M'Askill, Miss M'Askill had eyes that would lift up
that way when she found something dirty drawn on a slate.
In lower East Wynd of a winter morning half the lane was
frozen to a slide, you took a long run from Peter Peat's shop
and shot down the Wynd on the frozen slide that came from
the leaking drains of Segget. By the Moultrie shop you'd
to plan your turn, else you'd batter yourself on the wall of
their house, as you'd done your second winter in Segget,
the whole of Segget seemed fallen upon you, and your face
had shifted, you sat on the ground and thought you had lost
it and felt it all over, it still was there, grown bigger than
ever, growing bigger and bigger every moment, it seemed.
It was while you were sitting there, licking the blood, it
trickled from your lips and tasted salt, and that old Mrs
Moultrie came out and found you, she'd heard the bang
as you struck the wall, she said to Chris when she took

you home she thought that it was a cart and horse. But you liked her in spite of clyping to Chris, her face, brown, old, and tired and quiet as she bathed you and *whished* as though you were a baby, till you sat up and said *I'm fine. Many thanks.* Old Moultrie was sitting in his corner, glaring, reading a Bible, and you said *Good day.*

He'd taken no notice at all before that, he glared some more, but you didn't mind, you saw he really was awfully shy underneath all the hair and the horns, so you said, while Mrs Moultrie went out for a towel, *Do you like the Bible? There's a lot of rot in it.* He stood up, shaking all over, funny, and asked, *And you're the minister's bairn?* And you shook your head, *Oh no, I'm not. Robert's only my stepfather, didn't you know? My father was a crofter down in Kinraddie. Much better than being a minister, I think.*

Funny, he was friendly enough after that, and started telling stories of Segget, when there weren't so many of the gentry dirt sossing about with their motor-cars. And you listened, polite, because he was old, a pity besides that he was so shy. But Mrs Moultrie said to Chris that you were the only soul in Segget he'd treated to a civil word for years.

There was the Arms, not worth looking at, you threw a stone at a cat in the Square and watched the dog up against the angel, funny that dogs were so fond of that. They really couldn't *want to*, so often. Every day that dog of Newlands came down, as you turned in the Square to go up the Close, and did that against the Memorial stone, you'd once told Robert, and he'd laughed and laughed and said that the dog was a pacifist, maybe. But one morning you stood and watched for the dog and sure as anything along it came, and stopped, and relieved itself by the angel; and the door of the Arms opposite opened, and Mrs Melvin came out and said that you were a dirty little brute to stand and look at a dog doing that— Weren't you black burning ashamed of yourself? She was soft in the head, why should you be ashamed? Maybe she was drunk, but you didn't say anything, just looked her all over, from top to toe, to see if she'd fallen while she was drunk, and then raised your cap and went on to school.

Round by here you could see the Mills, in the big, glass

windows across the field the whirr of the wheels as they
caught the sun, the spinners at work in the dust and the
smell; but you liked the Mills, you'd been down there
twice, with Charlie, he said the folk in New Toun were
daft to speak of the folk in the Mills as only spinners,
there were foremen and weavers, and a lot more besides;
but they all *looked* like spinners.

To the right, in the Spring and most of the year, as you
passed up The Close you would see in the park the donkey
that was kept by MacDougall Brown. If you whistled one
note, high up in your throat, you'd found that the donkey
would bray every time. So nearly every day as you passed
you whistled that note and the donkey brayed, and you
laughed, and he'd bray some more and come trotting and
push his long nose through the fence and snuffle, but he
never bit you as once Mabel Brown. Mrs Brown spoke
funny, and she called her May-bull, and had a long story
how the donkey once *bat May-bull* when she went to play
in the park.

There was the smiddy and it once was great fun, when
you were a kid, to lean up by the door and look at old Leslie
blowing the bellows, he'd turn round and sweat, *Ay man,
is that you?* He'd called you *man*, but he blithered a lot,
you would hardly heed at all what he said—about Chris,
was she ill-like of late, would you say? and *The minister'll
be gey fond of her, eh?* and *D'ye mind your own father that
was killed out in France?* And you said you didn't know
to all of these questions, because you couldn't be bothered
with them, and he said, *Eh man, when my father died I just
roared and howled—ay, loon, I'd a heart. And you said Like
the Roarer and Greeter, Miss Moultrie?* And he stopped and
stared with his mouth fallen open, and muttered that you
were an impudent get.

You'd take the West Wynd through the Old Toun then,
with its crumbling white houses and its washing to dry, there
was always washing to dry, never dried. You knew a lot of
the kids in West Wynd, they'd be finishing porridge and
pulling on boots, and they'd cry *Wait, Ewan!* but you'd
never wait, except for young Cronin, he'd come slouching
out and say *Ay, Ewan,* and you'd say *Hello, Charlie,* and go

on together, not saying a thing till he'd ask, as always, *Have you done your sums?* Then you'd know that he hadn't done his and would bring out your book so that he might copy.

Funny that he couldn't do things like sums, you could nearly do them with both eyes shut, and lean back and go off on a think on flints while the other scholars were finishing theirs; and Miss M'Askill would cry out, *Ewan! Have you finished already? Show me your sums.* And you'd show them to her, she'd stand over close, with an arm around your shoulder, like so; and you'd move away, though as slow as you could; and she wrote in your report to the Manse that you were brilliant, but you hadn't enthusiasm; you supposed because you hadn't enthusiasm for cuddling.

It had been different in the first two years, the youngest room with Miss Jeannie Grant, Miss Grant was pretty and laughed at you, and at everyone else, and kept her cuddles for Charlie's brother, or so you supposed. She was going to be married some time to him, Jock Cronin, that was only a railway porter, Chris said that job was as good as another. But you didn't think much of John Cronin, yourself, he didn't believe what he himself said, he just said things and then tried to believe them—you knew that well while you watched him sit, with Robert, up in a room at the Manse, and talk of Segget and socialism coming—it was all a fairy-tale, and he knew it, why didn't he say the things that he thought?

You said that to Chris and she took your two shoulders, and shook her head and looked at you, strange, *Oh Ewan, you're hard and cool as—grey granite! When you too grow up you'll find facts over much—you'll need something to follow that's far from the facts.* And she said something else, about a pillar of cloud, and was suddenly angry, *Don't stare at me so!* And you said *I'm sorry,* and she shook you again. *So am I, Ewan—but oh, you're so cool!*

Well, you saw nothing to make you excited, except now and then a broad-flake flint. It was worth reading history to get at these people, the makers of flints and their lives long ago. Though most of the histories were dull as ditchwater, with their kings and their battles and their dates and such muck, you wondered how the people had lived in those times. But especially before the history-book times you wanted to know how men had lived then and had read all the books you could find in the Manse, and got money from Chris to send and buy others, the lives of the people ere history began, before the Venricones came to the Mearns. And young Cronin would listen and say *What's the use? Father says that the only things we should learn are how to fight the ca*PIT*alists*. You didn't know about them, you asked who they were, and Charlie said *Folk like that mucker Mowat*.

Mr Mowat lived sometimes in Segget House, but most of the time he was down in London, sleeping with whores, Charlie Cronin said. You asked what whores were and he told you about them, what they did, how they slept for money with men. You said that you didn't see why they shouldn't, and Charlie said you'd a dirty mind, and would soon be doing the same as Mowat. That was rot, you hadn't any use for girls, they could only giggle and drift along roads, with their arms twined, and screech about nothing. Or they played soft games in their own playground, once you'd run through there for a cricket-ball and the bigger girls were playing a game, *When will my true love come from the sea;* and the silly fools pulled you in the middle and kissed and slobbered you one after the other, you stood it as long as you could, then pushed out, you didn't want to hurt the fools and you didn't; but you had felt almost sick in their hands. You told Chris that when she heard about it, she laughed and said *All lassies aren't fools, and they think you a good looking lad, I believe*. So you said that you didn't care about that, could you have a piece now and go up to the Kaimes?

You went often up there to seek round for flints; when they dug the Kaimes they must have dug deep, in a squatting-place of the ancient men, and mixed the flints with the building-earth. You had nearly thirty specimens already, properly labelled in a press in your room, and each described on a ticket near. And you had a catalogue, fairly complete, with diagrams of the ripples, hinge-fractures, the ovates and such, and a drawing of the best, a tortoise-core from the Leachie bents. Most of the stuff was late Bronze Age, when the hunters in Scotland had still only flints.

Dinner-times you went home by the near way, quick, stopping to throw up a stone at the rooks. Robert would sometimes be there at the table, and sometimes was out and about the Mearns, trying to raise his fund for the miners, and raising little but temper, he said. Chris never went with him at the dinner-hour, she would stay at home and help Maidie at work, Maidie couldn't cook a dinner for toffee.

Sometimes Chris would be out at night when you came back from the school for tea. So Maidie would give you your tea, like a mouse, and you'd have it and help her to clear and she'd say, *Oh, Master Ewan, I'll do it myself,* but you took no notice, just went on and helped, not heeding her blether you should do your lessons, any fool could do the lessons in ten minutes. Then you'd climb to your room and look in your press, and dust here and there that tortoise-core, and a fabricator-cone you had gotten near Brechin, and take them out and turn them with care, the light waning and dying in from the window as the day waned west from the slopes of the Howe. And sometimes you'd raise your head and look up, when the sun grew still on the peaks of the Mounth, by the glens and the haughs you had searched for flints, and think of the men of ancient times who had made those things and hunted those haughs, running naked and swift by the sunlit slopes, fun to live then and talk with those people. Robert said that they hadn't been savage at all, but golden hunters of the Golden Age.

And once Chris came up as you stood and looked at a new ripple-flake you had newly found, a summer night ere you went to bed, you'd taken everything off, to be cool, and stood by the window and traced out the whorls on the red and yellow of the antique axe. Chris opened the door, and you felt the air waft, and turned and looked at her, her standing so still. You asked was anything wrong, she said *No,* giving a laugh as though wakening up. *Only you looked like a hunter yourself, strayed and lost from the Golden Age!*

And Else went by, and looked through the door, and suddenly flushed and ran up the stairs; that was just a week ere she went from the Manse.

FAITH, THAT HAD fairly set folk agog, when that coarse
quean Else was sacked from the Manse. It just showed you
the way that the world was going, dirty spinners that gave
you their lip, work hard to get, so many sweir—and
ministers that couldn't look after their queans. Folk said
they'd been at it a year and a half, her and Dalziel of
the Meiklebogs, afore that Sabbath night in July when Mr
Colquohoun came in on the pair, right bang in the Manse's
own kitchen it was, Meiklebogs in the way you'd expect a
man in, Else Queen in a way that no quean should be in,
with a two-three bits of her rig laid by. The minister had said
This won't do, Else, fair mad with rage at old Meiklebogs,
for he himself had slept with his maid, and was over-mean
to share the lass out.

Some said that that was all a damned lie, the minister
had nothing to do with the quean, she'd left the Manse of
her own free will. The Reverend Mr Robert Colquohoun
wouldn't bed with an angel sent down from heaven, let
alone a red-faced maid in his house, he was over decent
and fond of his wife. But you shook your head when you
heard that, faith! it clean took the guts from a fine bit
tale. If he wasn't the kind to go to bed with any bit quean
could you tell a man why he was chief with the Cronin dirt,
socialists that said you might lie where you liked and didn't
believe in morals or marriage?

And if some childe said that THAT wasn't true, you
knew right well that he was a liar, you'd seen it all in the
People's Journal, what the coarse tinks did in Russia with
women—man, they fair had a time with the women,
would you say 'twould be easy to get a job there?

Well, whatever the thing that took place at the Manse,
and well you might wyte it wasn't just prayer—with that
scowling brute, the minister himself, and his wife with her
proud don't-touch-me face, and that meikle red-haired bitch
of an Else—whatever happened Else left the Manse and
took a fee at the Meiklebogs. And what the two of them did
when alone, with the night in about and the blinds pulled
down, you well might guess, though you didn't ask. All but
Dite Peat, and he said one night, when Dalziel came taiking
into the Arms, with that shy-like smile pon his unshaved

face, and the yellow boots that he wore for scuddling, *Ay, Meiklebogs, you'll sleep warm now. She's a well-happèd quean, Else Queen, I should think.* Dalziel said nothing, just smiled like a gowk and drank at his dram and syne had another, he hadn't a yea or a nay to say, it showed you the coarse old brute that he was, and you nearly bursting your bladder to know.

Some said they didn't believe it at all, Dalziel of the Meiklebogs a decent-like childe, and an elder of Segget kirk forbye. So he might be, but you knew a man's nature, he needed a woman just now and again—no, no you didn't blame *him* overmuch, but she fairly must be an ill tink, that Else Queen. And you'd look at her hard the next time that you met, not a bit of shame she would show as she passed, just cry *Ay, Fusty Face, so it's you?* and go swinging by with her meikle hips on the sway like stacks of hay in a gale, well-fleshed and rosy, disgusting, you thought, you'd feel as mad as a mating tyke at Meiklebogs and his shameless sin.

But faith! 'twas the same wherever you looked. There was Mr Mowat up at the House, folk said he'd come back from a London jaunt with *two* of the painted jades this time, you'd hear their scraichs all over the House; and once the servant went in of a morning and what do you think he saw in the bed? Young Mr Mowat with a quean on each side, he'd slept with the two and he fairly looked hashed, the bitches just laughed as the servant gaped, and one slapped Mr Mowat in a certain place and cried *Hi Solomon, here's the head eunuch!*

But you couldn't believe all the lies that you heard. Young Mr Mowat was fairly a gent, and right fine if you met him outbye, and speak civil; and say he Rahly was glad that you'd met. He was maybe a bit daft about Scotland and such, and a lot of dirt about history and culture. But couldn't a gent please himself with his ploys, it kept him from wearying and did no harm? When the Mills closed down for a fortnight once, they had over-much stock already on hand, he said he was Jahly sorry for the spinners—and he couldn't say fairer than that, could he now? So you couldn't believe about the two queans, and even were it true 'twas a different thing—wasn't it?—a gent with his play, and a randy old brute like that Meiklebogs man sossing about with a quean half his age?

THEM THAT SAID Dalziel was an innocent childe fair got a sore shock ere the year was out, Else at her new place worked outdoor and indoor, she'd to kilt her skirts (if they needed kilting—and that was damned little with those short-like frocks) and go out and help at the spreading of dung, and hoeing the turnips and anything else, she was worth her own fee and a joskin's as well. Well, the harvest came and it came fell heavy, Else helped at the stooking and syne at the leading. That was a windy September day, the other childes were down in the fields, Else and Meiklebogs managed a cart, out in the park Meiklebogs forked sheaves, big and thick, into Else Queen's arms; and she built them round and about the shelvins till they rose four high and syne it was time for Meiklebogs to lead home the horse, Jim, the roan, a canny old beast. So home they would go and the stour would rise under the grind of the iron wheels, up above the Mounth in its mist of blue, Dalziel would look back now and again and see that the corn was biding in place, and see Else as well, lying flat on the top, with her eyes fast-closed, the meikle sweir wretch.

So he led the roan, Jim, up the Meiklebogs close, and round to the back of the Meiklebogs barn, high in the wall a window was cut, and he planned that this load be forked through the window for early threshing with his new oil mill. He stopped the horse and he backed it canny, the roan was old and he gave a bit groan, and Dalziel gave the roan a belt in the mouth, the brute of a beast to groan out like that, folk would think that it was ill-treated. The roan looked surprised, as though he'd done nothing; and Dalziel cried to Else Queen, *Come on, you'll have to be up and doing some work*.

She cried, *I'll soon do that, you old mucker*, she called him the terriblest names to his face, and all he would do would be to smile shy, and stroke at his chin, neither shaved nor unshaved. So he held, splay-footed, to the front of the barn, and got himself in and climbed to the loft and keeked from the window, and there was Else Queen, standing atop of the rows of sheaves, her fork in her hand, waiting to fork. She cried *You're fair getting old in the bones!* and flung in a sheaf that near hit his face, he smiled and said nothing, they both set to work, her working as fast and as fleet as you liked, Dalziel inside was bigging the sheaves, ready for the first bit thresh at the place, the sun a blind fall on the cart outside. And once when Dalziel took a keek out he saw the sweat in a stream from Else, and her eyes looked glazed, it would take down her creash.

Well, there happened near next the kind of a thing that surely Else Queen had expected to happen, unless she were innocent as the Virgin Mary, Ake Ogilvie said: and he doubted that. And even She was hardly that now, with Burns a hundred years in heaven.—Folk said *What's that?* and Ake looked surprised—they had surely heard of their own Great Poet? Well, the creature died and he went to heaven and knocked like hell on the pearly gates. And St Peter poked his head from a wicket, and asked *Who're you that's making a din?* And Burns said *I'm Robert Burns, my man, the National Poet of Scotland, that's who.* St Peter took a look at the orders, pinned on the guard-room wall for the day; and he said, *I've got a note about you. You must wait outbye for a minute or so.* So Robbie sat there cooling his heels, on the top of the draughty stair to heaven, and waited and waited till he nearly was froze; syne the gates at last opened and he was let in. And Burns was fair in a rage by then, *Do you treat distinguished arrivals like this?* And St Peter said *No, I wouldn't say that. But then I had special orders about you. I've been hiding the Virgin Mary away.*—That was a real foul story to tell, it showed you the tink that Ake Ogilvie was, interrupting the real fine newsy tale of the happenings down at the Meiklebogs.

For when they had finished with the forking, 'twas told, Dalziel took a bit of a look round the barn and saw he would need a hand to redd up. *Get up from the cart and come round,* he cried down, *I'll need you to lend me a hand in the loft.* Else cried back, *Havers! Do you think I can't jump?* And she put the end of her fork on a stone that stuck out a bit from the wall of the barn, and the prong-end under her arm, *so,* and next minute sailed through the air like a bird and landed

neat by Meiklebogs' side. And then she went white and then
red of a sudden and Meiklebogs thought of the groan he'd
heard, it hadn't been Jim the roan after all, 'twas Else had
been groaning afore, as just now. And he stood looking sly
as she sat on the sheaves, her face beginning to twist and
to sweat, she said *I'm not well, send off for the doctor*. Then
her time came on her and they heard her cry, the fee'd men
out in the Meiklebogs fields, and came tearing home to see
what was up. But by then the thing was nearly all done, the
bairn born out in the barn, and Meiklebogs looking shyer
than ever and getting on his bike to go for the doctor.

But faith! that was all he would do in the business.
He wouldn't register the bairn his; and when the young
doctor, McCormack, came up, and Else was moved to
her room in the house, and McCormack said *Is the bairn
yours?* Meiklebogs smiled shy, *No, I wouldn't say that*.
And McCormack said *Whose is it, then?* And Meiklebogs
never let on a word, just looked past the doctor and smiled
shy and sly; and the doctor said *Huh—immaculate con-
ception. Something in the air of the Meiklebogs. You've had
other housekeepers ta'en the same way*.

Well, the story was soon all about the place, as scandalous
a thing as ever you heard, Ag Moultrie, the Roarer and
Greeter of Segget, knew every damned thing that had
happened in the barn, more than an unmarried woman
should know, she said the bairn was Meiklebogs' image,
with his eyes and his nose—and Ake Ogilvie said *Ay,
faith! and his whiskers as well I could warrant*. So Ag told
him if he couldn't be civil and listen she wouldn't bother
to give him the news; and Ake said *D'you think I'll suffer
for that?*—not a neighbourly way to speak to a woman
that was trying to cheer you up with some news.

Soon Else was up and about the place, and the bairn,
a loon, tried to get its own back on its father Dalziel, if
father he was. Its howl was near fit to lift off the roof,
Else let it howl and worked in the parks: as the season
wore on, were the weather fine, she'd take the creature out
to the parks, and when it came to its feeding time suckle
the thing on a heap of shaws. When the fee'd men blushed
and looked bashful at that, she'd cry *What the devil are you*

reddening for? You sucked the same drink before you met beer,
fair vulgar and coarse she'd turned to the bone, you'd never
have thought she'd worked in a Manse. Dalziel would hark,
with his shy, sleekèd smile, saying neither yea nor nay to
her fleers, she would tongue him up hill and down dale
when she liked, and call him the foulest names you could
hear. But the foreman said she still went to his bed, or he
to hers—ay, a queer carry-on!

Till the business of Jim the roan put an end.

THAT CAME WITH the second winter's close, when Meiklebogs carted his grain to the station, he'd sold the stuff for
a stiff-like price, and put a young fee'd loon, Sinclair his
name, on to the carting with the old roan, Jim. He fair
was a willing old brute, the roan, he'd pant up a brae till
an oncoming body might think from the other side, out
of sight, that a steam-mill and thresher was coming that
way. But he never would stop, would just shoggle on, with
his great wide haunches shambling and swinging, he'd a
free-like way of flinging his feet, but he wasn't cleekèd;
and he fair could pull.

Ah well, it came white weather of frost, the ground as
hard and as cold as iron, ribbed with a veining of frost
each morning, folk that you met seemed most to be nose,
and red nose at that when it wasn't blue-veined, Melvin at
the Arms did a roaring trade, the water-pipes were frozen
in the Manse, and the horses of all the farmers out about
were brought to the smiddy to have their shoes cogged.

But Meiklebogs was over busy for that, on the Monday
morning, the worst of the lot, he sent off Sinclair with the
last load of corn; and afore he had gone very far the loon
was all in a sweat and a bother with his job, old Jim the
roan on the slide all the time, and the weighted cart going
showding and banging. Sinclair tried to lead the old horse
by the grass that grew stiff-withered by the side of the road;
and that for a little while eased up the beast, till they turned
into Segget at the top of East Wynd. There was devil a speck
of grass grew there, and near Ake Ogilvie's the ground was
like glass, and young Ewan Tavendale that came from the
Manse had been sliding there a half hour that morning. So

when Jim the roan came on that with the cart he did the same as the Manse loon had done—took a run and a slide, and cart, horse, and all shot down past Ake's like a falling star—so Ake Ogilvie said, a daft-like speak. The lot fetched up near the Sourock's house, the roan fell shaken, but he didn't coup; and nothing of the harness by a miracle broke. Young Sinclair had fairly got a fell fright and he leathered old Jim round about the head with the reins and kicked him hard in the belly, to make the old brute more careful in future.

Peter Peat looked out and he nodded, *That's it, nothing like discipline for horses and men;* and he looked fierce enough to eat up old Jim, that was bending under the ding of the blows to his patient old head—ay, a fierce man, Peter. And Sinclair, that was only a loon and a fool, said, *I'll teach the old mucker to go sliding about,* and gave the old roan another bit kick, to steady him up, and got on the cart, and sat him down on a bag of corn and cried to the roan *Come on, you old Bee!*

So old Jim went on and he fair went careful, flinging his great meikle feet down canny, the loaded cart swinging and showding behind, the road below like a sheet of glass. And he went fell well till the East Wynd sloped, down and round by the Moultrie shop, and there they found it—a slide once again! all the lasses and lads of Segget had been there, the night before, with their sleds and skates, and whooped and scraiched and dirled down the wynd, on their feet sometimes, on their backsides next, near braining themselves by the Moultrie wall, young Ewan Tavendale the worst of them all—he fair could slide, that nickum of a loon, with his black-blue hair and his calm, cool eyes, he'd led the lot and could wheel like a bird just in time to miss the bit wall that was waiting there to dash out his brains.

Well, young Tavendale might, but old Jim mightn't, no sooner did his great bare feet come down on the slide than the same thing happened as before. He started to slip and the cart went with him, it half wheeled round with the weight of its load, and reeled by the wall of the gardener Grant and stotted from that, and the roan was down, braking with its feet, that did little good. Sinclair jumped off and fell on all fours. As he picked himself up he heard the crash, and the scream that rose with the breaking shafts, and he scrambled erect and looked down the lane; and the sight was a sickener, old Jim the roan had run full tilt in the Moutrie wall, and one of the shafts of the cart had snapped and swung back right in the horse's belly, as though the old brute were a rat on a stake. He lay crumpled up, the cart broken behind him, young Sinclair started to greet at the sight: and the noise of the crash brought folk on the run.

Afore you could speak a fell concourse was round, old Moultrie came hirpling out with his stick, and cried, *What do you mean, malagarousing my house?* and Jess Moultrie peeped, and looked white and sick; and Ag came out and then nipped back quick, no doubt in order to Roar and Greet. Will Melvin took Sinclair over to the Arms and had a drink down him afore you could wink; and young Sinclair stopped sniftering and habbering about it, he was feared he'd be sacked by Dalziel for this. *And what can I do in the middle of the season if I lose my job?—I'll just have to starve. You can't get a fee for love or money, right in the middle of the winter, you can't. And that old mucker Meiklebogs—* But Mrs Melvin came into the bar and said *None of your Blasting and Blaspheming in here. You'll have to go out with your swearing, young man.*

So Sinclair went out and gaped like a fool at the folk that had come in around to see Jim. He lay with his eyes half closed and at last he'd stopped from trying to rise from the ground, the end of the shaft was deep in his belly and there was a smell fit to frighten a spinner; folk took a good look and went canny away, you hadn't time to stand there and stare, you might be asked to help if you did, let Meiklebogs look to his old horse himself. Sim Leslie, the policeman that folk called Feet, came down and took his bit note-book out and asked young Sinclair how it all happened; and wrote it all down and looked at old Jim, and frowned at him stern; and then wrote some more—no doubt the old roan's criminal record. Syne he said he'd ride out and tell Meiklebogs, and he did, and when Meiklebogs heard of the news he smiled canny and shy, and got on his bike, and came riding to Segget to see the soss.

By the time he did it was nearly noon, Ake Ogilvie down
with his gun at the place, a crowd had gathered to see the
brute shot; but Dalziel wouldn't have it, *No, bide you a
wee. If the beast should be shot there would be no insurance.*
Ake Ogilvie said *Can't you see it's in hell, with the shaft of
the cart driving into its guts?* But Meiklebogs just smiled shy
and said nothing, except to Feet—that the horse was his
property, and he lippened to him it wasn't destroyed. And
Feet said *Ay. D'you hear, Mr Ogilvie? You'd better take
home that gun of yours.* And Ake Ogilvie stood and cursed
at them both, and folk were shocked at the words he used,
calling Meiklebogs a dirty mucker when the man was only
seeking his insurance.

Well, there the roan lay all that afternoon, sossing up
the road, and it wouldn't die. Folk came from far and near
for a look at old Jim the roan as he lay on his side, as the
afternoon waned he turned a wee, and the blood began to
freeze round the shaft that was stuck so deep in his riven
belly. But what with the folk that came in such crowds, a
birn of the spinners down from the Mills, and the bairns as
they left the school at four, the roan was splashed an inch
deep with glaur and hardly twitching or moving by then.
Meiklebogs had sent off a wire to Stonehive, to ask about
the insurance, like; but no answer came, and he didn't
expect one, he'd the corn loaded on another bit cart and
went off home to the Meiklebogs, attending to his work
with his shy, sleekèd smile, the insurance his if the horse
died natural. Once or twice Jess Moultrie came out to the
beast and held a pail for it to drink out of, it slobbered at
the warm water and treacle, syne would leave its head lying
heavy in the pail, till Jess lifted the head and put it away;
and all the while her face was like death, the fool was near
greeting over the horse, if she couldn't stand the sight of
the soss, why did she ever go near the beast?

It looked like a hillock of dirt by dark, and then Ake
Ogilvie that half the day had been seeking the minister,
that was off down the Howe, found him at last and told him
the tale. And folk said that the Reverend Colquohoun swore
awful—*The bloody swine, the* BLOODY *swine!*—a
strange-like thing to say of a horse. But Ake Ogilvie said

it wasn't the horse but the folk of Segget the minister meant. And that was just daft, if Ake spoke true—that Mr Colquhoun could mean it of folk, real coarse of him to speak that way of decent people that had done him no harm. It just showed you the kind of a tink that he was, him and his Labour and socialism and all.

And he said to Ake Ogilvie *Get out your gun,* and Ake got it again, and the two came down, the roan lay still in its puddle of glaur, the cart behind and the night now close. And the circle of folk drew off a wee bit, and the roan seemed to know the thing that Ake meant, for it lifted its head and gave a great groan. The minister looked white as a drift of snow, he cried *Stand back there—damn you, stand back! Ake, aim canny.* And Ake said nothing, but went up to the roan, and folk looked away as they heard the bang.

Soon as Meiklebogs himself had heard of what happened, and he did that in less than the space of an hour, he was over at the Manse to see the minister, with the shy, sly smile on his half-shaved face. And he said *They tell me, Mr Colquhoun, that you've had my horse shot down in East Wynd.* The minister said *Do they? Then they tell you the truth.* So Meiklebogs said he would sue him for that, and the minister said he could sue and be damned—*And I'll tell you a thing that I am to do—report you for cruelty by the very first post. You're the kind of scoundrel over-common in Scotland.* And Meiklebogs for once lost his shy-like smile. *Say of me again what you said of me now! Mind, there's a witness to hear us, minister.* The Maidie was near in the hall, he meant her, but Mr Colquhoun was blazing with rage. He said *Get out or I'll throw you out,* and made at Dalziel, and he shambled out, not such a fool as face up to a madman, a creature that fair went mad on a horse.

Nor was that the end of his troubles that day, for when he got home the news had reached Else, she was waiting in the kitchen when Meiklebogs came. He smiled at her shy, *Have you nothing to do but stand about there and be idle, then? Get my supper ready, or I'll need a new housekeeper.* The foreman had come in at the tail of Meiklebogs, and he heard every word that the two of them spoke. Else said *Is this true that I hear of the roan?* and Meiklebogs said *Ay; will you give*

me my supper? and Else said *No, but I'll give you my notice.
I've stuck queer things at your hands, Meiklebogs. I've been
crazed or daft that I've stuck them so long. But I wouldn't bide
another night in your house.* And Meilkebogs smiled sleekèd
and shy, *Ah well, just gang—with your fatherless bairn.*
And Else said she'd do that, but the bairn had a father,
God pity the littl'un, the father it had.

She was greeting by then, she'd been fond of the roan.
She hardly looked the Else that the foreman knew well,
raging and red-haired and foul with her tongue, she stared
at Meiklebogs as a body new waked out of the horror of an
ill-dreamt dream; and she packed her things and wrapped
up her bairn.

The foreman met her out in the close and asked her where
she would spend the night, and he made a bit try to give her
a cuddle, maybe he hoped that she'd spend it with him, her
a tink-like quean, him buirdly and brave. But instead she
banged her case at his legs, near couped him down in the
sharn of the close, and held up through Segget and down
to the station, and took the late train to her father's in
Fordoun—the ill-gettèd bitch that she was, folk said,
to leave Meiklebogs without warning like that, her and her
blethering over a horse.

THERE WOULDN'T HAVE been half the steer and stour if
Mr Colquohoun had kept to himself. He'd need to leave
other folk a-be and heed to his own concerns, him, that
tink-cool stepson of his, for one—wasn't *he* the loon that
had led the others in making the slide that mischieved the
horse? He led most of the bairns in ill-gettèd ploys, folk
told after that, though you hadn't heard even a whisper
before. 'Twas said he would sneak in the lassies' playground,
and cuddle and kiss them when they were at games, the
ill-gettèd wretch, and at his age, too. Ay, Mr Colquohoun
was more in need of trying to reform young Ewan Tavendale
than interfering with a good, quiet childe like old Dalziel of
the Meiklebogs.

Old Leslie said *Ay*—it was down at the Arms—*or
getting that proud-looking wife with a bairn—damn't! is
that an example to show, none of a family and married five*

years? Now, when I was a loon up in Garvock. . . . and
folk began to hem and talk loud, and look up at the roof
and hoast in their throats, and you couldn't hear more, and
that was a blessing, the old fool could deave a dog into
dysentery. But still there was something in what he was
saying, other folk had bairns, they came with the seasons,
there was no escape were you wedded and bedded. But Dite
Peat said *Isn't there, now? Let me tell you*—and he told
about shops in *that lousy hole, London,* where things were
for sale that a man could use, right handy-like, and what
happened then? You never fathered a family, not you,
you could sin as much as you liked and pay nothing. And
Dite said forbye it was his belief that's what that couple
did up at the Manse, that was why Mrs Colquohoun went
about like a quean, with a skin like cream and a figure like
that, hardly a chest on the creature at all; instead of the
broadening out and about, looking sappy and squash like a
woman of her age. Damn't, what was woman in the world
for, eh?—but to make your porridge and lie in your
bed and bring as many bairns into the world as would help
a man that was getting old? Not that the London things
weren't fine for a childe when he went on a holiday, like.
But if he himself were tied up, b'God, he'd take care he'd
his wife in the family way—ay, every year, with a good
bit scraich when it came to her time, that fair was a thing
to jake a man up.

That was a dirty enough speak, if you liked. Folk looked
here and there and Jim the Sourock, that had gotten religion,
cast up his eyes, he had grown so holy with MacDougall's
crush that he called the watery the w.c., and wouldn't have
it that women had bodies at all more than an inch below the
neck-bone. But Hairy Hogg had come in and sat down, folk
cried, *Ay, Provost, and what would you say?* And Hairy said
he thought Scotland was fair in a way, and if Burns came
back he would think the same; and the worst thing yet they
had done in Segget was to vote the Reverend Colquohoun
to the pulpit—him and his Labour and sneering at folk,
damn't! he had said we were monkeys, not men.

Some folk in the bar took a snicker at that, the story
was growing whiskers in Segget, but the Provost had never

forgiven the minister. And Hairy said it was his opinion,
from studying folk a good fifty year—and mind you, he
was no fool at the job—the minister took up with some
other woman. They said that the father of Else Queen's
bairn was old Dalziel of the Meiklebogs, but he, Hairy
Hogg, had his doubts of that. Had the minister ever cast
out with the quean? No, when he'd meet her out and about
he'd cry to her cheery, as though nothing had happened. If
he couldn't give a bairn to his mistress, the minister, it was
maybe because he was hashed other ways.

Damn't, that was a tasty bit story, now, queer you yourself
hadn't thought of that. But long ere another day was done
the news was spread through the Segget wynds that the
Reverend Mr Colquohoun, the minister, had fathered the
bairn of that quean, Else Queen, the Provost had seen the
two of them together, him sossing the lass like a dog at
its pleasure.

Ake Ogilvie heard the tale from the tailor, and Ake said:
*Blethers, and even if it's true what has the business to do with
old Hogg? He himself, it seems, has done a bit more than just
lie down by the side of his wife—or that gawpus he has for
a son's not his.*

That was just like Ake Ogilvie, to speak coarse like that,
trying to blacken the character of a man that wasn't there
to defend himself. Peter Peat said *Well, I'm a friend to
my friends, but a man that's once got himself wrong with
me*—and he looked fierce enough to frighten a shark;
but Ake Ogilvie laughed, *And what's Colquohoun done?*
And Peter said *Him? A disgrace to Segget, that should be
a good Conservative. What is he instead?—why, a Labour
tink.* But Ake Ogilvie just said *To hell with their politics, I
don't care though he's trying to bring back the Pretender, same
as that snippet, Jahly young Mowat.*

But Peter wouldn't hear the gentry miscalled, and he
said that Jahly would come to himself, and take his right-
ful place, you would see—at the head of the Segget
Conservative branch. Ake said *He can take his place on a
midden if he likes—and he'll find they've much the same
smell.* Peter asked what had much the same smell and Ake
said *Tories and middens, of course,* and Peter Peat looked at

him fierce, and left; that would learn the ill-gettèd joiner, that would.

Well, the news reached Cronin, the old tink in West Wynd, him that was aye preaching his socialist stite; and he said that he thought the whole thing a damned lie, an attempt to discredit the socialists of Segget. Jock Cronin at the station heard it and said *He's all right, Colquohoun*, in an offhand way, to let you know he and the Manse were fell thick and slobbered their brose from the very same bowl.

Ag Moultrie, the Roarer and Greeter (for short), took the news to the servants at Segget House; and it spread about there, and when young Mr Mowat came home from a trip he had gone to Dundon, he laughed out aloud. *Some have all the luck. But if Mrs Colquohoun's in need of a bairn I'll give half a year's profits to provide her with one.*

And you couldn't but laugh at the joke of the gent.

ROBERT WAS AWAY that New Year's Eve, into Aberdeen, he wouldn't say why; but Chris could guess and had laughed at him. *Mind, nothing expensive.* And he'd said *What, in drinks? I'm going to squat in a pub and swizzle confusion to all the sour sourocks in Segget!* Chris wished that it wasn't a joke, and he would; he kissed her and went striding away down the shingle, turning about to wave from the yews, his kiss still pressed on her lips as she stood, and tingling a bit, like a bee on a flower.

It was frosty weather as the day wore on, the sky and the earth sharp-rimed with steel, no sun came, only a smoulder of grey, Chris cooked the dinner with Maidie to help, and remembered Else, she'd have been more use. Maidie still *Memmed* like a frightened mouse, and once when up and above their heads there came a crash like a falling wall, she nearly jumped from her skin with fright. Chris said *It's just Ewan, he's moving his press*, and Maidie said, *Oh, I got such a fright!* and looked as though it had lifted her liver. Chris left her and went up to Ewan's room, and knocked at the door, he bade her come in, the place was a still, grey haze with dust. She saw Ewan through it by the window ledge, he'd stooped to look in the press he'd moved, it was filled with his precious array of flints.

Chris asked what else he was moving to-day? He said *Everything* and set to on the bed, she sat down and didn't offer to help. His hair fell over his eyes as he tugged, funny to look at, funny to think he had been your baby, been yours, been you, been less than that even—now sturdy and slim, with his firm round shoulders and that dun gold skin he got from yourself, and his father's hair. He stopped in a minute and came where she sat: *I think that'll do. I'll dust after dinner.*

So the two of them went down and had dinner alone, Ewan said he'd have everything moved in his room ere the New Year came and Chris asked why. He said *Oh, I like a new angle on things,* and then he said *Mother, you wanted to laugh. What about?* and Chris said *You, I suppose! You sounded so grown-up like for a lad.*

He said nothing to that, but went on with his meat, they didn't say grace when Robert wasn't there, that was funny when you came to think of the thing, Robert knew and knew that you knew he knew. But he was too sure to vex about that, sure of himself and his God and belief, except when the angry black moments came—seldom enough in this last three years. Once he'd raved *Religion—A Scot know religion? Half of them think of God as a Scot with brosy morals and a penchant for Burns. And the other half are over damned mean to allow the Almighty even existence. You know which half you belong to, I think.* Hate and fury in his face as he said it, the day after the killing of Meiklebogs' horse. Chris had looked at him cool and remotely then, as she'd learned with the years, and he'd banged from the room, to return in an hour or so recovered. *What a ranter and raver I am, Christine! I think you'll outlast me a thousand years!*

And now, on a sudden impulse, she said, *Do you ever think of religion, Ewan?*

He never said *What?* or said your last word the way other boys of his age would do; he looked up and shook his head, *Not now.* She asked when he had and he said, long ago, when he was a kid and hadn't much sense, he used to be worried when Robert was preaching. Chris said *But he never tried to fear you,* and Ewan shook his head, *Oh no, it wasn't that. But I hated the notion God was there, prying into every minute of my life. I wanted to belong to myself, and I do; it doesn't matter a bit to me now.* She understood well enough what he meant, how like her he sometimes was, how unlike! *So you think God doesn't matter, then, Ewan?* and he said, *I don't think He's worth bothering about. He can't make any difference to the world—or I should think He'd have made it by now.*

The evening came down before it was four, up in the Mounth the snow came thick, sheeting hill on hill as it passed on the wings of the howling wind from the haughs. But the storm passed north of Segget, lying lithe, Chris in the kitchen looked out at it pass, she was making cakes and pies for the morn, Maidie tweetering about like a bird *Eh, Mem, but that's* RICH, *that'll be a fine one!*

Chris said *Then be sure you eat a good share, you're still thin enough since you came to the Manse. Are you sure you are well?* And Maidie said *Fine.* She blushed and stood like a thin little bird, Chris looked at her quiet, a thin little lass—what did she think, what did she do in her moments alone, had she a lad, had she ever been kissed—or more than that, as they said in Segget? Not half the life in her that poor Else had; what would Else Queen be doing to-day?

Dark. As they took their tea together, Ewan and Chris, they left the blinds drawn and could see the night coming stark outbye, growing strangely light as the daylight waned and the frost, white-plumed, walked swift over Segget. Ewan sat on the rug by the fire and read, his blue head down-bent over his book, Chris stared in the fire and tired of that and finished her tea, and wandered about, and went to the window and looked at the night. Then she looked at the clock. She would go and meet Robert.

She turned to the door and Ewan jumped up, she said not to bother, she was going to walk. He said absent-mindedly, *See you keep warm,* and his eyes went back again to his book.

Outside, she went hatless, with her coat collar up, she found at the door of the Manse a wind, bright, keen, and edged like a razor-blade, the world sleeping on the winter's edge, about her, dim-pathed, wound the garden of summer, she passed up its aisles, the hoar crackled below her, all Segget seemed held in the hand-grip of frost. A queer thought and memory came to her then and she turned about from going to the gate, and went back instead by the side of the Manse, up through the garden where the strawberry beds lay covered deep in manure and straw, to the wall that girded the kirkyard of Segget.

Here the wind was still, in the Manse's lithe, she put out a hand on the hoar of the dyke, it felt soft as salt and as cold as steel; and idly, standing, she wrote her name, though she couldn't see it by then in the dark, CHRISTINE COLQUOHOUN in great capital letters. And she minded how once she had stood here before, four years or more, after Segget Show; and she and Robert were there together and she'd thought of the vanished folk in the yard, and planned to add to those that supplanted. And the War-time wound that was seared on Robert had seared that plan from her mind as with fire. . . .

It seemed this night remote from her life as the things she'd dreamt as a quean in Blawearie, when she was a maid and knew nothing of men, the kind of play that a bairn would play: for her who stood here with life in her again, unexpected, certain, Robert's baby and hers.

And she found it strange in that icy hush, leaning there warm, her hair bare to the cold, to think how remote was that life from her now, even bairn for the thing that lay under her heart was a word that she'd hardly used a long time, thinking of it as a baby, in English—that from her books and her life in a Manse. She seemed to stand here by the kirkyard's edge looking back on the stones that marked the years where so many Chrises had died and lay buried—back and back, as the graveyard grew dim, far over those smothered hopes and delights, to that other Chris that had been with child, a child herself or so little more, and had known such terror and delight in that, young and raw and queer and sweet, you thought her now, that Chris that had been—the Chris far off in that vanished year who had lain in terror as nights came down with knowledge of the thing that moved in herself, the fruit of her love for the boy she had wed, Ewan sleeping so quiet and so sound in her bed. Remote and far to think she was YOU!

Quiet in the dark she wrote with her finger another name

she wrote far up in the Kaimes a peesie wheep—maybe a lost memory from those years in Kinraddie, a peesie that had known that other Chris! She heard a long scuffling through the long grass, silver beyond the rim of the dyke, some rabbit or hare, though it made her heart jump; and slowly she felt her finger rub out the name she had written in hoar on the dyke—ill-luck to have done that, she minded folk said.

A month ago since she'd known for sure, had puzzled for days with the second no-go. Robert would frown, *What on earth's gone wrong? You're dreaming, Christine!* and smile, and she'd smile, and puzzle again when he'd left her alone. So it came on her in the strangest places, she stood in MacDougall Brown's to shop, and MacDougall asked thrice what thing she might want—*Now, Mem*—and she said—*Did I want it at all?* and then came to herself at his cod-like stare. So she gave her order and went out and home, she supposed MacDougall would manage to make out that was another proof of her pride!—all Segget for some reason thought her proud, maybe because she had taken to thinking, not stayed as still as a quean in a book or a quean in a bothy, from year unto year.

And when once Stephen Mowat came down to see Robert, and she gave them supper and sat by to listen, Mowat broke off the talk to say *Rahly, Mrs Colquohoun, do tell us the joke!* She said *What joke?* And he said *The one that's making you smile in that charming way.* She'd said *Oh, I suppose I am full up of supper!* And he'd said he thought that a Jahly untruth, joking, polished as a mart-day pig.

So at last she had known and woke one day sure; and lay and dreamt; and Robert got up—*Feeling all right?*—and she had said *Fine. Robert, we're going to have a baby.* He stared—*We?*—the thing had staggered him, she lay and watched, something moved in her heart, laughter for him, a queer pity for him—oh, men were funny and just boys to be pitied! *Well, I am,* she'd said, *but you had a share.* He was standing half-dressed, with his fair hair on end, he sat on the bed and stared and then smiled, slowly, with that crinkling about the eyes she had loved near the very first time she met him. *Really and honest-to-God that we are?* And she'd said it was real enough, how did eyes she had loved near the very first time she met him. *Really and honest-to-God that we are?* And she'd said it was real enough, how did it happen? And he'd said he hadn't the least idea, and that struck them as funny, they giggled like children; and after 'twas Robert that went into long dreams. She'd say *What again?* and he'd say *But Christine! A baby—Good Lord, I hope it's a girl! What does it feel like being as you are—a nuisance, just, or tremendous and terrible?* And Chris had said that it made you feel sick, now and then, and Robert had laughed at that, he wasn't so easily cheated as Mowat. *Oh Chris Caledonia, I've married a nation!*

Now, standing beside the dyke in the dark, she minded that, it was true enough, somehow you did hide away the great things, Scots folk had always done that, you supposed—in case they'd go blind in their naked shine, like a soul in the presence of Robert's great God—that God he followed unfaltering still, and was getting him deeper in dislike than ever, with his preaching in Segget the cause of the Miners. These were the folk that were going on strike, in May, unless their wages were raised. Robert said their case was a testing case, the triumph of greed or the triumph of God. Chris herself had hardly a thought in the matter because of that nameless doubt that was hers—doubt of the men and method that came to change the world that was waiting change—all the mixed, strange world of the Segget touns, with its failing trade and its Mills often idle. The folk of the Mills would hang round the room where their dole was paid by a little clerk, they'd laze there and snicker at the women that passed, and yawn, with weariness stamped on each face; and smoke, and whistle, and yawn some more. Once she'd passed and heard some of them quarrelling out loud, she had thought it must surely be over politics; but instead 'twas the chances of a football match! She'd told Robert that and he'd laughed and said *Demos!—didn't you know that the chap was like that? But we'll alter these things forever in May.*

May: and the baby wouldn't come till July, a good enough month for a baby to be born, though Robert said if they had planned it at all they would surely have planned

it better than that. July might be far too hot for comfort. But
he didn't fuss round her, stood back and aside, he knew it
her work and that he'd little help—oh, different as could
be from the Ewan long ago, the frightened boy who had
so fussed about her—how they'd quarrelled, how wept,
how laughed in that time of the coming of that baby that
was now in the Manse—a boy, grown up, remote from it
all, remote enough with his books and his flints, far enough
off from being a baby, rather like a flint himself in some
ways, but of a better shape and grain, grey granite down to
the core, young Ewan, with its flinty shine and its cool grey
skin and the lights and the flashing strands in it. Different
from that, Robert's baby and hers—

   She stamped her feet and woke from her dreaming as
down through the dark she heard on the shingle the coming
footsteps of Robert himself.

AND NEXT MORNING he said, *Let's go out a walk, up in
the hills somewhere—are you keen?* Chris said she was and
well before eight they were off, they met with Ewan in the
hall as they went, he said nothing at all about going out with
them, he always knew when he wasn't much wanted. Chris
kissed him and said they'd be back for dinner; syne she
and Robert went up by the Kaimes, and Ewan stood and
looked after them—you could hardly believe that Chris
was so old.

   Underfoot the frost held hard and firm in the rising
sun of the New Year's Day, that sun a red smoulder
down in the Howe, the hoar was a blanching on post
and hedge, riming the dykes, far up in the Mounth the
veilings of mists were draping the hills, except that now
and then they blew off and you saw the coarse country deep in the haughs, remote with a flicker of red on
the roofs of some shepherd's sheiling high in the heath.
Robert was walking so fast that Chris for a while could
hardly keep up with his stride, then she fell into that and
found it easy, the Kaimes was past and above it the path
opened out through the ragged fringe of the moor that
came peering and sniffling down at Segget as a draggled
cat at a dish out of doors, all the country-side begirdled

with hills and their companions the moors that crept and
slept and yawned in the sun, watching the Howe at its work
below.

They passed a tarn that was frozen and shone, Chris tried
the edge with her stick and it broke, and she saw herself for
a minute then, with the looped-up hair and the short-cut
skirts and the leather jacket tight at her waist, high in the
collar; and the blown bronze of her cheeks and hair and
the stick in her hands and the fur-backed gloves, she smiled
at herself, for this Chris that she'd grown. Robert stopped
and looked back and was puzzled, and came, and stood by
her side and looked down at that Chris that smiled remote
in the broken ice. *Yes, not at all bad. See the childe by her
shoulder? Do you think the two can be decently married?*

Chris said that she thought not, they'd something in their
eyes—and Robert kissed her then, iron, his hard, quick
kiss, the kiss of a man with other passions than kissing:
but wonderful and daft a moment to stand, on the frozen
moor, her head back on his shoulder, and so be kissed,
and at last released, Robert panting a little, and they both
looked away; and then they went on, swinging hand in
hand for a while till they tired and needed their sticks.

Robert went first, bare-headed, black-coated, he was
whistling *Over the Sea to Skye*, clear and bright as they
still went on, up through the wind of a sheep-track here
where the Grampians pushed out their ramparts in fence
against the coming of life from below.

By eleven they were high in the Culdyce moor, winding
the twist of its slopes in the broom that hung thick-rimed
with unshaken frost; for the sun had died away in a
smoulder, the Howe lay grey in a haze below, as they
climbed that haze betook itself from the heights to the
haughs, Leachie towered high, its crag-head swathed with
a silk-web mutch. Trusta's ten hundred feet cowered west
as if bending away from the blow of the wind, the moors a
ragged shawl on her shoulders, crouching and seated since
the haughs were born, watching the haze in the Howe below,
the flicker of the little folk that came and builded and loved
and hated and died, and were not, a crying and swarm of
midges warmed by the sun to a glow and a dance. And

the Trusta heights drew closer their cloaks, year by year, at the snip of the shears, as coulter and crofter moiled up the haughs.

Once Chris and Robert came to a place, out in the open, here the wind blew and the ground was thick with the droppings of sheep, where a line of the ancient stones stood ringed, as they stood in Kinraddie far west and below, left by the men of antique time, memorial these of a dream long lost, the hopes and fears of fantastic eld.

Robert said that they came from the East, those fears, long ago, ere Pytheas came, sailing the sounding coasts to Thule. Before that the hunters had roamed these hills, naked and bright, in a Golden Age, without fear or hope or hate or love, living high in the race of the wind and the race of life, mating as simple as beasts or birds, dying with a like keen simpleness, the hunting weapons of those ancient folk Ewan would find in his search of the moors. Chris sat on a fallen stone and heard him, about her the gleams of the wintry day, the sailing cloud-shapes over the Howe; and she asked how long ago that had been? And Robert said *Less than four thousand years,* and it sounded long enough to Chris—four thousand years of kings and of Gods, all the dark, mad hopes that had haunted men since they left the caves and the hunting of deer, and the splendour of life like a song, like the wind.

And she thought then, looking on the shadowed Howe with its stratus mists and its pillars of spume, driving west by the Leachie bents, that men had followed these pillars of cloud like lost men lost in the high, dreich hills, they followed and fought and toiled in the wake of each whirling pillar that rose from the heights, clouds by day to darken men's minds—loyalty and fealty, patriotism, love, the mumbling chants of the dead old gods that once were worshipped in the circles of stones, christianity, social-ism, nationalism—all—Clouds that swept through the Howe of the world, with men that took them for gods: just clouds, they passed and finished, dissolved and were done, nothing endured but the Seeker himself, him and the everlasting Hills.

Then she came from that thought, Robert shaking her

arm. *Chris, you'll be frozen. Let's climb to the camp.* He had
once been here with Ewan, she hadn't; the moor shelved
smoothly up to its top, as they climbed in view Chris saw two
lines of fencing climbing each slope of the hill, new-driven
and stapled, the fences, they met and joined and ended up on
the crest. But before that meeting and joining they plunged
through the circles of the ancient camp that had been, the
turf and the stones had been flung aside, Robert told that
the hill had been recently sold and the lands on either side
as well, and two different landowners bought the hill and
set up those fences to show their rights—what were dirt
like the old heathen forts to them? Symbols of our age and
its rulers, these clowns, Robert said, and the new culture
struggling to birth—when it came it would first have to
scavenge the world!

Then he started talking of the Miners, of Labour, of the
coming struggle in the month of May, he hoped and believed
that that was beginning of the era of Man made free at last,
Man who was God, Man splendid again. Christ meant and
intended no more when He said that He was the Son of
Man, when He preached the Kingdom of Heaven—He
meant it on earth. Christ was no godlet, but a leader and
hero—

He forgot Chris, striding up and down the slope; excitement kindled in his harsh, kind eyes. And Chris watched
him, standing, her stick behind her, her arms looped about
it, saying nothing to him but hearing and seeing, him and
the hills and the song that both made. And suddenly she
felt quite feared, it was daft—as she looked at the scaling
heights high up, the chasms below, and her Robert against
them! She put out her hand and caught him, he turned,
something in her face stopped questions, all else, the pity
and fear that had been in her eyes. He didn't kiss her now,
his arms round about her, they were quiet a long moment
as they looked in each other, they had never done that
that Chris could remember, seeing herself globed earnest,
half-smiling, and with trembling lips there in the deep grey
pools that hid away Robert—never hers for long if ever
at all, unceasing the Hunter of clouds by day. The men of
the earth that had been, that she'd known, who kept to the

earth and their eyes upon it—the hunters of clouds that
were such as was Robert: how much was each wrong and
how much each right, and was there maybe a third way to
Life, unguessed, unhailed, never dreamed of yet?

Then he said *Now we surely know each other*, and she came
from her mood to meet his with a laugh, *If we don't we've
surely done shameful things!* And they sat in the lithe of a
heath-grown dyke and ate chocolate Robert had brought
in his pocket, and Chris fell fast asleep as she sat, and
awoke with Robert sitting still lest he wake her, one hand
around her and under her heart, but far away from her in
his thoughts, his eyes on the sailing winter below and his
thoughts with the new year that waited their coming down
through the hills in the Segget wynds.

CHRIS WATCHED THE coming of that Spring in Segget
with her interests strange-twisted back on themselves, as
though she relived that Chris of long syne, far from the
one that had taken her place, that Chris of kirks and Robert
and books—they sank from sight in the growing of the
Spring, quick on the hills, on the upland parks, you saw
the fields of Meiklebogs change as you looked from the
window of that room in the Manse that John Muir had set
with Blawearie gear. It was there you intended the baby be
born, the only sign of insanity yet, said Robert, laughing,
and helping you change.

He seemed to have altered too with the Spring, the
black mood came seldom or never now, nor that red,
queer cough that companioned it. You'd hear him of a
morning go whistling away, under the yews, on some kirk
concern, blithe as though the world had been born anew.
It wasn't only the coming of the baby that had altered him
so and kindled his eyes, all the air of the country was filled
with its rumour, that thing that awaited the country in May,
when the Miners and others had threatened to strike. Robert
said that more than a strike would come, the leaders had
planned to seize power in May.

The red-ploughed lands steamed hot in the sun as
Meiklebogs' men drove slow their great teams in the
steam of the waiting world of Spring, the rooks behind

them, Chris stood still and watched, and remembered, and put her hand up to her heart, and then lower, by belly and thigh: and slow, under her hand, that shape would turn, May close and July coming closer now, she felt fit and well, contented, at peace.

Ewan knew now, he had stared one morning; and then asked if she was going to have a baby. Chris had said *Yes, do you mind very much?* and he had said *No,* but hadn't kissed her that morning, she watched him go with a catch of breath. But by night he seemed to have got the thing over, he put cushions behind her when she sat at tea, grave, and with care, and Robert winked at her. Ewan saw the wink and flashed his cool smile; and they all sat silent in front of the fire, with its smouldering glow, they had no need to speak.

Then Maidie knew, as she watched Chris at work, and tweetered the news to some quean outbye, and the quean gasped *Never!* and told Ag Moultrie, the Roarer and Greeter, met in the street. And Ag had nearly a fit with delight, and before that night came down in Segget there was hardly a soul in both touns but knew the minister's wife had taken at last—ay, and must be fell on with it, too, by her look, so the lassie Moultrie had said. Had Ag seen her? you'd ask, and they'd tell you Ay, she'd fairly done that, and Mrs Colquohoun had told the bit news to Ag Moultrie herself; and syne broke down and just Roared and Grat on Ag's shoulder.

Old Leslie said 'twas Infernal, just, you'd have thought a minister would have more sense. He never had thought it decent in a minister to show plain to his parish he did *that* kind of thing; and he minded when he was a loon up in Garvock— Those nearest the door of the smiddy nipped out, Ake Ogilvie near was killed in the rush, and he found old Leslie habbering to himself, hammering at a horseshoe, and far off in Garvock. *What's up then, Leslie?* Ake Ogilvie asked, and Leslie said *What, have you not heard the news?* and told of the thing that was on at the Manse, and might well have begun to tell of Garvock, but that Ake, the coarse brute, said *Well, what of it? Didn't your own father lie with your mother—the poor, misguided devil of a childe?*

Syne out he went swaggering and met with John Muir, and asked if he'd heard what the scandal-skunks said? Muir gleyed and said Ay; and it made him half-sick, and Ake said the same, they were both of them fools, and cared nothing at all for a tasty bit news.

John Muir went home, never told his wife, she found out herself nearly three days late; and fair flew into a rage at that, to be so far behind with the news. *Did you know the news of Mrs Colquohoun?* she speired of John and he gleyed and said *Ay*. And she asked could he never tell her a thing, her that had to bide at home and cook, and wash and sew and mend all the time, with himself and two meikle trollops of daughters, working her hands to the very bone? And John said *Well, it's nothing to me if Mrs Colquohoun has been ta'en with a bairn—I'm not the father, as far as I know.*

Mrs Muir reddened up, *Think shame of yourself speaking that way in front of the lassies.* Tooje was standing with her meikle mouth open, drinking it up, afore she could close it her mother took her a crack in the gape. Tooje started to greet and Ted in the garden heard the greeting, as aye she would do, and came tearing in, and started to greet to keep Tooje company; and John Muir got up with his pipe and his paper and went out to the graveyard and sat on a stone, and had a fine read: decent folk, the dead.

In the Arms Dite Peat said *Wait till it comes. She's the kind that takes ill with having a bairn—over narrow she is, she'll fair have a time. I warrant the doctor'll need his bit knives.* Folk thought that an unco-like speak to make, he'd a mind as foul as a midden, Dite Peat: but for all that you went to the kirk the next Sabbath and took a gey keek at Mrs Colquohoun—ay, God! she fairly was narrow round there, more like a quean than a grown-up woman, with her sulky, proud face and her well-brushed hair, she'd look not so bonny when it came to her time.

Then Hairy Hogg heard it and minded the story of what Mr Mowat had said he would give—to take the minister's wife with a bairn. *You well may depend that was more than a speak.* Folk had forgotten it but now they all minded, it was said in Segget it was ten to one the bairn wasn't the minsiter's at all, young Mr Mowat had been heard to say he'd given half of a whole year's profits for lying with that proud-like Mrs Colquohoun. MacDougall Brown said 'twas a black, black sin, and he preached a sermon in the Square next Sabbath, about scarlet priesthoods living in shame; and everybody knew what he meant by that, his son Jock wabbled his eyes all around, and Mrs Brown shook like a dollop of fat; only Cis looked away and turned red and shy, and thought of Dod Cronin and his hands and lips.

The spinners didn't care when the news reached *them*, though an unco birn came now to the kirk that had never attended a kirk before, the older men mostly, disjaskèd, ill-dressed, with their white, spinner faces and ill-shaved chins, like raddled old loons, and they brought their wives with them—the minister was fairly a favourite with them. So might he be, aye siding with the dirt and the Labour stite that the Cronins preached; and twice he had interfered at the Mills and forced Mr Mowat to clean out his sheds. But the younger spinners went to no kirk, just hung about of a Sabbath day, and snickered as a decent body went by, or took their lasses up to the Kaimes as soon as the Spring sun dried the grass.

Most of the gossip Chris heard of or knew, and cared little or nothing, folk were like that, she thought if you'd neither books nor God nor music nor love nor hate as stand-bys, no pillar of cloud to lead your feet, you turned as the folk of farm and toun—to telling scandal of your nearest neighbours, making of them devils and heroes and saints, to brighten your days and give you a thrill. And God knew they were welcome to get one from her, she found herself liking them as never before, kindled to new interest in every known face, seized again and again in the Segget wynds—looking at the rat-like little Peter Peat, at MacDougall's bald head, at the lizard-like Mowat—with the startling thought, *He was once a bairn!* It nearly put you off having one sometimes; and then again you'd be filled with such a queer pity, as you passed, that Hairy Hogg would go in and say to his wife—*That Mrs Colquohoun she goes by me and* SNICKERS! and his wife would say *Well damn't, do you want her to go by you and greet?*

So April was here, with its steaming drills and the reek of

week that he put them on Stephen Mowat came down to
the Manse, with a paper in his hand and a list of names.
He wanted Robert to join the list, the O. M. S., a volunteer
army, that was being prepared all over the country to feed
the country in the Miners' strike. And he said that they
didn't always see eye to eye, him and Colquohoun, but that
this was serious: you Jahly well couldn't let a push like the
miners dictate to the country what it should do. And he said
that Rahly Robert must join, and Mrs Colquohoun as well,
if she would; and he smiled at her charming, and showed
all his teeth.

Robert said *Well, Christine, what do you say?* and Chris
didn't much care, for she didn't much hope. Then she looked
at Mowat, elegant, neat, in his London clothes, with his
tended hair and his charming look; and the saggy pouches
under his eyes. And it seemed she was looking at more than
Mowat, the class that had made of the folk of Segget the
dirt-hungry folk that they had been and were—made them
so in sheer greed and sheer grab. You had little hope what the
Miners could do, them or the Labour leaders of Robert, but
they couldn't though they tried make a much worse mess
than Mowat and his kind had done, you knew. So you just
said *No;* Robert smiled at Mowat. *That's Chris's answer, a
trifle abrupt. And I can't help the* O. M. S. *myself—you see,
I've another plan afoot.* Mowat said that was Jahly, what
was the plan? And Robert said *Why, do all that I can do
to hinder the* O. M. S. *or such skunks as try to interfere with the
Strike.*

Chris had never admired Stephen Mowat so much, he
kept his temper, charming, polite, she and Robert watched
him stride from the door, down under the yews, and they
later heard he had gone to the Provost and gotten his help,
and the same from Geddes, and the same from Melvin that
kept the Arms. Near everybody that counted would help,
except the spinners, the Manse, and Ake Ogilvie—Ake
had told Mr Mowat they could hamstring each other, strik-
ers and Government, for all that he cared. And neither
would MacDougall Brown give his name, he said his living
depended on spinners: and if all the world renounced its
sin the cares of the world would be ended tomorrow.

And all the time he was saying this he was mixing sawdust under the counter, canny-like, in a bag of meal.

CHRIS PUT THE whole thing out of her mind, busied in making the baby's clothes, busied in going long walks by herself, the last day in April she took Ewan with her, across by Mondynes, till they saw far off, crowning the hills, the roofs of Kinraddie. *You were born over there twelve years ago,* she thought aloud as they sat to rest, Ewan with his head cupped up in his hands, his arms on his knees, his black-blue hair rumpled, untidily tailed, in the glow of the sun. He said, *Yes, I know,* and then looked at her sudden—*but I say! I never really thought of that. . . . Or anyway, never as I thought just now.* She asked how was that, and he looked down the Howe. *Well, that I once was a part of you; though, of course, I know all about how babies come.*

And for almost the first time in years he seemed troubled, her boy, the fruit of herself, so cool, so kind and sure and so stony-clear, troubled to a sudden, queer brittle pity. *Mother!* And he looked at her, then away, then came and cuddled her tight for a moment, his arms round her throat Chris nearly was stifled: but she didn't move, didn't say a word at that strange embracing on the part of Ewan.

And May and to-morrow waited their feet as they turned back quiet up the Segget road.

EWAN IN HIS bed; in the May-time dark Chris wandered the sitting-room of the Manse, looking again and again from the window at the mist that had come and grew thicker each minute. Beyond her vision the yews, the hedge: she could see but a little space from the window, a space translit by a misty star, the lights far up in Segget House.

What had happened to Robert—had he been in time?

And at last she could bear it no longer, went out, into the hall and put on her coat, and opened the door and went down through the path, through the slimy, slow crunch of the shingle, mist-wet. A light gleamed faint in the house of John Muir and a dog barked loud from old Smithie's shed as he heard her footsteps pass in the mist, it came draping its cobwebs across her face, she put up her hand and wiped

off the globes, from her lashes, and stopped and listened on
the road. Nothing to be heard, the mist like a blanket, had
Robert come up with the spinners in time?

They had gone to blow up the High Segget brig, a birn
of the spinners and one of the porters, the news had been
brought to the Manse by John Cronin, panting—*They've
gone to blow up the brig and prevent the trains that the blacklegs
are running reaching beyond this, or south from Dundon*. Robert
had jumped up—*When did they go?* and Cronin had said
*Ten minutes ago, I heard of it only now in the Old Town, this'll
mean the police and arrest for us all*. Robert had said *Oh, damn
the fools, and their half-witted ploys—blowing up brigs!
Right, I'll be with you*, and hadn't waited his coat, had told
Chris not to worry and kissed her, and ran, long-striding
down through the shingle, Cronin at his heels and the mist
coming down.

Where were they now, what had happened at the brig?

She pressed on again, that fear for an urge—a fool to
be out, maybe Robert would miss her. The mist was so
thick she could hardly see a thing on the other side of the
Wynd, she kept the leftward wall and held down, past the
locked-up shop of little Peter Peat, the shop of the Provost
locked up as well, and Dite Peat's as well, all three of them
specials enrolled by Mowat to help Simon Leslie. But the
station folk and the spinners were out, so Robert had told
her, and here in Segget, as all over the country, the Strike
held firm.

Had he and Cronin reached the brig in time?

Now she was down in the Square, so she knew, the lights
of the Arms seeped up through the mist, the Arms crowded
with spinners as usual, few of them knew of the thing at the
brig, John Cronin had said the folk who had gone to blow
up the place were no more than boys, and daft at that, with
their blasting-powder gotten or thieved from the quarry at
Quarles.

As Chris crossed the Square she met in the mist two men
who were holding up to East Wynd, Sim Leslie was one, and
a man with a brassard, one of the specials, she thought it Dite
Peat. They peered in her face and Sim Leslie coughed, and
the man with the brassard laughed a foul laugh. Chris felt

her blood go cold at that laugh, she heard them engage in a mutter of talk as she hurried down the road to the station.

There were lights down there, but still as the grave, she stood and looked down, her heart beating fast. And so, as she stood, slowly, quietly, under her heart her baby moved. She gasped a little, she must go more slow, she shouldn't be out in the mist at all. Robert and Cronin must have reached them in time.

But even yet she could not go back. She stood and listened in the mist and heard the fall of it on the grass, on the hedge, beyond the wall where she stood and leaned—soft, in a feathery falling of wet, blanketing sound away from her ears. She ought to go home, but how could she, unsure?

In that minute, far to the south the mist suddenly broke and flamed: she stared: the flame split up through the mirk from the ground. Then there came to her ears the crack and crinkle of such explosion as she'd heard before up in the Mounth-side Quarles quarry. She knew what it meant; and started to run.

Beyond the railway lines was the path that wound by the lines till it reached Segget Brig. Here the hawthorns brushed her face and the grass whipped wetly about her legs as she ran, not thinking, trying hard not to think, to run fleetly, and gain the Brig, as she must—Robert was there—Oh, and those fools!

The second explosion laid hand on the night and shook the mist as a great hand might. Then it died, and Chris found the true dark had come, it had seeped through the mist like spilt ink through paper, and she couldn't run now, but walked and stumbled, and heard no more for it seemed an hour.

Till far behind her there rose a whistle, a long-drawn blast remote in the night.

She stopped at that and turned about, a whin-bush lashed her face as she turned and then stood listening and looking beside her. And far away north up the side of the Mounth a line of lights twinked suddenly bright, and moved and slowed and came to a stop.

Clenched hand at her throat, for that seemed to help, she gasped and stared at that cluster at halt—some Dundon train that had halted at Carmont, in five minutes more it

would be in Segget, and the brig was down, and it wouldn't
know——

Running again she felt that change, slow and dreadful and
sick in her body, her arms held out as she kept the path;
and she cried to the thing unborn in her womb, *Not now,
not now;* and it moved again. Then up the line she heard
the skirl of the starting train, its windows flashed, it purred
from sight as it climbed through the woods—she never
could do it, try though she might!

Yet, so at last, running, she did; and gained the road
with the station below. Down there was a flurry and scurry
of lights, behind on the road a scurry of feet. She turned at
that sound, saw a drift of men, she seemed to know one:
and cried out *Robert!*

THE NIGHT quietened away in a mist of faces and a kindled
lantern and Robert's voice. So later Chris minded, and then
the next hours closed suddenly up as a telescope closes. One
minute she was standing, her teeth in her lip, harkening
Robert tell how he'd gained the brig, just in time, they'd
done no more than test off the powder, he and Cronin had
stopped them at that; and the next she was up in the Manse
with Robert, as she stood in the hall and he closed the door
the hall rose up and spun twice round her head, she stared
at the grandfather clock in the hall, for a minute she couldn't
breathe, couldn't move. Something suddenly flooded her
mouth, she sopped the stuff with her handkerchief—red,
and saw as last thing Robert's startled scowl as he leapt to
catch her; and then he quite vanished.

She opened her eyes in bed the next time, sick and weak
with the May light high and pouring into the room in a flood,
somebody she didn't know near the bed. Then the somebody
turned and looked and Chris knew her, she whispered *It's
Else!* and Else said *Shish! You mustn't move, Mem,* and
crinkled her face as though she would cry. Chris would
have laughed if she hadn't been weak, so she closed her
eyes for another rest, maybe another day, maybe a minute,
and woke, and the dark was close outbye, the first thing she
heard as she came from the dark the rake and tweet of the
rooks in the yews. She looked round about and saw Robert

and Ewan, Robert was over by the window, hunched, with his shoulders and head black-carved in the light, Ewan was sitting by the side of her bed, a hand on his knee, his head down-bent, looking at a little flint in his hand. She coughed: and both of them turned at the sound, and she coughed again and saw with surprise the stuff that spilt from her mouth on the sheet, not red, it was brown, and she suddenly saw, vividly clear and distinct, it was awful, horror and horror in Robert's face.

NIGHT, WITH a setting of stars, all alone, in the May time dark, she knew it still May. There was a hiss of rain on the roof, light rain, and all the house set in silence but for that whisper of the falling rain. She lay and suddenly knew the Thing close, a finish to the hearing of rain on the roof, a finish to knowing of that hearing at all, the world cut off, she felt free and light, strung to a quivering point of impatience as she waited and waited and the night went by—ready and ready she waited, near cried, because the Thing didn't come after all. And grew tired and slept; and the Thing drew back.

Lord, Chris, you've given us a devil of a time!
She lay and looked at him and suddenly she knew, wakened wide, she said *And what happened to my baby?* Robert said *You mustn't worry about that. Get well, my dear*—he was thin as a rake, and near as ungroomed, his hair up on end, she asked if Maidie had been doing the cooking, for him and Ewan—and where was Ewan? He said that Ewan was at school today, seeing the doctor had found her much better. As for Maidie, she'd proved no use at all, and he'd sent for Else, Else had done fine. . . .

So it hadn't been a dream Chris lay and knew as the hours went by, and Robert went out and Else came in; and later the doctor and all fussed about her; below the sheets her body felt flat, ground down and flat, with an empty ache; and her breasts hurt and hurt till they saw to them, she hadn't cried at all when she knew what had happened, till it came for them to see to her breasts, for a minute she nearly was desperate then. But that was just daft, she'd given plenty of trouble, said the Chris that survived all things that came to her. So she gave in quietly, and they finished at last, and she slept till Ewan came back from the school, and came up after tea, and looked in and smiled.

Hello, mother, better?

He came to the bedside and suddenly cuddled her; for a minute she was hurt with the weight of his head on her breast, though she put up her arms about him. Then something hot trickled on her breast, and she knew what—Ewan to cry! that was dreadful. But he did it only a minute while she held him, then drew away, and took out his handkerchief and wiped his eyes, and sat down, calm, but she didn't care, reaching out and touching his hand as he sat. Funny she should ever have feared she would lose him, that already she'd done so, him no longer a baby, remote from her thoughts or from thought of her. How nearer he was than any there were! She said *You must tell me, Ewan, what happened. When was the baby born, was it dead?*

So he told her the baby was born that morning after the spinners went to blow up the brig. Robert had gone for the doctor and Ewan had stayed at home and tried to look after her, though he didn't know much of the things he should do: as for Maidie, the girl was a perfect fool. At last the doctor and Robert arrived, Robert sent off a wire to Else at Fordoun, and they put Ewan out of the room—he was glad, even though it was Chris, he'd a beast of a headache. The baby had been born then, it wasn't born dead, though it died soon after, or so Ewan heard. Else said that it was a boy, like Robert, but Ewan hadn't seen it: that was days ago, two or three days before the Strike ended.

Chris remembered: *What, is it ended, then? Who won?* and Ewan said the Government, Robert raved the leaders had betrayed the Strike, they'd been feared that they would be jailed, the leaders, they had sold the Strike to save their skins. Robert hadn't believed the news when it came, that was the morning that Chris was so bad and the two of them had sat in her room—

Chris lay still and said *Thank you, Ewan*, with a little ghost of a laugh inside to know that he called her Chris in his thoughts, as she'd thought he did; and soon, wearied still, she slept again, sleeping till supper-time, it brought Else up with a tray and hot bottle, and all things needed, she cried, right pleased, *You're fine again, Mem?* and Chris said she was, she had to thank Else with others for that.

Else said *Devil a thanks—if you'll pardon a body mentioning Meiklebogs' cousin in a Manse. I liked fine to come 'stead of biding in Fordoun, with the old man glunching at me and my bairn.* Chris asked how the baby was, and Else kindled, *Fine, Mem, and fegs you should see how he grows.* And then suddenly stopped and punched up the pillows, and set Chris up rough, and began to chatter, like a gramophone suddenly gone quite mad, with her ears very red and her face turned away.

Chris knew why she did it, she'd thought of that baby she'd carried out dead from this room a while back, she was feared that Chris might take ill again were anything said to mind her of babies. But Chris had never felt further from weeping, appalled at the happening to Robert, not her.

Else told how the Strike had ended in Segget, folk said that the spinners who went out that night and tried to blow up the brig would be jailed. But there was no proof, only rumours and scandal, and the burnt grass in the lee of the brig. Sim Leslie, him that the folk called Feet, had come up to the Manse like a sow seeking scrunch, but the minister had dealt with him short and sharp and he taiked away home like an ill-kicked cur. The spinners and station folk wouldn't believe it when the news came through that the Strike was ended, they said the news was just a damned lie, John Cronin said it, and they wouldn't go back, he and the minister kept them from that till they got more telegrams up from London. And Mr Colquohoun and Ake Ogilvie the joiner, John Muir and some spinners had organized pickets to keep Mr Mowat's folk from getting to the Mills. Syne they heard how the leaders had been feared of the jail, and the whole thing just fell to smithereens in Segget. Some spinners that night went down the West Wynd and bashed in the windows of the Cronin house, and set out in a birn to come to the Manse, they said the minister had egged them on, him safe and sound in his own damned job, and they'd do to the Manse as they'd done to the Cronins.

But coming up the Wynd they met in with Ake Ogilvie, folk said that he cursed them black and blue; and told them how Chris was lying ill and wouldn't it have been a damned sight easier for Mr Colquohoun to have kept in with the gentry, instead of risking his neck for the spinners? The spinners all sneered and jeered at Ake, but he stood fast there in the middle of the road, and wouldn't let them up, and they turned and tailed off. A third were on to the Bureau again, and Jock Cronin sacked from his job at the station, and Miss Jeannie Grant hadn't gone to the school, through all the nine days she'd been helping the spinners: and when she went back Mr Geddes said *No*, and folk told that she would get the sack, too.

Chris said *So it ended like that? Else—was my baby born dead, and was it a boy?* Else went white and wept a little at that, Chris lay and watched and Else peeked at her, scared, she looked strangely un-ill with that foam of bronze hair, and the dour face thin, but still sweet and sure. Else said that it wasn't, it lived half an hour, the minister came up and baptized it Michael, a bonny bairn, tiny and quiet, it yawned and blinked its eyes just a minute—*oh, Mem, I shouldn't be telling you this!*

Chris said *But you should. Where is it buried?* and Else said 'twas out in the old kirkyard, there were only the minister and Muir and herself, the minister carried the coffin in there, and read the service, *bonny he did it, if it wasn't for that fool John Muir that stood by, like a trumpet, near, blowing his nose. And when the minister came to the bit about Resurrection—I don't mind the words—*

Chris said *I do*, and heard her own voice tell them with Else near weeping again: *I am the Resurrection and the Life. He that believeth in me, though he were dead, yet shall he live.*

Else gulped and nodded. *And after he said that—he didn't know what he was saying, Mem, with his bairn new dead and his Strike as well—he said* AND WHO SHALL BELIEVE? *quiet and queer. . . . I shouldn't be telling you this, but oh! you'll have to hurry and get well for him!*

COMING OUT OF those memories given to the years, Chris moved and looked at the waiting Segget, quiet in the lazy spray of June sun, the same land and sun that Hew Monte Alto had looked on that morning before Bara battle. You were waiting yourself in a halt before battle: all haltings were that, you thought, or would think if you weren't too wearied to think now at all.

But that would pass soon, you'd to get better quick—quick and quick for the sake of Robert. Better, and take him out of himself, Ewan would help, maybe Segget even yet—

She rose slowly to her feet and smiled at herself, for that weakness that followed her when she stood up, with the drowse of the June day a moment a haze of little floating specks in her eyes. Then that cleared, and a cold little wind came by, she looked up and saw a thickening of clouds, rain-nimbus driving down upon Segget.

FOUR

Nimbus

NOW, WITH THE coming of the morning, the stars
shone bright and brittle on the Segget roofs, the rime of
the frost Chris saw rise up, an uneasy carpet that shook in
the wind, the icy wind from the sea and Kinneff. Under her
feet the dark ground cracked, as though she were treading
on the crackle of grass, and she passed through the Kaimes'
last gate—far up, in the dimming light of the stars, there
fell a long flash from the arc of the sky, rending that brittle
white glow for a moment, its light for a second death-white on
the hills. Then she saw the sky darken, and the corpse-light
went: behind the darkness the morning was coming.

So, walking quick to keep her feet warm, and because she'd
but little time left for this ploy, she gained the Kaimes and
halted and looked—not at them, but up at the heights of
the hills, sleeping there on the verge of a dawn. Nothing
cried or moved, too early as yet, but a peewit far in a hidden
hollow, she minded how it was here she had come—almost
at this very hour she had come—the very first night
she had lain in Segget. And here she climbed from those
ten full years, still the same Chris in her heart of hearts,
nothing altered but space and time and the things she had
once believed everlasting and sure—believed that they
made her life, they made her! But they hadn't, there was
something beyond that endured, some thing she had never
yet garbed in a name.

She put up her hand to her dew-touched hair, she'd
climbed bare-headed up to the Kaimes, she had seen a
grey hair here and there last night. But it felt the same hair
as she felt the same self, its essence unchanged whatever its
look. Queer and terrible to think of that now—that all
things passed as your life went on, but the little things you
had given no heed.

The wind goeth towards the south, and turneth about unto the north; it whirleth about continually, and the wind returneth again according to his circuits.

That was Ecclesiastes, she thought; stilled; the dawn pallid on her coiled, bronze hair.

In Segget below a cock crew shrill, she turned and looked down at the shining of frost, remotely, and saw it gleam and transmute, change and transmute as though Time turned back, back through the green and grey of the years till that last time here when she'd climbed the Kaimes, her baby new dead and herself a live ache—

SHE HAD SHOWN as little of the ache as she might, in spite of the waste, she had hated that. So she told to Robert and he laughed and said *You sound like a woman in an Aberdeen joke,* his eyes with the beast of the black mood in them. *Waste? Good God, do you think that is all?*

He flung away from her and walked to the window, beyond it the smell and blow of the hay in the sleeping parks of Dalziel of Meiklebogs. Then suddenly he turned—*Christine, I'm sorry. But I'm weary as well, let's not speak of it more.*

And she left it at that, he'd drawn into himself, lonely, he sat for hours in his room, with impatience for either her pity or help. So she buried herself in the work of the house, and sought in her pride a salve for the sting of the knowledge she counted for little with Robert, compared with his cloudy hopings and God. She could be strange and remote as he could. . . .

And it came with hardly an effort at all, they were hurrying nods that met on the stairs and went to bed at uneven hours; yet sometimes a hand seemed to twist in her heart as she watched him sit at his meat in silence, or at night when she woke and he lay asleep, with it seemed the tug of lips on her breasts and the ghostly ache of her empty womb—silent the yews in the listening dark.

SEGGET CROWDED THE kirk the first Sunday in May after the General Strike collapsed, to hear what that cocky billy Colquohoun would say of his tink-like socialists now. But he never mentioned the creatures at all, he preached a sermon that maddened you, just, he said there was nothing new under the sun: and that showed you the kind of twister he was. Hairy Hogg, the Provost, came out of the kirk, and said that the man was insulting them, sly, trying to make out that the work they had done to beat the coarse Labour tinks was a nothing. Instead, now the Strike was ended so fine, you'd mighty soon see a gey change for the good, no more unions to cripple folks' trade, and peace and prosperity returning again; and maybe a tariff on those foreign-made boots.

But damn the sign of either you saw as that year went on and the next came in, there was little prosperity down at the Mills, they were working whiles, and whiles they were not, young Mr Mowat went off to London and syne from there he went off on a cruise, as a young gent should; but he fair was real kind. For he wrote that he'd soon be back home again, and would see about pushing the Segget trade, that would mean more men—*but no union men*.

It wasn't his wyte that he had no work, in spite of the spinners and their ill-ta'en grumblings. For they grumbled still, though their union was finished—faith! that was funny, for you'd got from the papers that the men would be fine if it wasn't the unions—the Tory childes nearly broke down and wept on the way the unions oppressed the workers. The Cronins had all been sacked from the Mills and no more of a Sunday you'd hear them preach about socialism coming, and coarse dirt like that. Jock Cronin, that had once been a railway porter, was down now in Glasgow, tinking about, it fairly was fine to be rid of the brute. Folk said that that Miss Jeannie Grant had gone with him, some childe had seen her, down there at a mart, all painted and powdered, she'd ta'en to the streets, and kept Jock Cronin, he lived off her earnings. Ay, just the kind of the thing you'd expect from socialists and dirt that spoke ill of their betters, and yet powdered and fornicated like gentry.

But young Dod Cronin, that was a mere loon, he heard the news, he worked out at Fordoun, and he went to the smiddy and tackled old Leslie, with the sweat dripping down from his wrinkled old chops. And Dod said *What's this you've been saying of my brother?* and old Leslie said *What? And who are you, lad?* And Dod said *You know damn well who I am.*

*And if ever I hear you spreading your claik about my brother or
Miss Jeannie Grant, I'll bash in your old face with one of your
hammers.*

Old Leslie backed nippy behind the anvil and said *Take
care, take care what you say! I'm not a man you must rouse,
let me tell you.* And he told later on that never in his life
had he heard such impudence—'twas Infernal, just, he'd
a mighty sore job to keep himself back from taking that
Cronin loon a good clout. Now, when himself was a loon up
in Garvock— And you didn't hear, more, for you looked
at your watch, and said you must go, and went at a lick;
and left him habbering and chapping and sweating.

Young Dod was as mad as could be on the thing, he went up
to the Manse and clyped to Colquohoun; and Else Queen,
that was back there again as the maid, told that the minister
said he was sorry, but what could he do? Young Cronin
shouldn't worry, you could only expect a smell from a drain.

Else said the minister was referring to Leslie: and folk
when they heard that speak were real mad. Who was he, a
damned creature that sat in a Manse, to say that an honest
man was a drain? There was nothing wrong with old Leslie,
not him, he'd aye paid his way, a cheery old soul, though he
could sicken a cow into colic with his long, dreich tales and
his habberings of gossip.

He'd aye been good to his guts, the old smith, and faith, he
grew better the longer he lived. At New Year he took a bit taik
down the toun, into the shop of MacDougall Brown; it was
late at night and what could Brown do but ask the old smith
to come ben for a drink—not of whisky, you wouldn't find
that at MacDougall's, but of some orange wine or such a like
drink, awful genteel, though it had a bit taste as though a stray
pig had eased himself in it. Well, Leslie went ben, and there
sat the creash, MacDougall's wife, and Cis, the fine lass, and
the other bit quean that folk teased and called May-bull. Mrs
Brown was right kind and poured out the wine, syne she went
and took out a cake from the press, there was more than half
of the cake on the plate, and Mistress Brown cut off a thin
slice, genteel, and held out the plate to the smith.

And what did he do but take up the cake, not the slice,
and sit with it there in his hand, habbering and sweating like

a hungered old bull, and tearing into MacDougall's cake, MacDougall watching him boiling with rage—faith! speak about washing in the blood of the Lamb, he looked as though he'd like a real bath in the smith's.

Well, old Leslie finished his bit of repast, and got up, though he hadn't near finished his story, about Garvock, but he never yet had done that, though you'd known him fine this last fifty years. But it was getting fell late-like by then and he thought he'd better go take a taik home, Mrs Brown had gone to her bed, and Maybull, and the fine lass Cis had gone as well. MacDougall showed him out to the door, and cried good-night, and banged it behind him; and old Leslie was standing sucking at a crumb that was jooking about in an old hollow tooth, when what did he see round the end of the dyke that sloped to the back of MacDougall's shop, but a body slipping over in the dark.

Old Leslie wondered who it could be, and stepped soft in the dark down the lithe of the dyke. Near to the end he stooped and stopped, and heard the whisp-whisp of some folk close by. And he knew one voice, but not the other, 'twas the voice of Cis Brown and he heard her say *Not to-night—Mabel is sleeping with me.* The voice that the smith couldn't put a name to said *Damn her, why doesn't she sleep with the cuddy?* Cis laughed and sighed and syne Leslie heard the sound of a kiss, disgusting-like, he himself had never all his married life so much as pecked at his old wife's face: and once when she saw him without his sark, he'd been changing it, careless-like, by the fire, she nearly had fainted, and so near had he, they'd never been so coarse as look at each other, shameless and bare, in their own bit skins. . . . Well, where was he now with this story of Cis?—Ay, her slobbering her lad by the dyke. In a little bit while they were whispering again, and the smith tried hard to hear what they said, they spoke over low, the tinks that they were, to make an old man near strain off his neck from his hard-worked shoulders to hear what they said. Syne that finished and Leslie heard footsetps coming and dodged in the shadow of the post-office door. And who should loup over the wall and go by but that tink Dod Cronin, that had so miscalled him, him it had been that was kissing Cis Brown!

But folk said that that was just a damned lie, Cis Brown was as douce and sweet a quean as you'd find in the whole of Segget, they said—old Leslie telling the tale in the Arms was nearly brained by Dite Peat himself. Dite said he liked a bit lie fell well, just as he liked to soss with a woman, especially a woman he'd no right to, but he wasn't to hear that kind of a speak of Cis Brown, he was fairly damned if he was. And others cried, *Ay, that's right, that's right!* and Feet, the policeman, said to his father *You'd better away home.* Off the old smith went, the coarse old brute; still habbering his lies and swearing he'd seen Dod Cronin and that fine quean Cis together.

CHRIS HEARD THE tale, but she paid it no heed, with long months of resting her strength had come back, she was out in the garden of the Manse each dawn, digging and hoeing as the Spring came in. Funny to think 'twas nearly a year since she'd walked this garden, her child in her body, and stood over there and looked in the kirkyard, and thought of the folk that had once been bairns, and died, and nothing of them endured. And now she herself walked free and young, slim as of old, if her face was thinner, but warm and kind, warm blood in her body, she could see it rise blue if she looked at her hands loosen their grip from the shaft of the graip, and her hair was alive, that had gone a while dead, and crackled its fire as she combed it at night, long hair that still came near to her knees. And the baby she'd brought in the world last year—

But she'd not think of that, not here in the sun, the rooks a long caw out over the yews, sailing, sun-winking, dots in the sun, the clouds went wind-laden down through the Howe, all the Howe wakening below them to hear the trill and shrill of the springs of Spring. So busied Chris was as the days grew warm, she'd found in a garden what once in the fields, years before, on the windy rigs of Blawearie, ease and rest and the kindness of toil, that she saw but little or nothing of Robert—no loss to him, with his bittered face, and no loss to her now, they went their own ways.

Ewan was shooting straight as a larch, narrow and dark, with a cool, quiet gaze, and a sudden smile that came seldom enough, but still, when it did— Else said she could warm her hands at that smile. He was out all hours of the day, was Ewan, still at his flints, he'd raked half the Howe, he 'd been down by Brechin and Forfar for flints. He was known in places Chris never had seen, the dark-faced loon from the Manse of Segget, that would ask if he might take a look at your fields, and would show the arrows and such-like of old that the creatures of hunters had used in their hunts. And the farmers would say, *Faith, look if you like,* and Ewan would thank them, charming and cool, a queer-like loon, not right in the head, folk that were wice weren't near so polite.

Some times, as the light of the Spring days waned he'd come back from school and find bread and milk, and bring them out to the garden to eat, and set them down by a bed or a drill and take the hoe or the fork from Chris, and start to work with quick, even strokes, the down of a soft, fine hair on his cheeks, Chris would sit with her knees hand-clasped, and watch him, the ripple of his smooth, dark skin, he'd long lashes as well, that were curled and dark, he worked with a cool and deliberate intent at digging the garden as he did at all else. Once Chris asked him, one of those evenings in April, what he would do when he had grown up.

He stopped at the turn of a drill and looked at her, he was leaving school and going to Dundon, up to the college in the summer term. He said *I'd like to be an archaeologist, but I don't suppose that I'll ever be that.* Chris asked *Why not?* and he said that he thought it unlikely you could be that without lots of money. He would just have to face up to things as they were, jobs scarce, and all the world in a mess.

Chris wondered what were his thoughts on the mess, he had read nearly every book in the Manse, had he read the books on Socialism yet? She asked him that and he said that he had, indifferently saying it, one of the books—by a Ramsay MacDonald, all blither and blah. Charlie Cronin, who had now left the school was a socialist, the same as MacDonald, they were both very muddled, they had no proofs and they hadn't a plan, it was spite or else rage: OR BECAUSE THEY WERE FEARED.

Chris looked at the fairy featherings of clouds that went south on the hurrying wind of the Howe, the green of the hedges trilled low in its blow, you could feel in your body the stir of the blood as the sap stirred sweet in the hedge, you supposed. Spring and the time of young folk and dreams, following cloud-pillars as they sailed the Howe! . . . And maybe Ewan was doing no more in that he refused all clouds and all dreams!

She said *What are* YOU *going to do with the mess?* and he put down his cup and said *Oh, nothing,* and started to weed in the strawberry patch: *Unless I just must,* and he whistled to himself, calm and cool, with his dark, cool face, he whistled and hoed in the evening light. And Chris felt for him a tenderness, queer, not as though she were only his mother but as though he were all young life in an evening of Spring—thinking the world would dare hardly intrude in their lives and years, but would stand back and bow, and slip to one side to let them go by. . . . She held out a hand—*Help me up, son, I'm stiff. Growing old, I suppose;* he stopped and looked at her, his gravity suddenly drowned in that smile. *I thought just now you looked like a girl. There are some at the school who look older than you.*

But he gave her his hand and she jumped to her feet, light enough still, and they looked at each other; and Chris put up her hand to his throat, making on that the button there needed re-sewing, it didn't, but she wanted to touch that cool throat. He let her, standing there quiet and alert, like the deer she had seen come down from the haughs, with brindled pelts, in the winter-time—not feared and not shy, cool, quick and alive, under her fingers a little vein beat as she fastened his collar, and Ewan said *Thanks,* and went on with his weeding, Chris went to the house and looked at the clock and made tea for Robert.

HE WAS OFF at Stonehaven, a meeting of ministers, called together to discuss the reason why every kirk in the Howe grew toom, a minister would sometimes rise of a Sunday and preach to a congregation of ten, in a bigging builded to hold two hundred. So Robert told Chris as he wheeled out his bike, that morning, under the peep of the sun; and Chris had said *Well, they surely know why? Do they need a meeting to find out that?*

Robert had looked at her withdrawn, remote, the brooding anger not far from his eyes. *Do* YOU *know the reason?* Chris had said *Yes, the reason's just that the times have changed.*

His unchancy temper quite went with him then, *By God,* he sneered, *isn't that profound?* Chris flushed, with an angry retort on her lips; but she bit it back, as so often she did, and turned indoors as he wheeled down the Wynd—what a fool she had been to say what she'd said! Like telling an angry blind man he was blind. . . . She would keep to herself, she was nobody's serf.

But sometimes she ached for kind eyes and kind hands. One night she had turned to him, kissing him then, and he'd shrugged away from her—*Not now, Chris, not now.* She had said in her hurt, *And maybe not again—when* YOU *would again,* and had turned her back and pretended to sleep, but had wept a little instead, like a fool. Spring was here, she supposed it was that, daft to desire what no one could give except with a flame of desire in the giving.

So she waited this evening, with pancakes new baked, they might live poor friends, with love and lust by, but she still ate his meat and she owed him for that. Else had the day off to go down to Fordoun, her baby bade there in its grandmother's care. In the cool of the kitchen Chris stood for a while and watched Ewan kneel to a thrawn-like weed, and saw him twist it up ruthlessly, sure; she sighed with a smile at herself for that sigh. Were she sure of herself as Ewan of himself, she might go her own way and not heed to any, have men to lie with her when she desired them (and faith, that would sure be seldom enough!), do and say all the things that came crying her to do, go hide long days in the haughs of the Mounth—up in the silence and the hill-bird's cry, no soul to vex, and watch the clouds sailing and passing out over the Howe, unending over the Howe of the World; that—or sing and be glad by a fire; or wash and toil and be tired with her toil as once she had been in her days on a croft—a million things, Chris-alone, Chris-herself, with Chris Guthrie, Chris Tavendale, Chris Colquohoun dead!

She lighted the lamp as she heard Robert come and carried it through to the hall for him to see to hang up his coat and his hat. He said *You look very sweet, Christine, there with the lamp,* and held her a moment, lamp and all, Chris felt her heart turn, with gladness—then, queerly, she felt half-sick. . . .

He loosed her and followed her into the room, soft happed in shadow in the loglight's glow, she put down the lamp and looked at him again. There was something about him that wasn't him at all—a *filthy* something, she thought, and shivered. He said *Not cold?* and smiled at her kind—ROBERT with eyes like a kind milch cow!

She went in a daze and brought in the tea, they sat and ate by the open window, the world all quiet out and about, except, sharp-soft in the fading light, the click and scrape of the tools of Ewan as he redded and bedded by the kirkyard wall. And again, as she looked at Robert, Chris shivered—*What's ta'en you, Robert—Robert what is it?*

He raised up his head and she saw his eyes smile. *Just something you'll think is quite mad when you hear.* . . .

And he told her then of the thing that had come as he rode from the minister's meeting at Stonehaven, grinding his bike through Dunnottar's woods, he had looked once or twice from the road to the woods and saw them green in the April quiet, the sunset behind him—*very quiet, Chris.* He had ridden up there till the way grew steep, the old bike was near on its last wheels now: and just as he gained the near edge of the woods he got from his bike and looked back at Stonehaven, in that corridor of trees the light fell dim, a hidden place, no sun came there. And, as he stood there and breathed in the quiet, he saw the Figure come slow down the road.

He came so quiet by the side of the road that Robert hadn't heard His coming or passing, till he raised his head and saw Him quite close, tired, with a white strange look on His face, no ghost, for the hair blew out from His head and he put up His hand to brush back the hair. And Robert saw the hand and the piercèd palm, he stood frozen there as the Figure went on, down through the quiet of Dunnottar's woods, unresting, into the sunset's quiet, a wood-pigeon crooned in a far-off tree, Robert heard the sound of a train in Stonehaven, he stood and stared and then leant on his bike, trembling, suddenly weeping in his hands.

OUTSIDE, THE NEXT day broke quick with wind, a grey
quick drive that was bending the trees, blowing its blow in
the face of the sun, Chris went to her room and dressed in
short skirts, the rig she'd once worn—it seemed years
before—that day she and Robert climbed up the Mounth.
She'd no fancy at all for that walk to-day, she found a stick
and went down through the shingle, and looked back as she
passed in the whisp of the yews, Ewan. in his room; he
stood near the window, some everlasting flint in his hands.
She waved to him, but he didn't see, then at the turn of
the dyke the wind caught at her breath and her skirts and
her hair.

Ake Ogilvie looked from his shop as she passed, and gave
her a wave and bent over his desk, his poetry maybe, Robert
said it was awful, the angry sneerings of a poet born blind. . . .
But Chris hurried on from the thought of Robert, swinging
her stick, the wind in her face, the Sourock's wife looked
out as she passed, and stared after the creature, that Mrs
Colquohoun, like a slip of a quean she was, not decent, her
that had had her two bairns, one dead the other upgrowing
and nearly a man. She said later on she was black-affronted
as Mrs Colquohoun reached the bend of the Wynd, the wind
blew up the creature's short skirts, all about her, and instead
of giving a bit scraich and blushing to the soles of her feet, as
she should, she just brushed them back and went hastening
on—what was *her* hurry, no hat on her head, and her fine
silk breeks and nought else below?

(And folk said *What, had she nothing else below?* and
the Sourock's wife said *Not a damned stitch, fair tempting the
childes, half-naked like that, not to mention tempting her death
with cold.*)

Past the shop of Dite Peat and Hairy Hogg's front, Alec,
the son of the Provost, stood there, he had lost his job in
Edinburgh, Alec, Chris liked him better than when she first
met him, she cried *How are you?* and he raised his cap;
and Chris sped on, Alec said that night when he looked in
on Else, that Mrs Colquohoun looked more of a boy than a
grown-up woman who had a fine son. Else said *She both looks
them, and makes them, my lad,* whatever she meant by that, if
she knew; but she kept him at sparring distance, did Else.

Down at the edge of the Moultrie shop, where Jim the roan had had such an ill end, Chris found herself in the lithe of the dyke that shielded the plots of the gardener, Grant. It was here she nearly ran into Cis Brown, running, with sober face and blown hair, Chris held her and laughed and they steadied themselves, Chris asked *And how are things at the college?* Cis coloured up sweet, she said they were fine. She loitered a moment and Chris looked in her face and caught there the glimpse of a desperate trouble.

Something (what Chris of them all?) made her say *I'm off for a long walk down through the Howe, I'm restless to-day, would you like to come?*

AT NOON THAT day they stopped at a place, a little farm high in the Reisk, over-topped by the wave of its three beech trees, standing up squat in the blow of the wind that came in a shoom from the Bervie braes. They were given milk there, and new-baked cakes, and rested a while, Chris glad of the rest, Cis lying back in her chair with her face flushed to colour from the walk they had come. They had come down the Howe from the Segget haughs, past Catcraig, out on the Fordoun road, Fordoun a brown, dull lour to the north, and so swung on down past Mondynes, Kinraddie to the left, and then reached the brig, Chris stopped and peered in the water below and minded how once she'd done that, long before, in a summer, and seen the school-bairns plash, naked and dripping, in the shadowed shallows. Now the water flowed under, free and unvexed, east, to twine to the Bervie mouths, Cis leaned beside Chris and stared down as well, and then said *There is something I want to tell you.*

And Chris had said, gently, *I think I know what.* Cis flushed up a moment and bit at her lip, she wasn't afraid, only troubled, Chris saw. And she said *We'll go on, to the right, I think;* and so they had done, and climbed up the brae to the Geyrie's moor, and looked back from there and saw all around the steaming teams a-plod in the parks, shoring the long red drills of clay. Up in the hills the mists had come down, as they watched they saw a rain-cloud wheel out, down from the Mounth on the roofs of Drumlithie, white-shining there on the road to the South. Back and still back, line on line, rose the hills, the guardian wall of the Mearns Howe, it came on Chris as she stood and looked she'd never been beyond that wall since a bairn. The peewits were flying in the parks outbye, in the wind that came racing up from the east was the smell, a tingle that tickled your nose, of the jungle masses of whins that rose, dark as a forest, on the Geyrie's moor.

Chris said that she thought they might take that way, Cis said *Is it safe?* she had heard it was nearly impassable with bog, holes in the earth where a cart could lair, they sat on a gate and looked into its stretch, dark-brown and green in the hand of Spring. And Cis's shyness and constraint had gone, she was calm and young, they smiled one at the other, and Chris said suddenly, *Oh, we're such fools—women, don't you think that we are, now, Cis? To worry so much about men and their ploys, the things that they do and the things that they think!*

Cis said *But what else is there to do? They count for so much*—and sat and thought, grave, shy and sweet as a wing-poised bird. *Or maybe they don't as much as they think, but there wouldn't be children without them, would there?* Chris laughed at that and jumped down from the gate. *I suppose there wouldn't, but still—we might try! Let's go through the moor:* and so they had done.

There they saw the cup of the Howe rise up to the Barras slopes that led to Kinneff, on their right, dark-mantled, lost in its trees, Arbuthnott slept on the Bervie banks, clusters of trees, with the sudden gleam in the wind and the sun of the polished gear, bridles and haimes, on the straining shoulders of the labouring teams. Like going back into your youth, Chris thought, and sighed at that thought and Cis asked why, and Chris said *Because I am getting so old,* and Cis said *That's silly, I sometimes think you're the youngest of all the folk in Segget.* And was shy, *Please don't ever cut your hair, though I've had mine cut: it's lovely, your hair.*

Chris said that she thought it wasn't so bad, and they came to a little bare patch in the moor, where the whins drew aside their skirts and stood quiet, and right in the middle a great stone lay, maybe a thing from the antique times, and Chris sat on it and clasped her knees, and Cis looked at her and then sat at her feet, Chris with her gold eyes closed in the sun, the run and wheep of the wind in her hair, the sun on her face: she could listen to it now, aloof and sure and untroubled by things. And she said to Cis *Is the boy Dod Cronin?*

So she'd heard it all as she sat knee-clasped, there, in the play of the wind and the sun, a tale so old—oh, old as the Howe, everlasting near as the granite hills, this thing that brought men and women together, to bring new life, to seek new birth, on and on since the world had begun. And it seemed to Chris it was not Cis alone, her tale—but all tales that she harkened to then, kisses and kindness and the pain of love, sharp and sweet, terrible, dark, and the wild, queer beauty of the hands of men, and their lips, and the sleeps of desire fulfilled, and the dark, strange movements of awareness alone, when it came on women what thing they carried, darkling, coming to life within them, new life to replenish the earth again, to come to being in the windy Howe where the cloud-ships sailed to the unseen south. She fell in a dream that went far from Cis, looking up and across the slow-peopled parks at the scaurs of the Mounth and its flying mists, beyond these the moving world of men, and back again to those clouds that marched, terrible, tenebrous, their pillars still south. *A pillar of cloud by day and a pillar of fire by night.*

She said *I must think, I'll get Robert to help;* and Cis said *The minister?* and looked still more troubled. *Oh, Mrs Colquohoun, what have men to do with it, it's not their concern, they don't understand. Dod doesn't—he's frightened—for me or himself, but he doesn't know this, how queer it all is, and sickening, and fine—maybe I'm sickening myself to say that?*

Chris said she thought she was sweet to say it, and put her arm round the shoulders of Cis, and the girl looked up, and her lips came to Chris's; and Chris thought at that moment that no men could kiss—not as they should, they'd no notion of kissing. . . . Oh men, they were clumsy from the day they were breeked to the day they took off their breeks the last time!

The wind was coming in great gusts now, driving the riven boughs of the broom, in times it rose to a scraich round about and the moor seemed to cower in its trumpet-cry. Cloud

Howe of the winds and the rains and the sun! All the earth
that, Chris thought at that moment, it made little difference
one way or the other where you slept or ate or had made
your bed, in all the howes of the little earth, a vexing puzzle
to the howes were men, passing and passing as the clouds
themselves passed: but the REAL was below, unstirred and
untouched, surely, if that were not also a dream. Robert with
his dream of the night before, that Face and that Figure he
had seen in the woods, Chris had listened to him with her
head bent low, knowing she listened to a madman's dream.
And Robert to dream it! Robert who once followed a dream
that at least had the wind in its hair, not this creep into fear
and the fancies of old. But she'd seen then, clear and clear as
he spoke, the Fear that had haunted his life since the War,
Fear he'd be left with no cloud to follow, Fear he'd be left
in the day alone and stand and look at his naked self. And
with every hoping and plan that failed he turned to another,
to hide from that fear, draping his dreams on the face of life
as now this dream of the sorrowing Face. . . . And she'd
shivered again at the *filth* of the thing, not looking as she
heard that crack in his voice, he was saying he could almost
have touched the Figure—*God, Chris, it was* HIM, *whom
I've never believed! I've thought Him only a Leader, a man,
but Chris—I've looked on the face of God.* . . .

She'd sat and said nothing till that was impossible, so to sit
silent, and raised up her eyes, misty with pity, yet repulsion as
well. Robert had said quiet, *And you don't believe?* And she
said *I don't know, I don't know—oh, I'll try!* And gripped
his hand tight that he mightn't ask more.

She jumped up then from that seat in the moor—*Come
on, I'm so hungry!* and the two of them went on, through the
whins with the scud of the clouds overhead, that patched their
faces in the sharp sun-fall, a snipe was sounding up by the
Wairds as they came to the shaven lands of the Reisk, shaven
and shorn in the greed of the War. So, as they climbed they
came on the farm, with the three beech trees, and, beyond
the horizon, poised and glistening, the tumbling sea.

And when they had finished with drinking their milk and
eating their cakes Chris offered to pay. But the farmer's wife
shook her head, she'd not have it, she'd heard of Chris from

her son, she said, he lived in London and wrote horrible
books: but he and Chris were at college together. Chris
couldn't mind much of the son at all, she supposed they'd
met some time or another, but she didn't say that, she and
Cis cried their thanks, and went on down the road, it was
afternoon, then, the sun had wheeled round and was on the
west slant.

Down in Arbuthnott they found a bus and with that were
carried down the road to Bervie, where the old brig hung
by the lazy drifts of smoke from the Mills that lay in the
hollow—mills half-idle, as were those of Segget, Bervie
above them, a rickle and clutter. They got from the bus
and looked at the shops, then went down to the sea by a
straggling lane, the sea was pounding into the bay where no
boats came because of the rocks—it frothed and spumed
like a well-beaten egg, out east a fisher boat went by, into the
mist and the Gourdon smell. Chris sat on a rock and looked at
the sea, very wakeful, but Cis went to sleep in the sun, till
Chris waked her up and they went back again, and found a
new bus to take them to Stonehaven, where they'd get yet
another to take them back, up the long roads, to Spring-green
Segget.

And so, by the fall of night, they came back; and Chris
was tired, but her mind made up. Not even for Robert could
she change and pretend, though she'd not say a thing that
would hurt, could she help. She had found in the moors and
the sun and the sea her surety unshaken, lost maybe herself,
but she followed no cloud, be it named or unnamed.

NEXT SABBATH THE minister stood up in the pulpit and
preached from the Sermon on the Mount to Segget, he
said that the Christ still walked the earth, bringing the
only message that endured—though all else faded, that
was undying, they must search out the Christ, each soul by
himself, and find in himself what the world denied, the love
of God and the fellowship of men.

Folk listened and thought the man a fair scunner, damn't!
you wanted a minister with spunk, whatever had come over
this childe Colquohoun, bleating there soft as a new-libbed
sheep? Once he'd glowered as though he would like to gut

you, and thundered his politics, and you'd felt kittled up, though you didn't believe a word that he'd said. But this Sunday he blethered away in the clouds, folk came out and went home and were real disappointed, minding the time when he'd said from the pulpit, right out, that Hairy Hogg was a monkey—damn't! he'd fair fallen away since then.

And some of the spinners that came to the kirk, they were few enough now, remembered the name they had called the minister a long time back, they said that Creeping Jesus was back, he'd got feared at the gentry, the same as some others. Old Cronin himself it was that said that, and by others he meant his own son Jock that had led the Strike but a two years back, and had aye been a right coarse brute, folk thought, though fair the apple of his father's eye. But Jock had gotten on well in Glasgow, where he'd lived in sin with Miss Jeannie Grant, he'd gotten a job on a union there and went lecturing here and went blethering there, in a fine new suit and a bowler hat, and spats, right trig, and brave yellow boots. And he'd married Miss Grant, a three weeks back, and they had a fine house on the Glasgow hills; and wherever he went Jock Cronin would preach alliance between all employers and employed, and say to the folk that came to hear him that they shouldn't strike, but depend on their leaders—like himself; and take a smug look at his spats. When news of that came up to old Cronin, he cursed his son in a sickening way, and he said he'd never guessed he had fathered a Judas that could sell out the workers for that—not even for silver or a hungered guts, but spats, and a house on the Glasgow hills, and a craze for a white-legged quean in his bed.

Folk took a good laugh when they heard the news, Jock Cronin was showing some sense, they said, he fair had changed since the days when he'd go and break up the meetings of MacDougall Brown. Next MacDougall himself got a sore stammy-gaster, and so did the whole of Segget; it gasped. That tale of old Leslie's had had the truth in it, though you'd hardly believe it again when you heard it—it was all a damned lie and Cis a fine quean.

But then, when you met with her out in the street, and looked, and heard the news from the Manse, she and Dod Cronin to be wed in a week—your throat went dry, you went into the Arms and had a bit dram and swore at the bitch, all the folk said she was a foul creature, but they said it with something catching their throats, they'd been proud of Cis, all Segget had been, and here she was showing herself in that way, no better than that tink Else Queen at the Manse.

Ake Ogilvie said it was only nature, Cis or Else or the whole jing-bang, what ailed the folk of Segget, he said, was that they'd seen Cis as *they* might have been—clean—and they'd liked her for what they had lost. He spoke that speak to John Muir, the roadman, Muir gleyed and skeuched and chewed the thing over, it didn't make sense, Ake seldom did.

He went out to dig a bit grave after supper, the moon far up out over the Mounth, the sunset still far, though the lines lay long, in long slants across the hayfields of summer, and smoke drowsed low on the Segget roofs. In the kirkyard the grasses lay scythed as he'd left them, and he walked through that grass, there was some of it clover, bonnily scented with dead men's manure. So he came to the kirkyard corner and stopped, and lighted his pipe and spat on his hands, and started in to dig the bit grave, for one of the old spinner wives of West Wynd.

All the land here about was thick with old graves, he'd soon have to stop or start carting the bones to a pit and bury them out and apart, to leave room for the rest of Segget down there, eating and sleeping and having its play, all coming to stour and a stink at the end. And Muir gleyed down at the grave and dug, and minded of Cis and the speak there was, Dod Cronin had been found a job in Dundon and he and the lass were moving up there, the best they could do to get out of their shame. God knew there wasn't much shame in the thing, a lot overrated, this bedding with a quean—you worked yourself up and you got damned little, and where did it end then, all said and all done? Down here with the clay and the grass up above, be you rich, be you poor, unwedded like Cis, or as bonny as Mrs Colquohoun was bonny, or a shameless limmer like one of the queans that young Mr Mowat would bring to the House.

HE FAIR WAS a devil among women, young Mowat, gents were like that, Peter Peat said; but he'd time yet to settle down bravely in Segget and take his natural place at its head : and that was the Segget Conservative branch. Maybe he *had* had more queans than he should, but he'd settle down bravely yet, you would see. Ake Ogilvie said, *No doubt—in his sharn,* a tink-like speak, just what you expected, he was jealous as hell of the gentry, Ake, nearly as bad as that creature Moultrie that was now over stiff to crawl out at all.

One of the Mills had been idle for months, though young Mr Mowat had come back from his sail. He was no sooner back than a birn of the spinners went up to the House in a deputation. But when the deputation got there, and the servant had shown them into the hall, and they stood there twisting their caps, fell shy, they heard the crackle of a falling bottle and a hooting and laughing as though lunatics were loose ; and out of a side-door a quean came running, without a stitch on, nothing but a giggle, she looked back and laughed at young Mowat behind her, running and laughing with his wee frog face ; and up the stairs the two of them went.

Well, the deputation blushed from head to heel; syne one of them, the oldest operative there, said *That's where the cash goes we make in the Mills,* and they looked from one to the other, old, hungry, and some of them were gey bitter, most of the dole, on starvation's edge; and they stood in the rich, warm hall and looked round, at the log-wood fire and the gleam of deers' heads, and the patterned walls and the thick, soft rugs. But the rest said nothing to the speak of the first, they knew it was useless trying to complain or to start that kind of socialist stuff that the Cronins of old had preached in the Mills, you'd seen the end of that with the Strike, young Mowat was the only hope of the Mills.

He came down at last and was charming, polite, and said it was Jahly to see them again. And he stood with his back to the fire and said *Hwaw?* and read them a lecture on the awful times, he said that taxation was killing the country, all they could hope at the coming election was that the Conservative folk would get back, stronger than ever in position and power, and reduce taxation on men like himself. Then perhaps he would manage to open the Mill. And he smiled at them, charming, with his horn-rimmed eyes, but he offered no drink, instead rang a bell, and the servant childe came and ushered them out; and young Mr Mowat said it had been Jahly; and that showed that he had a real good heart.

Now, that was the first Peter Peat had heard about young Mr Mowat and the wishes he had that the Tory Party should get back again, they'd been holding office but a bare five years and hadn't yet had time to set things right, being busied with breaking strikes and the like, and freeing the working men from their unions, and seeing that we had a real strong navy, and trying to get the coarse foreign tinks to reduce their armies, a danger to Europe. . . . Peter Peat had these facts at his finger-tips and went up to the House to see Mr Mowat, and ask a subscription for the Segget branch. And Mr Mowat said it was Jahly to see him, Rahly Jahly, and sipped at his wine, and the quean did the same, exploding a giggle, sitting bare-legged on the back of his chair. Yes, he believed in Devolution for Scotland, but not this mad nationalism now rampant, only the Unionist Party would see that Scotland got her just dues in the end. And he told Peter more of the coarse new Nationalists, not the flower of the country's gentry, as once, Scotland had lost her chance once again, the new leaders a pack of socialists and catholics, long-haired poets, a fellow called Grieve, and Mackenzie and Gunn, hysterical Highlandmen. Well, he had Jahly soon finished with *them*, and would be glad to give a donation some time to the branch of the Unionist Party in Segget.

And Peter Peat was fell happy at that—ay, the old blood flowed in the gentry's veins.

THE AUTUMN CAME, the Election's results, and Segget was fair stammy-gastered at them, the Labour tinks had gotten in power, led by that coarse brute Ramsay MacDonald. You minded him and the things he had said, long before, when the War was on?—that we shouldn't be fighting the Germans, no, no, but leave them a-be, they were much too strong. Ay, that's what he'd said and here he was now, at the head of the country, lording it about, and not even maybe saying Sir to the King. But others said the creature would fairly swank now, and get the King to make him a lord, or a duke or something: and Ake Ogilvie said he'd heard the title was Lord Loon of Lossie.

But that was just one of his ill-natured speaks, damn't! was he against this Government as well?—after going to all that stour to vote Liberal, instead of decent and Tory like others. Hardly any of the spinners had voted at all, they just hung about and smoked their bit fags, or dug in their gardens back of the wynds, or stared at the Mills with their hungry eyes. But Ake Ogilvie had said he was voting Liberal, and had canvassed Segget for the Liberal childe, doing him a sight more harm than good, he said there was good in none of the parties, Labour or Tory or Liberal or any: but the Tory name fair stank in your throat, it was built on the purses and pride of the kind of half-witted loon that mismanaged the Mills; the Liberals were damn little better, he knew, but they *had* a great name that was worthy a vote.

Hardly a soul paid heed to his blethers, just smiled at him canny and said *Well, we'll see;* and got ready for the polling day to come to ride to Laurencekirk in the Tory cars. Ake Ogilvie borrowed a Liberal car, and its driver, and waited in Segget Square; and the Tory cars piled black with folk, getting off to vote for the gentry childes that had promised them reischles and reischles of tariffs; but not a damn soul looked near Alec Ogilvie, sitting with a sneering look in his car. And then the door of the Moultrie shop was flung wide open and who should come out, hoasting and hirpling slow on his stick, but that thrawn old billy, Rob Moultrie himself, leaning on a stick and his old wife's shoulder, he hobbled and hirpled over to the car, near bent down double, Jess Moultrie beside him. Ake jumped from his seat and helped the two in, and stood back with a queer-like grin on his face—were these all who championed Liberty here?

But there was a fourth; Ake had grown tired and was crying to the shover that they might as well go, when he heard a hail and looked over his shoulder. And there was Mrs Colquohoun of the Manse, crossing the Square, running like a lad, with a spray of blood on her dark, soft skin. *Sorry I'm late, Ake,* she said, and jumped in; and Ake got in himself and could nearly have cuddled her.

But the Liberal man got a mighty few votes, the Tory got in, as you knew he would do, if the rest of the country had done half as well, where would these tinks of socialists have

been? Selling spunks in the London streets, or that coarse
brute Ramsay MacDonald's tracts. And the Provost said in
the Segget Arms 'twas an ill day this for our Scottish land.
What was it the poet Robert Burns had written?—an
ancestor, like, of the Hoggs, Rabbie Burns. *A man's a man
for a' that,* he wrote, and by that he meant that poor folk of
their kind should steer well clear of the gentry and such,
not try to imitate them at all, and leave them to manage the
country's affairs.

DEEPER AND DEEPER as that year slipped by, Robert
slipped from the life of his parish, he hadn't bothered to
vote at all, he locked himself up long hours in his room,
dreaming or reading or just sitting still—alien to Chris
as that Figure he dreamt he'd met in the dark of Dunnottar
woods.

Nor was that meeting the only one, there were others
haunting the paths of his feet, times when he'd know that
Presence in his room, once in the midst of a sermon he
stopped, not staring or wild, but all the kirk watched him,
and he watched the door, and his eyes moved slow as though
following a figure that came down the aisle; and folk turned
round and stared where he stared, and saw nothing at all but
the winter gleam of the cold kirk floor, and beyond that the
glass of the far, stained window that looked on the tossing
boughs of the trees. Chris half-rose from her seat in that
silence, she saw the sweat bright on Robert's still face. Then
his eyes left the aisle and he wiped his forehead, and went on
in an even voice with his sermon.

For outside these moments he was quiet and kind, with a
kindness Chris hated—for it was not his. It was something
borrowed from his unclean dream, not Robert at all, a mask
and a pose, a kindness he followed with Fear for an urge. And
a dreadful loneliness came upon Chris, and a shivering hate
for that cloud he followed, that sad-faced Figure out of the
past, who had led such legions of men to such ends up and
down the haughs and hills of the earth. Christ? So maybe
indeed He had lived, and died, a follower of clouds Himself.
That Figure she minded from school-time days, and even
then it had not moved her, it seemed a sad story, in mad, sad

years, it was over and done: and it left her untouched. And it left her so still, it was only a dream that could alter nothing the ways of the world. . . . Oh, why wasn't Robert like other ministers?—easy and pleased and hearty and glib, with no religious nonsense about them, they led hearty lives and ate well at table, and took the days as they found them come, and didn't leave their wives to think daft thoughts, and cry here, quiet, in the dark, like a child, sometimes with the fear of a child for the dark.

But she just had to meet it: and her life was still hers. So she worked through that autumn tending the garden, till almost the earth rebelled from her touch, she thought with a smile, and welcomed the winter. New Year's Eve came in a bluster on Segget, in snow and a breaking of sleet for sharp hours, there were spinners starving down in Old Toun John Muir told Chris as he came in on Sunday. And he said that another twenty were sacked, it was likely the second Mill would close down.

Robert heard that story as well, and listened, and said not a word, who once would have flamed into curses and anger on the cruelty of men. But now he stood up in the pulpit and preached, his text the saying of Chirst, *Feed my lambs*. And Chris sat and listened to the gentle voice, and shivered as though at a filthy thing. And she looked round quiet at the people he preached to—the Provost Hogg with his heavy face, John Muir, with his skeugh and his puzzled eyes, Peter Peat the tailor, red-eyed, like a rat, and the mean, close face of the publican, Melvin. What hope in appealing to them for help?—were there but a flicker he had sold his soul to that fancy and Figure for something at least. But they heeded as little the whine of his Christ as the angry threat of his Struggling God.

And that New Year's night as she lay by Robert, in the quiet and the dark, she knew fear again, fear for the year new come to birth, for the man who lay so quiet in his sleep, beside her, turned away from her touch, low in the grate the coals were drooping, in a little red glow, she watched them sink and fade and grow grey as the dawn came dim over a world that was wrapped in white; and out in the yews the frozen rooks stirred: and down in the kitchen Else Queen did the same.

THAT YEAR BROUGHT plenty of changes to Else, before it began there were rumours about her, Ag Moultrie one morning was going by the Manse when she saw the door of the kitchen open, and out, as quiet as an ill-gettèd cat who should come stepping but that loon Alec Hogg? And he turned and gave a bit nod of his head, and Else Queen looked out and nearly saw Ag, but she dropped down smart in the lithe of a bush, and watched the two part, and was fairly ashamed—to think that the son of a man like the Provost should have taken up with a harlot, just. And the more Ag thought of it, the more she was shamed, till she just broke down and fair Roared and Grat.

Well, she passed the news on in a neighbour-like way, and folk were fair shocked, and snickered at the Provost—ay, that was a nasty smack in the face for old Hairy Hogg: had he heard the news yet? And when it came out that he hadn't, just yet, there were half a dozen that took him the news, you yourself were nearly killed in the rush, there was never such a birn of boots needing mending, Dite Peat went in with a pair, and his brother, and Bruce the roadman, and syne Will Melvin. And old Hairy sat like a monkey and blew on how well he could sutor, and Dite Peat said *Ay, and we hear you'll be sutoring soon for a marriage. Or is it a christening?* And they all took a sly bit look at the Provost; and he habbered and said *What?* and so he was told.

Well, he couldn't believe that speak about Alec, the loon might be a bit of a fool and had lost his work in the Edinburgh office, the place had closed down, that wasn't his wyte: but he wasn't such a fool as take up with a quean that once warmed the bed for that wastrel Dalziel. And as soon as young Alec came home that day from some gardening work he had gotten outbye the Provost cried out, *Come into the shop,* and told him the coarse-like speak in Segget. Alec Hogg said, *Well, then, there's something in it. I like Else well and I mean to marry her.* When he heard him say that old Hairy near burst, and he asked Alec Hogg did he want to bring them, respectable folk, in shame to the grave? And Alec said No, he didn't think so, he only wanted to bring Else to tea. And the Provost said 'twould be over his dead body if he did.

When that got around folk fair took a laugh—faith,

man! that would fair be a funny-like sight, Else Queen
stepping over old Hairy Hogg's corpse, and the old ape,
dead or alive, you could swear, taking an upward keek as
she passed. Else and Alec were watched fell close after that,
and once, when they took a walk up the Kaimes, that Spring,
a windy Sunday in March, and sat in the lithe to have a bit
crack, there was nearly a dozen that kept on their track,
and Ag Moultrie, the Roarer and Greeter of Segget, was up
in the Schoolhouse watching the pair with a spy-glass she'd
borrowed at racing speed. And the childes that had crept up
the Kaimes to watch near froze to death, for they didn't dare
move, and Alec and Else did not a damn thing, they didn't
even kiss all the time they were there; and you well could
warrant if they didn't kiss then, it was only because they had
come to a pass when neither kisses nor cuddles contented.

Well, Alec couldn't marry, he hadn't a meck, Else's wages
went to the keep of her bairn, Dalziel of the Meiklebogs
wouldn't pay a penny. When Else had written and asked
him for that he had just smiled sly, and torn up the letter.
So things might well have stood as they were but for the tink
row that broke out in the house of Smithie, the whiskered
old roadman of Segget.

He hardly had seemed to alter at all, except that his
whiskers looked more and more still like the birns of hay
he would pinch from the parks. He still bade on with his
daughter and goodson, Bruce, folk said he had hell for a life,
though the house was his and all the gear in it, the kye in the
byres and the kirns in the creamery. But he'd come home
still of an evening from work and get no friendly greeting
from any, unless 'twas the kye, and only from them if he
brought them their meat: otherwise, they would sulk. In
his house his daughter would say, *Oh, it's you? Then clean
your nasty big feet on the mat.* And old Smithie would glower
at her sore, but say nothing, it was years since the old bit
creature broke out.

But one Saturday afternoon in April, just as old Smithie
had stopped from his chapping out on the road that led to
Stonehive, and had wiped his long whiskers and took a keek
round, a lorry came down the road and went skeugh, and
nearly went into the west-side ditch. Well, the lorry-driver

swore like a tink, which wasn't surprising, he probably was one, and cried on old Smithie to give him a shove. And he shoved, and old Smithie, they shoved and they heaved, and swore at the lorry, and chaved a good hour, 'twas a lorry-load of crates of whisky and beer going north to Dundon, the lorry-man told. And he said that he hoped that their guts would rot, them that would drink but a drop of the stuff.

Well, at last they got the wheel from the ditch, and the lorry-driver said he was bloody obliged. He looked at his watch and said he must go, but syne he reached back in a small bit crate. *Here, I pinched two bottles of this for myself, but you try one, it's a fine-like drink.* And he said some more and syne he drove off, leaving the bottle in old Smithie's hands.

Old Smithie took a bit keek at the thing, a fattish bit bottle of an unco-like shape; and he took off the cork and gave it a lick. That tasted as unco as the bottle looked, sugary and sweet, and old Smithie thought, *Well, damn it, he surely thinks I'm a bairn, it's a lemonade drink, this Benny Dick Tine.*

So held the bottle to his mouth for a suck, and down the stuff gurgled, and old Smithie paiched, and wiped his long whiskers and curled up his nose—feuch! it was sickening; but he fairly was dry. So he drank down a half of the lemonade stuff, and corked the bottle and put it in his pouch, and got on his bike and rode home to Segget.

God knows what happened atween there and Segget, he rode through the Square at the awfullest lick, and nearly killed Melvin opposite the Arms. He was singing that his heart was in the Highlands, not here, Will Melvin sore vexed to see him like that, if the coarse old creature wanted to get drunk why couldn't he come down and get drunk at the Arms? Will Melvin cried *Hi!* and louped like a goat, and Smithie cried back *That'll teach you, I hope, to bide out of my way, you whiskied old wife!* Syne he wheeled round and up the East Wynd like the wind and narrowly missed running into the dyke, and swung the bike over to the other bit side, and nearly killed a lone chicken there; and vanished through Segget in a shower of stour, with Will Melvin and the angel gaping together.

Ake Ogilvie told that he saw him go by, like a Valkyr

riding the wings of the storm—whatever that fool of a
joiner meant. But the next thing that happened for sure was
that Smithie got off at the door of his house and went in. His
goodson Bruce sat canny by the fire and hardly looked up as
he heard Smithie's step. Then Smithie said *Just a minute, you,
the sweir swine there, and I'll deal with you!* and Bruce looked
round and there was old Smithie, with a bottle upended,
sucking like mad. And then he had finished and flung off
his coat, the daft old tyke, and let drive at Bruce, and near
knocked him head first into the dinner that was hottering
slow on the swey by the fire. Well, Bruce got up, he would
soon settle this, and his wife, old Smithie's daughter, cried
out *Crack up his jaw—don't spare the old tink!*

But God! she nearly died at what followed. Old Smithie
had fair gone mad of a sudden, he didn't heed the bashings
of Bruce, not a bit, but took him a belt in the face that near
floored him, syne kicked him right coarse, and Bruce gave a
groan and caught at himself, and as he doubled up old Smithie
took him a clout in the face with a tacketty boot, and for weeks
after that it looked more like a mess in a butcher's shop, than a
face, that thing that the childe Bruce wore. Bruce was blinded
with blood, he cried *Stop—I can't see!* But old Smithie
had gone clean skite, what with his wrongs and the Benny
Dick Tine. *Oh, can't you? Well, then, you can damn well
feel!* And he took Bruce and swung him out through the
door, and kicked him sore in the dowp as he went, and
threw a chair at him, and Bruce had enough, he ran like
a hare, half-blind though he was, and the Muirs all stood
next door and gaped, Mrs Muir and Tooje and Ted, all but
John, he sat indoors and gleyed quiet up the lum.

The next thing the Muirs saw was Mrs Bruce herself,
kicked out like her man and running like him, and syne the
bairns, and syne they heard sounds inside the house like a
wild beast mad. Then old Smithie started to throw out the
things that belonged to his daughter and his goodson Bruce,
a sewing machine and their kists and clothes, a heap in the
stour outside the door. Bruce had cleared his eyes by then and
come back, but old Smithie saw him and chased him away,
with a bread-knife, and came back and danced on the gear,
he looked like the devil himself, said Ake, who had come up

to see what the row was about—if you could imagine the
devil in whiskers raising worse hell than was usual in Segget.

Well, he closed the door next and after a while some folk
went over and chapped at the door, but they got not a cheep,
and waited for Bruce, he'd gone to the smiddy to borrow an
axe. He came back with a fair-like crowd at his heels, Feet
the bobby came with him as well, and just as they started in
on the door Ake Ogilvie cried *No, damn't! that won't do.*
And he said to Bruce *Is this your house, or his?* Bruce told
him to mind his own mucking business, and was raising his
axe to let fly at the door when Ake Ogilvie said, *All right,
then, all right. It's up to you, Feet. You're supposed to defend
the law here in Segget. Here's a man that has locked himself up
in his house, and you're standing by and aiding and abetting a
burglar trying to get into the place.*

That hadn't struck folk afore, now it did, they cried, *Ay,
that's right,* and Bruce glared around; and Feet scratched at
his head and took out his notebook. And he said to Bruce that
he'd maybe best wait, he himself would call on old Smithie
for a change, to open the door in the name of the Law. But
all that they heard after Feet had cried that were the snores
of old Smithie asleep on his bed.

He wasn't seen in Segget till the Sunday noon, when he
crawled out to give some meat to his kye. But he never left
the house but he locked up the door, the Bruces got tired of
trying to dodge in, they said they couldn't bear the old brute,
anyhow, him and his stink, and they flitted to Fordoun, and
Bruce got a job on the railway there; and old Smithie at last
had his house to himself, thanks to the lorry-man's Benny
Dick Tine.

And what all this clishmaclaver led to was Alec Hogg
getting the job on the road that had once been Bruce's, and
the seat by the fire in old Smithie's house that was Bruce's
as well. For young Alec Hogg was a skilly-like childe, right
ready and swack and no longer polite, he called a graip by
its given name. As for looking around for slop-basins these
days, he'd have eaten tea-leaves like a damn tame rabbit, and
munched them up with contentment, too. And he said to old
Smithie as they mended the roads there was nothing like a
damn good taste of starvation to make you take ill with ideas

you'd held, he had starved down south when he lost his job,
and near starved when he managed to get back to Segget, his
father, the old mucker, would glunch and glare at every bit
mouthful he saw his son eat—*his* hands had never held
idleceit's bread. He'd sneer at the table, the monkey-like
mucker, *And what have your fine friends, the Fashers, done for
you?* And it was but the truth, they had done not a thing;
as for Fascism's fancies on Scotland and Youth—well,
starvation's grip in your belly taught better. Scotland and
its young could both go to hell and frizzle there in ink for
all that he cared.

And old Smithie thought that a fell wice speak, and so did
John Muir, and they'd sit and crack, the three of them by the
side of the road, and watch the traffic go by to Dundon, the
cars with gentry, the buses with folk. And John Muir would
gley *Ay, God, and that's sense. I was once myself a bit troubled
about things—fair Labour I was, but to hell with them all.
Poor folk just live and die as they did, we all come to black flesh
and a stink at the end. . . . And like fools we still go with the
soss, bringing grave-fodder into the world. For I hear that you're
courting Else Queen, are you, Alec?*

Alec reddened up a bit and said maybe he was; and John
Muir said Well, and he might do worse, since women there
were you'd to bed them sometime. And he asked when Else
and Alec were to marry, and Alec said *Christ, I haven't an
idea—we've no place to bide though we married to-morrow.*

And 'twas then that old Smithie said *Have you no? You're
a decent-like childe and I like you well. Let you and your wife
come bide in with me.*

ELSE CAME TO Chris and told her the news, Chris said
she was glad—*and I know you'll be happy.* Else tossed
her head, *God knows about that. There are worse folk than
Alec—at least, so I hear. And as for being happy —och,
nobody is!*

Chris laughed at that and said it wasn't true, but she
wondered about it in the fresh-coming Spring, maybe it was
Else had the sense of the thing—not looking for happiness,
madness, delight—she had left these behind in the bed of
Dalziel; only looking to work and to living her life, eating

and sleeping and rising each dawn, not thinking, tiring by night-time and dark—as Chris did herself in the yard of the Manse. And Chris raised her head as she thought that thought, and heard the trill of a blackbird, shrill, and saw the spirt of its wings as it flew, black sheen of beauty, across the long grass: and the ripple and stilly wave of the light, blue sunlight near on the old Manse wall. And she thought that these were the only glad things—happiness, these, if you found the key. She had lost it herself, unlonely in that, most of the world had mislaid it as well.

She minded then as she worked at that tree, an apple tree, and set smooth the earth, and reached her hands in the cling of the mould, that saying of Robert's, long, long ago, the day he unveiled the new-hallowed Stones up by the loch on Blawearie brae—that we'd seen the sunset come on the land and this was the end of the peasants' age. But she thought, as often, we saw more than that—the end forever of creeds and of faiths, hopes and beliefs men followed and loved: religion and God, socialism, nationalism—Clouds that sailed darkling into the night. Others might arise, but these went by, folk saw them but clouds and knew them at last, and turned to the Howe from the splendid hills—folk were doing so all over the world, she thought, back to the sheltered places and ease, to sloth or toil or the lees of lust, from the shining splendour of the cloudy hills and those hopes they had followed and believed everlasting. She herself did neither, watching, unsure: was there nothing between the Clouds and the Howe?

This life she lived now could never endure, she knew that well as she looked about her, however it ended it could not go on; she was halted here, in these Segget years, waiting the sound of unhasting feet, waiting a Something unnamed, but it came. And then—

She stopped in her work and looked down at herself, at her breast, where the brown of her skin went white at the edge of the thin brown dress she wore, white rose the hollow between her breasts, except where it was blue-veined with blood; funny to think that twice in her life a baby had grown to life in her body and herself changed so to await that growth, and still she looked like a quean, she thought, breast, hips, and legs, and she liked her legs, even yet, as she looked at them with a smile, at the line of herself as she squatted to weed, nice still to cuddle spite her sulky face! Had she lived in the time of the golden men who hunted the hills by the Trusta bents there would have been cuddles enough, she supposed, fun and pain and the sting of the wind, long nights of sleep in a heath-hid cave, morns shining over the slopes of the hills as you stirred by your man and peered in his face, lying naked beside you, naked yourself, with below the Howe just clearing its mists as the sun came up from an alien sea—the Howe, unnamed and shaggy with heath, with stone-oak forests where the red deer belled as the morning grew and the Bervie shone; and far over the slopes of the Howe you could see the smoke rise straight from another cave, and know your nearest friends a day off; and you'd not have a care or a coin in the world, only *life*, swift, sharp, and sleepy and still, and an arm about you, life like a song, and a death at the end that was swift as well—an hour of agony, or only a day, what woman feared death who had borne a child? And many enough you'd have borne in the haughs and been glad enough of their coming in that day, undreaming the dark tomorrows of the Howe that came with the sailing ships from the south. . . .

And, kneeling and cutting at a wallflower clump that had grown over-large for its portion of earth, Chris smiled as she thought of her talk with Else on this matter of humankind itself growing over-large for *its* clump of earth. Else had stood and listened with red-tinted ears, and stammered and blushed, it was funny and sad, Chris knew how she felt, she had once felt the same. Else said *Oh, Mem, but I couldn't do that—it wouldn't be right to do anything like that!* Chris said *It's surely better to do that than have the bairns that you can't bring up?* Else shook her head, *They'll just come, and we'll manage. But I couldn't do things to myself like that.*

Robert had overheard Chris as she talked, he had heard the talk through the kitchen door, coming down the stairs in his silent way. And when he and Chris were alone together, he said *You shouldn't have said that, Christine*, gentle and quiet and even of speech. Chris had shivered a little and drawn further away. *Why not?* she asked, and he said *Because*

*we have no rights in these matters at all. We have meddled
too much with our lives as it is; they are God's concern, the
children who come.*

For a minute Chris hardly believed what she heard, she
had stared at him, at his maskèd face; they themselves had
done this thing he denounced. . . .

ALL THE NEXT afternoon, as it seemed to Chris, she heard
the rumour and hum of the wedding, down in the hall of the
Segget Arms. It had turned to a day sun-blown and clear, the
earth was hard as she weeded the beds, clumps of begonias
under the dykes, back of the Manse the chickens of Muir
were deep in a drowsy scraiching, well-fed. Chris went and
looked over the wall and watched, and laughed a little at the
courting play of an over-small cock with a haughty, shamed
look, as though it thought mating a nasty thing, but yet was
right eager to make half a try. There were lots of folk who
had minds like his!

Robert and Ewan were both at the wedding, Robert
returned as soon as he might, Chris heard him climb up
the stairs to his room. The noise went on far into the night,
stirring in sleep towards the Sunday morning Chris heard the
light step of Ewan go by. Next morning he wasn't stirring as
usual, and she carried a cup of tea to his room, and knocked
and went in and he still slept fast, lying straight, his dark
hair thick as a mop, she stood and looked at him and tickled
his arm, and he woke up lightly, as he always woke. *Oh, it's
you, Chris!* and stared a moment: *I'm sorry, Mother!*

She said *Oh, I'm Chris as well, I suppose,* and sat on the
side of the bed while he drank, the morning growing in the
yews outside, promise of another day of summer yellow on
the ivied walls of the Manse. She asked how the wedding had
gone, and he yawned, so grown-up, and stretched while she
caught the cup; and he said that the wedding had gone off
fine, except that folk were afraid of Robert, he'd changed so
much, with never a laugh. Ewan had heard Dite Peat say of
Robert—

Chris said *Yes, what did he say of Robert?* and Ewan lay
and looked at her, calm and cool. *He said that Robert had
lain with Else, he knew bed-shame in a man when he saw it.*

Chris said *You didn't believe that, did you?* Ewan yawned
again, *I don't know; he might. Though I shouldn't think it
likely, he has you to sleep with: and you must be very nice, I
should think.*

Chris felt the blood come swift in her cheeks, and a moment
the wildest feeling of fear; and then that went by, she'd be
honest as him. She said *Oh, I think I am nice to sleep with.
You've to be terribly in love with someone for that—it makes
all the difference, as you'll know some time.*

He said, politely, *Yes, I suppose so*, he hadn't much interest
in the matter at all; and told some more of the fun at the
wedding, the Provost and MacDougall Brown had both sung,
the Provost banking and braeing, bass, MacDougall strong
on the Blood of the Lamb. There had been lots to eat and
lots of dancing, Ewan had danced with most of the women,
rather fun, though most were too fat round the hips, the hips
were the things that counted, he'd found. He'd told Else that
and she'd said she was shocked, but he didn't suppose that
she was, very much. And then Alec Ogilvie and Dite Peat
had quarrelled, it seems they had hated each other for years,
and kept away from each other for years, neither one nor the
other sure that he'd win. It was round about seven o'clock
that it happened; they went out to the back of the Arms to
fight, Ewan didn't hear till the fight was near done and went
out and saw Dite Peat on the grass, his eyes closed up and
rather a mess, Ake Ogilvie being helped into his coat and
wiping a trickle of blood from his nose. And Ewan had felt
a bit sorry for Dite—goodness knew why, the *dirtiest* rat.

Chris asked what time he'd reached home and he said *Not
till this morning some time, nearly two. I took a friend of Else's
to Frellin, the servant-maid at the Manse up there.* Chris asked
was she nice? and Ewan gave a shrug, *I thought her rather a
boring young beast, she wanted me to make love to her—up to
a point, I suppose, I don't know.* Chris asked *And did you?*
and Ewan said *No, but I thought I would try to teach her a
lesson. You know I've got strong wrists?—I get them from
you—so I held her with one hand and smacked her with the
other, and patted her all neat and nice again, and put her in
through the Frellin Manse gate, and came home to my bed: I
felt a bit tired.*

FOLK SAID HE fair was a nickum, that loon, young Ewan Tavendale that came from the Manse, and went to the college at Dundon each day, cool and calm you'd see him swing by, no hat on his head be it sun, be it sleet, folk said he was proud as dirt: and for why? He was only the son of a crofter, just, killed in the War, and only his luck his mother had married into a Manse. He never went by with a loon-like slouch, or reddened up, loon-like, over the lugs, if he met with a covey of queans in the Square—damn't, there was something unnatural about him, a sly young brute, you could well believe. And what though they said he did well at college? No doubt his step-father, the minister Colquohoun, did all his lessons and he got the credit.

Then the speak got about from the Frellin Manse that he'd taken a lass from the wedding of Else, the lass that idle young thing Jeannie Ray, and she'd thought to have a bit play with the loon—she often would play about with the loons and get them sore in a way to have her, syne leave them looking and habbering like fools. But she'd got a sore stammy-gaster with Ewan, the coarse young brute assaulted the quean, and left her greeting on the Manse door-mat. And she told the news to a crony in Frellin, and the crony giggled and passed it on, and it reached Ag Moultrie, the Roarer and Greeter, and she nearly exploded with shame and delight. And next time she met in with Ewan she cried, *Ay, Ewan, what's this that I hear about you and that lass Jeannie Ray down at Frellin Manse?* And the loon said *I'm sorry I don't know what you'd heard, Miss Moultrie, but no doubt Segget soon will. Good morning.* And he smiled, polite, and passed on, not a bit ashamed, and left Ag to gape. And not only that, she felt a bit feared, it was fair uncanny, a loon like that.

And a queerer thing followed, her father was dying, Rob Moultrie that said he wasn't her father, the coarse old brute still tormented his wife with the speak that Ag was no daughter of his. Well, he was down and fast sinking at last, about time that he was, the snarling old sinner. And near to the last, when he'd got gey low, he said that he'd like to see the young man, Ewan Something his name was, up at the Manse, he'd like to see him and nobody else. Ag sat by his bed and she heard the bit blither, and she said to him, soothing, *You're wandering a bit. He doesn't know you, the young man at the Manse.* And Rob Moultrie said *Go get him at once, you goggle-eyed gowk, with your claiking tongue. He's more kin of mine than you'll ever be, you with your half-dozen fathers or more.*

So Jess Moultrie trudged away up through Segget, and gave in the message, and young Ewan came down, and went in and sat by the bed of old Moultrie, not feared as a loon at the breath of death, but cool and calm, as though it were nothing. Folk sat outbye and couldn't make out the words that the two spoke one to the other, except that they heard Ewan Tavendale say *Yes, I've noticed that,* and *Yes, that's worth knowing.* And he shook hands with Rob when at last he stood up, and didn't make on, as any other would, that old Rob would soon be up and about, instead he shook hands and wished him Goodbye, and went out as calm as he had come in—ay, a heartless young mucker if ever there was one, whatever could Moultrie have wanted with *him?*

Rob wouldn't hear of the minister coming, and died without a prayer in the house, and that was queer in a childe like him, fell religious and fond of his Bible. Ag cried that her father had died unblessed; and when he was dead she just Roared and Grat.

They buried the old tyke on a hot, quiet day, Mr Colquohoun thinner and quieter than ever; but he had a fine voice as he read out the words, lower than once it had been, more genteel, he fairly had quietened down, had Colquohoun. Once on a time at a burial service folk said the minister would speak out as though he fair meant that the dead would rise up some day, and live once again, and it made your hair crawl—it was all in the Bible, no doubt, and right fine, but you knew the whole thing just a stuttering of stite. But now the minister spoke earnest and low, with a kind of a whine that you heard undisturbed as they lowered old Moultrie down in the clay, with his ill-led life and his ill-gettèd ways, his hatred of gentry, his ill-treating of Jess. Well, that was his end, and you felt undisturbed, all but John Muir, as he told to Ake later.

For it came on him when the folk had gone, and he worked there alone in the stilled graveyard, and watched the figure

of Colquohoun move off, that something was finished and
ended in Segget, more than old Moultrie, older than him.
And a queer qualm came in the pit of his wame, he stopped in
the sun to gley in a dream, 'twas as though they were shadows
in the sunblaze he saw, nothing enduring and with substance
at all, kirk and minister, and stones all around graved with
their promised hopes for the dead, the ways and beliefs of
all olden time—no more than the whimsies a bairn would
build from the changing patterns that painted the hills.

AND FAITH, THERE were more than enough of those
changes, folk woke to the fact of ill changes in Segget,
you'd to count your silver now ere you spent it, there wasn't
a soul but was hit some way, prices so high and the spinners,
the dirt, with hardly a meck to spend in shops. Whiles one
of the Mowat mills still joggled along, as it wore to Autumn
you'd see its smoke like a lazy snake uprise in the air. But it
joggled half-hearted, there was fell little traffic, the stationy,
Newlands, said so little jute came in he wondered the Mill
kept going: and he tried to get spinners to do what he did,
bawl for the Blood of MacDougall's Lamb; and no doubt
he fair was a pious childe, though you thought yourself that
praying for blood was hardly the way to start a jute mill.
    The Segget wynds were crowded with spinners, lolling
about in the sun, the dirt, you turned one moment from
cursing the brutes for their sweirty and living off the like
of yourself, and the next you had nearly moaned your head
off that there wasn't a thing they now bought in your shops.
Dite Peat was the first to feel the bit nip, he'd never done
well with the spinners, Dite, since that time long back he'd
mishandled his father. But up until late he'd managed to
live, with trade from the rest of Segget New Toun, though
most from the countryside out around. Well, he found that
the farms were failing him now, cottar folk got their meat
from the vans on the roads, and all the farmers had gotten
them cars and went into Stonehaven or even Dundon: in
the end Dite Peat was rouped from his door. It lent a bit
of excitement, that, Dite's stuff sold up while he stood and
looked on, still bearing the marks of the knocks he had got
in that tink-like fight with the joiner of Segget.

Folk wondered what would become of him now, it was said he hadn't a meck of his own: and though when it seemed he owned a bit shop folk bore with him and his dirty jokes, they weren't such fools as to do that now and cold-shouldered him everywhere that he went. And down in the Segget Arms one night when he started in with his dirty tales, Alec Hogg was there and he said *You shut up, we're sick of you and the things you can do—though you can't keep your shop-roof over your head*. Dite bared his rotten brown teeth like a dog, but other folk were crying *That's right,* and he didn't dare make a set at young Hogg. That was near the end of the brute in Segget, he went to Meiklebogs and asked for a fee, folk told that Dalziel had ta'en him on cheap—Dalziel whose new housekeeper was in the old way; faith! with Dite Peat at the Meiklebogs as well, the question of fatherhoods in the future would be more of a complication than ever.

For bairns came thick as ever they'd come, folk cut their costs in all things but cradles, down in Old Toun they squawked into life, the bairns, in rooms that were packed out already. The less the work the more of the creatures, they bred fair disgusting old Leslie would say, and it showed you the kind of dirt that they were, living crowded like that, four-five in a room, in houses that were not fit for pig-rees. 'Twas Infernal, just: the men should be libbed: now, when he himself was a loon up in Garvock—

But his trade at the smiddy was failing as well, though he habbered and blethered as much as ever, you'd fell often hear the anvil at rest and look in and see old Leslie sit there, sitting and staring down at his pipe, it gave you an unco-like feeling to see him. There were fell few jobs came down from the Mills and a mighty few from the farms outbye, with their new-like ploughs that needed no coulters, if they broke a bit they looked in a book and sent away to the makers for't. Not like the days of the crofter childes, when in and about from Kinraddie, Arbuthnott, and half the hill-land betwixt Segget and Fordoun, the folk of the lost little farms would ride with plenty of trade in a small-like way.

The only creature that seemed to flourish as the harvest brought a dour end to the weather and the clouds rolled slower over the Howe was Will Melvin that kept the Segget

Arms, him and that sharp-tongued besom his wife, the spinners would go down to the Arms and get drunk, instead of biding at home in their misery and cutting their throats, as decent folk would.

Mr Mowat came suddenly home to Segget and sacked every servant he met in the House: he said that he Jahly well must, he'd no choice, he was taxed to death by those Labour chaps. Then he went to the kirk, the first time in years, and sat and listened to a dreich-like discourse—God! there was something queer with Colquohoun. But he kept his eyes, Mr Mowat, folk told, on Mrs Colquohoun and not the minister, as she sat in the choir with her sulky-proud face, and her swathings of hair, ay, she'd fairly fine hair, herself looking up at the pulpit as though she didn't know Mr Mowat looked at her—and didn't know, as everybody else did in Segget, that he'd been the father of that bairn of hers that died away a three-four years back.

Mr Mowat never went near the Manse now, he hadn't done that since the days of the Strike, nor the Geddeses either since Mrs Colquohoun had raised a row at the w.r.i. And what do you think that row was about? A socialist creature had offered to come down from Dundon and lecture on birth-control: and all the folk were against it at once, except the tink bitch the minister had wed. . . . And what might IT be? you asked, and folk told you: just murdering your bairns afore they were born, most likely that was what *she* herself did.

She did her own work in the Manse nowadays, they had had to draw in their horns as well, no other maid took the place of Else. And the Sourock's wife was fairly delighted, she said getting down on the floors to scrub would be an ill-like ploy, she would warrant, for the brave silk knickers that Mrs Colquohoun wore. For the Sourock's wife had never forgiven the minister's wife her bit under-things, and the way she voted at the General Election.

But syne news came that fair raised a stir, the Labour Government thrown out at last, and that fine-like childe, Ramsay MacDonald, was in with the Tories, and said they were fine. And them that had wireless sets listened in, and Ramsay came on with his holy-like voice and maaed like a sheep, but a holy-like sheep, that the country could yet be saved: and he'd do it. Ay, he'd grown a fine chap and had got back his guts, you were pleased to hear as the maa went on, now he had jumped to the gentry's side. And no doubt you would see fine changes in Segget.

BUT CHRIS WATCHED that and the life in Segget with a queer apprehension holding her heart. One evening she climbed up to Ewan's back room, where he sat at a little desk he had there, reading a text-book, his head in his hands. He jumped up when she came and found her a seat, polite and kind, though remote with his book till she asked him what the book was about. So he told her the stuff was geology, he was studying the strata of the last Ice Age that came in Scotland long years ago, when the bergs came drifting down by Dundon and folk looked out from their mountain eyries and saw the peaks and the glaciers come. Chris sat and listened, hands clasped round her knees, looking at Ewan's head in the light, smooth and dark and yet shot with gold, the pallor of the lamplight upon his hair—grey granite below as grey granite above.

Then her mind switched away to what he was saying, she thought *And the thing is happening again*—all over the world the Ice was coming, not the Ice-time that ended the Golden Age, but the Ice of want and fear and fright, its glacier peaks on the sky by day, its frozen gleam on the sky by night, and men looked out bewildered to see it, cold and dank, and a dark wind blew, and there was neither direction, salvation, nothing but the storming black lour of the Clouds as the frosts and the fog of this winter came. . . .

Ewan had twisted around, he said *Mother!* sharp, and jumped to his feet and shook her. Chris came to herself with a start, and stared. *What's wrong?* she asked, and he said *You looked—fey.*

She seldom heard a Scots word from Ewan, he brushed them aside as old, blunted tools, but the word had come on his lips as though sudden he'd sought in English and English had failed. She laughed and said *Did I?* and ruffled his hair, and he grinned at her, quiet, he'd been quick, but not feared—he'd do strange things yet in the world, Ewan,

who hadn't a God and hadn't a faith and took not a thing on
the earth for granted. And she thought as she held him (he
endured that, polite) he was one of the few who might save
the times, watching the Ice and the winter come, unflustered,
unfrightened, with quiet, cold eyes.

And she smiled at that and her prideful dreamings for the
child of her womb, an idle woman's pride: and bade Ewan
good-night and went down to the kitchen to leave it neat for
the morning's work. 'Twas then that there came a knock at
the door and Else Queen that was now Else Hogg stamped
in, with the washing she did each week for the Manse, she
cried *Well, Mem, have you heard the news?*

Chris asked *What news?* and Else sat down and gasped,
*I fair had to run to tell you. It's about Mr Mowat—but surely
you've heard?*

The story, she said, was all over Segget, Mr Mowat was
ruined and hadn't a penny, the whole of Segget mortgaged
to the hilt. The last time he came back from London he'd
tried to raise a bit loan at any damn price; and he'd gone
to his Dundon bankers and tried, and they'd said they must
see the jute in his mills. So they sent a man down, Mr Mowat
met him and dined him and wined him up at the House, it
minded old Sinclair, the last of the servants, of the good old
days when young Jahly Mowat would come back with a half
dozen whores in his car. Ah, well, the banker childe was fell
canny, he drank but little, and that with suspicion; but Mr
Mowat soaked like a drouthy fish, and then said *Right O,
we'll go down to the Mills.*

There were two main storage sheds at the Mills, one was
near empty, said young Mr Mowat, the other well filled with
new bales of jute. And Mr Mowat showed the first of the
sheds, there was only a bale or so in the place, but when
they came to the other bit shed, and the sliding doors slid
back in their slots, there were the bales packed up to the
roof, so tight they nearly bulged through the door. *You see,
we've a Jahly good stock at the Mill*, said Mr Mowat, and the
bank man agreed.

So the bank childe went back to Dundon and reported,
and they loaned Mr Mowat a five hundred pounds. And the
creature vanished, none knew where he'd gone; and this last

week or so the bank grew suspicious. It sent a man down to
Segget yestreen, and he went to the Mills and what did he
find, down there at the shed that had seemed so packed?
That there was no more than a curtain of bales, stacked up
to the roof at the shed's near end, the rest of the shed was as
toom as your hat, Mr Mowat had swindled the bank to the
end: and now the bank had ta'en over the Mills.

Chris asked what that meant and Else didn't know, except
that all the folk left at the Mills had been sacked that evening
and the Mills closed down. And folk were saying they never
would open, it wouldn't be worth it, with trade so bad; and
nobody knew what the spinners would do that had waited for
years for their jobs to come back.

And the winter was coming. Down in the Old Toun a weary
indifference lay on the wynds, they paid no heed to the new
Election, Chris herself didn't bother to vote—were the
liars and cheats called Labour or Tory they'd feather their
own nests and lie to the end.

Rain held the sky at November's end, she saw the
streaming parks of Dalziel lift and move under the freezing
haze that sailed and swam by the base of the Mounth, the
curlews had ceased to cry on the Kaimes and of nights the
sounds of the trains came blurred, those nights that the great
lighted buses would lighten, suddenly, firing the walls of the
room where she lay by the side of Robert unsleeping, him
sleeping so sound that he sometimes seemed dead. How to
sleep, how to sleep, when your mind took hold, in the dark,
of the plight of the Segget wynds?

They had brought in a thing they called the Means Test,
spinners who had had the dole over long were told that their
relatives must keep them in future. Chris had stopped by
the door of Ake Ogilvie's shop, and he told her that things
were black in Old Toun, the Wilsons had been cut off the
dole altogether because their old grannie had the Old Age
Pension—the three of them to live on ten shillings a week.
How could they pay their rent on that? Since the Mowat
creditors took over the place they were forcing payments
right through the nose, they'd already had Feet up at the
eviction of a two-three families out of their houses, if houses
you could call them—they smelt like pig-rees. Old Cronin

had been cut off the Bureau as well because young Charlie
was fee'd up at Frellin, and stayed at home to look after his
father: and how could they live on the pay of a loon? And
there were worse cases than these, far worse, God damn't!
you had never much liked the spinners, but the things that
were happening near turned you sick, it was kicking in the
faces of the poor for no more than delight in hearing the
scrunch of their bones.

Chris said *They won't stand it, there'll be revolution*, and
Ake sneered *Revolution? They'll starve and say nothing. Or
'Come walk on my face and I'll give you a vote!'*

Then the news went round that old Cronin was dead, found
dead in his bed by his young son Chae, Chae blubbered the
old man had no firewood for days, and nothing but a pot
of potatoes to eat. Folk wouldn't believe that blither at
all, it couldn't be true, for it made you shiver—no, no,
'twas only another damned lie, that kind of thing never
happened in Segget. Would you find that news in the *Mearns
Chief?*—you wouldn't, so you knew that it couldn't be
true, the *Chief* said week by week we were fine, and Scotland
still the backbone of Britain, and the Gordon Highlanders
right gay childes, not caring a hoot though their pay was
down, and Progressives just the scum of the earth that
planned to take bairns out of the slums and rear them up in
Godless communes, and a woman Naomi Mitchison coarse,
for she said not a word about Christ in her book. . . . Ay, the
Mearns Chief was aye up-to-date, and showed you a photo of
Mrs MacTavish winning the haggis at a Hogmanay dance.

That son of old Cronin's, Jock was his name (you surely
minded when *he* was in Segget?) had done right well for
himself, folk said. He was now a National Labour supporter,
one of Ramsay's new men down in Glasgow, and would likely
get into the Parliament soon: and he was starting on a lecture
tour—*The Country First, Parties Must Wait*. By that, of
course, he meant the political parties, not the kind he would
hold in his Glasgow house—he spoke and acted the gent
to the life.

But Charlie said his old father had seemed to shrivel up
when he heard of the tour; and the last time Charlie had
been to his father he hardly had spoken a sensible word,

just muttered over one of his socialist books, by Ramsay
MacDonald, till the light grew dim, so faint that he couldn't
have seen to read.

He told that to Ewan when he came to the Manse to arrange
the burial in Segget kirkyard, he and Ewan hadn't met for a
long time past, chief enough though they'd been at the school
together. And Charlie was shy and he said to Ewan, *I hear,
Mr Ewan, you've clever at college,* and stood and shuffled his
great glaured boots, and his hands were heavy and calloused
and cold, holding the clumsy cap in his hands. Ewan said
I'm all right. Sit down. Like some tea? and went ben to the
kitchen where Chris made a cake. *It's young Charlie Cronin,
and mother, he's hungry.* Chris said she'd bring some food on
a tray, but Ewan said *No, you see he would guess I knew he
was hungry and that would offend him. I'll take in some and
we'll eat it together.*

So he did, though he'd only new-finished his dinner, Chris
peeped at the two of them, sitting and talking, with a twinge
of pride and wonder for Ewan, and a twist of pity in her heart
for his friend, with his shy red face and his clumsy hands.
Then she went back to her work, and they ate; and when
Charlie Cronin at last went away she heard Ewan make a
dive for the bathroom and be suddenly, exceedingly, very
sick there. She took him a glass of water to drink, and he
smiled and drank and said that was better: white-faced
and black-haired, but still cool enough. Chris thought at the
time 'twas because of the food he'd eaten to keep the Cronin
lad company; but she wasn't sure later, for she found out
that Charlie had told him black tales of the things in Old
Toun.

And that night she went up to his room and found Ewan,
staring out at the fall of sleet, a pelt and a hiss in the moving
dark, his head in his hands, not reading as usual. She touched
him, quiet, and he started a little.

Oh, nothing, he said, *I'm fine, don't worry. I was trying to
remember old Cronin's face.*

He was turning to look in the face of Life.

THAT WAS THE Sunday; on Monday folk woke to a blind-
ing pelt of rain-sheets on Segget and down and across the

steaming Howe where the churned earth lay with its quag-
mired pools, the hills corona'ed dark with their clouds.
Robert went early up to his room and Chris was making
the dinner in the kitchen when she found John Muir at the
kitchen door. He looked stranger than ever she had seen him
look, John Muir, and forgot to call her Mem. He said a gey
thing had happened last night; and gleyed at her queer and
gave a queer cough.

Chris said, *What's happened? Sit down, you look queer*.
And he sat and told her the unco-like tale.

SHE HAD HEARD of the Kindnesses? Well, they were folk
that bided down in Segget Old Toun. At least they had done
till a three days back, Kindness himself was an ill-doing
childe, and weeks behind with his rent, folk said. His wife
was a lass from Kinraddie way, she'd a bairn only a three
weeks old, and had near gone daft when the landlord's folk
came down to the house to turn them out. Sim Leslie had
gone to see it was done, and thought nothing of it, he was
used to that now.

Well, out they'd been turned, their bit gear in the streets,
you minded that Saturday streamed with sleet, and the house
they'd been in was at Segget's tail end, and few folk saw the
thing that went on, or cared to be out in weather like that, and
Kindness himself was a surly brute. He got sacks and happed
up the most of his gear, and prowled Segget for hours to look
for a place. But he wasn't well known and he wasn't well
liked, so he came back at last somewhere about midnight,
and broke in a window and put his wife in, she had stood in
the lithe all those hours in the sleet with her bairn in her arms
and must near have been dead. She sat in the kitchen the rest
of the nignt, Kindness himself had brought in a chair, then
he prowled some more, for he couldn't sleep.

But worse was to come with the Sunday morning; the
policeman, Sim Leslie, that folk called Feet, came on them
early and miscalled them for tinks, and took Kindness's name
in his little note-book, as though the fool didn't know it by
now, and said there would a court-case about this. Syne he
turned them out and boarded the window, and went off and
left them, and a neighbour nearby took in the wife and bairn

for a while. But she hadn't an inch of space to spare, and at
last, as the night came, Kindness came back and said he'd
gotten a place where they'd bide, he didn't say more, a surly
bit brute.

Well, his wife went with him through the pelt of the sleet,
and got to the end of Old Toun to the place, and that was an
old deserted pig-ree, from the time when folk in Segget bred
pigs, long ere the Mills or the spinners came. You could get
inside if you got down and crawled, Kindness had taken a
mattress in there and a stump of a candle and some of their
things. Mrs Kindness was feared at the dark and the sounds
that the old ree made as the night wore on, but they put out
the light at last, fell tired, and went to sleep in the sound of
the rain.

It must have been somewhere near morning they woke,
Mrs Kindness woke up with her bairn screaming, not just
the cry of a bairn in unease but a shrill, wild cry that near
feared her to death. She tried all she could to comfort its
wail, then the light began to peek in the pigsty and they saw
the reason for the bairn's screams, the rats in the night had
gnawed off its thumb.

JOHN MUIR CRIED *Mistress, don't take on like that!* and
caught Chris's arm and put her in a chair. And then as he
straightened up from that he saw the minister stand in the
door, he'd come quietly down as he came these days, and
he looked like Chris, he had heard it all. But he only said
John, where are they now?

Muir skeughed and said that he didn't well know, he'd
heard that folk had ta'en meat to the ree, and Kindness
was off for a doctor, 'twas said, walking all the way
to Stonehive. Robert said *Walking?*—his face looked
queer—WALKING? *Chris, I'll go for those folk. Will you
get a room ready before I come back?*

She worked as quick as she could when he'd gone out
into the shining pelt of the rain. But it nearly was noon ere
Robert came back, the woman looked only a slip of a quean,
Robert carried the bairn, it had ceased to cry, whimpering
and weeking soft like a kitten. The woman stopped and
looked at Chris with the shamed, strange eyes of a frightened

beast, Chris squeezed her hands for a moment, just, and was rough, and told her where her room was, and was rough that she mightn't break down and weep. And she took the bairn and bathed the torn thumb, though it nearly turned her sick as she worked; and the bairn weeked like kitten hurt. Then she carried it up to its mother, waiting, in the spare bedroom with the blazing fire.

She left them there and came down to find John Muir come back with the Kindness gear. He told her the minister was off to Stonehaven, on his bike, to try and overtake Kindness, the minister himself would hold on for the doctor.

Kindness reached back to the Manse about three, and an hour or so later Robert and McCormack, Robert soaked and shivering from his ride in the rain. The doctor went up and bade a long time and them came down to the hall and Chris. He shook his head and snibbed up his bag.

I came over-late. Poison and shock. The woman didn't know it though she had it beside her. The baby's been dead this last hour or more.

IN THE DEAD of the night three nights after that, Chris woke, she was sharply and suddenly awake, Robert beside her coughing and coughing. She got up and padded to his side of the bed, and he had not known that her warmth was gone, all his body was in such a heat; but he saw her against the light from the windows. He said *I'm all right, go back to your bed* and instantly fell to his coughing again.

Chris put on a dressing-gown and went down, and made and brought up a hot lemon drink, he drank it and thanked her, she put out the light, his body still burned as she lay by his side. But presently the cough died away and she slept, and didn't awake till the morning came, Robert's cough awoke her, that and the sound of the wind as it swept the snow down on Segget, piled up on the edge of another New Year.

With the coming of the day the wind rose and rose and rattled at the window-hasps of the house, the skirl of it in the old roof-tops and wailing down the long, winding chimneys. Robert kept to his bed, Chris had made him do that, almost by force, he had suddenly smiled—smiled so that her bowels had seemed turned to water, with that flare of the hot old love that was gone. *If I was a man again, I'd hold* YOU, *you wretch of a woman to bully me like this!* Chris said *You'll be welcome to hold me as you like—when that cough's better, not until then.* He stroked her arm, the flame in his eyes: *Strong and comely still—I've neglected you, Chris!* Then he coughed for a while and when he came to, lay quiet, listening to the day go on.

The Kindnesses had gone to friends in Dundon, and left no relic but a snow-happed grave, and this cough that Robert had got in his throat, and that memory that woke you, sick in the night, of the rats that fed on a baby's flesh. And men had believed in a God and a Christ, men had believed in the kindness of men, men had believed that this order endured because of its truth and its justice to men. . . . Robert was sound beside you in sleep, but once he moved and muttered in dreams. He said *Oh, I can't, I can't—oh, my God!* Chris happed him close and again sought sleep, and the next day came, and he woke to that coughing, and Chris saw a spray of blood on the pillow.

She said *I must send for a doctor, Robert,* fear in her heart, though none in her voice. But he shook his head, his eyes grown remote. *I'll be all right, I'll look after myself.* And after he'd eaten a slice of toast and had drunk some tea, he didn't cough more, and asked for a pad of paper and pencil, he wished to write out his to-morrow's sermon.

Chris knew he wouldn't be able to speak it, a week at least ere he'd rise from his bed; but she took him the paper and pencil to quiet him, and stood by a while till at last he looked up—*Yes, Christine?* his eyes far from her again. So she turned to her work with a daft, dull pain, daft ever to think that THAT could come back.

Ewan helped her that morning, scrubbing the hall, bringing in coal, the wind still raged, a steely drive that was edged with sleet; as the day wore on it froze up again. When she went up that afternoon to Robert's room the door wouldn't open a while though she pushed, then it did, and the stinging air smote her face, the window wide open, the room ice-cold, Robert lying half-naked alseep in his bed. He woke as he heard the sound of her come, his face was flushed in spite of the cold, he said that he'd tried to sleep and couldn't, he'd felt choked and opened the window and slept. Where had the pad for his sermon gone?

Chris went down to Ewan to wire for the doctor. When he came in the evening he sounded Robert's lungs, Robert lying quiet, his eyes far away; and the doctor was puzzled, though he chatted and joked. But later, downstairs, he said to Chris, *There's something queer in Mr Colquohoun's lungs—oh no, this cold's not on to them yet. Was he ever gassed in the War, do you know? There's the strangest contraction in both upper lungs. I'll be back fell early the morn's morning, keep him in bed and keep him warm.*

Ewan went up about six and came back and said that Robert was sleeping again, but there was blood on his pillow, fresh. Chris got up to change it, she ached in each limb, but Ewan said that he'd done that already, and Robert wasn't waked up from his sleep. *Sit down and rest,* and he forced her to sit, and they sat a long time looking into the fire, hearing the blast of the wind over Segget. But near eight or nine when they went to their beds the wind seemed to die in the cry of the yews, Ewan went to the window and called Chris to look. So she did, and stood by his side in the dark, and looked on a sky that was burnished in steel, rimed with a pringling frost of stars, nothing moved or lived, the yews stood black, the garden hedges rose up in the silence as if to listen to the void star-glow. . . . Ewan said *You'll catch cold,* and blinded the window, and above their heads they heard Robert cough.

NEXT MORNING John Muir came early to the Manse, he said that he'd tell the congregation there wouldn't be a service; and Chris agreed. But then, as they stood together in the hall they heard the sound of an opening door, and looked up, and Chris gave a gasp and cried, *Robert!* He was coming down slowly, his hand on the rails, he said *I'm all right; I* MUST *take the service.* He'd a handkerchief up to his mouth, saying that, and stopped and coughed, and Chris wrung her hands. *Robert, go back to your bed—you must.*

He shook his head, he was fully dressed, even shaved, *I'll take the service as usual. There's nothing in a cough to stop me, is there?* AND I HAVE SOMETHING TO SAY TO THE FOLK.

Chris had stood enough, now she knew at last if she didn't
win now she never would win. She said *Robert, for me. I've
never asked much—for me, and I'll never ask another thing:
Will you please go back?*

Ewan had come out of his room and looked down, and
he saw Robert's face for a moment twist, as if in pain, then
it altered again, back to the dark, dreaming look that they
knew. *It's you or the kirk, Chris, and I'm the kirk's man.*

For a second it seemed to Chris she'd be sick, she gave
the funniest dry laugh at that thought, with that gripping
in her stomach and that pain in her throat. Then that went
by, she was suddenly cool, she heard herself say, *All right,
here's your coat;* and found a coat for him in the hall, and a
muffler, and wrapped it about him, as she finished with that
he stared at her queer, the ice broke round his eyes. He said
suddenly, *Chris—my dear, dear Chris!* and kissed her with
that look, not with his lips, not in front of John Muir, and she
smiled at him, white. Then he went out across the chill blow
of the wind, his feet rang sharp on the frozen ground. Chris
caught Ewan's arm and shook it—*Go with him! I'll come
as soon as ever I'm dressed.*

She fled and changed in a flurry and was down, and across
through the snow-wrapped garden before the kirk bells had
ceased from their sudden clamour. She raised her eyes as she
hurried through the kirkyard, and saw the Mounth as though
suddenly halted, watching, and staring down at Segget, the
far peaks under their canopy of cloud, the nearer bare but
for a snow-pillar she saw rise up from the Leachie bents and
whirl in the icy blow of the wind.

FOLK SAID THAT the kirk at Segget nowadays was a fine
bit place to go for a sleep, the Reverend Colquohoun was as
quiet as a cow with his blethers of Jesus and Brotherhood
and Love and the Sacred Heart that still bled for men. You
could pop a sweetie or so in your mouth and take a bit snore
as the sermon went on; even hairy Hogg confessed it was
quiet, they had fairly tamed that creature Colquohoun, with
his coarse-like suggestings the Hoggs came from monkeys,
when instead they were all descended from Burns. And Ake
Ogilvie said *Well, monkeys for me!*

They were both of them there, both Ake and the Provost, that Sunday, and Mistress Hogg came as well, she was failing a bit, but still as sharp-tongued, she had said to her son when he married Else Queen—*Ay, you're keen on the bowl in spite of the slop*. She sat by her man, Else and Alec sat near, and it tickled you a bit to see Meiklebogs—behind, ill-shaved, smiling shy to himself, he had come back to kirk since Colquohoun quietened down.

The kirk began to fill up a bit, old Leslie came in, he was getting fell done, and you thought as you watched him paich down the aisle he never would finish that story about Garvock. And damn't! you felt almost sorry about that, worse folk than old Leslie, his son Sim for one, promoted now, he was leaving Segget, if it wasn't he had such feet as he had you'd have said he'd grown overbig for his boots.

That fair was a hell of a clamour Muir raised, Will Melvin came in in the middle of the ring, like a pot-bellied cat, his thin mistress behind, they were making money like dirt, folk said. *Dirt unto dirt, 'twas the way of all flesh* was Ake Ogilvie's speak about that—aye the same, he'd miscall both the good and the bad in Segget, and didn't seem to see any difference at all 'tween an ill-doing brute like that tink, Dite Peat, and his brother, Peter, that owned his own shop.

There was wee Peter Peat up near the choir, looking round him right fierce to see folk were quiet, his mistress beside him, and the Sourock's wife, the Sourock himself would be down in the Square, singing about Blood in MacDougall's band—he'd never gotten over that mess in his bed when Dite Peat had left the pig he had killed.

God! the frost was fair driving the folk to the kirk; you moved over a bit to let a childe in; young Cronin, you saw, from the manse at Frellin, the only one of the spinners that had come; the coarse creatures hadn't a care for religion. Charlie Cronin blushed and opened his Bible and sat like a duck on the edge of egg-laying, fell decent-like and shy; and you thought to yourself that Geddes, the headmaster, might well take a lesson, there he was, all asprawl in his pew, showing no respect or example at all; and that nasty bit sneer on his face as he sprawled.

Syne you saw the choir was beginning to fill, Miss

Ferguson first; God! how she still blushed. Ake Ogilvie said she'd have a blush on her face if ever they exhumed her corpse from its coffin. Beside her Miss M'Askill sat down with a jerk that couldn't have been good for her spine, you'd have thought, especially as the bottom of that looked ill-padded. She hadn't got a man, and there seemed little chance that she ever *would* now, things as they were—damn't, Segget affairs were fair in a state, you could only hope, with the National Government, they'd alter some time afore Segget was dead. Ramsay MacDonald had said that they would, if we all went poorer, ate less, and spent more—ay, fair a fine childe, with a right clear mind, Ramsay MacDonald, as the English knew well, they couldn't breed the like of Ramsay in England: though Ake Ogilvie said they smothered them at birth. But that was just one of his tink-like says, the English aye needed the Scots at their head, right holy and smart at the same bit time.

John Muir had finished with his ringing at last, and went gleying down the aisle as of old, one shoulder first, and brought in the minister. Faith, he looked white, you'd heard he'd been ill, some cold or such like, a nothing at all. He climbed to the pulpit and coughed and sat down, and looked down the kirk—damn't! a queer-like look, near the kind he would give in the days long syne when he was so keen on changing the world.

Syne you saw that you'd fair been mistaken in that, he was praying, with his head laid down in his hands; you felt a bit better to see him like that, decent and douce, as a minister should be—not trying to alter things as he'd done—who the hell wanted alterations in Segget? Folk were fine, if it wasn't that there wasn't any work, and meat a bit scarce, and you hadn't a notion what your bairns would find to do in the world, when they grew up and found it full up of the ill-gettèd bairns of spinners, and such. Ah well, they'd just have to gang their own gait, with the help of some guts and the rock of Christ's kirk.

Young Ewan Tavendale came in and sat down, and looked round the kirk and up at the pulpit as though he owned both and was frightened at neither—faith, folk were right, an impudent get, with no respect for God or man. Then, as the playing on the organ stopped, the far door opened to Mrs Colquohoun, white-faced and proud, like a proud quean still, hurrying to take her seat in the choir. Half-way to that she stopped and looked up at her man who sat so quiet in the pulpit—folk saw the look and kittled to interest, could the two of them have had a row in the Manse?

The minister gave out the psalm, but so low you hardly heard the words that he said; and you spent so long looking up the passage that the singing was over afore you had found it. Syne the minister was praying, you bent your head, a fell dreich prayer and only half-heard. But then as he finished and gave out his text folk fairly louped in their seats as he spoke, his voice had a ring like a sudden bell:

My text is from the twenty-third chapter of St Luke, verse forty-two: AND HE SAID UNTO JESUS, LORD, REMEMBER ME WHEN THOU COMEST INTO THY KINGDOM.

It is nineteen hundred years since that cry was heard, it is sixteen hundred years since the holy Catholic Church was established in temporal power. In the early days after the death of Christ His return was hourly awaited—His followers, scanty, assured, looked to His coming within a few months or years at the most, they were certain He would come again and redeem the evil of the world that had murdered HIM. *And the years went by: and He tarried still. But that Hope and that Promise it was that bore the Cross to triumph at last in Rome, all over Europe; that uplifts it still. And still the Christ tarries and the world remains.*
LORD, REMEMBER ME WHEN THOU COMEST INTO THY KINGDOM.

In Segget a week ago to-night, in this Christian village, a man and a woman were driven from their home and had no place to lay their heads. In the night a rat came and fed on their child, eating its flesh in a sacrament of hunger—
LORD, REMEMBER ME WHEN THOU COMEST INTO THY KINGDOM!

In the years when the Great War ended the world seemed to turn in its sleep and awake, a new promise cried all about the earth, the promise of the Christ fulfilled in Man—fulfilled in the movements of pity and hope that men called by many names, meaning the same. Against ignoble oppressions and a

*bitter tyranny the common people banded themselves at last—in
a Christ-like rage of pity to defend their brothers who sweated
their blood in the mines, to give warmth and light and ease to
us all. And the leaders of the great Nine Days, days filled with
the anger and pity of the Christ who drove the money-changers
from the Temple courts, looked in their hearts and found there
fear, heard the crunch of the nails that were driven in through
the shrinking hands of the Christ. And they sold Him again, his
promise in Man, each for their thirty pieces of silver.*

LORD, REMEMBER ME WHEN THOU COMEST INTO THY
KINGDOM.

*This year, when hunger and want filled the land, the coun-
sellors of the nation told for our guidance that more hunger and
poverty yet must come, an increasing of stripes in the name of
the Law, of Good Government, Order, in this Christian land,
in this nineteenth century since the Christ died and came into that
Kingdom of the Soul which the Churches proclaim that he came
into—*

LORD, REMEMBER ME WHEN THOU COMEST INTO THY
KINGDOM.

AND IT WAS ABOUT THE SIXTH HOUR, AND THERE
WAS A DARKNESS OVER ALL THE EARTH UNTIL THE
NINTH HOUR.

AND THE SUN WAS DARKENED AND THE VEIL OF THE
TEMPLE WAS RENT IN THE MIDST.

*So we see, it seems, in the darkened sun, in the rending veils
of the temples and kirks, the end of Mankind himself in the
West, or the end of the strangest dream men have dreamt—of
both the God and the Man Who was Christ, Who gave to
the world a hope that passes, and goeth about like the wind,
and like it returns and follows, fulfilling nothing. There is no
hope for the world at all—as I, the least of His followers see—except it forget the dream of the Christ, forget the
creeds that they forged in His shadow when their primal faith
in the God was loosed—and turn and seek with unclouded
eyes, not that sad vision that leaves hunger unfed, the wail of
children in unending dark, the cry of human flesh eaten by
beasts. . . . But a stark, sure creed that will cut like a knife,
a surgeon's knife through the doubt and disease—men with
unclouded eyes may yet find it, and far off yet in the times to*

be, on an earth at peace, living and joyous, the Christ come back—

His voice had sunk near to a whisper by then, so that folk in the back of the kirk couldn't hear, all the kirk sitting and staring in silence. Then he started again, he said, very clear, and once again, slowly, terrible to hear, as a man who cried from his soul on a friend who had passed beyond either helping or help:—

LORD, REMEMBER ME WHEN THOU COMEST INTO THY KINGDOM.

CHRIS WAS NEVER exactly sure of what followed. But she got from the choir stalls and ran up the aisle, the frozenness gone that had hemmed her in—took scarcely a second to move from that moment when Robert had stopped, the queer look on his face. For he stared down the kirk as though Someone stood there. And then a bright crimson thing came on his lips, and down at the kirk's far end a loon screamed.

John Muir reached the pulpit as quick as she did, she saw Ewan, swift and dark, stand up, Ake Ogilvie as well, the rest of the folk stared and stared in a frozen silence, from them to the silent figure up there. Chris ran up the pulpit-stair, opened the door, Robert's head had fallen forward in his hands, and all the pages of the Bible below she saw soaked in the stream of blood from his lips.

And somehow it did not matter, she had known, she put out her hand and put back the hair, from his forehead, gently; and looked at the faces of the congregation. She wetted her lips and tried to speak, to be cool and tell them the minister was dead, and the service was ended, would they please go? And then at last she heard herself speak, in strange words not her own, unbidden to her lips:

It is Finished.

NOW, WITH THE broadening of the day, she could see the peaks of the Mounth wheel one by one into the line of the flow of the light, dun and sun-riding they rode down the Howe. Trusta towered first and north and north the peaks came fast, sun on the Howe and day on the Howe, her last day in Segget ere she went elsewhere, to new days and ways,

to changes she could not foresee or foreknow. Round her the
new year wakened to life, she saw the steam of a ploughing
team, a curlew was calling up in the broom.

She moved and stretched in weariness then, the morning
weariness before you right woke, so standing she minded the
way that Robert would bless the folk of Segget on Sabbath.
And queerly, her hands shaped into that gesture, with Segget
rising in its driftings of smoke, and the hills behind, and all
time before.

Then that had finished; she went slow down the brae,
only once looked back at the frown of the hills, and caught
her breath at that sight they held, seeing them bare of their
clouds for once, the pillars of mist that aye crowned their
heights, all but a faint wisp vanishing south, and the bare,
still rocks upturned to the sky.

Notes

Black = G. F. Black, *The Surnames of Scotland* (New York 1946)
Kinnear = G. H. Kinnear, *Glenbervie* (Laurencekirk 1895)
OGS = *Ordnance Gazetteer of Scotland*, ed. F. H. Groome (Edinburgh 1901)
SND = *Scottish National Dictionary*, ed. William Grant and David Murison (Edinburgh 1931–76)
Watt = J. C. Watt, *The Mearns of Old* (Edinburgh and Glasgow 1914)

p. 1   *borough of Segget*. Gibbon got the name from his birthplace, the croft Hillhead of Segget in Auchterless parish, Aberdeenshire, and he has anglicised the Scots 'burgh'. The location is deliberately vague; the town and its industries are fictitious, blending some of the characteristics of Auchenblae, Inverbervie and Drumlithie.

the Mounth. The great SE spur of the Grampian mountain system.

Mearns Howe. That part of the great valley of Strathmore contained in Kincardineshire.

Fordoun. Village on the main Stonehaven-Forfar road, some three miles NE of Laurencekirk.

Drumlithie. Village seven miles SW of Stonehaven.

the Kaimes. A 'kame' or 'kaime' is a long narrow steep-sided ridge, or the crest of a hill or ridge (SND). There is a sandbank with this name between Glenbervie and Arbuthnott parishes which looks 'as if it had been cast up by human art' (Kinnear, p.5), but the choice of name may also have been influenced by the Kaim of Mathers, a fortress in the parish of St Cyrus, though it rises above the sea and these Kaimes are inland.

Laurencekirk. Market town on the main road between Aberdeen and Perth, some thirteen miles SSW of Stonehaven.

Finella. The daughter of the Mormaer (High Steward) of Angus and wife of the Mormaer of the Mearns, who is traditionally supposed to have slain Kenneth III in 964 at Fenella Castle, one mile W of Fettercairn. Her name occurs in at least three other Kincardineshire place names (OGS).

p. 1   *Wyntoun*. Andrew of Wyntoun (?1350–?1420), whose vernacular metrical history tells the story of Scotland from the beginning of the world to the accession of James I in 1406. In the Scottish Text Society's edition of his *Original Chronicle*, Fenella is called 'Fembel'.

p. 2   *Iohannes de Fordun* (?d. 1384). Probably a chantry priest at Aberdeen, he was part author of the Latin *Scotichronicon* and continued it as *Gesta Annalia*. He naturally says nothing about these Kaimes, since they are fictitious, or about Hew Monte Alto and the ruined camp. But he does tell us that the town of Fettercairn was reduced to ashes in revenge for Kenneth's murder (*John of Fordun's Chronicles*, ed. W. F. Skene, 1872, ii. 167).

    Bara. A hill of this name in E central Aberdeenshire, with a prehistoric fort and three concentric earthworks, is traditionally linked to Robert Bruce's victory against Comyn Earl of Buchan and other magnates in 1308 (OGS).

    Monte Alto. The derivation of Mowat from Monte Alto is generally accepted. The first of the family in Scotland is said to have come from Wales, and the name appears frequently in chartularies of Arbroath and Brechin between 1198 and 1218 (Black, p.614). In Gibbon's boyhood Mowats owned the tanworks in Stonehaven.

    Mathers. The family name of the lairds of Mathers and of the builder of the Kaim of Mathers referred to above, was Barclay (Kinnear, p.21).

p. 3   *Fettercairn*. Village and parish in SW Kincardineshire, five miles NNW of Laurencekirk.

    King Grig. Sometimes written Greg, sometimes Circ: a Pictish king said to have reigned c. 877 (Watt, pp.4, 95–8).

    Mearniae decurio. Sheriff of the Mearns.

    Bannock burn. The site of Robert Bruce's decisive victory against Edward II of England, 1314.

    Melville. The Mearns Melvilles were supposedly descendants of James Melvill, a Hungarian noble (Kinnear, p. 20).

p. 4   *four fierce lairds*. Daniel de Berkeley (1406–37), laird of Berkeley, with Arbuthnott, Lauriston, Pitarra and Halkeston, were accessory to the slaughter by boiling of John Melville of Glenbervie (Watt, p. 8).

    Garvock. The hill of Garvock, a small range of high land covered with heath, rises to 810 ft. and runs through the Kincardineshire parish of that name, approximately $1\frac{1}{2}$ miles E of Laurencekirk. It forms the eastern boundary of the Howe (OGS).

Killing Time. The period of the greatest persecution of the Covenanters, 1685. The term was later extended to cover the whole period 1679–1688, during which Charles II and James VII tried to put down by force those Presbyterians who refused to worship in a Church headed by bishops.

p. 6   *Bervie.* It flows from the N E corner of Fordoun parish past Glenbervie, Mondynes, Arbuthnott and Inverbervie to enter the sea at Bervie bay.

O Segget it's a dirty hole. In *Sunset Song* Drumlithie church is said to have no steeple (p. 76, Canongate Classics edn), though the original rhyme was about Tarland parish in Aberdeenshire (Note by Gibbon in NLS MS Acc. 26041).

p. 8   *strange happening.* Her love-making with Long Rob of the Mill (*Sunset Song*, pp. 232–3, Canongate Classics edn).

p.17   *Stonehive.* The traditional pronunciation of Stonehaven.

p.21   *Mondynes.* About one mile s w of Drumlithie, which is seven miles w of Stonehaven.

Christ tempted of the devil. See Matthew 4 and Luke 4.

p.22   *a dead.* Pronounced 'deid'; a corpse.

try for his pulpit. In the Church of Scotland congregations have the right to choose their ministers, which is done only after they have heard the candidates preach.

p.23   *Judges* Chapter xvi. 25–30.

p.26   *Dalziel.* Pronounced 'Dee-yel' or 'Dalyel'.

p.27   *option.* The right of a town or district to decide whether and how many licences to sell liquor should be granted within its bounds.

p.29   *Wallace.* Sir William Wallace, Scottish Independence leader (executed 1305).

p.30   *Blawearie.* The Guthrie farm-croft in Kinraddie, whose lease was continued by Chris after her father's death and on which she lived after her marriage to Ewan Tavendale, her first husband.

blue. Chris's favourite colour. She had worn blue underwear and a blue dress for her first wedding.

p.33   *salt and savour.* 'Ye are the salt of the earth: but if the salt have lost his savour, wherewith shall it be salted?' (Matthew. v.13).

p.34   *her father.* John Guthrie had lusted after Chris when she was a young girl.

p.38   *all that were in their gates.* 'Gather the people together, men, and women, and children, and thy stranger that is within thy gates' (Deuteronomy xxxi. 12).

p.39   *certificated.* Malapropism for 'certified'.

p.40   *Dundon.* A made-up name for a city with some of the features of Aberdeen, such as the barracks that were the headquarters of the Gordon Highlanders.

p.48   *Tipperary*. Though it will always be associated with the 1914–18 War, the song was first published in 1912.

p.49   *Old Kirk*. The established (Presbyterian) Church of Scotland.

        the Frees. Originally members of the Free Kirk, which broke away from the established church at the Disruption of 1843, but at this time (and now) applied to the minority which refused to enter the union between the Free Presbyterian Church and the United Presbyterian Church in 1900.

        came from the south. She has a southern Scottish, not an English, accent.

p.50   *Blood of the Lamb*. 'Have you been to Jesus for the cleansing power? Are you washed in the blood of the Lamb?', from a nineteenth-century evangelical hymn by Elisha B. Hoffmann.

        Whiter than – the whitewash on the wall! From 'The Top of the Dixie Lid', an anonymous soldiers' song of the 1914–18 War.

p.51   *Ananias*. He means old Leslie is a hypocrite, like the Ananias of Acts v.

p.53   *but they knew*. Without knowing.

p.54   *High Places*. In the Old Testament, 'high places' are associated with temples, altars, the prophets' communion with God, and with worship and spiritual experience generally.

        Trusta. A hill (1052 ft) in Fetteresso Forest, some six miles E of Stonehaven.

p.60   *east-windy, west-endy*. Fashionable ('west-endy') attire for active leisure, such as golf at St Andrews, where the chill east wind often blows in from the North Sea.

p.61   *Skite*. Contemptuous name for Drumlithie. The most pejorative meanings of 'skite' are 'mad' (adj.) and 'soil with excrement' (vb.)

        Arbuthnott. Kincardineshire rural parish in whose churchyard Leslie Mitchell's ashes are interred, and on which the Kinraddie of *Sunset Song* is largely based.

p.63   *W.R.I.* Properly S.W.R.I., the Scottish Women's Rural Institutes. They encouraged domestic skills through classes and competitions in baking etc. and were centres of leisure activity.

        Annie S. Swan, David Lyall. The two are one and the same. Annie Shepherd Swan (Mrs Burnett-Smith, 1860–1943), an immensely popular romantic novelist with a colossal output, also published under the pseudonym of David Lyall.

p.64   *Catcraig*. There seems to have been no Catcraig in the Mearns, but Gibbon did not invent the name. There is a farm called Catcraig $^1/_2$ mile S of Auchnagatt in Aberdeenshire.

p.69   *Drops of Brandy*. The steps are danced to a Scottische (J. M. and T. M. Flett, *Traditional Dancing in Scotland*, 1964, p. 20).
        when she did the line. The dancers were in two parallel lines facing each other. Each couple had a chance to lead the line and pass down the set in turn – 'down the middle and up'.

p.93   *slew . . . the French*. Burns welcomed the French Revolution at first, but partly owing to fear of persecution and the possible loss of his job in the excise, swung round to support 'the defence of the realm' after France declared war on Britain. He helped to organise the Dumfries Royal Volunteers in January 1795, but his song for them – *Does haughty Gaul invasion threat?* has a refrain with radical undertones: 'For never but by British hands/ Must British wrongs be righted.'

p.94   *pillar of cloud and fire*. On the Israelites' road to the promised land, 'the Lord went before them in a pillar of cloud, to lead them the way; and by night in a pillar of fire, to give them light' (Exodus xiv. 21).
        trumpet had cried. Robert has in mind God's colloquy with Moses on Sinai: there were 'thunders and lightnings, and a thick cloud upon the mount, and the voice of the trumpet exceeding loud' (Exodus xix. 16).

p.96   *shrouded dead in red*. The allusion is to *The Red Flag*, anthem of the British Labour Party: 'The people's flag is deepest red/ It shrouded oft our martyred dead' (lines 1–2). The words are by James Connell (1852–1929) and the tune is that of the German folk song, 'O Tannenbaum'.

p.97   *on the bureau*. Drawing unemployment pay. The 'bureau' (pron. 'burroo' in Scotland) was the local Labour Exchange, which paid out unemployment benefit.

p.98   *Chae Strachan*. The well-travelled socialist crofter of Peesie's Knapp in *Sunset Song*.

p.107   *Dunnottar Castle* see *Sunset Song*, pp. 125–6 (Canongate Classics edition).

p.111   *Edzell*. A village some six miles N by W of Brechin. The magnificent ruined castle on its outskirts was formerly a seat of the Lindsays.
        Brechin. A 'city' with a cathedral in E Forfarshire.

p.113   *Twin Daughters of the Voice of God*. Wordsworth's 'Ode to Duty' begins 'Stern Daughter of the Voice of God'.

p.119   *Venricones.* The ancient inhabitants 'who, according to Ptolemy, occupied the country south of the Water of Carron, with Forfar as their capital' (Watt, p. 14).

       ovates. Handaxes elliptical in shape, relatively thin in section, and sometimes with a twisted edge due to alternate flaking.

       tortoise-core. Tortoise-shaped nodule of stone from which flakes have been intentionally removed.

p.120   *fabricator.* Piece of stone used for detaching flakes from a core.

       Golden Age. According to Diffusionist theory, men were organised in happy, peaceful groups of nomadic hunters before civilisation with all its corruptions was created in ancient Egypt.

p.121   *People's Journal.* Published in Dundee from 1858, it became the most popular weekly printed in Scotland until overtaken by *The Sunday Post.*

p.141   *Culdyce.* Evidently a made-up name. 'Culdors' occurs in what appears to be a short list of such names in NLS MS Acc.26041, a notebook containing fifty numbered ideas for *Cloud Howe*, and there is a Culdees Castle in Perthshire.

       Leachie. A hill (1289 ft.) some four miles WSW of Trusta.

p.142   *Pytheas.* A reference back to *Sunset Song*, where this Greek navigator and geographer of the fourth century BC is a potent historical symbol. (p.39, Canongate Classics edition).

p.148   *The O.M.S.* The Organization for the Maintenance of Supplies emerged in 1925 and had registered about 100,000 volunteers in the nine months before the General Strike of 1926. They drove cars, buses, lorries, and even trains, and also acted as electricians, mechanics and other maintenance staff (Patrick Renshaw, *The General Strike*, 1930, p. 130 and *passim*).

p.150   *Quarles.* Gibbon has brought this name in from outside; there is no Quarles on any of the 1:50,000 Ordnance Survey Maps of Scotland.

p.151   *Carmont.* A farm-settlement some four miles W of Stonehaven, below Carmont Hill (774 ft.).

p.158   *Kinneff.* A coastal hamlet eight miles S of Stonehaven.

       ten full years. The year is now 1932.

p.159   *The wind goeth towards the south.* (Ecclesiastes i. 6).

p.166   *went with him.* Ran away with him, took over.

       and watch. The first edition and all others have 'and to watch', but the intrusive 'to' is clearly an error not picked up at the proof stage.

p.169   *the Reisk*. An upland area between Arbuthnott and Mondynes. The croft of Bloomfield where Gibbon lived between
the ages of eight and sixteen was on the Reisk road, two
miles N of Arbuthnott.

        Geyrie's moor. The hill of Gyratesmyre and the farm of that
name are just south of Bridge of Mondynes on Bervie
Water.

p.170   *Barras slopes*. About three miles inland from the coastal
village of Catterline.

p.172   *the Wairds*. Upland farms and moorland about 1 mile SE of
Gyratesmyre.

p.173   *he lived in London and wrote horrible books*. A sly reference to
Gibbon himself and his disapproving mother.

        Bervie. Inverbervie, ten miles S of Stonehaven. Like the
Segget of the novel, it mainly consisted of three small
irregular streets forming three sides of a rectangle. It had
woollen, flax, and tow mills, as well as wincey and sacking
factories (OGS).

p.177   *Grieve*. Christopher Murray Grieve ('Hugh MacDiarmid',
1892–1978), poet, essayist and publicist, was the dominant
figure in Scottish literature from the mid 1920s to the 1950s.
During the time-span of the novel he had sat on the
Montrose town council as an Independent socialist, and was
at various periods a member of the Scottish Nationalist and
Communist Parties.

        Compton Mackenzie (1883–1974), popular novelist and
publicist, was a founder-member of the Nationalist Party.

        Gunn. Neil Miller Gunn (1891–1973), novelist and excise-
officer, joined the Nationalist Party in 1929 and had
campaigned actively in 1931 for John MacCormick,
Nationalist parliamentary candidate for Inverness-shire.

        Lord Loon of Lossie. James Ramsay MacDonald
(1866–1937) was a native of Lossiemouth, a fishing port on
the Moray coast. He had been prime minister of a minority
Labour government in 1924, but now (1929) had a
parliamentary majority. In 1931 economic collapse and
massive unemployment caused him to combine with the
conservatives to form a 'National' government to solve the
crisis.

p.179   *A man's a man for a' that*. Hairy Hogg perverts the
revolutionary message of the song.

p.183   *his heart was in the Highlands*. The reference is to a song by
Burns, 'My heart's in the Highlands, my heart is not here;/
My heart's in the Highlands, a chasing the deer.'

p.188   *sailing ships*. In Gibbon's Diffusionist mythology, these
contained the bearers of that corrupt, enslaving civilisation

p.188   that had spread northwards from Egypt, destroying the idyllic life of the primitive hunters.

p.190   *banking and braeing*. The reference is to Burns's 'Ye banks and braes o' bonie Doon', with a pun on 'brae' (bray).

   Frellin. There is no such village in the Mearns, but Gibbon may have taken the name from the old pronunciation of Freeland in the Forgandenny parish of SE Perthshire.

p.198   *Means Test*. The National Government reduced unemployment benefit by some ten per cent. After a claimant had been twenty-six weeks on benefit the income of the entire household was examined by the local Public Assistance Committee. All forms of income—pensions, contributions from sons and daughters, even household possessions—were taken into account (John Stevenson and Chris Cook. *The Slump*, 1977, p. 68).

   cut off the Bureau. His dole had been stopped.

p.199   *Mearns Chief*. The local paper's name was, and still is, *The Mearns Leader and Kincardineshire Mail*.

   Naomi Mitchison. Novelist, social critic and travel writer (b. 1897). Her anthropological and historical novel *The Corn King and the Spring Queen* had just been published (1931).

p.208   *rock of Christ's kirk*. 'Thou art Peter, and upon this rock I will build my church; and the gates of hell shall not prevail against it' (Matthew xvi. 18).

p.211   *It is Finished*. (John xix. 30).

Glossary

Definitions followed by CSD are from the *Concise Scottish Dictionary*,
edited by Mairi Robinson (Aberdeen 1985), and by LGG are from the
glossary Gibbon provided for the 1933 American edition of *Sunset
Song*. (There was no glossary for *Cloud Howe*.) Scots words which
are generally known throughout the English-speaking world (e.g.
auld, *bairn*, *brae*) are not defined.

a-agant, all agape
affronted, humiliated
afore, before
agley, off the straight, awry
Ake, dim. of Alexander
ashet, oval serving-plate
a-skeugh, (of shoulder)
   twisted
bap, soft bread roll
Bee, bugger
ben, inside, towards the inner
   part of the house
Benny Dick Tine, Benedictine
bents, slopes covered with coarse
   grass
besom, impudent hussy
bide, dwell, stay; *bade*, stayed
bigging, (of kirk) building; (of
   sheaves) stacking
billy, fellow
birkie, conceited fellow
birn, heap, pile, crowd
bit, 'a mildly deprecatory adjec-
   tival handle' LGG
blatter, storm, pelting
blether, chatter, talk nonsense
bodies, people

bothy, separate building for
   housing unmarried male farm
   workers
braws, fine clothes
breeks, trousers
britchen, breeching (strap
   around hindquarters of a
   shaft horse to let it push back-
   wards)
broch, large round tower with
   hollow walls of stone,
   erroneously thought to have
   been built by the Picts
brose, oat or pease meal mixed
   with boiling water
brosy, (of morals) 'homespun'
buirdly, burly, vigorous
bull's eye, policeman's lantern
   with thick central lens
by, (adv) near, close
calthrop, instrument armed
   with four spikes, arranged so
   that one always stands
   upright, used to obstruct an
   enemy
canny, careful(-ly)
carle, man, fellow

chapping, knocking, striking

chave, 'toil back-breakingly'
 LGG

childe (*Sc.* chiel), 'a full-grown,
 responsible male' LGG

chirk, (to horses) make a harsh,
 strident noise

claik, gossip

cleck, hatch, give birth to

cleekèd, (of horse) crippled by
 leg-cramps

clishmaclaver, hubbub of talk

close, farmyard, courtyard

clour, blow, thump

clout, blow

clype, tell tales, inform on

cog, (for feeding calves)
 wooden container made of
 staves

cogged, (in horse's shoes) have
 wedges fixed

cole, haycock

coulter, blade in front of a
 ploughshare

coup, overturn

couthy, comfortable, sociable,
 friendly

crack, crazy

creash, fat, fat person

crush, 'set' of people

cry, call, shout

cuddy, donkey; sometimes
 horse

dander, stroll, temper

deave, deafen, bore

dickey, false shirt front

dirl, rattle

ding, strike, (of rain) pelt

disjaskèd, dejected, dilapidated

Dite, fam. form of George

Dod, fam. form of George

dole, state pay to unemployed

douce, quiet, gentle, respectable
 (-ly)

dour, severe and humourless

dowp, posterior

dreich, dry, dreamy, prolix

drouthy, thirsty

eirde, iron age underground wal-
 led dwelling

engraffed, engrafted

fair, (adv.) very, really

fairely (*ferlie*), strange sight,
 marvel

fairly, (adv) marvellously,
 wonderfully

fash, hurry, make an effort

fast-snecked, tightly-fastened

feare, price of grain for the year
 used to determine ministers'
 stipends up to early 20th century CSD

fecht, (past, *faught*), fight

fee, an engagement as a servant

fee'd, hired

fegs, (interj) indeed, sure

fell, great, very

fey, visionary, other-worldly

fleer, 'to scoff, to flare' LGG; to
 ogle

fleers, temper-fits

forbye, besides

futret, weasel, stoat

gait, way, road extent

galluses, trouser braces,
 suspenders (U.S.)

gang, go

gant, yawn

gape, the extent to which the
 mouth can be opened

gawk, awkward, clumsy person
 (often a teenager)

gawpus, clumsy, stupid lout
 CSD

get (Sc. 'giet'), child, brat

gey, strong, terrible; disreput-
 able, wild '(sardonically)
 rather, very' LGG

glaur, 'black, viscid mud' LGG

glaured, muddied

gley, squint

glower, scowl

glunch, 'to mutter half-threateningly, half fearfully' L G G

goodfather/son, -in-law

gowk, stare foolishly; a fool

graip, iron-pronged fork used in farming or gardening

greet, (past, *grat*), weep

greip, open cowshed drain

gurring, snarling

habber, stammer, gabble nonsensically

haimes, 'the two curved pieces of wood or metal forming or covering the collar of a draught horse' C S D

half-tirred, half stripped

hap, wrap, enfold, cover

hashed, tired out, 'dead beat'

hasps, fastenings

haugh, meadowland by a river or stream

haver, talk nonsense

heritor, landed proprietor

heuch, deep glen

hiddle, *hiddling*, huddle, cluster

hippen, baby's diaper

hirple, limp

hoast, cough

Hogmanay, New Year's Eve

hotter, simmer

hubbley-jock (or *bubbly-*), turkey

idleceit, idleness

ill-gettèd, misbegotten, mischievous

jagger, 'jigger', upset, ruin

jake up, raise, lift

jook, dodge in and out

jookery-packery, trickery, underhand scheming

joskin, male farm worker, bumpkin

keek, glance, look

kirn, churn

kist, chest

kittle, excite, stimulate; (n) excitement

kye, cows, cattle

lair, bog down, stick fast, soil

lave, the rest of them

lead, carry harvested grain in from the field

leather, flail, wallop

leet, list of selected candidates for a post

let gang, allowed to go

ley-park, meadow field

lib, castrate

lick, speed

lipped, leapt

lippen, trust

lithe, shadow, protection

loon, [farmer's] boy, fellow

loosening-time, end of the working day

loup, jump, leap

lowe, glow

lum, chimney

malagarouse, dishevel, damage

meck, halfpenny

meikle, big, much

mind, remember

moil, toil

mucker, bugger L G G

muffler, scarf for the throat

neist, next

nickum, mischievous boy

nip, small quantity of whisky

outbye, out in the fields, out of doors

paich, gasp, pant

park, field

peek, tiny bead or point of light, little tongue of flame C S D

peesie, lapwing

pickle, few

piece, sandwich

pig-ree, pigsty

press, large cupboard
prig, urge
pringling, prickling, tingling
purviews, grounds
push, gang, rabble
quean, girl
raddled, fuddled, stupefied
rash, disease of pigs
redd up, epitomise, tidy, clear (throat)
ree, perch, pen, midden, pigsty
reek, smoke
reischles of, 'oodles', abundance of
rickle, loose, ramshackle pile
rig, furrow, dress
rouped (of possessions), sold up
rousting, blustery
row, roll
salts, a purgative
sark, shirt
scaur, 'sheer rock, precipice; a steep, eroded hill' CSD
schlorich, 'a wet, disgusting mess' CSD
scone (vb), beat
scraich, screech
screw, wage, salary
scrunch, pig's food
scuddle, do dirty work
scunner, disgust; loathsome person
shargar, youngest of a brood or litter, weakling
sharn, 'dung in a semi-liquid state' LGG
shaws, stalks and leaves of potatoes or turnips
shelvin, part of the sides of a farm cart
shoggle, sway unsteadily
shoo, send away, usher in (from word used in driving animals)
shoom, hum, buzz
shover, chauffeur

showd, swing to and fro
skeuch, (n) squint; off-course
skilly-like, competent, practical
skite, mad, 'daft, used flippantly' LGG
skitter, 'slither in a jerky, awkward way' CSD
sleekèd, sly and cunning
slider, ice-cream wafer
slocken up, quench thirst
slummock, 'a lumpish slattern' LGG
smeddum, energy, 'guts'
smiddy, smithy
smore, smother
sneck, door-latch
snib, fasten
snicker, snigger
snifter, snivel
sodden, boiled
sonsy, (of woman) buxom (of kirk) roomy, substantial
soss, (n) a dirty, wet mess (vb) to foul, dirty, mess about with (sexually)
sough, sigh
sourock, sorrel, 'a little sour plant' LGG; a perverse, surly person
spank, move briskly
speak (n), rumour, talk, piece of idle gossip
spirit, spurt, flutter
spleiter, 'a wettish mess' LGG; contemptuous term for a group
spunk, match, spark
stamash, uproar, 'blind fury' LGG
stammy-gaster, (vb) flabbergast (n) disagreeable surprise
stationy, (railway) stationmaster
steer, commotion
stirk, bullock, heifer
stite, nonsense
stiter, stagger

stook, shock of cut sheaves set up to dry in a field

stot, (n) bullock (vb) bounce, rebound

stour, dust

sumph, idiot

supped, eaten

sutor, cobbler (vb) cobble

swack, nimble, brisk

sweir, lazy, idle

sweirty, sloth, slack period for tradesman

swey, movable iron bar over a fire, on which pots, kettles etc. can be hung CSD

swither, (of a pig's head) move uncertainly

swop, (of a pen) swing, move quickly

syne, then, next, ago

tacketty, hob-nailed

ta'en, taken

taik, walk, stroll

thrapple, throat

thrawn, obstinate

thummikins, thumbscrew, in which one or both thumbs were compressed

tink, tinker, 'contemptuous term for a person, *specif*, a foul-mouthed, vituperative, quarrelsome, vulgar person' CSD

tint, lost

Tooje, a local pet (girl's) name

toom, empty

toun, farm-settlement, town

trig, tidy, neat

twine, twist, meander

ulster, long, loose overcoat

unchancy, ill-omened, dangerous

unco, strange, outlandish, enormous

vest, undershirt

wame, stomach

well-happed, well-fleshed

wice, sensible

wynd, narrow, often winding street leading off a main thoroughfare in a town CSD

wyte, (vb) know (n) fault

yammer, whine, clamour

yestreen, yesterday

yherne, eager

yowl, howl, yell

CANONGATE CLASSICS
TITLES IN PRINT

1. Imagined Corners by Willa Muir
   ISBN 0 86241 140 8   £3.95
2. Consider the Lilies by Iain Crichton Smith
   ISBN 0 86241 143 2   £2.95
3. Island Landfalls: Reflections from the South Seas
   by Robert Louis Stevenson
   ISBN 0 86241 144 0   £3.95
4. The Quarry Wood by Nan Shepherd
   ISBN 0 86241 141 6   £3.95
5. The Story of My Boyhood and Youth
   by John Muir
   ISBN 0 86241 153 X   £2.95
6. The Land of the Leal by James Barke
   ISBN 0 86241 142 4   £4.95
7. Two Worlds by David Daiches
   ISBN 0 86241 148 3   £2.95
8. Mr Alfred M.A. by George Friel
   ISBN 0 86241 163 7   £3.95
9. The Haunted Woman by David Lindsay
   ISBN 0 86241 162 9   £3.95
10. Memoirs of A Highland Lady Vol I
    by Elizabeth Grant of Rothiemurchus
    ISBN 0 86241 145 9   £3.95
11. Memoirs of A Highland Lady Vol II
    by Elizabeth Grant of Rothiemurchus
    ISBN 0 86241 147 5   £3.95
12. Sunset Song by Lewis Grassic Gibbon
    ISBN 0 86241 179 3   £2.95
13. Homeward Journey by John MacNair Reid
    ISBN 0 86241 178 5   £3.95
14. The Blood of the Martyrs by Naomi Mitchison
    ISBN 0 86241 192 0   £4.95
15. My First Summer in the Sierra by John Muir
    ISBN 0 86241 193 9   £2.95
16. The Weatherhouse by Nan Shepherd
    ISBN 0 86241 194 7   £3.95
17. Witch Wood by John Buchan
    ISBN 0 86241 202 1   £3.95